Guarded Hearts

A Surrender to Love Romance Collection

Alison Reid

Guarded Hearts - A Surrender to Love Romance Collection

by Alison Reid

ISBN: 978-1-7644837-6-6

First edition

Independently published

Introduction to...

Guarded Hearts

A Surrender to Love Romance Collection

Walls. Resistant. Reluctant.

Welcome to **Guarded Hearts**—a collection of emotionally charged romances where love tests even the most guarded men and surrendering to desire comes at a risk. From protective heroes to high-stakes danger and slow-burning passion, these stories follow men who have never given their hearts… until the women they cannot resist force them to.

Each novel in this collection is a complete standalone romance, written in the spirit of classic Mills & Boon with a modern edge. You'll find reluctant heroes, slow-burn attraction, enemies-to-lovers sparks, and situations where giving in to love feels both impossible—and inevitable.

Inside these pages, desire collides with secrets, trust is challenged, and hearts must decide whether surrendering to love is worth the risk. There is no cheating, and every story delivers a guaranteed happily-ever-after.

Whether you're discovering these characters for the first time or returning to favourite heroines and heroes, **Guarded Hearts** invites you to immerse yourself in a binge-worthy collection where passion cannot be denied, and love conquers even the most guarded hearts.

Enjoy the journey.

Table of Contents

Billionaire Bodyguard

Alison Reid

A complete standalone romance
Previously published individually

Chapter One

Chad Morgan had mastered the art of distance. Emotional detachment wasn't a flaw—it was armour. He moved through life with the same precision he'd once led Marines into combat: focused, calculated, always in control. Feelings were unpredictable. Dangerous. And he'd learned—painfully—that getting too close meant risking everything.

So, he didn't.

Duty was his compass. It grounded him when memory threatened to pull him under. Mission objectives, protocols, logistics—those were easy. Clean. Predictable. It was far simpler to bury himself in work than confront the war still waging inside. His company, his discipline, his silence—those were the walls he'd built to keep the guilt at bay.

Because no matter how many lives he saved, one debt still bled beneath the surface.

Lance.

Lance had taken the bullet meant for him and lost the use of his legs. While Chad walked away intact, Lance was left in a wheelchair—a hero grounded, because of him. That truth lived deep in Chad's bones. It haunted his sleep. Shadowed his every move. Happiness, peace, even love—those were luxuries reserved for men who hadn't cost their best friend everything.

Chad Morgan was a man forged in fire and tempered by discipline. At thirty-five, he didn't need to speak to command a room—his presence did that for him. Tall and broad-shouldered, his physique still bore the hallmarks of war: lean muscle, taut control, and a posture so precise it seemed carved from steel.

His face was all sharp lines and clean edges—a hard jaw, high cheekbones, and a scar slicing through his right brow, a souvenir from his final mission overseas. His eyes were steel-grey, always watching, always calculating. When he smiled—which was rare—it never quite reached his eyes.

Dark tactical gear—quiet, utilitarian, like the man himself. No tailored suits. No cufflinks. Just a military-grade watch, an armoured SUV in the garage, and a presence honed by war. His wealth whispered, never begged for attention. His power was quiet, absolute. He could disarm a man in five seconds or dismantle a security system in less. But beneath all that controlled force was something deeper—a storm of loyalty, regret, and pain he never gave voice to.

After retiring from the Marines as a decorated captain, Chad had built Morgan Security from the ground up—a global powerhouse in cyber and personal protection. Governments, CEOs, and royalty trusted him with their lives because he never failed.

He couldn't afford to. Not again.

Now, he stood alone in his Manhattan headquarters, arms folded behind his back, staring out at the city through floor-to-ceiling glass. Below him, New York pulsed with relentless energy—alive, chaotic, and utterly unaware of the man watching from above.

His office was a study in control—matte black walls, polished concrete, and a single glass desk glowing with real-time threat analysis. Behind a reinforced door, servers hummed quietly. No clutter. No chaos. Just silence.

Chad didn't do chaos anymore.

The shrill buzz of the encrypted line cut through the quiet.

He turned from the window, his expression unreadable but alert. Only a handful of people had access to that line.

He crossed the office in three long strides and pressed the call through. "Morgan."

A beat of silence.

Then a familiar voice, lower now—wearier. "Hey, Cap."

No one else called him that anymore.

Chad's jaw flexed. "Lance."

"I need a favour," Lance said.

But before the weight of those words could settle, a memory surged forward—unbidden, sharp as shrapnel.

Kandahar, six years ago.

The air was thick with heat and dust. Gunfire cracked like whips through the valley. Chad's team was pinned—visibility zero, comms scrambled. He moved instinctively, leading the flank, covering his men—until the explosion.

The IED tore through the Humvee behind him. The force threw him forward, ribs cracking on impact. Dazed, ears ringing, he reached for his sidearm—too slow.

From the smoke, an enemy fighter emerged. Rifle raised.

And then Lance was there.

A blur of fury and instinct, screaming his name as he lunged. He fired—once, twice—dropping the insurgent. But not before a bullet slammed into his back.

"Cap!" Lance's voice, ragged with pain. "Move—move!"

Chad dragged them both behind cover, blood slicking his hands. Lance's legs weren't moving. His jaw clenched, refusing to scream.

Chad had never felt more helpless.

He called in the medevac. Held pressure on the wound. Kept Lance conscious with a stream of swears and promises he wasn't sure he could keep.

They both made it out.

But only one of them walked again.

Chad exhaled slowly, grounding himself in the present. The weight of that moment never left him. It lived beneath his skin—etched into every decision.

"Come in tomorrow," Chad said into the phone. "We'll talk."

A pause stretched.

Then Lance's voice, low and even: "You're not gonna like it."

Chad's mouth tugged into something that wasn't quite a smile—more a flicker of dry amusement edged with grit. "Doesn't matter what I like. You saved my life, Gunny. I owe you."

And Chad Morgan never left a debt unpaid.

A rustle on the other end—Lance shifting, maybe bracing for impact.

Then the words hit harder than any bullet.

"It's about Violet."

The line went dead.

Chad stood motionless. The silence of his office turned deafening. Outside, the city pulsed on. Oblivious. But inside him, everything had gone still.

Violet.

The name landed like a punch to the chest.

Fire in her eyes. Steel in her spine. Trouble in heels and a mouth that didn't know how to back down. The woman he'd kissed once—just once—and hadn't been able to forget since. The one who had no idea how close she'd come to unravelling the control he wore like armour.

The one who still haunted him.

It had been five years ago. Not the first time they'd met—he'd known her as Lance's kid sister. Too young. Too fierce. Far too beautiful for her own good. But that day at the VA hospital, everything changed.

Chad had just come back from the field—raw, wrecked, blaming himself for the bullet that took Lance's legs. Violet was there—angry, grieving, sharp as a blade. She confronted him, challenged him, then crumbled in his arms. One second, she was crying into his shoulder, and the next, her mouth was on his—wild, desperate, real.

That kiss… it cracked something open inside him.

She'd been all fire and vulnerability, heartbreak, and heat. And it terrified him.

Because for a heartbeat, he'd wanted more.

So, he did what he always did when something felt too good. Too dangerous.

He pushed it away.

Told himself it was better that way. That a man like him—haunted, broken—had nothing to offer someone like her. But deep down, in the part of himself he refused to look at too closely, he knew the truth.

He hadn't just walked away from Violet Miller.

He'd run.

Fast.

And he hadn't seen her since.

But he'd never stopped thinking about her.

It wasn't that he didn't date—he did when time allowed. But it was never serious. Never close. He made the rules clear up front: no promises, no illusions, no overnights. He never stayed, and he never let them stay.

It was convenient. Controlled. Safe.

Just the way he liked it.

Because connection came with risk. Vulnerability. The kind of emotional exposure Chad Morgan had spent his entire adult life avoiding.

Casual was manageable.

Detached was survival.

Anything more?

That led to chaos.

And Chad Morgan didn't survive chaos.

He buried it.

He stood in the centre of his office, the silence pressing in like a vice. The name still echoed in his mind.

Violet.

He didn't move. Didn't blink. Just stood there, locked in place while something sharp and electric twisted in his gut.

He hadn't heard her name in years, and yet it hit like a live wire—unexpected, unwelcome, and unmistakably powerful. For a man who lived by discipline, who compartmentalised with surgical precision, this was dangerous ground.

His hands curled into fists at his sides. Not from anger. From memory.

She was sunlight and thunder—warmth wrapped in danger, impossible to ignore. The only woman who'd ever gotten under his skin without even trying. And now—after all this time—Lance was calling about her.

What the hell kind of favour did he need?

Chad crossed the room in two strides and dropped heavily into the black leather chair behind his desk. He leaned forward, elbows on his knees, hands steepled, eyes locked on the dark floor.

This wasn't supposed to happen. Not her. Not now.

He'd buried those feelings the same way he buried everything else that hurt—with silence, work, and a steel wall so high nothing could get through.

But that kiss…

He could still feel the press of her mouth—urgent, searing, unforgettable. Still remember the way her fingers had gripped the front of his shirt, knuckles white, like she was holding on to the last solid thing in a world that had fallen out from under her. She'd clung to him with a desperation that undid him, not because she was weak, but because she was raw. Real. Human. And when the tremble in her shoulders gave way to that flash of fire in her eyes—defiant, unyielding—he'd known something with terrifying certainty.

Even broken, Violet Miller didn't break.

She rose.

She burned.

And God help him, part of him admired the hell out of that.

And for a few breathless seconds in that hospital hallway, she made him feel something he hadn't felt in years—alive.

Another part had been terrified of it.

Because she'd seen too much. Seen him—not the soldier, not the CEO, not the weapon in a suit—but the fractured man underneath.

And she hadn't flinched.

That's what made her dangerous.

That's why he left.

But now she was back in his orbit, not by chance, not by fate—but because Lance needed him. And if Violet was in trouble…

He raked a hand through his hair, the movement abrupt, almost angry. This wasn't about feelings. It wasn't about the past. It was about duty.

And Chad Morgan always showed up when it mattered.

Even when it hurt.

Especially when it hurt.

He straightened, spine rigid again, breath steady. The moment of weakness passed like a shadow across his face.

Then he picked up the secure phone, dialled his assistant, and said the words that made it real.

"Reschedule my meetings for tomorrow. And I want a file on Violet Miller on my desk by morning. I want everything you can find on her."

He ended the call and sat back in his chair, the city lights flickering beyond the glass like distant stars.

Some debts were professional.

Others, personal.

This one? It was both.

And something told him—it wouldn't stay clean for long.

Chapter Two

Violet Miller is strikingly beautiful in an understated, effortless way. She stands tall at 5'9", with an athletic build shaped by years of morning runs—strong legs, defined shoulders, and a natural grace in her movements that hints at both discipline and power. Her complexion is smooth with a sun-kissed olive tone that rarely needs makeup.

Her long, wavy dark brown hair falls past her shoulders and is usually pulled back in a high ponytail or braid when she's working or running. It frames a heart-shaped face with high cheekbones and expressive, deep chocolate-brown eyes—eyes that are perceptive, guarded, and quietly intense. They often give away more than she intends when she lets her guard slip, which isn't often.

Her lips are full and naturally pink, though she rarely wears more than tinted balm. Her style is polished and elegant—sharp trousers, silk blouses, and low heels—professional without being flashy. She wears confidence like armour and beauty like an afterthought.

There's an aura of quiet strength around her—people notice her not because she demands attention, but because she doesn't need to.

She runs five miles every morning before the city has fully woken up—before the sirens start and the horns blare, before the courtroom heels and briefcases swallowed the sidewalks. She liked the quiet, the solitude, the rhythm of her own breath as her sneakers hit the pavement in a steady cadence that grounded her.

Today, the sky was slate grey. Mist clung low to the streets like the city was still dreaming. Violet cut through the early morning chill in a faded hoodie and leggings; her long dark hair twisted into a high braid that bounced between her shoulder blades. Her earbuds pulsed with low-tempo rock, but her focus wasn't on the music. It never was.

Running wasn't about cardio. It was control.

A way to outrun the chaos.

She slowed at the corner of Lexington and 92nd, chest rising in even, practiced breaths. Her chocolate brown eyes scanned the street—not nervously, but with the sharp awareness of someone who didn't take safety for granted. The same instinct that made her a damn good lawyer. She didn't miss things.

Not the man loitering too long outside the bodega.

Not the same black sedan that had parked across from her building three times this week.

Not the way her doorman had started asking if everything was all right.

Violet shook off the thought and crossed the street. By the time she stepped into her brownstone, the sun was beginning to burn through the mist. The warmth was welcome. Her apartment was quiet, clean, minimal. She lived alone by choice—just enough furniture to be comfortable, nothing unnecessary. The walls were lined with law books and legal briefs, framed photos of her and Lance, and one old snapshot of her parents smiling on a beach in Cape Cod.

No trace of Liam.

She'd erased him. Or tried to.

Two years ago, she'd been engaged to a man her friends swore was perfect. Wealthy, polished, charming. He said all the right things, kissed her hand in public, sent flowers to her office. But under the surface? There were cracks. Possessiveness disguised as protectiveness. Subtle guilt trips. A growing need to control—where she went, who she saw, how much time she spent with Lance.

He hated that she still ran every morning. Said it wasn't "feminine."

Violet broke the engagement three months before the wedding.

It had cost her. Friends. Reputation. Half the guest list at her firm holiday party stopped speaking to her. But she didn't regret it.

She would never belong to a man who tried to own her.

Not Liam.

Not anyone.

Her stomach twisted slightly at the thought, but she ignored it. She always did.

After a shower and a quick breakfast—black coffee and peanut butter toast—she dressed for court. Tailored slacks, low heels, and a navy silk blouse that framed her face without drawing attention. She was beautiful, but modest about it. Always had been. She didn't flaunt it. She didn't need to. She didn't need stilettos or red lipstick to make a statement.

She made hers with precision. With facts. With a voice that could slice through arrogance like a blade.

By nine, she was seated in her office overlooking Fifth Avenue, reviewing case files, and sipping her second cup of coffee. Outside, the city moved fast. Inside, she moved faster.

A light knock at the door broke her focus.

"Morning," Damien said, stepping inside with the Peterson file in hand and his usual eager smile. He was still relatively new, but sharp, attentive, and already picking up her rhythms—something not everyone managed.

"Morning," Violet replied, glancing up just long enough to meet his eyes. "You're early."

"I figured you'd want this before your meeting with Chambers."

She reached for the file, flipping it open. "Good thinking."

He hovered a second longer. "I flagged the witness inconsistencies and highlighted the financials from '21. Want me to draft a rebuttal outline?"

Violet looked at him properly now, a faint smile curving her lips. "I like how your brain works."

Damien grinned. "I'll take that as a yes."

"You can," she said, then nodded toward the conference table. "And leave the hard copy over there. I'll mark it up myself."

He set it down, then paused in the doorway. "You slept at all this week?"

"Define 'slept.'"

"More than four hours in a row."

She snorted. "You're getting bold, Damien."

"I like working here. Just trying to make sure my boss doesn't keel over mid-deposition."

Violet smirked, the warmth in her eyes rare but genuine. "Duly noted. And appreciated."

He gave a mock salute and backed out of the room. "Coffee is on me tomorrow if you win this one."

"I always win," she called after him, and turned back to her file, smile lingering just a little longer than usual.

As the door clicked shut behind her assistant, Violet sat still, her gaze fixed on the window. The Manhattan skyline stretched beyond the glass—silver and sharp, glittering in the late morning haze. But she wasn't looking at the city. Not really. She was watching its reflection, her own faint silhouette framed against it, like a ghost in a life that sometimes didn't feel entirely her own.

The phone on her desk rang, the screen lighting up with a name that brought a flicker of something real.

Lance.

She picked up the receiver. "Hey, big brother."

"Hi, Violet. How are you?"

"I'm good." She leaned back in her chair, letting the tension in her shoulders ease just a little. "How are you?"

"I'm fine." A pause. "Are you still getting those gifts and letters?"

Violet's jaw tensed, just enough for the muscles to tick. Her eyes flicked to the bouquet on the corner of her desk—white lilies and deep red roses in a crystal vase. The scent was faint but persistent, clinging to the air like memory.

"Yeah," she said softly. "I got chocolates yesterday."

It had started three months ago. First, a single red rose in a black box, left with the receptionist—no card, no signature. Then came handwritten notes, all poetic and vague, describing how she reminded someone of "grace under fire" and "the calm inside the storm." Beautiful, if not a little dramatic. They were always printed on thick ivory stationery, always unsigned.

Then the flowers came. Orchids. Peonies. Roses. Always arranged perfectly, like something out of a high-end catalog—no grocery store bouquets, no casual wrapping. These were deliberate. Expensive. The kind you sent when you wanted to make a statement. After that, the chocolates—Belgian truffles in gold foil boxes, delicate and rich and clearly imported. Violet had given most of them to the secretarial staff, laughing it off when they teased her about her secret admirer.

"I don't know," she said now, tucking her legs under her chair. "It's kind of... sweet? Whoever it is, they've got great taste."

There was a pause on the other end of the line. "Violet."

She sighed, already hearing the warning tone in Lance's voice.

"I'm serious," he said. "This doesn't sound like a harmless crush. It sounds like someone who's watching you."

"You're being dramatic." Her voice was light, easy. Dismissive, even. "It's probably just someone at the office too shy to say something face-to-face."

"This has been going on for months."

"And they haven't done anything weird," she countered. "No creepy phone calls, no stalking, no threats. Just flowers and chocolate and a few anonymous notes. That's pretty harmless."

"Nothing about this is harmless," Lance said, his voice low and tight. "Vi, I know you're trying to play this off but come on. You work late. You run alone in the mornings. You walk to your car by yourself. You don't even have a security system in that apartment."

Violet rolled her eyes, a fond smile tugging at her lips. "Okay, now you sound like Dad."

"Dad never took a bullet overseas, Violet. I did. So, forgive me if I don't like the idea of someone lurking in your blind spot."

Her smile faded, just a little. She rubbed the back of her neck, suddenly aware of the silence in her office, the faint hum of the city beyond the glass.

"I get it, Lance," she said softly. "But I'm fine. Really. Whoever it is probably just likes the mystery. I'm not losing sleep over it."

Lance didn't respond right away, and when he did, his voice had cooled into something she knew too well—Marine-serious.

"Just promise me you'll stay alert. If something feels off, you call me. No brushing it off. No tough-girl routine. Promise me."

She hesitated. Then sighed.

"I promise."

"Do you think it could be Liam?" Lance asked, his voice dropping a shade lower, edged with suspicion.

Violet let out a soft laugh. "Doubt it. He was seriously peeved when I broke our engagement."

"I'm glad you did," Lance muttered. "Didn't like that guy."

"Neither did I, in the end," she admitted, leaning back in her chair. "Too controlling. Always had to know where I was, who I was with… like I was a project to manage, not a person."

There was a grunt of agreement on the other end.

"But no," she added. "I don't think it's Liam. He's not the secret admirer type. He was more the 'buy you a gym membership and suggest a meal plan' kind of guy."

"Ass," Lance said flatly.

Violet smiled. "Yeah. Took me a while to see it. But I'm not looking back."

"Good," Lance said. "But whoever's sending those flowers? He's watching you. And I don't care how pretty the notes are—people like that don't usually stay in the shadows forever."

"You worry too much."

"You're my sister, Vi. I will always worry."

"And I love you for it," Violet said, her voice softening. Then she pivoted, needing the shift. "How's Jenny?"

"She's good." Lance paused, then chuckled. "Nice change of subject, too. Smooth."

Violet smiled. "I try."

"You succeed," he said, affection threaded through his voice. "But seriously, Vi… just promise me you'll keep your guard up, okay? Whoever this secret admirer is, I don't like that he knows where you work. That he's getting through."

"I promise," she said quietly, even though part of her still thought it was harmless. Maybe naive—but a little mystery had always appealed to her.

Chapter Three

It was early morning, and the office was still cloaked in silence. No ringing phones, no footsteps in the corridor—just the low hum of the city waking up outside the floor-to-ceiling windows. Chad Morgan sat behind his desk, the soft glow of his monitor casting pale light over the sleek surface of his workspace.

In front of him was a single file.

Violet Miller.

The name was printed in bold across the tab. He didn't open it right away. Just stared at it, jaw set, eyes unreadable.

He already knew what she looked like—had known her for years, though it had been a while. But he needed more. He needed to understand the woman Lance had asked a favour for. The woman who'd once stirred something in him that no one else ever had.

After a long moment, he flipped the file open.

Name: Violet Rose Miller

Age: 26

Occupation: Defence Attorney

Firm: Whitaker & Rowe LLP, Fifth Avenue, Manhattan

Education: Columbia Law School, graduated top of her class

Win Rate: 93%—specialises in criminal defence and high-profile litigation.

Current Residence: Upper East Side, NYC – brownstone, third floor, owns property.

Family: One sibling – Lance Miller, 34, former USMC Gunnery Sergeant (retired, disabled). Parents deceased.

Known Associates: No criminal ties. Close to veteran community through brother and father.

Recent Activity:

Appeared in court 18 times last quarter—won 16 cases, 1 mistrial, 1 pending.

Spotted running Central Park Loop between 5:30–6:15 AM on weekdays; also jogs along the East River Trail

Lives alone; minimal building security—no cameras, no doorman present overnight.

No pets. No roommates. Keeps a tight, predictable schedule.

Romantic History:

Formerly engaged to Liam Hudson, 33, hedge fund partner. Engagement ended three months before scheduled wedding.

Chad's eyes paused here.

Liam Hudson.

Even the name made something cold shift behind his ribs. Too polished. Too political. Too possessive. Chad had read enough about the man to know he was the kind of guy who wore charm like a mask and buried threats in silk.

Violet had walked away.

That told Chad more than any background check could.

Notes:

No reported threats, but recent anonymous deliveries to her office: roses, imported chocolates, handwritten notes.

Same black sedan seen circling her block multiple times over past two weeks.

Subject dismisses concerns. Brother disagrees.

Chad leaned back in his chair, fingers steepled under his chin.

Now he understood why Lance had reached out—not just as a fellow Marine, but as a brother.

This wasn't a coincidence. It was a pattern.

A red flag.

And if Lance—stoic, level-headed Lance—was worried, Chad trusted that instinct without question.

Violet Miller.

Smart. Disciplined. Fiercely private. She played life like chess—precise and unflinching. But the same strength that made her a force in the courtroom could also make her blind to the shadows gathering behind her.

Chad had seen it before—women who believed strength alone could keep danger at bay.

But Violet didn't need saving.

She needed someone who could read the shift in the wind before the storm hit.

Someone who understood the game behind the scenes.

Someone willing to disappear into her blind spot and stand guard.

His jaw flexed.

If someone was circling her life, waiting for the right moment—they'd have to get through him first.

His gaze drifted to the photo paper-clipped inside the file. Violet, mid-stride on a running path. Hair tied back, jaw set, eyes blazing with that guarded fire he remembered.

He closed the file.

The soft ping of the elevator echoed, followed by the quiet hum of wheels over polished marble. Chad didn't look up right away—he knew the sound. Knew the pace. Controlled, purposeful.

Lance.

A moment later, the door opened, and Lance rolled in—straight-backed, broad-shouldered, same buzzed haircut he'd worn since boot camp. Time hadn't dulled him.

"Hey," Chad said, standing. "It's good to see you."

"You too, man." Lance offered a rare smile, wheeling forward. Chad rounded the desk and clasped his hand in a firm shake.

"You look good," Chad said.

"Better than I was last year," Lance replied. "Actually… I'm seeing someone."

Chad's brows lifted, surprised. "Yeah?"

"Jenny. Met her at that adaptive sports event last fall. Physical therapist. It's serious."

A grin pulled at Chad's mouth. "I'm happy for you."

"She's good to me. Keeps me grounded."

Chad chuckled, motioning toward the chair across from him as they both settled in. "So, what's the favour?"

Lance's smile faded. His jaw ticked. "It's Violet."

Chad's expression sharpened. "Is she alright?"

"She's… okay. For now. But something's not right." Lance exhaled hard. "She's been getting things—roses, chocolates, handwritten notes. No sender. All expensive. And lately, it's been happening more often."

Chad's eyes darkened. "You think she's being stalked?"

"I know she is," Lance said quietly. "She just doesn't see it yet."

Chad waited, letting him speak.

"At first, I thought it might be her ex-fiancé. Liam Hudson. Little prick."

"You didn't like him."

"He tried to control her," Lance said flatly. "Always watching. Always second-guessing her. I could've told him that wasn't going to work. Violet's strong—doesn't like being handled."

Chad nodded. "Glad she dumped him."

"Three months before the wedding. I was proud of her. But I don't think it's him. Liam's a narcissist, sure—but he's not subtle. This feels… different. Someone creeping behind the curtain."

Chad's jaw flexed. "Then we're dealing with someone who enjoys the shadows."

"Exactly. And Violet doesn't even see him coming."

Lance's voice dropped a notch. "She thinks it's harmless. But her life's too predictable— same running route every morning, late nights at work, walking to her car alone. No security at her building. No backup. I've kept quiet too long. Whoever this guy is… he's not backing off. And the kind of gifts he's sending? That's not casual. That's obsession with a bank account."

Chad nodded. "I'll need to talk to her. Try to get her to cooperate."

Lance let out a half-laugh. "Yeah, good luck with that. You know how stubborn she is."

Chad's mouth quirked. "Always has been."

"She's strong—maybe too strong sometimes. Hates asking for help. But I can't stand by anymore. She's all I've got, Chad."

Chad leaned forward, voice steady. "Then I'll make sure she's safe. Whether she likes it or not."

"I can't lose her," Lance said, barely above a whisper.

A long silence settled between them.

Then Chad gave a single nod. "I'll handle it. Personally."

Lance blinked. "You? I thought you didn't do fieldwork anymore."

"This is different," Chad said. "You're family."

Lance swallowed, emotion flickering behind his stoic mask. "Thank you."

Chad leaned back again. "I'll go see her tomorrow."

But as the words left his mouth, his gut coiled tighter.

The signs were all there—escalation, obsession, control. And Violet… she wasn't the type to see it until it was right in front of her. Maybe not even then.

Convincing her to let him help?

That might be harder than keeping her safe.

Especially since the last time she looked at him, she'd said she never wanted to see his face again.

The office fell quiet again after the elevator doors slid shut behind Lance.

Chad stood by the window, hands in his pockets, staring out over the city but not really seeing it.

Instead, his mind drifted backward—five years ago, to the last time he'd seen Violet Miller.

She'd been twenty-one. Just barely out of law school, all fire and fearlessness in that way only someone untouched by failure could be. And he... he'd been thirty, already jaded, already carrying the scars no one saw. One look at her had cracked something wide open inside him.

It had been the day after that kiss.

He remembered every detail—the way her lips had tasted like champagne and wild impulse, the heat of her hands tangled in his shirt, the way she'd pulled him closer like she didn't care about anything but him. For one brief moment, he hadn't felt broken. He'd felt wanted. Alive.

And then the next day, she'd come to see him.

She'd stood in the doorway of his apartment, face flushed, words tumbling out before he could even speak.

"I'm attracted to you," she'd said. "I want to see where this goes. Don't pretend you didn't feel it too."

God, he had.

But he'd looked her dead in the eye and lied through his teeth.

"I'm not interested," he'd said. Cold. Final.

She'd stared at him like he'd slapped her.

They'd argued. He'd said it wasn't a good idea. That she was too young. That he wasn't the kind of man she thought he was.

What he hadn't said was the truth.

That he wanted her so badly it terrified him.

That he didn't believe he was worthy of something that pure, that hopeful.

That loving her might destroy him—and worse, ruin her.

He could still see her expression—etched in his memory like a scar. First hurt, raw and wide-eyed. Then fury. Then something colder than either. Her chin had lifted, mouth trembling with restraint, but her eyes... her eyes had burned with betrayal.

"I never expected you to be a coward," she'd said, voice low and shaking. "I never want to see your face again."

Then she'd turned and walked away.

She hadn't looked back.

And he hadn't stopped her.

Now, five years later, he was about to step back into her world. Not as the man she once kissed. Not even as the one who broke her trust.

But as her last line of defence.

And he didn't know if she'd ever forgive him for that—or if she'd let him close enough to try.

Chapter Four

The late afternoon sun slanted through the tall windows of Whitaker & Rowe's upper-floor office, casting a golden glow over the polished surfaces and shelves of leather-bound case law. Violet sat at her desk, sleeves rolled to her elbows, hair pinned in a no-nonsense twist that had started coming loose hours ago. She stared at the latest delivery.

Another bouquet of long-stemmed red roses, perfectly arranged, fragrant, and bold. A crisp cream-coloured envelope was attached, her name written in delicate script.

Congratulations on another win.

No signature. No card. No company logo.

She smiled, recalling the court victory from just hours ago—an aggressive embezzlement case she'd nearly lost on a technicality until she'd shredded the opposing counsel's witness on cross. The ruling had come down just after eleven. This bouquet had arrived by two.

How did this person know?

She stared at the petals, beautiful and blood-red, but all she could think of was how curated it was. The timing. The message. The implication.

It was someone she knew—it had to be.

She picked up the note again, eyes scanning the neat handwriting for the third time. The unease that had been simmering all afternoon crept closer to the surface.

The roses were beautiful. The message was polite. But something about it felt... off.

She told herself she'd call Lance later. Maybe. He was already worried—no point in adding fuel to the fire.

Her phone buzzed, cutting through the quiet.

"Ms. Miller," said the receptionist's voice over the line, polite but vaguely uneasy. "There's a Mr. Chad Morgan here to see you."

Violet's entire body went still.

She hadn't misheard. Couldn't have.

Chad Morgan.

The name hit her like a blow, sudden and sharp, ricocheting off the past and slamming her back into a memory she'd buried five years deep.

What the hell was he doing here?

Her fingers gripped the edge of her desk, breath stalling in her chest.

The last time she'd seen Chad; he'd looked her in the eyes and told her he didn't want her. She'd walked away from him, pride burning through the pain. Walked out with his taste still on her lips, with the echo of a kiss that had wrecked her for months. They had barely touched—but God, it had been everything.

And now he was here?

She should tell reception to send him away.

She should refuse to see him, keep her armour intact, let the years and bitterness do their job.

But instead—dammit—curiosity tugged at her like a thread unravelling something she wasn't ready to face.

Her voice came out cool, clipped. "Send him in."

She ended the call and stood before she could second-guess herself, smoothing her hands over her navy pencil skirt. She caught her reflection in the glass wall—composed, professional, sharp as ever—but her pulse was a wildfire beneath her skin.

A moment later, the door opened.

And there he was.

Chad Morgan.

Broader than she remembered. Harder, somehow—his presence more carved than chiselled, like life had taken a scalpel to him instead of a sculptor's hand. That same unreadable intensity lived in his eyes, the kind that made you feel seen—and judged— without a single word.

He wore dark pants and a fitted black shirt, the top button undone as always. No tie. No pretence. Just lethal confidence wrapped in clean lines and quiet power. The clothes were tailored to perfection, but it was the man inside them who made the air in her office feel too thin.

Still impossibly composed.

Still maddeningly calm.

Still the man who had kissed her like she was the only thing in the world that had ever made him feel anything.

Her throat tightened.

"Violet," he said, his voice like smoke—low, smooth, and entirely uninvited.

She didn't move. Didn't blink. Just stared him down, let him see the ice she'd forged over old wounds. Let him feel the chill she'd sharpened for five long years.

"Why are you here?" she asked, her tone flat, clipped, lethal.

His jaw flexed. "Lance came to see me yesterday."

She blinked.

And just like that, her balance shifted. The ground beneath her tilted, ever so slightly.

Chad's eyes dropped to the bouquet on her desk. "It's about that."

His gaze darkened, his whole posture tightening like a storm was about to break.

She didn't wait for more.

"Get out, Chad," she snapped, her voice rising. "I don't need your help. And I sure as hell don't need your protection."

The wind was nearly knocked out of his lungs.

There she was.

Tall. Strong. God, so beautiful it almost hurt to look at her. The kind of beauty that didn't just turn heads—it stole breath, rewired memories, haunted dreams. But it wasn't just her looks that hit him like a punch to the chest—it was the fire in her eyes, the strength in her posture, the way she held herself like no one would ever knock her down again.

She had changed.

But so had he.

And yet, in that split second, standing in her office doorway, he was thirty again—aching, unworthy, and utterly undone by Violet Miller.

He had an almost violent urge to walk right up to her and kiss her. Not just because he wanted her—he always had—but because he needed to tell her the truth. That he had lied that night. That he had been scared, broken, convinced he had nothing to offer her but damage and regret.

He wanted to tell her that not a day had passed when he hadn't thought about her. Wondered if she was okay. Wondered if she hated him. Hoped she did—because it made it easier.

But he couldn't.

And he wouldn't.

Not when she was looking at him like that. Like he was the last man she ever wanted to see walk through her door.

So, he held the words back. Buried them deep, where they'd lived all these years.

Because this wasn't about his guilt or his longing.

This was about keeping her safe—even if she hated him for it.

"You do need it, and I promised Lance, I would keep you safe."

She turned away, arms crossed, staring out the window like it was easier to face the skyline than him. "You can go," she said flatly. "I was curious about why you were here. I now know. But I don't want you anywhere near me."

"Tough," Chad said, voice low.

She spun around. "Excuse me?"

"I said tough," he repeated, nodding toward the roses on her desk. "These gifts you've been getting. Classic stalker behaviour. You're in danger, even if you don't want to admit it."

"I can take care of myself."

He stepped closer, jaw tight. "Can you? If I walked over there right now and grabbed you—could you fight me off? Do you know self-defence? Do you carry a weapon?"

Her chin lifted, defiant. "I don't need to. Because no one is going to do that. Especially not you."

For a moment, silence crackled between them—charged, electric.

His voice softened, but the intensity didn't waver. "No. Not me. But someone out there might. And you need to be ready for that."

A knock interrupted the tension.

"Come in," she called, without looking away.

The door opened and a young man stepped in, holding a cup of coffee. "Hey, boss—great job this morning. I brought you the coffee I owed you." He paused when he spotted Chad. "Oh, sorry. Didn't realise you had company."

Violet turned to him, her whole face lighting up. "Thanks, Damien. You didn't have to."

That smile—warm, easy, unguarded—hit Chad like a punch to the chest.

She'd never smiled at him like that.

"Anytime," Damien said, setting the cup gently on her desk.

"Thanks for the coffee, Damien," she said again, her voice softer now, the smile still lingering on her lips.

Damien cast a quick glance at Chad—curious, maybe a little wary—before slipping back out the door.

Chad didn't move. His jaw clenched, something sharp and unfamiliar twisting in his gut.

Jealousy. Possessiveness. Regret.

He wasn't sure which felt worse.

Not because the guy had brought her coffee. But because—for a moment—he'd seen the version of her that used to exist before he ruined everything.

She turned her eyes on him, the warmth from moments ago wiped clean. "You can go now, Chad. I can't say it was a pleasure seeing you again. I'll call Lance and tell him to stop worrying. And you—you can go back to forgetting I exist."

"No."

Her brows lifted. "No?"

"I told you—Lance is worried. And honestly, after seeing how quick you are to brush this off, I am too. You need to take this seriously."

"What? Because someone sent me flowers? Because they're interested? That's not a crime, Chad. They haven't threatened me. Haven't done anything but be… polite."

She didn't tell him about the tightness in her chest when she read the note. Didn't mention how the roses—lush, crimson, and pristine—had started to feel less like affection and more like surveillance. Like someone was keeping score. Watching. But she wasn't about to admit that. Not to him. Not after everything.

She didn't want him here.

Not when just looking at him reminded her of the kiss she never forgot.

Not when the sound of his voice still echoed in the part of her that remembered what it felt like to want him.

Chad stepped closer, his tone calm but firm. "This isn't about someone liking you. It's about patterns. You win a case this morning, and by the afternoon, there's a bouquet of roses with a personalised note. I'm guessing it mentioned the verdict."

She said nothing, but the silence was enough.

"That's not flattery, Violet. That's fixation. That's someone tracking you."

She crossed her arms, jaw tight. "Still doesn't mean I need you."

His jaw ticked. When he spoke again, his voice was quieter. "I know you don't want me here. I earned that. But this isn't about us."

"There is no us, Chad. There never was," she snapped.

For a moment, silence stretched between them.

He looked at her—really looked—and she caught the flicker of pain behind the practiced calm. The crack in the armour.

"You think I don't regret how I left things? You think I haven't replayed that day a thousand times, wishing I'd handled it differently?"

"Don't." Her voice hitched before she could catch it. She turned away quickly. "Please. Just go."

Chad's hand hovered in the air between them. He didn't touch her. He never would again.

"I won't leave you alone," he said quietly. "Even if you hate me."

And then he turned, striding for the door.

Violet's breath was unsteady as he stepped through it.

The second it clicked shut behind him, she sank into her chair, face buried in her hands, fighting against the emotions threatening to overwhelm her.

Chad Morgan was back.

And everything she thought she had buried was rising to the surface.

Chapter Five

Chad watched.

From the shadows near the exit ramp of the underground parking garage, he saw her step into the dim light that barely cut through the stale concrete air. She walked alone, her heels clicking against the pavement, sharp and steady like the beat of a warning bell.

She didn't know he was there.

The garage beneath her office tower was half-empty at this hour, echoing with silence and humming fluorescent lights. Too many blind corners. Too many places for someone to hide. Chad had done the sweep himself earlier. No cameras past the entrance. No security guard at night. Just Violet and a hell of a lot of open space.

And she thought she didn't need protection.

Her keys were already in her hand—metal glinting between her fingers like claws. She scanned the row of cars but didn't look behind her. Didn't see him, standing behind a concrete pillar, clothed in darkness and patience.

He could've called out to her. Could've made her look over her shoulder. But she would've resented him for it. She'd made herself clear.

I don't want your help. I'm not yours to protect.

Maybe not. But he was here anyway.

Because she was his to watch over, whether she wanted him or not.

He stayed silent, watching her slip into her car and lock the doors with one quick press of her thumb. The taillights flared red as she backed out of her spot and rolled toward the ramp, headlights sweeping the shadows.

Only once she was gone did Chad move.

He stepped out into the open, his boots scuffing the concrete floor as he walked toward his own vehicle—a black SUV tucked into the shadows near the service elevator. He didn't follow her immediately. He knew where she was going. Knew her route. Knew the layout of her apartment building. Knew that there was no security there either. Just another underground garage. Another chance for something to go wrong.

She hadn't admitted she needed help. Not yet.

But until she did, this was what he would do. Watching from afar. Silent. Unseen. He wouldn't press her again. Wouldn't force himself into her space.

But he wasn't leaving.

Not until the threat was gone.

He'd show up at her office every damn day if that's what it took. Quiet. Unyielding. Present.

Earning her trust again wouldn't be easy—he knew that. She was stubborn, proud, and scared in ways she hadn't admitted yet. But Chad didn't care how long it took. He couldn't afford to fail. Not with Lance.

And especially not with Violet.

She was more than just a promise to an old friend. She was the one thing in his life he couldn't afford to lose.

Violet sat on the edge of her couch, shoulders hunched, the weight of the night pressing heavily against her. The city sprawled before her window, its glittering skyline a deceptive illusion of magic and movement. Manhattan pulsed with life, but from where she sat, it all felt impossibly far away—like she was watching someone else's world unfold, not her own.

The silence in her apartment was oppressive. Too quiet. Too still. It only amplified the storm inside her head—the echo of his voice, the tension in his jaw, the unspoken things in his eyes.

Chad Morgan had walked into her office like a ghost, but he hadn't come to haunt her. No, that would've been easier. He'd come to protect her. To tell her she wasn't imagining it—that the bouquets, the notes, the carefully chosen words weren't gestures of affection. They were warnings. A pattern. A growing danger.

But that wasn't the part that had her heart twisted into knots.

It was his eyes. That quiet sorrow behind them. The restrained emotion he tried—and failed—to mask. The regret. The longing. It was all still there, as if no time had passed at all. As if the years hadn't changed a damn thing between them.

She hadn't wanted him there. She didn't want anyone. She had built walls too high, wrapped herself in independence like armour. She was a Miller—strong, resourceful, capable. But tonight, her strength felt like a lie. And Chad… he shattered her defences without even touching her.

She pressed her fingertips to her lips, as if she could still feel the ghost of that kiss.

God, that kiss.

It hadn't been planned. It hadn't been smart. It had been raw, impulsive, and completely, heartbreakingly real.

One moment she was breaking down in his arms, the sobs wracking her body in a way she hadn't let anyone see in years. And then—then she'd looked up, and something inside her had snapped. Or maybe it had finally broken free. Her hand curled into his shirt, desperate for something solid, something that wouldn't slip through her fingers. And when his mouth met hers…

It had been fire, ache, and longing—all those years of wanting him, crushed into one breathless collision.

His lips were warm, firm, achingly gentle at first. As if he was afraid to take too much. But when she deepened the kiss, he responded—his hands anchoring her, pulling her closer until there was no space left between them. It was a kiss that wasn't supposed to happen. A kiss full of everything they hadn't said, everything they'd buried.

But then he'd pulled away. Said it didn't mean anything. That it was a mistake.

Only, it hadn't felt like a mistake. Not to her. And not, she was certain, to him.

And now he was back. Not as the man who kissed her, but as the one trying to save her.

She just didn't know if she was ready to let him.

Her phone buzzed on the coffee table. A reminder that she wasn't alone in this. Lance.

Her fingers hovered over the screen for a moment, then she swiped to answer, swallowing hard as she pressed the phone to her ear.

"Violet?" Lance's voice was strained, his concern obvious even through the phone. "How are you?"

She didn't answer immediately. She couldn't. She was still so raw from the visit. From everything.

"Violet?" he pressed again, his tone softer this time. "Talk to me."

"I'm fine," she finally said, forcing the words out. "Just... it's been a long day."

Lance was silent for a beat, the kind of silence that carried weight. Then came a long exhale. "I don't buy that for a second. Chad was at your office today, wasn't he?"

Violet's spine stiffened at the mention of his name. "Yes," she said quietly. "He was. Why did you ask him to protect me? I don't need him."

"You do, Violet—and deep down, you know it." Lance's voice sharpened, threaded with a steely protectiveness that only her brother could wield. "Let me guess. You told him to stay the hell away from you, right?"

She looked out the window, the city lights swimming in her vision. Her chest tightened, a familiar ache clawing at her ribs. "Yeah. I told him."

She hated how much Chad's presence rattled her. Hated the way it made her feel like she was standing on the edge of a cliff—terrified but strangely safe. Like if she fell, he'd catch her. And that scared her even more. Because she didn't want to need him. Not again.

"I told him I don't need his help," she said, the words brittle. "I don't need anyone's help. Especially not his. I can take care of myself."

There was a pause, then a sharp breath on the other end of the line. "Violet... don't do this."

"I'm not doing anything," she shot back, her voice cracking under the weight of everything she wasn't saying. "I don't want him here, Lance. And I don't want you worrying about me either. I'm fine."

"No, you're not," Lance said flatly. "And this isn't one of your courtroom battles where you can argue your way out. This is real, Vi. This is dangerous. And I'm not going to sit back and watch you get hurt."

Her grip on the phone tightened until her knuckles whitened. Her throat burned. "I'm starting to see that," she admitted, her voice barely a whisper. "But I've handled worse."

"This isn't about what you've handled. It's about what you shouldn't have to face alone."

The silence between them stretched. And for once, Violet didn't try to fill it. Because maybe… maybe he was right.

And maybe the part that scared her most wasn't the danger.

Maybe it was the way she still felt when she heard Chad's name. The way it made her pulse stutter. The way her stomach twisted with something sharp and unspoken.

Lance didn't know what had happened between her and Chad. She'd never told him. And she was sure Chad wouldn't have either—he wasn't the type to spill something so personal. So, Lance had no idea how much having Chad around unsettled her, how it stirred up feelings she'd locked away and buried deep.

He didn't know about the kiss. The weight of it. The aftermath.

He didn't know that seeing Chad again had unravelled her in a way that felt both terrifying and inevitable.

And he certainly didn't know how hard she was fighting not to care.

Lance broke the silence, his voice rough with emotion. "Vi, I love you. I can't let anything happen to you."

Her heart clenched. "I love you too," she whispered. "But why Chad?"

"Because he's the best," Lance said without hesitation. "You know he is. He's smart, dangerous when he needs to be, and loyal as hell. If anyone can keep you safe, it's him. Why do you hate him so much?"

She opened her mouth, then closed it again, the words catching in her throat. There were a thousand things she could say—things about feelings and regrets, about the kiss that changed everything, about the way Chad made her feel exposed just by being near. But none of that would make sense to Lance. None of it would justify the storm brewing in her chest.

So, she said the only thing that would. The only truth she knew Lance would understand.

"He put you in a wheelchair, Lance."

Lance's breath caught—sharp and audible through the line—and Violet immediately regretted the words. She hadn't meant to say it, not like that. Not with that edge of bitterness that didn't belong to Lance's story, but to her own.

"Chad didn't put me in this chair, Vi," Lance said quietly. "You know that."

She knew that. Deep down, she'd always known. She had blamed Chad at first—that's why she had found herself in his arms that day, before the kiss. She remembered the way her body had given in, how his presence had grounded her when everything else felt like it was falling apart.

But it still didn't make it easier.

She closed her eyes, her chest tightening as long-buried wounds surged to the surface. "He gave the order," she whispered, the words slipping out before she could stop them. They tasted bitter, like poison on her tongue. "It was his call. And it cost you your legs."

A long silence stretched between them. Violet could hear Lance breathing, a steady rhythm that filled the void, and in that silence, she could feel the weight of their shared past, of everything they'd gone through, pressing down on her.

"Yeah," he said finally, his voice quiet but resolute. "But I'd follow that order again, Vi. Because it was the right one. And Chad knew it too."

Violet stood, pacing across her apartment, rubbing her hand down her face as emotions tangled inside her. "I can't see him, Lance. I can't even think about him without remembering that day. The call, the hospital, seeing you like that. I—" her voice broke.

A silence stretched between them, heavy with shared history.

"I get it," Lance said finally. "You're angry. You're scared. But Vi, I need you to separate what happened to me from what's happening to you. Chad didn't do this to me. The enemy did. And if you can't let go of what happened for your sake, then do it for mine. Because if something happens to you… I don't think I'll survive it."

Tears stung her eyes, her throat thickening with guilt and love all at once. "Lance…"

"I don't need you to forgive him," he said gently. "But I need you to let him protect you. Just until this threat's gone. Please."

And for the first time in a long time, Violet didn't have a response. Because maybe—just maybe—he was right.

"I'll think about it," she murmured, her voice barely above a whisper.

"For me, Vi," Lance said, his voice thick with emotion. "Think hard."

She closed her eyes, sinking back onto the couch, her fingers trembling around the phone. "I'll try."

Chapter Six

Violet was deep in her notes when a knock sounded at the door.

"Come in," she called without looking up.

"Morning, boss."

Damien stepped inside, balancing a coffee cup and a manila folder. His tie was slightly loosened, sleeves rolled, casual as always—but his energy was dependable, focused. He handed her the file and set the coffee down next to her laptop like he did every morning.

She looked up and smiled faintly. "You're a lifesaver."

"Just trying to keep you caffeinated and sane." He gestured to the file. "Harrington depositions. I highlighted the sections with conflicting timelines—pages eleven through fourteen."

"Perfect. I'll take it into prep this afternoon." She flipped it open, scanning the first page. "Nice work."

Damien grinned but didn't move to leave. "So… not to pry, but the guy who's been around all week—tall, looks like he was probably carved out of granite?"

Violet glanced up, brows lifting slightly. "Chad."

"Right. Chad." Damien nodded like he'd heard the name before. "He's been… very present lately."

She gave a soft laugh. "He's a friend of my brother's. Former military. Runs a private security firm now."

"Ahh." Damien leaned against the doorway, curious but casual. "Bodyguard vibes make sense, then. He's got the whole silent-sentinel thing down."

Violet shrugged, tone still light. "There's been some… concern. A few incidents. Nothing major, but my brother overreacts when it comes to me."

"Overreacting doesn't sound so bad if it keeps you safe." He sipped his coffee, gaze thoughtful. "Still. Hope it's nothing serious."

"I'm hoping the same." She smiled, more softly this time. "And I appreciate you checking in."

"Of course." He pushed off the doorway. "Gala's still on for Saturday, right?"

"Unfortunately." She grimaced. "You know how much I love evening wear and schmoozing with clients."

Damien chuckled. "You'll crush it, as always. Want me to come early? Help set up?"

She hesitated, then nodded. "Sure. That'd be helpful."

"I'll be there." He smiled but didn't move right away. "Big night for you. Wouldn't miss it."

Something in his tone flickered—too warm, too certain. But Violet was already glancing at her laptop again.

"Thanks, Damien."

He paused at the door. "You know I've got your back, right?"

She looked up, blinking. "Yeah. I know."

He smiled again—just a little too long. "Good."

Then he slipped out, and the door clicked shut, and Violet sat back in her chair, tapping her pen thoughtfully against the folder.

She hadn't told him everything—not about the texts, or how Chad had shown up uninvited and now refused to leave her side—but part of her was grateful for the normalcy Damien brought into the room. A steady rhythm. No questions asked.

She needed that—just a little space to breathe before things spiralled again.

Chad couldn't tear his eyes away from the underground entrance as he leaned against the matte-black SUV parked in the shadowed corner of the carpark, just out of view. Every morning for the past week, he'd done the same—arriving before the sun broke the skyline, waiting to catch sight of her.

Violet moved with the same quiet determination every day. Her heels echoed across the concrete as she crossed the garage and stepped into the elevator that would carry her up to her office.

He'd had her phone cloned on the second day. She knew—he'd told her. No secrets, not when it came to her safety. His tech team monitored every call, every message, every ping. It wasn't about control. It was about prevention. Anticipation.

He visited her office daily, always with the same objective: convince her to let him in. Not emotionally—though God knew that temptation simmered beneath the surface— but logistically. Access. Proximity. Safety. She pushed back at every turn—stubborn, sharp-tongued, throwing up walls that only made his job harder.

Still, he didn't stop.

He followed her to court, stayed long after she left work, always close, always silent. Watching. Waiting. Studying.

And damn if she wasn't brilliant. The way she moved in a courtroom, the fire in her voice, the unshakable conviction in her eyes—it was like watching a blade forged in fire. She was the kind of woman you wanted in your corner when the storm came.

And the storm was coming.

He could feel it.

That low hum of danger beneath the surface—quiet, but insistent. His mind cycled through a thousand worst-case scenarios, each one darker than the last. But none compared to the one where he failed. Where Violet got hurt on his watch.

There had been no more flower deliveries. No more cryptic notes.

Nothing—since he'd shown up.

Violet had said he should take that as a win.

But he didn't.

Silence didn't mean the threat was gone. It meant the stalker had gone underground—angry, watching, recalibrating.

And that was always when things got dangerous.

He was just about to enter her building when his phone buzzed—sharp, insistent. A jolt of tension snapped through his spine. He glanced down.

A message. Sent to Violet's phone. Unknown number.

Five words.

Get rid of the boyfriend.

His grip tightened. Jaw locked.

He stormed into the office building, nodding curtly at security as he passed. Calm on the outside—always—but inside, the storm was already here.

By the time he reached her floor, his pulse was a drumbeat in his ears.

Her door was cracked open. He didn't bother knocking. She was at her desk, back straight, typing—deliberate. Composed. But her shoulders stiffened when she sensed him.

"You're late today," she said, not turning. Clipped. Cool.

"I'm not here for a social call." He stepped inside, voice low. "Did you see the message that came through?"

She glanced at her phone, frowning. "Not yet. Why?"

She picked it up, thumb swiping across the screen.

Silence.

Five words stared back at her.

Get rid of the boyfriend.

Colour drained from her face. Her reaction was subtle—a flicker in her eyes, a catch in her breath—but enough.

"It's probably nothing. Just some idiot," she muttered.

Chad stepped closer, his voice quiet but edged. "Don't insult both of us, Violet. That's not nothing. That's a warning."

She didn't argue. Not really.

"I'll block the number."

Before she could, he took the phone from her—firm, not rough. "No. You don't block this. You show it to me. You let me handle it."

She looked at him like he'd just peeled back something she wasn't ready to face.

"You don't have to do this," she said softly.

"I know," he replied. "But I'm doing it anyway."

She stood suddenly, the movement sharp, brittle. "I never asked for you to protect me, Chad. I didn't ask for any of this."

"I know," he said again. "But you need it."

She turned toward the window. Her silhouette against the city was sharp and solitary. Her hands trembled—just slightly—but she said nothing.

Chad pulled out his phone. "Yeah. I need a trace on the message that just came through to Violet Miller's phone. Get me everything—location, carrier, burner status."

He ended the call, eyes never leaving her.

"You're not getting rid of me, Violet. No matter what you say."

She turned back, her expression finally cracking—frustration, vulnerability, fear. "Okay," she whispered. "I see it now. This is a problem."

His voice was steady. "So, are you going to let me protect you properly now?"

A long pause.

Then— "Okay. You win. But you better own a tux."

He blinked. "A tux?"

"I've got a gala Saturday night," she said. "Work thing. I'm not cancelling."

"Security nightmare," he muttered.

"You'll fit right in," she said dryly. "You look like you could break a man with a wine flute."

Violet kicked off her heels the moment she stepped into her apartment, the click of the door behind her like the exhale of a day finally over. Court. Client calls. A mountain of paperwork. And the constant, stupid sidelong glances at her phone every time it buzzed—hoping it was nothing. Dreading it might be something.

She was exhausted. Bone-deep, soul-weary. Finally—home.

She had just begun unbuttoning her blazer when a knock sounded at the door.

Her fingers paused.

One heartbeat.

Two.

No one was supposed to be here.

She crossed the room quietly and checked the peephole.

Of course.

Chad.

Black Henley stretched over broad shoulders, dark jeans that made him look more like a bodyguard than a billionaire, a small duffel bag slung in one hand. His other hand was tucked casually into his pocket. He looked like someone who wasn't going anywhere.

With a muttered curse under her breath, she unlatched the door and pulled it open. "What are you doing here?"

"You said I could protect you." His voice was calm, even as he stepped inside like he had every right to be there. "I'm following through."

She backed up instinctively, frowning as the duffel hit her hardwood floor with a soft thud. "Is that an overnight bag?"

"Smart and observant," he said, not missing a beat. "I'm staying."

Her brows shot up. "No. Chad—this isn't how this works."

"It is now." He met her gaze with that same quiet intensity he always carried, like he could stare down bullets and win. "That text changed things. I'm not protecting you from across the street anymore. I'm staying close."

She folded her arms across her chest. "I don't want you here."

"Too bad."

There was no heat in his voice—just steel. A soft-spoken certainty that left no room for argument.

"You're not safe," he added, more quietly this time. "And I'm not taking chances. Not with you."

She opened her mouth, the rebuttal already formed—but then she saw it.

In his eyes, beneath the calm and control, was something raw. Real. A flicker of fear he didn't want her to see.

For her.

That stopped her.

She sighed, deflated. "Fine," she muttered. "Spare room. And keep your boots off my rug."

It wasn't a victory. But it was a door cracked open.

A faint smile ghosted across his lips. "I was hoping you'd say that."

She rolled her eyes and turned on her heel, walking toward the kitchen with more irritation than purpose. "You're unbelievable."

"I've been called worse."

She didn't respond. Just pulled a bottle of water from the fridge and leaned against the counter, trying to ignore the tightness in her chest. She should've pushed harder. Should've made him leave.

But for the first time in days, she didn't feel alone. And that terrified her—because needing him was starting to feel too easy.

Chapter Seven

The morning started awkward. Tense.

Violet had been in the kitchen, bleary-eyed, wearing her striped cotton pyjama shirt—the one that barely reached mid-thigh—focused on buttering her toast and trying to forget that Chad Morgan was currently occupying her spare room.

She'd almost succeeded.

Until his voice came from behind her, smooth and amused.

"Nice sleepwear. Very… professional."

She jumped slightly, spinning around, her cheeks flushing as she saw him—fully dressed, freshly shaven, and looking like he'd just stepped out of a GQ photoshoot. Meanwhile, she was barefoot, hair a mess, and wearing nothing but that damn shirt.

"Oh." It was all she could say.

Chad's gaze lingered just a second too long. His eyes swept over her legs—bare and endless beneath the hem—and then back up to her face. There was a flash of something in his expression—quick and hot. Desire. He didn't try to hide it.

Violet cleared her throat and crossed her arms. "It's just sleepwear. Don't make it weird."

"I didn't," he said, that smirk still curving his lips. "You did."

She shot him a withering glare and turned back to her toast, pretending her skin wasn't tingling under his gaze.

Chad didn't say anything else. Just grabbed his keys off the counter and said, "I'll be back when you're ready to head to court."

And then he was gone.

Leaving her in the quiet kitchen, toast in hand, heart pounding harder than it should've been.

Chad walked out of the apartment, pulling the door closed behind him with more force than necessary. The moment it clicked shut, he exhaled a breath he hadn't realised he'd been holding.

God, she was going to kill him.

That shirt. That damn shirt. Soft cotton, clinging like a second skin—innocent and lethal. She'd been standing there like some sleep-tousled dream, barefoot and completely unaware of how sexy she looked. The hem barely skimmed the tops of her thighs, and her long, bare legs seemed to stretch on forever. Her hair was up in some messy twist that should've looked careless but instead made him want to bury his hands in it.

And her eyes—still soft from sleep, wide with surprise—had nearly undone him.

He rubbed a hand across his mouth as he strode down the hall, trying to shake the image. But it was burned into his brain. That tiny crease between her brows when she realised, he was watching. The way her arms crossed, trying to cover herself—but also not really.

It was going to be a long damn day. And an even longer night if he had to spend it under the same roof again.

This was about protection. That was the line. But with every look, every crack in her defences, that line was starting to blur. And with each passing moment, he was starting to forget why he'd drawn it in the first place.

Chad stepped into his office, already loosening the cuffs of his dress shirt as the door shut behind him. Jared, his head of IT, and Nolan, one of his top investigators, stood near his desk, their faces set.

"What did you find?"

Jared opened his laptop. "The message came from a burner. No registration, prepaid SIM, cash transaction. But here's the kicker—he was close when he sent it. Same towers pinged as Violet's phone. Within a block of her office."

Chad's jaw tightened. "So, he was watching."

"Most likely," Jared confirmed. "And the second the message went out; the phone went dark. Powered off. Hasn't come back online. He's not just angry—he's careful."

Nolan added, "I backtracked the phone. Corner store purchase. Went for security footage—but the cameras were vandalised. Spray paint, wires cut. And not just any day—the night before the phone was bought."

"You think it was him?" Chad asked.

Nolan nodded. "Too much of a coincidence. This guy covered his tracks before he made a move."

"He's planning something," Chad muttered. "He's escalating."

Jared asked quietly, "You think he'll try to make contact again?"

"Oh, he will," Chad said. "Next time, we'll be ready."

He straightened. "Double surveillance on her apartment and office. Facial recognition scrubbing every camera near that store. If he showed his face, I want it. Pull everything from the gala guest list—if he plans to get close, that's when he'll try."

They nodded, and the door shut behind them.

Chad stayed behind, staring out over the city with his hands in his pockets. Everything looked calm.

But Violet wasn't safe.

And he was going to change that—no matter what it took.

He got back to Violet's apartment right on time, pulling up in front of the building and heading upstairs with the same purposeful stride he wore in combat zones.

Inside, she stood near the kitchen island, dressed in a sleek navy pencil skirt with a matching blazer. Her heels were on. Her hair was twisted back into a neat knot. She looked like power and polish—like elegance wrapped in steel.

She was on the phone, her voice light and professional. "Thanks, Damien. You're a lifesaver," she said, still unaware of the way Chad's entire body tensed at the name.

A pause.

"Yes, I'll be there. See you then."

She ended the call and turned just as Chad stepped closer.

Without a word, they made their way downstairs to his black SUV. He opened the door for her, his movements smooth, a little too composed.

"How long has Damien worked for you?" he asked as she climbed in.

"Six months," she replied without looking up.

Six months. Chad's mind sharpened. The first anonymous gifts had started showing up three months ago.

"You like him. Damien, I mean," he said, too casually.

"Yes. He's good at his job."

"That all?"

She looked up then, brow arched. "What else?"

He didn't answer right away.

"I don't date coworkers," she said flatly. "If that's what you're implying."

"Who do you date?"

She blinked, caught off guard. "I haven't been on a proper date since Liam."

A beat of silence.

"What happened with your ex-fiancé?"

She sighed. "He got controlling the second the ring was on. Questioning my schedule. My decisions. I didn't like it. So, I walked."

"That must've been hard."

She looked out the window. "No… it actually wasn't. I don't think I was ever close to marrying him."

"Why say yes, then?"

She laughed under her breath. "All my friends thought he was perfect. Handsome, intelligent, wealthy, good family. On paper, he was everything. But honestly? He bored me."

Chad glanced over at her. "You don't seem like the kind of woman who settles."

"I didn't," she said simply. "That's why I left."

"Lance didn't like him."

"Oh, I know. He made that perfectly clear," Violet said, tucking her phone into her bag. "Used to—and probably still does—call him a little prick."

She let out a low laugh. "And honestly? He wasn't wrong."

The car slowed at the courthouse, Chad pulling smoothly to the curb. Violet was already reaching for her briefcase, her demeanour shifting back into that razor-edged professionalism.

"What courtroom are you in?" he asked.

"Six. Thanks for the lift."

"I'll be in as soon as I park."

She waved a hand, already halfway to the steps. "Yeah, yeah," she tossed over her shoulder.

Chad stayed behind the wheel for a moment, watching her walk away.

She looked unshakable.

But he knew better.

And he wasn't going anywhere.

Courtroom Six was a tall, cold chamber—oak-panelled and echo-prone, with sunlight leaking through the high windows in dusty beams.

Chad stepped inside quietly, his broad shoulders filling the doorway for a heartbeat before he moved to a seat near the back. He didn't want to distract her.

Not when Violet was in her element.

She stood at the front, spine straight, heels planted, voice clear and cutting with purpose.

"…and that's what this case is about, Your Honour. Not just negligence—but accountability."

Her tone was cool, precise. Every word fell like a stone in still water, leaving ripples.

Chad watched her, quietly impressed. This wasn't the Violet from the apartment—the one who smirked in her pyjamas, toast in hand, hair messy and soft.

This was Attorney Violet Miller.

Unshakable. Controlled. Fierce.

She moved slightly as she spoke but never paced. Never fidgeted. Her hands were measured, expressive without flourish. Her client sat at the defendant's table beside her—a nervous woman in her fifties, clutching a tissue and blinking rapidly. Violet's presence alone seemed to steady her.

"The opposition will try to paint my client as careless," she continued. "They'll say she overreacted. That she wasn't paying attention. But what they won't say is that the safety protocol she reported—twice—was ignored both times."

She turned to the judge now, calm, and focused. "She did her part. The company didn't. And now she's paying the price."

There was a murmur from the plaintiff's side. Chad's eyes flicked that way. A tight-jawed man in a corporate suit, arms crossed, was glaring holes into the back of Violet's head.

Chad made a mental note of his face. He didn't like the way the guy looked at her. Like he wanted to tear her down, not argue facts.

Violet stepped back slightly. "We're not asking for sympathy. We're asking for justice."

She paused. Let it breathe. Let the words land.

"Thank you."

She returned to the table, and her client reached for her hand. Violet gave it without hesitation, a quick squeeze of silent reassurance before slipping back into her seat.

The opposing attorney stood now. A tall, grey-haired man with the hollow confidence of someone used to getting his way. He smiled too easily. Addressed the judge like an old friend. His opening remarks were filled with platitudes and misdirection.

Chad listened for less than a minute before tuning him out.

His focus was entirely on her.

Violet didn't look back. Didn't notice him sitting there in the back row. But she straightened her papers. Lifted her chin. Tapped the edge of her pen against the table— once, lightly. A nervous tick, maybe. Or maybe it was the only hint she gave that she wasn't made of marble.

He leaned forward slightly, elbows on his knees.

She didn't need him.

But he was here anyway.

And no matter how many cases she tried, how many closing arguments she delivered, Chad Morgan knew he'd never get tired of watching Violet Miller command a courtroom.

The verdict came down in just under three hours.

Liability. Full.

Violet won.

It wasn't a dramatic moment. No gasps or courtroom fireworks. Just a few exchanged glances, a quiet sob from her client, and the gavel's final thud. Justice delivered in clean, clinical strokes.

Violet offered her client a soft smile, murmured something that made the woman nod tearfully, and gathered her files. She was calm. Unflappable. Even now.

But as she stepped out onto the courthouse steps, the bright April sunlight cut across her face—and there it was.

A flicker of something fragile behind her eyes.

Chad saw it. Even through the confidence. Even through the heels-clicking, sunglasses-on, cool composure she wore like armour.

He started down the steps toward her, his intent just to congratulate her and maybe, selfishly, soak in the sight of her a little longer.

But he wasn't the only one approaching.

"Miss Miller."

The voice was sharp. Male. Clipped with condescension.

Violet turned slightly. "Counsellor," she said coolly.

The opposing attorney stood a few steps above her, his briefcase in one hand, a sheen of frustration clinging to his too-stiff smile. "Enjoy your win," he said. "Just don't get too comfortable. You got lucky."

She arched a brow, unimpressed. "Luck had nothing to do with it."

"Oh, I think it did," he replied, his tone dropping. "You spun a good story. Played the jury with that doe-eyed client of yours. But next time, you won't be so lucky."

Violet gave a small, disbelieving laugh. "You lost. Get over it."

"Careful," he snapped, stepping down toward her now, invading her space. "You climb too fast, and people start waiting for you to fall."

That was when Chad moved.

He didn't say a word. Just appeared at Violet's side, his presence sharp and immediate like a drawn blade. He didn't touch her. He didn't need to.

The other man faltered slightly. "And you are?"

Chad's voice was quiet, deadly calm. "The guy who'll make sure she doesn't."

A beat of silence stretched. The lawyer hesitated—calculating—and then scoffed. "Of course," he muttered. "Your boyfriend. Should've known."

He turned on his heel and walked off, muttering under his breath.

Violet let out a breath through her nose, her jaw tight.

"You okay?" Chad asked softly.

"I'm fine," she said. Then—after a pause— "Thank you."

He didn't smile. Just looked at her for a long moment.

"You don't have to handle every fight alone, Violet."

She looked away but didn't argue.

Instead, she nodded once and started walking down the steps, heels clicking steadily. Chad followed, just a half step behind.

And he knew—after today—he'd follow her anywhere.

Chapter Eight

Violet hadn't expected a limousine.

She stepped out of her apartment building clutching a satin clutch, her wrap drawn tight around her bare shoulders against the evening chill. She was prepared for Chad's black SUV idling at the curb, maybe a nod from the driver, something low-key.

Instead, a sleek black limousine gleamed under the amber halo of the streetlamp.

The back door opened smoothly, and Chad stepped out—immaculate in a midnight tuxedo, dark hair neatly combed, his presence arresting without trying. His gaze swept over her like a tide, quiet and consuming.

"You didn't have to—" she began.

"I wanted to," he said simply, offering his hand.

She hesitated, just for a moment, then placed her fingers in his. His grip was warm, confident—steady in a way that made her pulse stumble.

"You look…" His breath left him slowly, his eyes lingering as if trying to commit her to memory. "Stunning."

The moonlight kissed her ivory gown, the silk moulding to her figure before cascading into a soft train that drifted over the sidewalk. Her hair was swept into an elegant twist, exposing the long, graceful line of her neck and the soft glint of pearl-drop earrings. The rest of the dress remained mostly hidden beneath her wrap—suggesting more than it revealed and somehow making it all the more dangerous.

"Don't look at me like that," she murmured, sliding into the back seat of the limousine.

"Like what?"

"Like you're about to cancel the evening and lock the doors."

He didn't answer. Just smirked faintly as he joined her, the sound of the door clicking shut like the start of something.

He poured champagne into two flutes, handed her one with a murmured toast.

Later, as they walked into the gala, Violet leaned in just close enough to brush his arm with her shoulder. "Try not to be too obvious," she whispered.

Chad arched a brow.

"You're staring already," she said, her voice low and amused.

And then—just like that—she slipped away into the crowd, hips swaying, confidence in every step. She didn't look back.

He watched her go, pulse ticking higher. He wasn't the only one watching.

The ballroom shimmered with light—golden chandeliers casting a warm, opulent glow over a sea of tuxedos and evening gowns. Crystal glasses clinked like soft percussion, and the gentle strains of jazz filtered through the air from a quartet playing beneath a canopy of white roses and pale hydrangeas. The gala was flawless, every detail curated to perfection.

But Chad barely noticed any of it.

His gaze swept the room, searching—only for her.

And then he found her.

His breath caught.

Violet stood near the edge of the crowd, her wrap gone, shoulders bare. A flute of champagne rested untouched in her hand. The gown was breathtaking—deceptively simple but perfectly cut, sleeveless with a plunging V that flirted with the edge of indecency, hugging her curves before fanning out in a silken whisper around her heels.

She wasn't trying to be the most beautiful woman in the room.

She just was.

And God help him; she was going to undo him.

Across the crowd, she turned—and their eyes met.

Heat bloomed in her chest. Her breath caught. Chad looked unfairly good in black, the tuxedo tailored to perfection, every inch of him sharp and lethal. But it wasn't the suit that undid her. It was the way he looked at her—like she was the only thing in the room worth looking at. Like he'd been waiting all night just to see her like this.

She forced herself to look away before she forgot how.

"Need rescuing?" came a voice beside her.

Violet blinked up at Damien, grateful for the distraction. "Only from myself."

He smiled and held out a hand. "Then let's dance."

The quartet slid into a sultry swing number as Damien led her onto the dance floor. She followed, grateful to be moving—to be focusing on anything but the weight of Chad's gaze still burning against her skin.

Damien was an easy partner. Confident, charming, always knowing just when to turn or dip. He made her laugh, complimented her earrings, even cracked a joke about her serious courtroom face. She smiled, she danced, she looked like she was having the time of her life.

But every time she spun, her eyes found Chad again.

And he was still watching.

Chad's jaw clenched slightly as he watched Violet laugh at something Damien said. It wasn't jealousy—he told himself—it was vigilance. Observation. Standard perimeter awareness. But when Damien's hand slid just a little too low on her waist, Chad's fingers curled into fists.

She was avoiding him.

He knew it. And she was using Damien to do it.

She danced with another lawyer after that—one of the younger hotshot litigators from a firm Chad didn't like. The guy was tall, polished, with a lazy smile and hands that lingered a beat too long. Violet seemed polite, maybe even amused. But when the guy leaned in, to whisper something into her ear, Chad's body moved before his brain caught up.

He crossed the floor in a few long strides and stopped just short of the edge of the dancers. His presence was immediate. Inevitable.

The lawyer clocked him, stiffening slightly. Violet turned at the same moment.

Their eyes met—and this time, she didn't look away.

"I'm cutting in," Chad said, voice low but clear.

The lawyer hesitated, then gave a short, clipped nod and stepped aside. Chad held out his hand.

Violet hesitated—but only for a second—before placing her fingers in his.

They moved together like they'd done it a hundred times. Her hand in his, his other hand settling lightly at her back. She felt the heat of him through the fabric of her gown, and it sent a shiver straight down her spine.

"You make ivory look like sin," he said, his voice low and deliberate.

Her cheeks flushed, but she didn't look away. The compliment stung with heat, a mix of desire and something darker she couldn't quite name. "You don't like it?"

His lips curled into the hint of a smirk. "Any man would like it." His voice was smooth, almost too smooth, but there was an edge to it—something raw that cracked through his usual calm.

She arched a brow, amusement flashing in her eyes, but there was something else—something quieter—lurking beneath the surface. "Is that so?" Her voice was playful, but the steadiness with which she held his gaze, unflinching, betrayed the undercurrent of something deeper, something that still lingered between them.

Chad's pulse quickened, but he kept his face neutral, unwilling to show how much the challenge in her tone affected him. "You have no idea what you do to the opposite sex."

Her lips tilted upward, but there was no warmth in the smile, just a cool, practiced expression. "I have a good idea. But I know I don't do anything for you. Remember, you told me five years ago that you were not interested in me."

Her words stung more than he'd like to admit. He shifted slightly, the weight of her hurt from all those years ago pressing on him, but he couldn't let it show. Couldn't let her see how much it bothered him. The truth was, he had been trying to protect her then—keep her away from the world he lived in, the one he knew was dangerous for someone like her. But now? He wasn't so sure if he could stay away. Or if he even had the right to ask her to.

"I remember," he said quietly, his voice tight. "I remember everything."

Violet's eyes softened ever so slightly, the flicker of something raw crossing her features before she masked it with a thin veneer of indifference. She took a half-step back, clearly unwilling to let him get too close again.

"Good," she said, her voice almost too casual. "Then I guess we both know where we stand."

Her words were a knife, slipping into the cracks of his carefully constructed defences. He wanted to tell her he was sorry—wanted to tell her that he regretted the way he'd pushed her away, that it had nothing to do with her. But the words caught in his throat. For one, he couldn't afford to make this about desire, not when her safety was still his primary concern. And for another, he wasn't sure if he deserved her—her strength, her warmth, the way she looked at him like she saw through the layers of armour he'd built around himself.

Instead, he just nodded, his gaze heavy, the weight of his regrets buried in the silence between them. "Maybe you're right," he said softly. "Maybe you don't do anything for me. But that doesn't mean I don't care."

Her eyes flickered, just for a second, and then she turned away, the elegance of her movement betraying the careful control she was exerting over the emotions she wouldn't let him see.

Chad watched her walk into the crowd, the sharp ache in his chest a reminder that some things—some people—he'd never be able to walk away from, no matter how hard he tried.

The evening wore on, the golden chandeliers casting their soft glow over the ballroom, but the excitement in the air had shifted, all eyes now focused on the stage. The awards ceremony was nearing its close, and the anticipation was palpable. Chad stood off to the side, his attention divided between the proceedings and the woman who had captivated his every thought since the moment they'd stepped into the room.

The announcer's voice cut through the murmurs, drawing all attention to the stage. "And now, the award for Attorney of the Year goes to... Violet Miller!"

A round of applause broke out as the spotlight turned to Violet. Her name echoed in the room, and for a moment, it felt as if the entire world had paused. She stood there for a beat, her breath catching in her throat, before the corner of her mouth lifted in a self-assured smile. The look in her eyes was fierce, confident—the woman who had fought for every success she'd earned.

Chad watched as she made her way to the stage, her ivory gown gliding behind her, every step measured with poise and grace. The moment she took the podium, the room seemed to hum with admiration, the clink of glasses and low chatter fading into a hush.

Violet accepted the award with quiet dignity, offering a brief but heartfelt speech that left everyone in the room in awe. She thanked her colleagues, her family, and the firm for their unwavering support. But there was a fierceness in her words, a reminder that she wasn't just here by chance. She'd earned this moment.

As the applause died down, she made her way back down the steps, her award clasped in her hands, her expression thoughtful. Her gaze swept over the crowd, and for a brief, fleeting second, her eyes met Chad's. He nodded, a small smile tugging at the corner of his lips, his pride for her undeniable.

Damien was the first to approach her as she descended from the stage, his tall frame looming over her as he offered his congratulations. His grin was wide, almost too eager, as he reached for her hand.

"Congratulations, Violet," Damien said, his voice smooth, his eyes lingering a bit too long on her face. "You deserve it."

Violet smiled politely, the smile never quite reaching her eyes. "Thank you, Damien."

Chad's gaze darkened as he watched the interaction. He couldn't place it, but something in the way Damien hovered over Violet didn't sit right with him. He had to force himself to look away, to concentrate on the gathering in front of him, but his attention kept drifting back to the two of them.

Violet's laugh was light, but there was a distance in it that made Chad's chest tighten. She was gracious as she listened to Damien, nodding in acknowledgment of his words, but there was a coolness in her posture, a subtle way she kept a bit of space between them. She had always been able to stand her ground, to navigate the complexities of any relationship with quiet strength, and tonight was no exception.

When Damien finally stepped back, Violet's gaze found Chad's again, a quiet acknowledgment passing between them. He saw the flicker of something—exhaustion, satisfaction, and maybe a hint of the barrier she'd built back up between them since their earlier conversation. But there was also something else in her eyes, something more than the award she had just received. It was the look of someone who knew their worth, who had fought to get to this point.

And in that moment, as the applause for her victory reverberated through the room, Chad couldn't help but wonder if he had been too late to realise what she truly deserved.

The night had wound down, the final notes of the jazz quartet fading into the quiet hum of the ballroom. The gala was coming to an end, and Chad could feel the pull of

Violet, the lingering tension between them as palpable as ever. They slipped out soon after the ceremony, the air cool and crisp as they made their way to the waiting car.

Inside the limo, the ride was silent but charged with the unspoken. Chad's gaze kept drifting to her, watching the way the dim lights reflected off her ivory gown, the way she held herself—poised, elegant, untouchable. Yet he couldn't deny the connection that still simmered between them, the warmth in the air that he could feel but not quite grasp.

When the limo finally pulled up outside her apartment building, the cool night air hit them like a breath of fresh reality. They both stepped out, the tension that had been building between them still crackling in the space between them.

As they walked toward the entrance, Chad couldn't help but reach out, his hand brushing against hers. The moment their fingers made contact, a spark surged between them—quiet but intense, like electricity waiting to ignite.

Once inside, the door clicked shut behind them, and the apartment was bathed in soft, amber light. Chad turned toward her, his expression unreadable for a beat as he looked at her with a gaze that was both appreciative and weighted with something more.

"Congratulations, Violet," he said, his voice low and warm, the words almost slipping into something deeper. "You earned that award. You're... incredible."

Her chest tightened at the sincerity in his voice, and for a brief, heart-stopping moment, she wondered if this was the time. If this was the moment when he'd finally close the distance between them that had been there for so long. She met his gaze, the pulse of her heartbeat quickening, and in the quiet of the room, she thought she saw it—the shift in his eyes, the flicker of desire, something raw and honest that made her stomach flutter.

For a second, she swore he was going to kiss her. He stepped closer, his presence overwhelming in the small space, and his gaze dropped to her lips. She held her breath, her own lips tingling in anticipation, her body instinctively leaning toward him.

But just as the air between them thickened, just as the tension seemed to snap and pull them together, he stepped back, a rueful smile on his lips. "I—" he started, his voice rough, the words lingering unfinished.

Violet swallowed, a quiet disappointment flickering in her chest. She had hoped for something more. Something real.

"I'll see you in the morning," he said, his tone shifting, distant once more.

It was as if the moment had been swallowed up by the space between them, the charged air dissipating as quickly as it had arrived. The flicker of something unspoken died in the quiet of the room, leaving only the soft hum of her pulse as a reminder of what almost was. Violet swallowed, her chest heavy, the flutter of hope she'd felt moments before slowly fading as she turned toward the bedroom door.

"Goodnight, Chad," she said, her voice steady but thin, betraying the quiet ache that settled in her heart.

He nodded, his jaw set, and for a moment, he just stood there, watching her. But then he turned away, moving toward the spare room with a deliberate slowness, as if the distance between them might give him room to breathe. The weight of the unspoken words hung in the air like a thick fog, neither of them willing to cross the line that had been drawn between them, even though they both knew how easily it could be erased.

The door to the spare room clicked shut behind him, leaving Violet alone in the soft glow of the apartment. She stood still for a moment, the silence pressing against her, her hand lingering on the doorframe. Despite the calm in her voice, her heart was a tangled mess of confusion, yearning, and the quiet sting of things left unsaid.

Chapter Nine

Violet awoke to the faint glow of morning creeping in through the windows of her bedroom. Pale light stretched across the hardwood floors, painting long shadows that danced silently along the edges of the room. The sheets beneath her were soft and clean, but they felt too crisp, too untouched. The air was still, the quiet pressing in around her like a weighted blanket.

She sat up slowly, her limbs heavy, the echo of last night's emotions still clinging to her like a second skin. Her eyes drifted toward the door, as if expecting something—or someone—to break the silence. But there was only stillness. The distant hum of city life filtered through the glass panes, muffled and far away.

Three days. She hadn't run in three days. Chad had asked her not to, his voice calm but firm. Not until they had something concrete—evidence, an identity, a damn name. "Just wait," he'd said. "Please, Violet. Just until I know you're safe."

She'd nodded. She always nodded. And then she'd sat. And waited. And felt herself unravel, one thread at a time.

Her body buzzed with nervous energy now, her thoughts looping on a relentless cycle—the sharp warning in Chad's eyes, the phantom weight of someone always watching. She couldn't breathe like this. Couldn't be like this.

The walls of the room, once a refuge, now felt like a prison. Too familiar, too safe. Her skin itched with the need to move, to push against the fear that had been stitched into her days like an unwanted seam.

She rose quietly, careful not to make noise, her bare feet padding across the cool floor. In the closet, she found her favourite black leggings and a faded hoodie, the cuffs worn soft from years of use. She dressed quickly, her movements deliberate, mechanical. She laced up her running shoes, fingers trembling slightly—not from fear, but from the weight of defiance curling low in her belly.

She needed this. Just a short run. A few blocks. A breath of normalcy. Something to remind her that she was still Violet Miller—the woman who argued cases in courtrooms, who faced judges without blinking, who ran five miles on bad days just to clear her head.

She slipped out the door quietly, pausing in the hallway just long enough to tap her phone into silent mode. No alerts. No calls. Just her and the pavement.

The world outside was still waking up, bathed in cool blue light and early shadows. She breathed in the crisp morning air, let it fill her lungs, steady her pulse.

One foot in front of the other.

She ran.

And behind her, the apartment door clicked softly shut—sealing in the safety she'd left behind.

Down the hall, Chad stirred, the quiet of the early morning broken by something intangible. The alarm hadn't gone off yet, but a shift in the air—or maybe just instinct—dragged him from sleep. Years of combat had taught him to trust that feeling, that subtle pull in the gut when something wasn't right.

He blinked against the dim light, the unfamiliar softness of the guest bed a sharp contrast to the alertness beginning to surge through him. Throwing back the covers, he swung his legs over the edge, bare feet meeting the cool hardwood. He ran a hand over his jaw, the scrape of stubble grounding him.

"Violet?" he called out softly, not wanting to startle her if she was awake.

Silence.

He moved down the hallway, his steps quickening, tension knotting tighter with every second. He pushed open her bedroom door and stopped cold. The bed was made. Neat. Untouched. His eyes swept the room in a practiced scan—closet doors closed, no sign of movement, no flicker of her presence.

His gaze dropped. Her running shoes were gone.

"Dammit," he muttered under his breath.

Crossing the room in three long strides, he grabbed his phone from the console table and checked for messages.

Nothing.

No note. No text. Not even a missed call.

She wouldn't just leave. Not now. Not after everything.

He was already moving, pulling on a black T-shirt, shoving his feet into his boots, holstering the Glock he kept locked in the drawer by the front door. Every movement was fast, efficient—muscle memory kicking in. But the panic was rising, cold and sharp.

He yanked open the door and barked into the comm system, "Did anyone see her leave?"

The answer crackled back a beat later. "Negative. No sign of Miss Miller since last night."

His jaw clenched. That meant she'd slipped past the team, somehow. Or someone had helped her.

No. No, she had helped herself. Because she didn't want to feel caged.

He pulled up her last known location—half a mile out. She was running. Alone.

Christ, Violet.

He hit the stairs two at a time, bypassing the elevator. His heart was hammering now, but not from exertion. This wasn't like the battlefield. There, he could control variables. Here, all he had were gut-deep dread and the knowledge that the woman he cared about was exposed.

He was out the building in seconds, eyes scanning, mind racing. The city had already begun to stir, traffic starting to thrum, the sidewalks speckled with joggers, dog walkers, delivery drivers.

But she wasn't just another morning runner. She was a target.

And someone out there had already threatened her once.

Chad didn't even notice he was running.

He just knew he had to find her—before someone else did.

Violet's breath came in ragged bursts, sharp and uneven. Her lungs burned, her hoodie clinging to her back with sweat. She'd pushed too hard, too fast. But the apartment was close now—just a few more blocks and she'd be home. Safe. Maybe she'd shower, make coffee. Maybe… talk to Chad.

She almost smiled at the thought.

Then she turned the corner—and everything changed.

A shadow shifted near the edge of a narrow alley, half-concealed by dumpsters and morning haze.

Too late.

A blur of motion. Rough hands. The ground vanished from beneath her feet.

She barely got a scream past her lips before a hard backhand cracked across her face, snapping her head to the side. Pain exploded in her cheekbone. Her knees hit the pavement with a sickening thud, the grit tearing through her leggings.

"Tell your boyfriend to back off," a voice snarled, breath hot and sour against her ear. "Get rid of Chad… or next time, you don't get up."

Violet choked on a cry. Her head swam. Blood filled her mouth. Her vision blurred with shock, fear, rage.

And then—

Footsteps. Pounding. Heavy. Fast.

"HEY!" Chad's voice shattered the air like a bomb.

The attacker bolted, melting into the shadows between buildings.

Chad didn't stop to chase. He dropped to his knees beside her, his arms around her before she even realised, he was there.

"Violet—Jesus—Violet, look at me. Look at me."

Her eyes fluttered open, dazed, and glassy. "I… I think I'm okay…"

But she wasn't. And neither was he.

Chad's hands trembled as they moved over her shoulders, down her arms, checking for injuries. His touch was gentle, reverent, but his jaw was clenched so tight it looked carved from stone. His eyes were wild with fury, but beneath it—pure, undiluted terror.

He gathered her close, holding her like a lifeline, like he was anchoring himself with her breath against his chest. "You're safe now. I've got you. He's gone."

Violet didn't resist.

For the first time, she let him hold her—really hold her.

She sagged against him, shaken to her core, the adrenaline crashing out of her system like a tidal wave. His heart thundered beneath her ear. One of his hands slid to the back of her head, cradling her protectively.

He pulled back just enough to look at her, to take in the angry bruise already blooming across her cheekbone.

Something in Chad snapped.

His control. His restraint. All of it.

His hand cupped her jaw with a reverence that made her ache, his thumb brushing over the swelling on her cheek as if he could soothe it, undo it—take it all away. His touch trembled, and then—without hesitation—his mouth was on hers.

Fierce. Urgent. Unapologetic.

There was no prelude, no question—just raw, explosive need crashing between them like a tidal wave. He kissed her like she was air and he'd been suffocating. Like every moment of holding back had been a wound—and she was the cure.

Violet gasped against him, her body jolting with the shock of it—but she didn't pull away. She couldn't. His kiss was fire, his mouth possessive and wild, and her own lips answered before her mind could catch up. It wasn't gentle, wasn't sweet—it was desperate, bruising, a release of everything they'd been holding in. Every argument. Every glance. Every time she'd wanted to close the space between them and hadn't.

His hand slid into her hair, tangling in it, angling her face closer. Her fingers curled into the fabric of his T-shirt, fisting it like she was afraid he'd vanish if she let go. She leaned into him, melting against his body as heat unfurled low in her belly, her fear momentarily eclipsed by something just as powerful—him.

The kiss deepened, grew messier. Hotter. Her breath hitched as his tongue stroked against hers, coaxing, claiming. She moaned softly into his mouth, her knees still scraped and throbbing, but none of it mattered. Not the pain. Not the alley. Not the shadows still echoing around them.

Only him.

Only this.

The world dropped away—fading into a blur of movement and breath, heartbeat, and heat. The pavement beneath them, the early morning hush of the city, the blood on her lip—all irrelevant now. All silenced by the storm between their lips.

Just heat.

Just breath.

Just him.

And for the first time in weeks, she wasn't afraid.

She was alive.

The kiss slowed, softened—like a wave drawing back after a storm. Still intense, but quieter now. Reverent.

Chad's lips lingered on hers a moment longer before he finally pulled back, just enough to look at her. His breath was ragged, eyes burning with a thousand emotions, but his hand stayed on her face—steady, grounding.

Violet blinked up at him, dazed. Her lips tingled. Her cheek throbbed. But her heart… God, her heart was racing.

Neither of them spoke.

The silence between them buzzed, not empty, but full. Of want. Of fear. Of everything that kiss had said for them.

Chad swallowed hard, his jaw flexing as he glanced at the bruise forming beneath her eye. Guilt stormed into his expression like a cold front.

"I shouldn't have done that," he muttered, his voice hoarse and low.

"But you did," Violet said, barely above a whisper. She didn't move, didn't step away. Her fingers were still caught in his shirt, her body still humming.

He closed his eyes for half a second, as if her words hurt. Or healed. Maybe both.

"You scared the hell out of me," he said finally, his voice rough. "I woke up and you were gone. I thought—" He broke off, shook his head. "Then I saw him grab you and—Christ, Violet. I lost it."

"I just needed to run," she whispered. "To feel normal for five minutes."

His eyes opened, searching hers. "You don't get to be normal right now. Not until this guy is caught."

"And kissing me?" she asked quietly. "Was that part of the protection detail?"

His lips twitched at the edge. Not a smile—something sadder. Something worn. "That was part of me losing control."

She nodded slowly, the ache between them stretching taut again.

"I'm not sorry," she said.

He blinked.

"I'm not," she repeated, softer now. "You might be. But I'm not."

Chad looked at her like she'd just cracked open the sky. His throat bobbed with the weight of whatever he wasn't saying. Then he stepped back, just a little—enough to let the cool morning air slide between them.

"We need to get you upstairs," he said. "You're bleeding."

She nodded, finally letting go of his shirt. But her eyes stayed on his face. The truth lingered there. That kiss wasn't just panic. It wasn't just fear.

It was real.

And neither of them could take it back, but Chad wanted to take it back because now everything's changed, and he can't protect her the same way anymore.

Chapter Ten

The elevator ride was silent, but every inch of air between them pulsed with what had just happened.

Chad stood at Violet's side, one hand braced against the wall, the other clenched in a tight fist by his thigh. He hadn't touched her since the kiss—not her waist, not her arm, not even her back when he guided her to the elevator. And yet she could feel him everywhere. The heat of his mouth still lingered on hers. Her lips still tingled from the bruising pressure; her cheekbone still throbbed from the attack—but it was the ghost of his kiss that haunted her skin.

She stole a glance at him as the elevator ascended. His jaw was set hard, his brow drawn tight. He was somewhere else now—shut off, locked down. It was a look she was starting to recognise. Battle mode.

The doors opened with a soft chime, and he gestured her out first, saying nothing.

In the apartment, the silence followed them in like fog.

"Sit," he said finally, his voice low, controlled. He pointed to the kitchen stool by the island.

Violet obeyed, mostly because her knees were starting to shake.

Chad moved with precision—grabbing the first aid kit from the cabinet, setting out gauze, antiseptic, butterfly bandages. Every movement exact, efficient. He didn't look at her.

"I can do it," she said, her voice rough, trying to pull the focus away from whatever had cracked open between them.

"No," he said. "You're shaking."

She hadn't noticed. She folded her hands in her lap, gripping them tight.

He knelt in front of her, the kit open at his side. His eyes finally lifted to hers. "This is going to sting."

"Most things do," she said softly.

His gaze flickered—but he didn't answer. Just reached for her knee.

His fingers brushed the torn fabric of her leggings, and her breath hitched. He glanced up, and for a second, something flickered between them again. Then it was gone. Replaced by the professional, clinical man she barely recognised.

He cut the fabric gently away from the abrasions on her knees, working in silence. The antiseptic burned, but Violet didn't flinch. Not from that. What made her wince was the careful way he handled her. Like she was fragile. Breakable. Untouchable.

"You regret it," she said finally, voice barely above a whisper.

His hand stilled against her leg. "I lost control."

"You kissed me."

"You were hurt. You were terrified. It was the worst possible moment and I—" He broke off, jaw flexing. "It was a mistake."

Violet blinked down at him, her throat tightening. "It didn't feel like one."

Chad looked up, his eyes storm-dark and tired. "Doesn't matter how it felt. It was."

He finished cleaning her knee and moved to her cheek. His thumb brushed gently under the swelling, just like it had before. But this time, he didn't linger. He dabbed the cut with antiseptic, avoiding her gaze.

"You kissed me like you meant it," she said quietly.

"And you've been through hell these past few weeks," he said, voice tight. "I'm not going to take advantage of that. I'm here to protect you, Violet. Not confuse you."

"You think I'm confused?"

He finally looked at her. "I think you're scared. And I think for five seconds, we both needed to feel something that wasn't fear."

She held his stare. "Speak for yourself."

The silence stretched between them, thick and electric.

"You're not scared?" he asked, voice lower now. "Not even a little?"

"I'm terrified," she said, "but not of you. Not of this." She reached up, her fingers grazing the front of his shirt where she'd clung to him in the alley. "I didn't imagine what I felt out there."

His breath caught.

But then he stood, abruptly, stepping away from her like she burned.

"You should get some rest," he said. "You've been through enough."

Just like that, the walls were back up. Reinforced.

Violet stayed on the stool, knees stinging, cheek aching. She watched him retreat to the living room, grab his phone, mutter something into his comm. Back to the job. Back to duty.

But even with his back turned, she could see it—the tension in his shoulders, the stiffness in his posture.

That kiss had rattled him.

And for all his regret, for all his restraint, it meant something. Just like it meant something to her.

She slid off the stool slowly, testing her legs. Didn't say anything more. Didn't push.

But as she passed him, she felt it—that unmistakable pull of his gaze. His head turned. His eyes followed her, lingering like he didn't want to—but couldn't stop.

Let him call it a mistake.

She didn't believe him.

And deep down, she was pretty sure he didn't believe it either.

She paused in the hallway, her voice calm but razor-edged. "You haven't asked what he said to me."

Chad's head lifted sharply. "He spoke to you?"

She met his eyes without flinching. "Yes."

A beat of silence.

"He said… 'Tell your boyfriend to back off. Get rid of Chad… or next time, you don't get up.'"

She let the words hang there—heavy, damning—and then turned and walked to her bedroom without another word.

She didn't look back.

But she knew he was still watching.

The door to her bedroom clicked shut.

Chad stood there, staring at the empty hallway, like maybe if he glared hard enough, he could burn through it. Like maybe he could undo it.

Get rid of Chad… or next time, you don't get up.

His jaw flexed. Once. Twice. The words ran on a loop in his head, each pass hotter than the last. He turned away from the hallway and planted his palms on the edge of the kitchen counter, head bowed.

His breath came rough through his nose.

She could've been killed. If he hadn't woke up when he did—

Chad squeezed his eyes shut, the burn of helplessness crashing into him like a wave he hadn't seen coming. He wasn't used to feeling powerless. He hated it.

And worse—he'd kissed her.

When she was still shaken. When she was vulnerable. When he was.

He slammed his fist down on the countertop—not hard enough to break it, but hard enough to feel it. The sharp bite of pain grounded him, barely.

He shouldn't have touched her.

But he had. And she'd kissed him back.

God help him, he could still feel the way she'd fit against him. The softness of her mouth. The way she'd looked at him afterward—like she wasn't afraid. Like she trusted him.

She shouldn't.

Because what lived in him now—this thing clawing at his chest, this need to protect her, to hunt the bastard who dared to threaten her, to keep her close—it wasn't part of the job. It wasn't about duty or loyalty to Lance.

It was something else.

Something he wasn't willing to name.

Not yet.

Violet shut the door quietly behind her and leaned against it, the wood cool against her back. Her heart was still thudding—not from fear this time, but from him.

That kiss hadn't been an accident. Not for her.

She moved toward the bed on unsteady legs and sat on the edge, fingers brushing the tender skin near the cut on her cheek. It stung, but it wasn't what she was thinking about.

She was thinking about the way Chad's hands had held her face like she was breakable. Like he didn't know whether to protect her or run from her. The way his mouth had crashed into hers like it was the only way to breathe.

And he regretted it.

She saw it the second their lips parted—the panic in his eyes, the way he put space between them like it would undo the heat still crackling in the air.

She exhaled slowly, pressing her fingers to her lips.

Let him regret it. Let him pretend it was a lapse in judgment.

But she'd felt something. And she didn't imagine the way his body had trembled against hers, like he was hanging on by a thread. The same thread she was holding now.

She lay back slowly, staring at the ceiling, the ache in her chest twisting tighter.

This wasn't simple anymore. It hadn't been the second she looked into his eyes and realised how scared he'd been for her. Not angry. Not just protective.

Scared.

And there was something about that—about knowing he cared more than he wanted to—that made it impossible to forget the taste of his mouth or the way he still looked at her when he thought she wasn't watching.

She closed her eyes.

Whatever happened next, the line was already crossed.

There was no going back.

Monday arrived wrapped in the dull hush of spring rain. Outside, the clouds sagged low, swollen with drizzle, casting a muted grey light through the apartment windows. Inside, the silence was heavier still.

Chad stood by the door, dressed in dark slacks and a black crewneck that fit him too well to be accidental. Arms crossed, spine straight. He didn't lean—Chad Morgan never leaned. He just waited. Watchful. Still. Like a soldier at the edge of a battlefield, bracing for whatever came next.

Except today, the stillness wasn't just vigilance.

It was tension. Regret. A weight he hadn't carried until yesterday.

Violet moved through the space with quiet precision. Her heels barely made a sound against the hardwood. She wore a black pencil skirt and a soft blue blouse, the collar buttoned neatly at her throat, her dark hair twisted up with clinical care. On the surface, she looked ready for court.

But Chad's eyes caught the details.

The faint smudge of fatigue under her eyes.

The bruise on her cheek, barely concealed by concealer.

The way her fingers trembled for half a second when she clipped her watch on.

The night had left marks.

They hadn't spoken much since the kiss.

Now, she shrugged into her coat and reached for her bag, careful not to meet his gaze. There was a pause—brief, uncertain—as if she wanted to say something but thought better of it.

Then her phone buzzed.

She glanced down, and her breath caught in her throat.

Chad was beside her in two strides. "What is it?"

She didn't answer. Just handed him the phone, her fingers tight around the edge like she couldn't bear to read it again.

I hope you took the advice. You won't get a second chance.

Chad's jaw locked hard. The phone lowered slowly in his hand, his other clenched into a fist so tight his veins stood out against his skin.

"Son of a—" He stopped himself, drawing in a sharp breath through his nose, trying to steady the fury building behind his ribs. "This isn't just a threat. This is an escalation."

Violet stood frozen, her eyes locked on the screen like the words might start bleeding. Her face had gone pale beneath her makeup, but her spine stayed straight.

"I'm not letting you go to work like this," Chad said, his voice low, clipped. A tone that brooked no argument.

"Chad, I have court this morning," she said, her voice quieter but no less firm. "I can't just cancel. My client is counting on me."

"I don't care." He turned to her fully now, his expression carved from stone. "You're not walking into a public courthouse with your name on the docket when some psycho is tracking your every move."

"I don't have the luxury of hiding," she snapped back. "This case is a year in the making—"

"And if something happens to you?" he cut in, stepping closer. "What then? What happens to your case if you're in a hospital bed? Or worse?"

She flinched—just a flicker—but she didn't back down.

"He's getting bolder," Chad said, lowering his voice again. "And the closer we get to finding out who he is, the more desperate he'll become."

"I know that." Her eyes flared, emotion finally cracking through. "Don't you think I know that?"

The silence that followed was thick and volatile.

Then she lifted her chin. "You either drive me, or I'll drive myself. You choose."

Chad stared at her for a long beat. Then another.

Without a word, he grabbed his keys.

Goddamn Miller blood. He didn't know whether to admire it or fear what it would cost her.

Chapter Eleven

Violet slumped back against the passenger seat of Chad's SUV, the courthouse already a shadow in the rearview mirror. Her blouse clung to her skin, sticky with sweat and courtroom stress, and her heels had long since become instruments of torture.

She hadn't broken today—not in front of the jury, or the smug opposing counsel. But it had been close. Her voice had cracked once. Her hands had trembled under the desk. She'd only just held it together.

And she had to do it all again tomorrow.

Beside her, Chad drove with one hand on the wheel, the other resting loosely against his thigh. His presence filled the space—solid, quiet, watchful. He hadn't pushed her to talk. He hadn't said anything at all until they pulled up in front of her office building.

"You want me to come up?" he asked, turning to look at her.

"No," she said quickly—then caught herself, softening. "I'll only be a few minutes. I just need to grab the Harrison deposition and update a couple of notes."

He hesitated, then shook his head. "No… I'll come with you."

Violet didn't argue. She was too tired to pretend she didn't need him. And the truth was, she didn't want to be alone.

They walked through the empty hallway of her law firm, the silence eerie in the after-hours hush. The scent of paper, old coffee, and floor wax clung to the air. Her office was dimly lit by the security lights filtering through the blinds.

Violet flicked on the lamp and shrugged off her blazer with a sigh. "Remind me why I ever thought trial work was a good idea?"

"You like a fight," Chad said simply, standing against the wall as she dropped into her chair.

Before she could reply, there was a knock at the door. Damien stepped inside with a small stack of folders in his hands and that usual faint, unreadable smile.

"Hey," he said. "Found these on the shared printer. I think you were looking for the supplemental motions in Harrison?"

"Perfect. Yes." Violet took the files, grateful. "Thank you, Damien."

He lingered a step closer. "Court went late?"

Violet nodded, rubbing her temple. "It's brutal. We're halfway through the witness list and opposing counsel keeps objecting just to throw us off rhythm."

"You looked composed in the hallway earlier," he said. "Strong. Calm."

She blinked at him. "You saw me?"

He shrugged. "I had to drop something at the clerk's office. I didn't want to interrupt. But... I saw you walking out." A pause. "You seemed tired. And—your cheek..."

Her hand went instinctively to the faint bruise on her face. "Oh, that? Just clumsy. I walked into a doorframe yesterday."

He frowned slightly, concern threading through his voice. "You sure you're okay?"

"I'm fine," Violet said, her smile polite. "Really. Just one of those days."

He nodded, eyes lingering on her a moment longer than necessary before stepping back. "Well, if you need anything... coffee, a break... someone to vent to... I'm around."

"Thanks, Damien. That means a lot."

He smiled, then glanced at Chad—still silent by the wall, arms folded, expression unreadable. Damien's smile faded a little as he nodded and quietly left the room.

The silence returned, but it felt heavier now.

Violet sighed and turned back to her desk, sifting through the folders Damien had brought. She was about to file them when she noticed an envelope in her in tray.

Her name typed neatly across the front.

She frowned. "What's this?"

She tore it open.

The letter was handwritten. The penmanship careful. Elegant.

You were beautiful in court today. So powerful. So strong. I can't wait to feel that fire when we're alone. When you finally stop pretending.

I think about touching you every night. I imagine the way you'll sound when I make love to you—when you realise no one will ever know you the way I do.

You're already mine. You just haven't accepted it yet.

The air drained from her lungs. Her hand trembled. Her heart slammed against her ribs like it was trying to escape.

Chad crossed the room in three strides.

He took the letter from her fingers, read it in seconds.

Then his voice dropped into a low, dangerous growl. "Where the hell did this come from?"

Violet swallowed hard. "It was in my in-tray."

Chad looked at her, then at the envelope, then at the door Damien had exited through.

He didn't say what he was thinking. Didn't voice the flash of suspicion that darkened his eyes the moment he glanced toward the door Damien had exited through.

Violet was too shaken to notice.

Too busy trying to breathe, trying to quiet the thrum of panic in her chest.

But Chad's jaw tightened.

His grip on the letter turned white-knuckled, like he was resisting the urge to tear it in half.

His whole body shifted—no longer just steady and protective, but tense, alert. Like a predator scenting something off.

Still, he said nothing.

Instead, he slipped the letter carefully into the inside pocket of his jacket, voice low and controlled. "I'm going to have this analysed. Fingerprints, ink, paper source—every inch of it."

Violet nodded, though her insides twisted like a knot.

Chad stepped closer, his tone dipping further, rough with something colder than concern. "I need you to think. Has anyone been hanging around more than usual? Watching you? Acting off?"

She hesitated, chewing on her bottom lip. "Not really. I mean… Damien's around a lot, but that's his job. He's my assistant. He brings me files, checks in—he's never made me uncomfortable."

Chad didn't respond right away, just studied her with that same unreadable stare.

Then he spoke again, brisk and firm. "We're leaving. Have you got everything you need?"

Violet glanced at her desk, then back at him. "Yes."

"Good," he said, already moving toward the door. "You're not coming back here alone. Not until I say it's safe."

And something about the way he said it made her feel, for the first time that day, just a little bit safer.

The drive back to Violet's apartment simmered with tension. Chad said nothing, but his jaw was clenched so tightly she could see the pulse beating in his neck. Violet didn't try to fill the silence—she couldn't have, even if she wanted to. The weight of the letter was still pressing against her ribs.

As soon as they walked through her front door, Chad pulled out his phone and ordered Chinese without asking, then tossed his jacket on the back of a chair like he was settling in for a stakeout.

"I'm going to take a shower," Violet said quietly.

He nodded once, already scanning the room, eyes sharp. "Leave your clothes out—I'll throw them in the wash."

There was something too intimate about that—too easy. Like they'd done this before. Like they might again.

And she didn't hate the way that made her feel.

Under the hot spray, she scrubbed the day off her skin, the grime of the courthouse, the adrenaline, the fear. But no matter how hard she tried, she couldn't wash away the memory of that letter. The words. The way Chad had looked at her—protective and furious and something else that sent heat curling in her belly.

When she stepped back into the living room in a soft tee and cotton shorts, her hair damp and curling at the ends, the smell of food hit her first—sweet soy, ginger, garlic.

Then she saw him.

Chad had set everything out on the coffee table—plates, chopsticks, the takeout containers all opened and steaming. He was sitting cross-legged on the floor, his broad shoulders outlined by the glow of the lamp. His shirt sleeves were still rolled up, revealing strong forearms and the veins in his hands that flexed every time he moved.

"Hope you're hungry," he said, handing her a plate without looking up.

"I'm starving," she murmured, sitting across from him. Her knee brushed his. Neither of them pulled away.

They ate in silence for a few moments, the clink of chopsticks and rustle of paper containers the only sound. But beneath it, something electric hummed in the air— unspoken words, unsatisfied tension, the kind of energy that vibrated between two people who were trying not to look too long, to feel too much.

Violet set down her food and reached for her water, her voice softer than she meant it to be. "This guy… he's dangerous, isn't he?"

Chad didn't answer right away. He watched her. The way her lips wrapped around the straw. The way her damp hair curled against her cheek.

Then he nodded. Slow. Measured. "Yeah. He is."

Something flickered in her eyes. Fear. But not just fear. A kind of vulnerable realisation. "He really thinks I belong to him."

Chad's jaw flexed. "Not for long."

She looked at him then. Really looked at him. "You sound so sure."

"I am," he said, his voice dropping into that low, gravel-edged tone that made her stomach twist. "Because I won't let him touch you."

Their eyes locked. The air thickened.

Neither of them moved, but everything shifted.

The container in her lap suddenly felt too hot. Her skin too sensitive. His gaze was a touch. His nearness a pull.

And in that small living room, sitting cross-legged on the floor, with half-eaten takeout between them and danger lurking just outside their door, Violet realised something terrifyingly simple.

She trusted him.

And she wanted him.

So badly it ached.

Chad closed the door to the guest room behind him with a soft click, but there was nothing soft about the way his body moved.

Everything in him was coiled tight. Rage, worry, restraint—they all warred beneath his skin, an unrelenting burn he couldn't shake. He paced once, then twice, then stood still in the centre of the room, fists clenched.

The letter was in his jacket pocket. Still there. Still mocking him.

He pulled it out and unfolded it slowly. His eyes scanned the words again, not because he needed to—he'd memorised every line the moment he read them—but because he couldn't help himself.

You were beautiful in court today. So powerful. So strong. I can't wait to feel that fire when we're alone...

The way it was written made his skin crawl. Intimate. Possessive. A man who thought he knew her. A man who thought he deserved her. Who felt entitled to her space, her body, her life.

Chad had seen this before. In warzones. In stalking cases. In men who wore the mask of normalcy while they obsessed from the shadows. It always started with attention. Then fixation. Then control.

He'd worked a case like this once—an heiress with a stalker who wrote her poetry and left flowers at her door.

Everyone thought he was harmless until he broke into her Hamptons estate with a knife and a wedding ring.

This guy wasn't playing games. He wasn't bluffing.

He was escalating.

And Violet—Jesus, Violet. The way she'd tried to downplay it. The faint bruise on her cheek she blamed on a doorframe. The fear she'd masked with sarcasm and a tired smile. The way she'd curled up on the floor tonight, legs tucked under her like she was trying to take up less space, even when she was trying to be brave.

She didn't want to be afraid. But she was.

And that enraged him.

Because it should've been his job to keep her safe. It was his job now, even if she hadn't asked for it. Even if she didn't want him to see how scared she really was.

Chad's jaw tightened as he folded the letter again, more carefully this time, and slid it back into the envelope.

He would run every trace possible on this. Paper fibres. Ink type. Fingerprints. He'd already texted his contact at the FBI to arrange a forensic review in the morning.

But that wasn't the part gnawing at him.

What gnawed at him—what kept him pacing like a wolf in a cage—was who had left it. How they'd gotten to her desk. Past her building security. Past the firm's internal access points.

That pointed to someone inside.

And he didn't say it earlier, but there was one name that kept floating to the top.

Damien.

Too convenient. Too close. Too observant. And that quiet little moment tonight—asking about her cheek, the way his eyes lingered. The way his tone shifted when he saw Chad in the room.

It hadn't sat right.

Chad's fists clenched again. He could feel the storm building inside him.

No one was going to hurt her. Not while he was here.

And if Damien—or anyone else—was behind this?

They had no idea what kind of hell they'd just unleashed.

In the dark, Damien watched her apartment window from across the street. His hood up, hands in his coat pockets. Just another silhouette in the night.

The glow from her living room lit the curtain in soft gold. He watched until her shadow moved past the window—slow, tired. Alone.

She was scared now. Good.

That meant she'd be ready soon.

Ready to see him.

Chapter Twelve

The smell of fresh coffee curled through Violet's apartment as she dabbed the last bit of concealer over the fading bruise on her cheek. It was lighter today, but still stubborn beneath the bathroom light. She adjusted her collar, checked her reflection, and tried to ignore the weight pressing against her chest.

In the kitchen, Chad was pouring coffee into two travel mugs, already dressed in crisp black slacks and a fitted shirt that made him look both dangerous and devastating. He moved with the quiet precision of someone who was always ten seconds ahead of trouble. She hated how safe that made her feel.

Her phone buzzed on the counter.

She glanced down and froze.

Lance.

Her brother never called before work. Texts, memes, the occasional grumpy voice note—yes. But a morning call? That meant something was wrong.

She swiped the screen. "Hey. Everything okay?"

His voice came through instantly—brisk, but with a rough edge of worry. "Vi. You alright?"

Her shoulders softened. "Yeah. I'm fine."

"You don't sound fine," he said. "Chad's been keeping me in the loop."

She sighed. "Has he?"

"He called last night. Told me about the letter. Said you were rattled… that you found it in your office."

Violet sank onto the edge of the bed, her fingers curling around the phone. "It was nothing. I mean—it scared the hell out of me. But I'm okay now."

"You don't have to be brave for me," Lance said, voice quiet. "You never did."

"I'm not."

"You are. You always are." He paused. "But this time, you don't have to. Not with this. Not alone."

"I'm not alone," she murmured.

Another pause.

"Good," he said, softer now. "So… you and Chad getting on?"

She smiled, despite the tightness in her chest. "Yeah. Surprisingly. He's… handling everything."

"Good," Lance said simply. "I trust him."

"I know." Her voice wavered.

Emotion swelled in her throat. She looked toward the kitchen. Chad glanced over, met her eyes, and gave a subtle nod.

"I don't want to worry you," she said quietly.

"You always say that," Lance murmured. "But Vi... you are my worry. Always have been. And you're not in this alone. Got it?"

She bit her lip. "Got it."

"Good. Now go kill it in court," he said, letting a note of big-brother swagger creep in. "And if that bastard sends another letter, you let me know. I love you, sis."

Violet laughed, and something inside her loosened. "Love you too, big brother."

"Always. Call me later."

She ended the call just as Chad stepped into the doorway, travel mug in hand. "You okay?"

She nodded and took the coffee. "Yeah. That was Lance."

"Worried?"

"Of course." She smiled faintly. "But he said he trusts you."

Chad's mouth curved, just a hint. "That's not easy to earn."

Violet met his gaze, steadier now. "You already have."

They left together moments later, the memory of the letter still lingering—but it no longer owned her.

Not completely.

Not anymore.

Another day in court, and Violet was wrung out. The proceedings had been gruelling again—tense cross-examinations, delays, the pressure of a case that was starting to feel like a weight pressed against her ribs. But at least it had ended a little earlier than yesterday.

When she and Chad stepped out of the elevator and into the law firm's reception, Kylie glanced up from her desk.

"Ah, Violet—this just came for you." She reached down and handed over a small package, brown paper, no markings except her name scrawled in ink across the top.

"Oh. Thanks, Kylie," Violet said, accepting it.

But as they walked toward her office, Chad reached out and took the package from her without a word.

She looked at him in surprise. His jaw was set, shoulders tense, expression grim.

Then it hit her.

He thinks it's from the stalker.

A flicker of dread climbed up her spine. Her stomach twisted.

When they reached her office, she opened the door—then stopped short, a sharp gasp catching in her throat.

There it was.

Another envelope.

Same as the one from last night.

It sat neatly in her in-tray, white, slightly crumpled, and chillingly familiar.

"I'll open it," Chad said, stepping forward without hesitation.

She nodded, silent, her pulse thudding in her ears.

He pulled on a glove from his jacket pocket and carefully tore it open. As he unfolded the note, his entire body seemed to go still—then rigid. His face turned to stone.

"What does it say?" she asked, her voice small, afraid.

He didn't speak. Instead, he placed the note on her desk with precise control.

"Just don't touch it," he said quietly.

She leaned forward and read:

I told you to get rid of Chad. He can't have you. Did you like the present I sent you? I can't wait to see you wear it. You'll look so sexy in it.

I dreamt of you again last night. I want to hear you moan in my arms when I finally take you.

I will make you happy. You'll see.

Violet recoiled, a sharp sob breaking from her lips. Her breath hitched. Her fingers flew to her mouth as her eyes darted to the package Chad now set carefully on the desk.

He opened it slowly.

Inside, nestled in crinkled tissue paper, was a red lace babydoll lingerie set.

Delicate. Intimate. Violated.

Matching g-string.

Violet backed away, a hand bracing the edge of her desk as her knees weakened.

"Oh my God…"

Chad didn't speak. His gaze was hard, cold, and deadly. The look of a man who had seen war and just declared one of his own.

Violet stumbled back until the edge of the couch hit the back of her knees, and she sank down like her bones couldn't hold her weight anymore. Her hands trembled in her lap, and her breath came in short, uneven bursts.

The lingerie lay open on her desk—a threat dressed as a gift. The letter sat beside it; each word seared into her mind.

Chad closed the box carefully, then slid the envelope into an evidence bag he'd taken from his inside jacket pocket. Always prepared. Always thinking three steps ahead.

She couldn't stop shaking.

"I can't do this," she whispered, voice cracking. "I can't keep pretending I'm okay."

Chad turned toward her slowly, his movements controlled, deliberate. He crouched down in front of her, resting his forearms on his knees so he could meet her eyes.

"Then don't," he said gently. "You don't have to."

Her vision blurred. "He's watching me. He's sending me underwear, Chad. He dreams about me. I don't even know who he is."

A sob rose up and broke loose before she could stop it. She covered her face with her hands, her shoulders shaking under the weight of all the fear she'd been holding in for weeks.

"I feel disgusting. Like he's in my head, in my home—like I'll never be clean again."

Chad didn't say anything right away. Instead, he reached up and wrapped his hands around hers, gently pulling them down from her face. Her eyes were red, tear-filled, desperate.

He moved closer, sitting beside her now, wrapping an arm around her shoulders and tugging her against him.

Violet didn't resist. She folded into him, her head against his chest, her hands fisting into his shirt like she needed something solid to keep from falling apart.

He held her.

Tight. Warm. Steady.

Like nothing could get to her while she was in his arms.

"You are not disgusting," he murmured against her hair. "You are smart, and brave, and still standing. He's the sick one. Not you."

Her voice was muffled by his shirt. "I hate that I'm scared. I hate that he can do this to me."

"You're allowed to be scared," he said, his voice low but unyielding. "But he's not going to win, Violet. Not while I'm here. I promise you that."

She looked up at him, her face wet, her heart in her throat. "How do you do that?"

"What?"

"Make me feel like I'm not falling apart when I am."

Chad's mouth curved just slightly, but his eyes stayed serious, intense. "Because I see you. Not just what's happening to you. You. And I'm not going anywhere."

A fresh tear slipped down her cheek. "I believe you."

He brushed it away with the pad of his thumb. "Good. Because you don't have to go through this alone."

She leaned into him again, her voice barely audible.

"Thank you."

"Always."

The apartment was quiet, save for the low hiss of water coming from the bathroom. Chad stood near the window, one hand gripping his phone, the other curled into a fist at his side. His jaw was tight; his shoulders coiled with tension that hadn't eased since the second letter.

He heard the faint sound of Violet moving in the shower—safe, for now—and pressed the phone to his ear.

Lance answered on the first ring.

"Well?"

Chad kept his voice low. "This guy's bloody smart."

He turned from the window, pacing a slow line across the hardwood floor.

"The cards and letters? No prints except Violet's. No DNA, no trace evidence. The phone he used to text her was a burner—unregistered, untraceable. Bought with cash. We tracked down the store, but the surveillance cameras were vandalised the night before. We checked nearby shops and traffic cams too—nothing. It's like he knew exactly how to avoid every angle. He planned every detail."

"Christ," Lance breathed. "He's always one step ahead of you."

Chad's gaze flicked toward the closed bathroom door, his voice low and razor-sharp. "Yeah. He's methodical. Calculated. And he's not going to stop."

"Bloody hell."

"He sent her another letter today," Chad said. "Worse than the last."

"Worse?" Lance asked, his voice tight.

Chad recited the message word for word, then added quietly, "The package he sent with it was lingerie. Red lace."

There was a pause. A long one. Just the steady sound of the shower running behind the door.

Then Lance's voice came through, raw and frayed at the edges. "Keep her safe, Chad."

Chad stopped pacing. His jaw clenched. "I will."

"She's all I got left," Lance said, quieter now. "I wouldn't survive if anything happened to her."

Chad closed his eyes briefly. When he spoke, it was with absolute certainty.

"She won't have to go through this alone. Not while I'm breathing."

Lance let out a shaky breath. "She trusts you."

Chad's gaze lifted to the door again, as if he could see through it. "I won't break that."

A pause.

Then Lance, gruff but grateful: "Good. Because you're the only one I'd trust with her."

Chad ended the call just as the water stopped running.

He slipped the phone into his pocket and crossed back to the kitchen, already pouring her tea by the time she emerged in an oversized sweatshirt, her hair damp and curling around her face.

She looked at him with tired eyes, but the faintest flicker of peace was there—just for knowing he was near.

And he swore to himself again, silently, that nothing—no one—would ever get close enough to touch her.

Not on his watch.

Chapter Thirteen

The apartment was still, wrapped in the breathless hush of three a.m. Shadows stretched long across the walls, and the only sound was the slow, metronomic tick of the old mantel clock in the living room—a reminder that time, unlike sleep, kept moving forward.

Chad hadn't managed more than a few restless hours. His body was conditioned for nights like this—wired to wake at the smallest sound, honed by years of midnight alarms and sudden threats. But tonight, it wasn't muscle memory or battlefield ghosts keeping him up.

It was her.

Violet.

A soft creak echoed through the quiet. Then a stifled sniffle. Chad sat up, instincts flaring, listening.

A shuffle of movement. The floorboard again. The unmistakable sound of someone pacing… someone trying not to fall apart.

He was out of bed in seconds.

Padding down the hallway, he paused outside her bedroom door, hand halfway to knocking. Then he heard it—barely audible—a choked sob, quickly smothered. A sound not meant for anyone else to hear.

He didn't knock.

He just opened the door.

She stood at the window, framed by moonlight, arms crossed tightly over her chest. One of her long-sleeve shirts hung loose on her frame. Her hair was in a messy braid, and her posture—usually so proud, so precise—had a tremble to it, like the scaffolding holding her up was buckling.

She didn't turn when he stepped in.

"I'm sorry," she said, her voice raw, barely above a whisper. "Did I wake you?"

"No." His voice was soft, even. "I was already awake."

She turned just enough for him to see her tear-swollen eyes, her skin pale in the moonlight. A sharp ache tightened in his chest.

This wasn't the woman who stood fearless before a judge or opponent. This was the woman behind the armour, unravelling beneath the weight of fear, doubt, and too many what-ifs.

"I feel ridiculous," she said, swiping at her cheek. "I keep telling myself I'm fine, but every time it gets quiet, it's like I can hear him breathing down my neck. What if he's out there right now? Watching?"

"You're not ridiculous," Chad said gently. "You're dealing with something real. And you're not alone."

Her gaze met his, and something inside her cracked. "I used to be stronger than this," she said, breath trembling. "I don't even recognise myself right now."

"You're strong," he said, taking a cautious step forward. "But even the strongest people break when they have to hold everything by themselves."

He didn't reach for her. He just waited.

She moved first.

Her fingers found his shirt, tentative, searching. Then her body leaned into his like a sigh, and Chad wrapped his arms around her, steady and warm. She fit perfectly—her head resting beneath his chin, her fingers curling into his chest as though grounding herself with his heartbeat.

"I hate that he's still in my head," she murmured.

"He won't be for long," he said, voice low and firm. "I won't let him win."

They stood there in silence, the kind that said more than words ever could. His arms around her, her breathing slowly calming against him, the air heavy with the kind of trust that didn't come easily.

When her knees gave slightly, he caught her without hesitation and led her to the bed. She didn't protest as he helped her beneath the covers. He sat on the edge, brushing a strand of hair from her damp cheek.

"Will you stay?" she asked, so softly he almost missed it.

He nodded, pulled a blanket from the nearby chair, and lay down beside her—on top of the covers, not touching, just close enough that she could feel his presence like a shield.

"I'll be right here," he said.

Violet reached for his hand.

She fell asleep holding it.

Chad stayed awake, watching the gentle rise and fall of her chest, the way her face slowly relaxed in sleep. And after a long moment, he whispered into the dark:

"I've seen warzones, Violet. But nothing terrifies me like the thought of something happening to you."

The first light of morning filtered in through the slats of the blinds, painting the room in soft bands of gold and shadow. The clock on the nightstand read 5:07. Outside, the world was still quiet—no traffic, no voices—just the faint stir of wind rustling the trees and the distant hum of a city not quite awake.

Violet blinked into the light, disoriented at first.

Then she felt it—the warm, steady weight of his hand in hers.

She turned her head slowly.

Chad lay beside her, still dressed, still on top of the covers. His brow was smooth in sleep, his breathing even. The sharp lines of his jaw and the faint scruff along it caught the dawn in soft relief. One arm was curled beneath his head, the other stretched toward her, hand loosely clasping hers as if even unconscious, he didn't want to let go.

For a long time, she just watched him.

There was something arresting about seeing him like this—unguarded, still. The man who'd stood between her and a hundred fears the night before now looked… peaceful. And younger, somehow. The weariness she always saw around his eyes had softened. The tension in his broad shoulders had eased.

He looked like someone who had finally stopped fighting.

And for once, it wasn't him doing the watching, the worrying. It wasn't him bracing for the next threat. It was him beside her, protecting her, anchoring her in the storm. The realisation twisted something deep in her chest—something grateful, aching, scared, and full of something she wasn't quite ready to name.

She brushed her thumb lightly over the back of his hand. He didn't stir.

"I don't know what I'd do without you," she whispered.

She wasn't sure if he heard her, if it registered somewhere in the edges of sleep, but his fingers curled around hers, just a little tighter. Like a promise.

Violet smiled faintly and let her head rest on the pillow again, still holding his hand.

For the first time in days, she felt like she could close her eyes and breathe.

She wasn't alone.

Chad's office was perched on the top floor of Morgan Global's security headquarters—floor-to-ceiling glass, sleek steel lines, and a direct view of the skyline that could be intimidating to some. But right now, he wasn't interested in the view.

He was behind his desk, sleeves rolled up, the tension in his jaw a clear sign that something had shifted.

He'd dropped Violet at the courthouse twenty minutes ago, watching until she disappeared into the building. One of his most trusted agents, Jenna Cruz, was tailing her discreetly—ex-military, sharp as hell, and instructed to intervene only if absolutely necessary.

But Chad had learned to trust his instincts. And something about all this—her stalker, the timing, the way she'd been targeted so precisely—didn't sit right.

He tapped his intercom. "Jared. My office."

Thirty seconds later, the door opened and Jared Beck strode in. Late thirties, with shaggy blond hair and the casual confidence of a man who could hack a satellite feed before his second cup of coffee. He wore jeans and a hoodie with a faded Star Wars logo, completely at odds with the high-level security clearance he held.

"You rang, boss?" Jared asked, shutting the door behind him.

Chad didn't look up right away. He was staring at a digital file open on his tablet—Violet's firm website, her bio, and a list of her coworkers.

"I need background checks on everyone who works in Violet Miller's office. Associates, paralegals, admin staff, even the guy who refills the coffee machine if he's on payroll."

Jared raised a brow. "Thorough."

"Someone's targeting her. I want to know if that someone is walking the same halls she is."

Jared dropped into one of the leather chairs across from Chad's desk, already pulling out his tablet. "You're thinking it's internal."

"I'm thinking it's someone who knows her schedule. Her habits. Someone who can plant things in her office without being seen."

Chad met his eyes then, voice low. "I'm not ruling out a coworker. Not until I've vetted every single one."

Jared nodded, the easy-going vibe fading. "Understood. You want full reports?"

"Anything that flags," Chad said. "Financial red flags, criminal history, recent large purchases, behavioural issues, sudden resignations, social media aliases—anything that smells off. Start with her assistant and whoever's been on her cases recently. Prioritise anyone with access to her calendar or office."

Jared was already typing. "I'll get my team on it. Couple hours, we'll have a preliminary sweep."

"Keep it quiet," Chad added. "I don't want anyone alerted. And don't touch Violet's own records."

Jared gave him a curious glance but didn't question it. "Got it."

As the door closed behind his IT lead, Chad leaned back in his chair. His eyes dropped to a still image on his desk—security footage from the building Violet worked in, timestamped three nights ago. A shadowed figure near the garage entrance. No clear face. Just enough to piss him off.

He'd promised her she wasn't alone.

And now, he was going to prove it—with facts, with strategy, with the full weight of the empire he'd built to protect people exactly like her.

Even if she didn't know just how far he was willing to go yet.

The gavel struck once, clean, and final.

Violet blinked. She sat still for a moment, as if waiting for the judge to amend the verdict, or for the ground beneath her to shift and call it all a mistake.

But it wasn't. She'd won.

The plaintiff's case had been dismissed. Her arguments—rushed, a bit disjointed at times—had somehow still landed where they needed to. The law had been on her side, but it had been a hell of a climb to this moment. She hadn't been sleeping, hadn't been eating much either. Her nerves were frayed, and her thoughts had been scattered like pages in a windstorm.

But she'd done it.

She gathered her files with a numb kind of grace, murmured a polite thank you to the opposing counsel, and stepped out into the courthouse corridor. Her heels clicked lightly on the polished floors, her pulse still a drumbeat in her throat.

She scanned the crowd instinctively—searching for a tall, broad-shouldered figure standing against the wall. But Chad wasn't there.

Instead, a woman with a sleek braid and dark blazer stepped forward, her stance professional but casual.

"Ms. Miller?" the woman said. "I'm Jenna Cruz. Chad asked me to bring you to your office. He's checking on a few things—said he'd meet you there."

Violet blinked. "Right. Okay. Thanks."

Jenna gave a quick, reassuring smile and motioned toward the exit. "Come on. Let's get you out of here."

The ride to the office was quiet, Violet's thoughts a tangle of exhaustion, relief, and anticipation. When they arrived, she made her way up to her floor, Jenna trailing behind like a discreet shadow.

Once inside, Violet tossed her case files on the desk and eased into her chair. Jenna remained near the window at first, then settled on the couch with a tablet in hand, legs crossed, seemingly at ease but clearly still alert.

Violet tried to focus on her inbox, on paperwork that had been piling up, but her eyes kept darting to the clock. She was proud of herself, sure. Grateful for the win. But a part of her wished Chad had been there—just to share the moment. Just to see her like this. Not broken. Not trembling in the dark.

She was halfway through replying to an email when a voice broke the quiet.

"You were incredible today."

She turned, surprised to see Damien standing just inside the doorway with two coffee cups in hand. She hadn't heard him come in. He must've slipped in while she was focused on her screen.

"I mean it," he said, stepping closer. "I know the last few days have been rough, but you pulled it off. You were sharp. Commanding. Classic Violet."

She smiled—small, grateful. "Thanks. I didn't feel that way, but… thanks."

Damien placed one of the cups on her desk, just within reach. "Vanilla oat milk, no sugar. Figured you could use something warm."

"You remembered." She took the cup, fingers brushing his for a second. "That's sweet of you."

He shrugged, casual. "You're easy to remember."

She chuckled softly and turned back to her screen, sipping the coffee as Damien leaned slightly against the corner of her desk, keeping just enough distance to seem respectful. Still, he remained in her peripheral blind spot—never quite in front of her, never too visible. But always there.

He didn't linger long. Just offered a final word before slipping away again. "Seriously… if you ever need anything, I'm here. You're not alone, Violet."

And then he was gone.

She stared at the doorway for a long beat, warmth from the coffee pooling in her hands.

From the couch, Jenna's eyes lifted from her tablet just briefly, watching the retreating figure with a barely perceptible narrowing of her gaze. But she said nothing.

Violet didn't notice.

She just kept sipping her drink, not realising that danger was standing in the room— and she'd thanked it with a smile.

The elevator dinged softly from outside Violet's office.

Inside, the late afternoon sun streamed through the windows, casting slants of golden light across the floor. Violet sat behind her desk, chin resting on her hand as she scanned documents, unaware of the change just outside her door.

Jenna rose smoothly from the couch, brushing invisible lint from her blazer. She moved to the door and opened it just as Chad stepped into the hallway.

They didn't embrace or exchange pleasantries. Just a quiet nod between two professionals used to operating in high-stakes environments.

"Hey," Jenna murmured, slipping out into the corridor and pulling the door closed behind her.

"Thanks for getting her here," Chad said, voice low.

"She did great today," Jenna replied, keeping her tone easy, but her expression sharpened slightly. "Nothing happened while I was with her."

Chad studied her for a beat. "But?"

She glanced briefly at the closed office door, then met his gaze again. "Damien."

His jaw tightened.

Jenna folded her arms loosely. "I don't have anything concrete. But something about him doesn't sit right. He was polite. Brought her coffee. Knew her order, which she seemed to appreciate." Her eyes narrowed just a touch. "But the way he moves around her? He stays in her blind spots. Keeps his tone soft. Subtle, but too subtle. Like he's practiced it."

Chad didn't respond right away. He looked down the hall, then back at Jenna. "I've been getting the same vibe. Too careful. Too convenient."

She nodded. "So, it's not just me."

"No." His voice dropped a little. "But I don't have anything I can take to Violet yet. She trusts him."

"She shouldn't."

"I know." Chad's expression darkened. "I'm getting someone to keep an eye on him. Discreet surveillance. Background checks are already underway."

Jenna exhaled softly, her tone turning protective. "She's vulnerable right now. I think she's trying to keep it together, but…"

"Hopefully she won't have to hold it together for much longer," Chad said, gaze firm. "I've got her."

Jenna gave a short nod, then backed up a step. "Let me know if you need anything."

"I will."

She turned and walked down the hallway, heels quiet against the polished floor.

Chad waited until she was out of sight before opening the office door. Violet looked up and smiled—tired, but radiant in a way that hit him right in the chest.

He stepped inside like he hadn't just plotted to take apart one of her closest work allies.

But the truth was simple now:

He didn't care how long it took—he was going to find out what Damien White was hiding. And he was going to protect Violet, even if it meant protecting her from someone she trusted.

Chapter Fourteen

That night, the apartment sat hushed beneath the dense veil of stars. The wind stirred softly through the pine trees, and inside, the lights were low, warm, comforting.

Dinner sat mostly untouched. Chad leaned against the counter, arms folded across his chest, watching Violet push her fork through the risotto without lifting a single bite to her lips.

"You need to eat," he said quietly.

"I can't," she murmured. "I've tried."

"Violet…"

She set the fork down and looked away, eyes glinting with unspoken things. "My stomach's in knots. Every time I think about tomorrow, about walking outside… about checking my phone… it's like I forget how to breathe."

He approached slowly, not wanting to spook her. "We're figuring it out. My team is tracking the messages, narrowing possibilities. Whoever this guy is, he won't get near you."

"But we don't know who he is," she said, her voice catching. "We don't know anything. Just that he keeps getting closer. That he watches me. That he knows things about my life no one should know."

Her voice trembled. "What if I miss something important? What if I let my guard down and someone gets hurt?"

"You won't let anything happen, Vi," Chad said firmly. "This isn't your fault. And you're not alone in this."

She shook her head, stepping back, wrapping her arms around herself like armour. "I'm tired of being afraid. But I don't know how to stop."

He moved to stand in front of her, careful not to crowd her. "Then lean on me until you can."

She looked up, tears brimming in her eyes. "You say that like it's easy."

"It's not," he admitted. "But it's worth it."

Something shifted in her expression—like a wall cracking just enough to let something softer through. She reached out, her fingers grazing his shirt, then flattening against his chest like she was anchoring herself there.

"I hate feeling weak," she whispered. "I've always handled my own problems. Always."

Chad's hand came up, brushing a strand of hair behind her ear. "This isn't weakness. It's survival."

She looked at him then, really looked—and whatever she saw in his face, it unravelled something in her. The fear, the isolation, the armour she'd built so carefully began to crack, and beneath it, raw vulnerability shimmered.

Her hand rose slowly, almost reverently, to the side of his face. Her fingers traced the line of his jaw, the slight roughness of stubble under her touch making her breath hitch. He didn't move. Didn't flinch. Just watched her with that steady, searching gaze that saw too much and never judged.

She leaned in, heart thudding, uncertain but drawn to him like gravity itself had shifted. When their lips met, it wasn't sudden. It was soft. Questioning. Like pressing her mouth to something sacred.

Chad stilled—but only for a breath.

Then he kissed her back.

His lips moved with devastating care, like he was afraid he'd break her if he pressed too hard. One hand found her waist, fingers splaying through the thin fabric of her shirt, anchoring her to him. The other slid up to the nape of her neck, thumb brushing the curve of her jaw, grounding and guiding her all at once.

The kiss deepened—slow and aching. Mouths parting just enough to let the truth of their hunger slip through. Her hand slid into his hair, and he exhaled sharply through his nose, as if he hadn't expected her to want this too.

There was no rush. No desperate fumbling. Just a long, restrained burn of emotion that hummed between their bodies like a live current. It was the kind of kiss that spoke in silences, which said: I see you. I feel this too. But I'm still holding back.

And then—he stopped.

Chad broke the kiss, but he didn't move far. His forehead pressed gently to hers, their breath tangling in the narrow space between them, both of them trembling—caught in the aftershock of what they'd almost let happen.

"Vi…" His voice came out rough, ragged with restraint. "We can't."

She blinked, dazed, lips still parted, the taste of him lingering. "Why?"

His eyes closed for a beat, as though it physically hurt to say it. "Because I can't protect you if I'm emotionally involved," he said quietly. "And I won't take advantage of you… not when you're scared, not when your whole world is coming apart."

His hand, still cupping her face, moved gently as his thumb swept across her cheek—catching a tear she hadn't realised had fallen.

"You deserve my full protection," he murmured. "I can't risk compromising that. Not even for this."

And in that moment—when he could've taken more but chose not to—something deep inside her broke open. Not with pain, but with trust.

Tears slipped silently down her cheeks. "You're the only thing that makes me feel calm."

His breath hitched. He brushed a reverent kiss to her temple, tender and impossibly gentle. "I'm sorry, Violet," he whispered. "More than you know."

He lingered a second longer, forehead still resting against hers, like he couldn't quite bear to let go. And neither could she.

He led her to the couch, pulled the blanket over her, and settled beside her without another word. She curled into his side, the thrum of his heart under her ear steady and sure.

For the first time in days, she let herself relax and close her eyes.

And for the first time, she believed she might wake up safe.

The next two days passed in a tense but quiet lull, as if the storm had taken a breath. Chad remained a constant, reassuring presence—checking doors twice, monitoring phone calls, walking the perimeter even in the rain. Violet didn't ask him to stop. She didn't want him to. But by Saturday morning, she realised her chest wasn't as tight, her sleep hadn't been so broken, and for the first time all week, she caught herself humming softly as she stepped out of the bedroom.

She padded barefoot into the kitchen, the scent of fresh coffee and toasted bread already in the air. Chad stood by the window, one hand on his hip, the other holding his phone to his ear. His tone was clipped, his brow drawn low. Something was wrong.

"I don't care who signed off on it, Dave. It never should've gotten that far without a double-check from legal. You know better."

A pause.

"No, I want the file on my desk when I get there. And send the security footage from the last forty-eight hours. All of it. If there's even a hint of tampering—"

He glanced over his shoulder then, catching sight of her, and his expression softened slightly. Still focused, but not cold.

"I've got to go," he finished shortly. "Text me the update."

He hung up, exhaling slowly as he set the phone down on the counter.

"Everything okay?" Violet asked gently, approaching with tentative steps.

Chad ran a hand through his hair. "Work issue. Someone accessed a classified client file they shouldn't have been able to touch. I've got to head to the office and handle it myself."

She nodded, her arms folding across her chest more from instinct than defensiveness. "That sounds serious."

"It could be." He reached for his jacket but hesitated. "There are two guys parked outside. I've got eyes on the building 24/7, but I can have someone come upstairs and stay posted inside with you if you'd feel safer."

She gave him a small, sincere smile. "No, it's okay. Just go handle what you need to. I'll lock the door and won't go anywhere, I promise."

His jaw worked for a second, the muscle ticking in restraint. He stepped close, his hand brushing her shoulder. "If anything feels off, anything at all—you call me. Or the team."

"I will."

Chad lingered a moment longer, eyes searching hers, then pulled out his phone again as he walked to the door. "This is Morgan. I'm leaving now—keep eyes on the building. She's inside, alone. You don't blink unless it's to reload. Understood?"

A firm "Copy that" crackled through the line.

Violet watched him leave, heart thudding just a little harder as the door clicked shut behind him. She locked it, just like she said she would, and stood there for a second longer—wondering if the quiet peace of the last two days was about to crack wide open.

The apartment was quiet, save for the soft ticking of the kitchen clock and the muted hum of the fridge. Violet sat curled on the couch, a blanket over her legs and a cup of cooling tea on the side table. Her book lay open in her lap, unread. For the first time in days, the tension in her shoulders had loosened just enough to let her breathe.

Then something shifted.

It was barely audible—a subtle click, the kind you might mistake for a settling pipe or the wind shifting a windowpane. But it wasn't that. Her spine stiffened.

She turned her head slowly, listening.

Click.

A door handle.

Her heart lurched.

She knew she'd locked it.

"Chad?" she called out, her voice thin and uncertain, hope clashing with dread.

No answer.

She stood, barefoot and trembling, eyes darting toward the hallway. Her phone was still on the coffee table. She snatched it up and fumbled to dial Chad's number, her fingers shaking so badly she almost dropped it.

The screen lit up. Ringing.

Her thumb hovered over the speaker icon, breath held.

Then—movement.

A figure stepped from the shadows of the hallway, slow and silent.

Her breath hitched.

The phone slipped from her hand, hit the floor with a dull clack.

She didn't even know if the call was still connected.

A man.

Inside her apartment.

"Get out!" she screamed, voice raw with terror as she stumbled back.

He lunged.

She turned to run—but he grabbed her arm and yanked her backward.

She shrieked, twisted, fought like hell. Her nails clawed at his face; her heel slammed into his shin.

He grunted, staggering. "You've got someplace to be, sweetheart. Someone's waiting for you," he growled in her ear, breath hot and foul. "Now be a good girl and stop fighting."

"Let me go!" she cried. "Chad! CHAD, HELP ME!"

Her scream echoed like a siren through the apartment.

She kicked again—hard—catching his knee. He stumbled, cursing. She bolted, heart pounding. But he tackled her from behind, driving her into the wall with a sickening thud.

"Stop fighting and this'll be easier," he snarled, yanking a set of zip ties from his coat.

"No—please, no—CHAD! CHAD!"

Her voice cracked, hoarse, still fighting. Still screaming.

He twisted her wrist painfully behind her back. "Shut up," he spat.

She refused.

Kicking. Scratching. Desperate.

She got one hand free and found the base of a lamp and she swung—hard. It cracked against his shoulder, and he howled in pain.

"You little bitch—" he hissed, rage lighting his face.

He shoved her into the wall again—hard enough to knock a picture frame to the floor with a crash. Violet sagged, dazed—just for a second.

But she didn't stop.

She clawed at his hands, dug her nails in deep.

He grabbed her around the waist, trying to drag her toward the door, but she kicked and twisted, refusing to make it easy.

Her foot caught on the rug—they fell, a tangle of limbs and fury.

"CHAD!" she sobbed again, one last time, before his hand clamped over her mouth.

Chapter Fifteen

Chad tapped the steering wheel with his thumb as he eased into traffic, replaying the morning's meeting in his head. The breach had been internal—a mid-level director in their Berlin office siphoning sensitive client data. It could've unravelled weeks of classified negotiations if Jared hadn't flagged it in time. Chad had spent the better part of two hours on calls with legal, internal ops, and the German security liaison, all while trying to stay calm enough not to punch someone.

They'd contained it, for now. But it had rattled him.

You can't afford to be distracted, he reminded himself. Not with Violet vulnerable. Not with a potential stalker still unaccounted for.

But damn, he was tired. And distracted, whether he admitted it or not. Violet had been quiet this morning, but there'd been a light in her eyes again. A bit more colour in her cheeks. And the way she'd smiled at him—soft, almost grateful—had pulled something loose in his chest.

He hadn't let himself touch her again. Not since that kiss.

Not since he'd felt himself start to fall.

The phone buzzed beside him on the console.

Violet.

Chad answered, already softening at the thought of hearing her voice.

"Hey, Vi. I'll be—"

Then he heard the sound.

A sharp crash. A muffled cry. Scraping. Screaming.

"Violet."

The name ripped from Chad's throat, urgent and sharp.

"Violet?" he barked, bolting upright. The scream on the other end of the line was raw—terrified—and then came the unmistakable sound of a struggle. Scuffling. Something crashing. Her voice, high and desperate:

'Get out!'

Then—

A man's voice, low and cruel.

'You've got someplace to be, sweetheart. Someone's waiting for you. Now be a good girl and stop fighting.'

'Let me go!'

'Chad! CHAD, HELP ME!'

His heart slammed against his ribs.

"Violet! Talk to me!" he yelled into the phone, panic detonating in his chest like a bomb. "Vi, I'm coming—just hang on—"

There was no answer. Only her sobs. The unmistakable sound of a struggle. A man's grunt. Another thud. Then silence.

"No—no—fuck!" He threw the SUV into gear and tore across the intersection on a red light, horn blaring. "Hold on, baby, hold on," he chanted, weaving between cars, heart hammering like gunfire in his chest.

His mind raced.

Someone got in. Someone has her. How the hell did they get in?

He barked into the comms. "Unit Two, come in—now. Violet's in trouble. I'm en route—ETA five minutes. Someone breached the perimeter."

"Copy that," came the terse reply.

His jaw clenched so tight it ached. This shouldn't have happened. She was supposed to be safe.

And as her final scream echoed through the phone still clutched to his ear, Chad's blood turned ice-cold with fury.

He wasn't just going to protect her anymore.

He was going to hunt whoever did this.

And end them.

Violet struggled, wrists bound painfully behind her back, the gag muffling her cries as the attacker dragged her toward the front door. Her heels scraped uselessly against the floor, panic rising like a scream inside her chest.

The lock clicked. The door swung open.

Then—

Footsteps. Heavy. Rushing.

Two voices shouted from below.

"How the hell did he get past us?"

"Shit!" the attacker spat, his grip tightening. But when the men charged up the stairs, appearing at the top with weapons drawn, he made a split-second decision.

He shoved Violet forward—hard.

She stumbled and fell straight into one of the guards. He caught her, breaking her fall, but the force of her body sent them both crashing to the floor.

"I've got her!" the guard shouted.

The other sprinted past them, taking off after the fleeing man.

Violet sagged in the arms of her rescuer, shaking violently, heart thundering like it would burst through her chest. The hallway spun. The gag pressed tight against her mouth, her breath coming in frantic gasps through her nose.

And then—

More footsteps. Faster. Heavier. Coming up the stairs like a storm.

"Violet!"

Chad.

His voice tore through the air like a lifeline, raw with fear and fury.

She turned her head just as he appeared at the top of the stairs, eyes locked on her—wide, wild, and unrelenting.

He ran to her.

Dropped to his knees beside her, ripping the gag from her mouth and pulling her into his arms. Her zip-tied wrists still behind her back, but she didn't care. She collapsed against him, sobbing, trembling so hard she could barely breathe.

"I've got you, Violet. I've got you." His voice was a low, shaken growl. He cradled her tighter, rocking her slightly as if he could somehow undo what just happened.

The guard holding her blinked, clearly unsure what to do with his furious boss suddenly wrapped around his principal.

Chad looked up at him, his jaw clenched so tight his words came out like bullets.

"How the hell did he get past you two?"

The guard swallowed, eyes wide. "No idea. Frank's chasing him now."

Chad cursed under his breath, held Violet tighter. His hand cupped the back of her head, shielding her from the chaos unravelling around them. Sirens echoed faintly from the street below. Doors were cracking open up and down the hall. But all Chad saw—all he cared about—was the woman shaking in his arms.

"You let someone get to her."

His voice was flat, deadly calm.

"That's not something I forget."

The guard paled. "We—we had eyes on the building. We don't know how—"

Chad didn't wait to hear the rest. His focus snapped back to Violet. He adjusted his grip, keeping her close as he helped her unsteadily to her feet. Her knees buckled, but he caught her, arms like steel around her waist. One hand reached into his back pocket, pulled out a slim tactical blade, and with one precise flick, sliced clean through the zip ties binding her wrists.

Her breath caught, a broken sob spilling out as she rubbed at the angry red marks on her skin. "Thank you," she whispered, voice wrecked.

"Come on," he said, his voice gentler now, steady in a way she needed. He guided her back into the apartment, one hand always touching her—her back, her arm, her waist— like he needed the contact to believe she was really there, alive, still his to protect.

But just as he reached the couch, her voice cracked through the silence.

"He had a key."

He froze.

Chad's head whipped toward her. "He what?"

She sank into the cushions, arms wrapped tight around herself, as if trying to hold her own body together. Her eyes met his—shiny with unshed tears, but unwavering.

"He had a key," she repeated. "He didn't break in. He… he unlocked the door. He walked right in like he belonged here."

Chad's entire body went rigid.

His fists clenched. The blade in his hand trembled before he slipped it away. For a beat, he didn't say anything—just stared at her, then the door, then the lock. Calculating. Boiling.

Then he turned to the guard still standing in the hallway like a stunned rookie.

"I want every inch of this building swept. Every camera checked. Every key accounted for. And find out who the hell has copies of hers."

He turned back to Violet, lowering himself in front of her until he was eye level. His knees hit the floor, uncaring of anything else, his hands braced firmly on her trembling ones.

His voice was quieter now, but no less intense. "Did you see his face?"

She swallowed hard, her eyes glassy, rimmed with red. A tremor passed through her shoulders.

Then she nodded, slowly.

Her lip quivered as she spoke. "It was the same man from the alleyway."

Chad's expression didn't change, but something in him shifted—tightened. A muscle ticked in his jaw. His grip on her hands firmed, not painfully, but possessively. Reassuringly.

"You're sure?"

"Yes." Her voice cracked. "He was tall. White. Maybe late thirties. Shaved head. He wore gloves. He knew my name. He acted like he'd been watching me. Like he knew I'd be alone. He said someone was waiting for me."

Chad inhaled through his nose, controlled, and measured, but his eyes betrayed the fury building beneath his calm exterior.

"He had a key," she whispered again, haunted now. "Chad… he didn't just get lucky. He knew exactly what he was doing."

Chad exhaled a long breath and cupped her face gently, his thumbs brushing tears from her cheeks.

"I swear to you," he said, his voice low and lethal, "I'm going to find out who gave him access. And when I do, no NDA, no lawyer, no goddamn soul on this earth will protect them from me."

He leaned in, forehead resting against hers for a brief second, grounding them both.

"You're safe now. You're not alone. And I won't let this happen again."

Violet closed her eyes, a sob catching in her throat as she leaned into him, clinging to the one thing that felt solid in the wreckage of her fear—Chad. His arms tightened around her, his hand never leaving the back of her head, sheltering her, shielding her.

Then came the heavy stomp of boots and the ragged sound of breath. Frank burst through the open door, panting, sweat slicking his brow. He bent over, hands on his knees, trying to catch his breath.

Chad looked up, his body tensing like a drawn bow.

"Well?" he snapped.

Frank straightened, shaking his head. "He got away. Took off through the back of the building. We didn't even know the rear stairwell was accessible."

"What the hell do you mean accessible?" Chad barked, his voice low and sharp.

Frank exhaled hard. "The doorman swore those doors were supposed to be locked. But the guy had keys—Chad, he had keys to the building. Not just Violet's place. He moved like he knew every damn entrance and exit."

Chad's jaw clenched.

"And there was a van waiting for him," Frank added grimly. "Dark grey. No plates. Driver peeled off before I could get a shot. I chased them three blocks before they disappeared."

Chad didn't respond right away. He just stared, his expression stone, one hand still on Violet, the other flexing like he was holding back the urge to punch a wall.

"He had keys," Chad repeated darkly, more to himself now. "To everything."

Violet shivered against him, and he pulled her tighter.

"This wasn't random," Frank said, voice lower. "He was organised. Prepared."

Chad nodded once, slowly. "Then we have to be."

Chapter Sixteen

The apartment door clicked shut with finality, the last guard slipping out with a grim nod. Chad turned the lock, the sound unnervingly loud in the hush that followed. For a long moment, he stood still, one hand braced against the frame, his chest rising and falling with shallow, uneven breaths. The adrenaline still coursed through his veins, but beneath it was something darker—pure, unfiltered fear.

She could've been taken.

He turned. Violet sat curled on the couch, knees drawn tightly to her chest, her body shaking. The bruises on her wrists where the zip ties had dug in, the red flush left by the gag—marks of violence. Marks of violation. They were evidence of just how close he'd come to losing her.

He crossed the room in three long strides, every instinct screaming to gather her up, shield her, never let her go again. But he paused. Just close enough to be near. Just far enough to let her come to him.

Then, slowly, as if approaching something fragile and sacred, he sat down and slid his arm around her shoulders.

Violet didn't resist.

She leaned into him, burying her face against his chest, her fingers clutching the front of his shirt like it was the only thing keeping her from crumbling. Her breath hitched against his skin, warm and tremulous. He wrapped both arms around her, one hand rising to cradle the back of her head, his fingers weaving gently into her hair.

"I could've lost you," he whispered, his voice raw and uneven. "Violet… I—"

She pulled back slightly, just enough to look up at him. Her eyes shimmered with unshed tears.

"I was scared," she said, barely audible. "I didn't think you'd get here in time. I thought… he was going to kill me. I thought I was going to die alone."

Something inside him shattered.

The iron control he always wore like armour broke into pieces. He cupped her face, his thumbs brushing away the tears sliding down her cheeks, and kissed her—fiercely, desperately, like she was the only thing tethering him to sanity.

The kiss was wild, unrestrained, all-consuming. Not gentle. Not careful. It was hunger and fear and aching love, tangled into a single breathless collision. She climbed onto his lap, straddling him, their bodies already seeking the comfort only closeness could bring.

Clothes fell away without thought. His shirt hit the floor, her sweater followed. Her skin was soft beneath his hands, and when he found the clasp of her bra, she arched into him. His mouth moved down her throat, desperate and reverent all at once.

When he carried her to the bedroom, it wasn't with ceremony—it was with purpose. He laid her down gently, reverently, but when their bodies met again, there was no slowness left.

Their lovemaking was nothing like the slow burn of fantasy. It was need and heat, two souls colliding in the aftermath of fear. He kissed her deeply, one hand sliding to cup her breast, teasing the nipple until she sobbed into his mouth.

"Chad," she gasped, breathless and aching. "I want you…"

He groaned, the sound guttural, feral. "God, Violet… I want you too."

His hands roamed her body, reverent yet greedy. Every curve, every breath, every sound she made drove him to the brink. When his mouth replaced his fingers, teasing her nipple with the flat of his tongue, her back arched, and a cry broke from her throat.

He moved lower, licking a path down her trembling stomach, until he reached the place, she was hot and slick with want. When his tongue found her, she cried out, her body arching, legs trembling.

"Chad…" Her voice was wrecked. "Please."

"You taste like heaven," he murmured, voice hoarse and reverent. Then he lost himself in her, every stroke, every suck designed to push her higher. She writhed beneath him, gasping his name, until she shattered against his mouth with a cry that made his blood burn.

He kissed his way back up, slow, and deliberate, his body pressing against hers. She was already trembling when he settled between her thighs, the tip of him brushing her entrance.

He kissed her, deep and hard. She could taste herself on his lips, could feel the tension in his muscles as he held back, just barely.

Then, with a long, controlled thrust, he entered her.

She gasped, arching, her body clinging to his in a way that made him groan. "Violet…"

He began to move, slow at first, savouring the feel of her wrapped around him. But it wasn't long before the urgency took over. His control broke. He drove into her, his mouth finding hers again, their moans swallowed in frantic kisses.

Their bodies found rhythm. Her nails dug into his shoulders. His name broke from her lips, over and over. He felt her tighten around him, her climax building, her breath catching on every thrust.

She shattered again, with a sob of pleasure, and he followed her over the edge, calling her name like a vow.

Afterward, he didn't move. He stayed inside her, holding her close, heart pounding beneath her ear.

She rested against his bare chest, her fingers lightly tracing the scar near his heart—a mark of a past he never spoke of, but one she now felt tethered to.

He kissed her hair, his voice low and fierce, like a vow spoken into the dark. "I'm not letting anyone near you again. Do you hear me? I swear to God, Violet—I'll burn down the world before I let anyone touch you again."

She didn't speak. But the way she clung to him, the quiet strength in her embrace, told him everything he needed to know.

And for now, that was enough.

They drifted off to sleep in each other's arms, tangled limbs and slowed breathing, hearts still echoing the fear of what could've been. But sleep didn't hold them long.

In the soft hush of the afternoon sun, golden light filtered through the curtains, casting a warm glow across tangled sheets and bare skin. Chad stirred first, brushing a tender kiss against Violet's shoulder, his lips lingering as if reluctant to break the quiet spell around them.

Violet turned in his arms, her lashes fluttering as her gaze met his. Her eyes were heavy-lidded, not from sleep, but from something deeper—something unspoken yet understood. Love. Gratitude. Relief.

They didn't need words.

This time, when they made love, it wasn't rushed or desperate. It was reverent. Slow.

Chad's hands moved over her like a benediction, fingers memorising the delicate map of her body with aching tenderness. Each caress was a vow. Each breath, a promise. Their mouths met in lingering, unhurried kisses, tasting each other with a hunger that had nothing to do with urgency and everything to do with presence.

His lips found her neck, her shoulder, the hollow of her throat—seeking not just her skin, but her soul.

Violet arched into him, her body yielding to his with quiet reverence. She opened to him completely, without fear, without hesitation. Trusting him not only with her body, but with every fragile piece of herself still healing from the terror of the morning.

He moved inside her, slow and steady, their fingers laced between them, their eyes locked in a silent conversation more intimate than words.

Every movement, every sigh and whispered name, wrapped around them like silk—soft and strong.

And when they came together, it wasn't with cries of desperation, but with shuddering breaths and tears they didn't try to hide.

They lay wrapped in each other, limbs tangled, breath mingling in the quiet aftermath. The golden hush of afternoon draped across their skin, warm and soft like a blanket of peace. Violet's head rested over Chad's heart, its steady rhythm grounding her, comforting her. His hand traced idle circles against her back, the silence between them sacred.

Then—

Bang. Bang. Bang.

A sharp, frantic knock shattered the stillness like glass.

Chad sat up in an instant, instincts firing like a live wire. Every muscle in his body tensed as the echo of that knock pulsed through him. Violet jolted upright beside him, heart leaping into her throat. Her fingers clutched the sheet to her chest, wide eyes darting toward the bedroom door.

Without a word, Chad swung his legs over the edge of the bed and moved—fluid, silent, precise. The soldier in him never slept. He tugged on his jeans and a T-shirt in seconds flat, his eyes cold and alert as he moved toward the hallway. He didn't have to tell Violet to stay close—she was already scrambling into her robe, hands trembling slightly as she gathered her hair into a loose tie and followed him barefoot to the door.

He paused at the peephole, body rigid with anticipation.

He exhaled, tension bleeding from his shoulders.

"It's Lance," he muttered.

He unlatched the door quickly, pulling it open—and there was Lance Miller on the threshold, wild-eyed and out of breath, his wheelchair rolling forward fast enough to nick the doorframe.

"Thank God," Lance breathed, pushing into the apartment without hesitation. His eyes scanned the room before landing on Violet. The relief on his face was immediate—and devastating.

"Violet," he choked, wheeling toward her. "Are you okay? Tell me you're okay."

She nodded, but the tears came anyway, unbidden, and hot as she crossed the room and dropped to her knees beside his chair. Her arms wrapped around him, clinging tightly.

"I'm okay," she whispered, her voice breaking, her face buried in his shoulder. "I'm okay now."

Lance gripped her just as tightly, his fingers threading into her hair. His jaw clenched hard. "When I heard… Jesus, Vi. I thought I was gonna lose you."

Chad stood off to the side, arms crossed tightly over his chest, but his eyes never stopped moving. He scanned the hallway behind Lance, then the windows, the corners of the room—his mind still in combat mode. Every creak of the building, every gust of wind beyond the glass sounded like a threat.

Someone had gotten in once.

And he hadn't been fast enough.

That failure was carved into his bones.

He couldn't relax—not yet. Not until he was certain the danger was truly over.

He glanced back toward Violet, watching the way her hand clutched her brother's, the way Lance held her like she was something irreplaceable. Chad swallowed hard, a fresh wave of resolve tightening his spine.

He'd never let it happen again.

Not to her.

Not ever.

Later, when the sun had dipped below the horizon and the shadows began to stretch across the apartment, Lance stayed for dinner. The mood was quieter, heavier—but there was comfort in the shared space, in the unspoken bond between three people who had each carried scars, visible or not.

Chad made something simple—grilled steak, roasted potatoes, and greens—and they ate around the kitchen island, Violet nestled between them. Her silence spoke volumes, but when she did speak, it was soft, thoughtful. Her presence anchored them both.

After the plates were cleared, Lance and Chad settled into the living room, the mood shifting from quiet comfort to quiet urgency. The lights were low, casting long shadows across the floor, but their voices carried a sharp edge.

"What happened?" Lance asked, his voice clipped, professional, the former Marine in him rising to the surface.

Chad leaned forward, forearms braced on his thighs, tension coiled through every line of his body. "Someone had her keys. Not just her apartment—the whole damn building. He didn't break in. He walked in. Like they belonged."

Lance's jaw clenched. "Bloody hell. And the cameras?"

"Didn't catch a damn thing," Chad said darkly. "Because my team wasn't watching the doors that are never supposed to be opened. They had access. Full access. Like they've been watching us long enough to know where the blind spots are."

Lance exhaled a slow, furious breath. "Lucky you got to her in time."

"I was lucky she called me," Chad said, voice rough with the weight of what could have been. "He was already inside. I don't know what his endgame was, but he's getting bolder. This wasn't a warning—it was a test. And we failed."

In the doorway, Violet stood barefoot and silent, arms wrapped around herself. The robe she wore hung loosely on her frame, her hair still damp from the shower. But her eyes—her eyes were sharp with fear and exhaustion.

"So, what do we do?" she asked quietly, like she already knew the answer but needed to hear it spoken aloud.

Chad stood and turned toward her, his expression resolute. "You come with me."

She blinked. "To your penthouse?"

"It's the safest place you can be. Biometric locks, reinforced entry points, full surveillance on every floor. Private elevator. No guests, no surprises. No one gets through without me knowing." His voice lowered. "Not even God."

Violet hesitated, gaze flicking between the two men. She didn't like being treated like a porcelain doll, didn't like the idea of hiding. But she also knew this wasn't about pride anymore—it was survival.

Lance met her eyes with a steady, quiet nod. "He's right, Vi. You'll be safer with Chad. Until we know who this guy is, we can't take any chances."

Her breath hitched, her arms tightening around herself like armour. She hated this—feeling exposed, hunted. But worse than that was the thought of Chad finding her too late next time.

She looked up at him, searching his face for the truth she knew he wasn't saying out loud.

His gaze didn't waver. There was something unspoken in it. A vow. A promise.

She swallowed hard, heart pounding beneath her robe. "All right," she whispered. "But I still need to work, Chad. I can't just… disappear."

"I know," he said, his jaw tightening. There was a flicker of tension in his eyes—not anger, but something protective, coiled and barely contained. "I'm not asking you to give up your life. Just to let me protect it while we figure out who's trying to take it from you."

Her gaze lingered on him, softening as she saw the war he was fighting—between giving her space and keeping her safe. Between respecting her independence and fearing for her life.

She stepped closer, voice quiet. "I need to feel like I still have control. That I'm not just hiding."

"You're not hiding," he said, gentler now. "You're surviving. And until this bastard is caught, I'll do whatever it takes to make sure you keep surviving."

He paused, his hand brushing hers. "I will still take you to your office and the courthouse."

Violet exhaled slowly, the knot in her chest loosening just a little. "Okay," she said, more firmly this time. "Okay."

Chapter Seventeen

Chad's penthouse was nothing like Violet had expected.

Towering floor-to-ceiling windows framed the glittering New York skyline, casting golden reflections over sleek, modern furniture in cool tones of slate and steel. The space was open and minimalist, all clean lines and quiet luxury. A fireplace flickered in one corner, illuminating a glass wall that led to a private terrace with views that stretched toward the Hudson. Every surface gleamed, every detail curated for function and discretion. It was so… him.

Violet stepped inside slowly, her heels clicking softly against the polished floor. "Wow," she whispered, more to herself than him. "This place is…" She trailed off, unable to find the right word.

Chad set her bag down just inside the door. "It's home," he said simply. But the word sounded hollow, even to his own ears.

He led her down a short hallway past the master suite, down to the far end of the apartment. When he opened the door to the guest room, Violet blinked. It was beautiful—soft grey walls, crisp white bedding, a view of the city—but completely unfamiliar.

"This is your room," he said.

She frowned, glancing at him. "My room?"

Chad nodded. "Yeah."

"I thought…" She hesitated, then folded her arms. "I just assumed I'd be sleeping with you."

He didn't answer right away. Just looked at her with those steady, unreadable eyes. Then he exhaled and rubbed the back of his neck. "We need to talk, Vi."

Her chest tightened. "That's never a good start."

"I shouldn't have touched you," he said, voice low and rough. "What happened between us—this afternoon—I shouldn't have let it happen."

She stepped back like he'd struck her.

"I'm supposed to protect you. That's the only thing that matters right now."

"Are you serious?" Her voice cracked around the edges. "You think that's the problem?"

Chad clenched his jaw, but he didn't answer.

She stared at him, trying to understand. "You don't regret what we did, do you?"

His silence was her answer.

Violet felt her stomach drop. "Unbelievable. You know, you might be big and tough and scarred from whatever the hell happened out there, but you're still the same damn man who ran away five years ago."

He flinched.

"You're a bloody coward, Chad Morgan," she spat. "And the worst part is, you think pushing me away is noble. Like it's some grand act of sacrifice instead of what it really is—fear."

"Violet—" he started, but she'd already crossed the threshold.

She turned to face him ready to close the door.

"Don't pretend you're doing this for me. You're doing it because it's easier than letting someone actually care about you."

The door slammed with a final, hollow thud.

And on the other side, Chad stood still, her words echoing in the quiet.

He didn't move for a long time. Didn't speak. He just stood there in his immaculate home, surrounded by all the armour money could buy—and still feeling like a man made entirely of broken glass.

By Wednesday, Violet and Chad had hardly said ten words to each other. They existed in the same space—shared morning coffee, crossed paths in the hallway, passed one another in the kitchen of his sleek, modern penthouse—but there was a distance between them that neither dared bridge.

Chad tried.

He lingered a second too long when she walked past him, cleared his throat when they were alone in the elevator, made half-hearted attempts at casual conversation. "Did you sleep okay?" "Do you want to go over your schedule for tomorrow?" "There's a new Italian place near the office—figured we could grab lunch, maybe?"

Each time, Violet offered a polite smile, a clipped nod, or a distracted "I'm swamped right now."

She was busy. She was. Between client calls, reviewing depositions, prepping for a hearing, and trying to feel like her life wasn't unravelling, she barely had time to breathe.

But it wasn't just the work.

She didn't regret making love to Chad. Not for one second. Hell, she had wanted him for five years. Every stubborn, intense, complicated inch of him. But the man could kiss her like she was the only thing holding him to the earth one moment—and then shut down completely the next.

He had chosen to pretend it meant nothing. That she meant nothing.

And that was frustrating.

Violet clenched her jaw as she highlighted a section of legal code, only half paying attention. Chad could stand there with all his stoic silence and pretend he was doing the right thing. That it was about her safety, or his responsibilities, or whatever damn noble excuse he'd cooked up to keep his heart on lockdown.

But the truth? He was denying it because he was scared.

And if he thought she was going to keep pretending she didn't notice—he had another thing coming.

Damien was the balm to her bruised ego.

While her personal life cracked and splintered in private places, she didn't have time to tend to, Damien became a steady hand in the storm. He was irreplaceable in the office— efficient, punctual, always one step ahead. Violet barely had to ask for something before it appeared on her desk, waiting.

Coffee made just right.

Briefs printed and tabbed in her meticulous, colour-coded system.

Reminders sent.

Filings done.

Court documents signed, sealed, and delivered—like clockwork.

She didn't notice how much she relied on him anymore. He had become part of the rhythm of her days.

"You're a godsend," Violet said that morning, glancing up as he placed her oat milk latte beside a fresh stack of depositions. Her fingers rubbed at a faint ache behind her brow. "Seriously, I don't know how I managed before you."

Damien smiled, modest, almost bashful. "Happy to help, boss. You've had a lot on your plate lately."

She gave a small, tired laugh, brushing hair from her face. "Haven't we all."

He didn't answer right away. Just straightened the cuffs of his pale-blue shirt—precise, deliberate movements. Almost military.

"I was going to drop those filings off at the courthouse for you," he said casually, lifting the folder from her outbox. "Save you the trip."

"That would be amazing," she said, glancing at her packed calendar. "Thank you, Damien."

"Of course." He hesitated then, turning slightly back toward her desk. "If you don't mind me saying something…"

She looked up, pen pausing above a sticky note.

"You've just seemed… off. A little tired. Stressed." His voice was soft, laced with just the right amount of concern. "Ever since Mr. Morgan turned up, actually."

Violet blinked. "What?"

He chuckled lightly, the kind meant to disarm. "Not in a bad way. I'm sure he's just trying to help. But… I guess I noticed the change. You used to breeze through court filings and client meetings like it was second nature. Lately, though, you've just seemed a bit—" he searched, careful with his tone "—weighed down."

"I've had a lot going on," she said briskly. "Personal things. My brother. Safety concerns."

"Of course." His voice was gentle, sympathetic. "I didn't mean anything by it. Just thought… maybe someone should say it. In case you didn't see it yourself."

She studied him for a beat longer. Damien was so composed—always composed. His suit jacket hung perfectly on his frame, his brown hair neatly combed back, a clean-cut profile. He didn't look like someone who stirred the pot. He looked like someone who handed you a spoon and offered to clean up the mess afterward.

He followed her gaze to the hall, where Chad stood with his back to the glass, phone to his ear, jaw clenched in profile.

"He doesn't look happy," Damien said mildly.

"No," she murmured. "He's always like that."

"Well, if there's anything I can do," Damien added, shifting the folder under his arm. "Don't hesitate. Take care of yourself, boss."

With that, he turned and left.

The door clicked shut softly behind him, and Violet sat there a second too long.

Something about his words stuck.

They crawled under her skin.

Was it true? Had she been more stressed since Chad arrived?

Or was it just that Chad made her feel things she didn't have time to process?

She shook the thought off like rain off her shoulders and turned back to her screen.

But in the hallway, Damien's steps echoed toward the elevator. His face relaxed into its usual calm expression. No trace of menace. No trace of malice.

Yet beneath the surface, something sharp gleamed.

Behind those friendly eyes, the storm was gathering.

Chad stood just outside Violet's office, half-shadowed by the hallway light, his eyes fixed on the easy exchange between her and Damien. His jaw tensed, fingers curling around his phone as Jared's voice crackled quietly in his ear.

"No red flags, Chad. I've run everything twice."

"That doesn't make sense," Chad muttered. "Someone's getting past Violet's security. Someone is sending her those messages, planting things. Someone is watching her. And it all started after she hired that new assistant."

"Damien White?" Jared asked, tapping keys on the other end of the line. "Yeah, I checked him out thoroughly."

Chad exhaled sharply. "Tell me again."

"Okay," Jared sighed. "Full name: Damien Charles White. Thirty-two. Parents died in a plane crash when he was twenty. Left him a decent inheritance—mid seven figures. Grew up in Connecticut, went to boarding school, then majored in business at Columbia. Joined the Army after college, served two years, honourably discharged. Administrative role. Logistics, mostly. Never deployed, never saw combat. His record's clean—no disciplinary marks, no psych evals that raise concern. Spotless."

Chad's brow furrowed as he watched headlights crawl along the highway far below.

"And since then?" he asked.

"Worked in corporate admin for a while, then pivoted to legal support," Jared replied. "He's bounced around high-end law firms in New York and D.C.—every exit amicable, letters of recommendation, the whole bit. No history of lawsuits. No criminal record. No financial issues, no flagged communications, no shady connections. His social media's practically textbook: clean, curated, private. This guy is either exactly what he looks like… or he's a damn ghost."

Chad's jaw tightened. "You ever meet someone who's too perfect?"

Jared chuckled. "You, maybe. But yeah. I know what you mean."

"There's something about him," Chad said, his voice low. "Something off. He watches people like he's cataloguing them. Always standing just close enough to listen but never quite saying anything real."

"Your gut talking again?" Jared asked.

"My gut's what kept me alive," Chad snapped, voice low. "And Violet's been off lately. Distant. On edge. I can't protect her if she starts trusting the wrong voice."

As the words left his mouth, a grim weight settled in his chest. He knew exactly why she was pulling away—because he'd pushed her. Again.

Jared was quiet for a moment. "Want me to keep digging? Deeper?"

Chad nodded, then realised Jared couldn't see him. "Yeah. Start with anyone from his past that suddenly cut ties. Old army contacts. School friends. Former coworkers. Somebody, somewhere has to have noticed something."

"Got it. But if this guy's hiding something, he's good at it."

"So am I," Chad muttered, ending the call.

He slid the phone into his pocket and stared out at the city again.

Damien might not raise alarms on paper—but Chad didn't trust paper.

He trusted instincts.

And his were screaming.

Chapter Eighteen

By Friday, the locksmith had confirmed everything was secure. Every lock on Violet's apartment and office had been changed. She'd been given a new set of keys—including one for her car—just in case. Chad had made sure of it. Nothing left to chance.

But by Saturday morning, the walls of Chad's penthouse were closing in around her.

Violet stood at the floor-to-ceiling windows, watching the city stretch below in sterile silence. The penthouse was stunning—sleek black marble, brushed steel accents, floating above Manhattan like a fortress in the sky. Expensive. Immaculate. Cold.

She hadn't said much in days. Neither had Chad.

She'd tried to bury herself in casework, tried to ignore how her skin ached every time he moved past her, careful not to touch. It was driving her mad.

He hadn't even kissed her since that night.

He regretted it—sleeping with her. That much was clear. He hadn't said it outright, but the message was written in every strained silence, in the way he looked at her like he was trying not to. Like he was ashamed of needing her.

She couldn't take it anymore.

Her bag was already packed—tucked behind the couch hours ago when she'd made up her mind. Violet rounded the corner into the open-plan living room and found Chad at the kitchen island, shoulders hunched over his tablet, the glow casting sharp shadows across his face. His jaw tightened the moment he sensed her.

"I need to talk to you," she said, her voice tight with barely restrained emotion.

He set the tablet down with careful precision. "What is it?"

She crossed her arms, every muscle strung tight. "I can't do this anymore."

Chad looked up, wary. "Do what?"

"This," she snapped, gesturing between them, the air suddenly charged. "Living in this penthouse like we're strangers. You barely speak to me. You barely look at me."

"You know why," he said, voice low and guarded.

"Do I?" She stepped forward, heat rising in her chest. "Because from where I'm standing, it looks a lot like you're running again. Running from something you want."

"That's not fair."

"No?" Her voice cracked. "You think protecting me and keeping your distance is noble? Like pretending what happened between us meant nothing doesn't tear me apart every single day?"

He didn't answer. His silence said it all.

Violet's hands shook. "None of this would've happened if you hadn't shown up."

His head snapped up, eyes narrowing. "What the hell does that mean?"

"It means ever since you came back, I've been watched, followed, threatened. I can't sleep. I can't breathe." Her voice broke. "This whole nightmare started the moment you walked back into my life."

Chad stood, slow and deliberate, muscles coiled tight beneath his T-shirt. "You think I wanted this? You think I planned for someone to come after you?"

"No," she whispered. "I think you make everything worse."

He flinched—just barely, but she saw it.

"I was doing okay," she pressed on. "I had work. Control. Then you showed up and ripped all of it apart. Not just the danger. You. You made me feel something again. You made me hope. And then you shut it down like it meant nothing. Like I mean nothing."

He stepped forward, jaw clenched. "So, I'm the villain for caring? For stepping up when your brother begged me to keep you safe?"

"No," she said, quieter now. "I'm blaming you for making me feel everything and then punishing me for it. Again."

She reached for her coat, slinging it over her arm, then bent to grab her bag.

Chad's eyes darkened. "What are you doing?"

"I'm leaving."

"Violet—"

"Don't follow me," she cut him off, voice sharp and trembling. "Find someone else to watch me. Because I can't stay here anymore. It hurts too much."

She turned toward the elevator. He moved to follow, then stopped short—like a soldier recognising a minefield.

"You're not safe," he said, voice raw.

She spun back, tears brimming. "I don't care. I'd rather be in danger than stuck here— twenty feet from a man who pretends I don't exist after holding me like I was the only thing keeping him alive."

The elevator doors opened with a soft chime. She stepped inside—back straight, chin high, heart breaking beneath the surface.

And then she was gone.

Chad stood frozen, the silence pressing in like concrete. For a long moment, he didn't move.

Then his hand went to his phone.

"She just left," he said to his lead operative. "I want eyes on her. Around the clock. I don't care if she screams, kicks, or calls you every name in the book. Don't let her out of your sight."

He hung up and let the phone fall to the counter.

The penthouse felt too quiet. Too empty.

And the weight of her absence hit like a blow to the chest.

She was gone.

And this time, it was his fault.

Violet closed the apartment door behind her and leaned against it, exhaling a breath she hadn't known she was holding.

Silence.

For the first time in days—no guarded tension, no quiet battles, no Chad standing a few feet away, looking like he wanted to reach for her but couldn't.

She dropped her bag and walked into the apartment. It was exactly as she'd left it—cold coffee mugs in the sink, papers on the table, a blanket draped across the couch. The familiarity didn't comfort her.

She was alone.

It should've felt like relief. After all, she'd asked for it.

Instead, it felt like grief.

That first night passed in a haze. She ran a bath, hoping to soak away the ache in lavender and steam, but all she could think about was the weight of Chad's hands on her skin. His mouth on her throat. The way he had held her like she was the only thing in the world that made sense.

And the way he had shut down after.

He didn't want her.

It didn't matter what they shared. What they felt. He would always choose distance. Duty. Control.

She was just a job again. A mission.

By Sunday morning, her eyes were puffy, her heart still split wide open.

She made coffee, sat on the couch, and tried to focus on case files. But her mind kept drifting. Kept replaying everything.

Five years ago, it had taken months to stop hearing his voice in the back of her head. She'd buried herself in work. School. Distractions.

But now?

Now she'd seen how his breath caught when he looked at her. She'd felt him tremble as he made love to her—like every inch of her mattered.

How was she supposed to forget that?

She stared down into her mug and whispered aloud to the quiet room.

"How am I supposed to forget you now?"

Only the refrigerator's hum and the ache in her chest replied.

She got up, paced the living room, folded laundry that didn't need folding. Every time she closed her eyes, she saw him—standing in his kitchen, torn between wanting her and pushing her away.

"Damn it, Chad."

She'd wanted him to fight for her. To say screw the job, screw the risk—I love you too much to let you go.

But he hadn't.

And Violet knew what that meant.

It was time to forget him.

Even if this time, it felt impossible.

Chad sat alone in his penthouse, the city lights sprawling out beneath him like a dream he couldn't wake from. He hadn't turned on the lights. He didn't need to see the empty space to feel it.

Violet was gone.

Because of him.

Again.

He scrubbed a hand down his face, jaw tight with frustration. Why did he keep hurting her? What the hell was wrong with him?

Because you don't know how to let anyone in.

The thought burned through him, sharp and unwelcome. But it wasn't wrong.

He had spent most of his adult life building walls—first as a Marine, then as a man running a company where trust could get you killed. He knew how to protect. How to plan. How to execute.

But feel? That was dangerous.

And Violet… Violet cracked him wide open.

He hadn't meant to fall into bed with her. He hadn't meant to need her like air.

But that day—the way she looked at him, touched him like he mattered—it had undone him.

And now, the silence she left behind was deafening.

He picked up his phone and hit speed dial.

"Yeah?" came the tired voice on the other end. One of the two men he had posted near her building.

"She still in her apartment?"

There was a beat of hesitation. "She hasn't left. Lights have been on. Got groceries delivered around four. That's the fifth time you've called tonight, Morgan."

Chad didn't flinch. "Keep watching."

"Yeah, yeah. I got it."

He hung up and tossed the phone onto the counter, exhaling hard. He could tell his guys were getting annoyed, and he didn't give a damn. He needed to know she was safe. That she was still breathing. That nothing had happened—because if it did, if she got hurt while she was out from under his roof, it would kill him.

And yet, she had to leave, didn't she?

He'd made it impossible for her to stay.

He couldn't stop thinking about the way she looked at him that morning—hurt and furious, trembling with betrayal.

'Don't follow me… it hurts too much.'

God. And it did hurt. Everywhere.

Chad leaned against the cold marble island, gripping the edge with both hands, breathing like it was the only thing keeping him from shattering.

He couldn't forget the way she felt in his arms. The warmth of her skin. The softness of her breath against his neck. The way she had said his name like a secret, like a promise.

He couldn't forget the feel of her beneath him. Her voice when he entered her—shaky, breathless, like he was the only thing she wanted.

And maybe that was what terrified him.

Because he didn't want to let her go either.

But he already had.

And now, all he had was an echo of her laugh, the ghost of her hands, and a list of regrets that seemed to grow by the hour.

He picked up his phone again.

This time, he didn't call his team.

He just stared at her number.

And did nothing.

Because he didn't know how to fix the damage he'd done. And the only thing he was sure of was that if Violet got hurt again—it would be on him.

And he wasn't sure he could survive that.

Chapter Nineteen

Chad didn't show up on Monday.

Which—of course—she expected.

No explanation. No call. Just silence where his presence used to be.

She told herself it didn't matter. She'd survived the weekend—she could survive a workday. So, she buried herself in motion practice and client files, drowning in legal briefs and colour-coded tabs.

Anything to keep her from glancing down the corridor expecting him to walk down it. But every time she did, her chest clenched.

And no matter how hard she worked, she couldn't drown out the echo of what they'd shared.

Damien, however, noticed.

And he interpreted Chad's absence differently.

He's finally backed off, Damien thought as he watched Violet move through the day with mechanical grace. Maybe she had come to her senses. Maybe she'd stopped chasing the man who treated her like a liability instead of a woman.

He'd been patient. Supportive. Always there.

He waited until the afternoon lull, when the office had gone quieter and the legal team had dispersed into meetings.

Violet was at her desk, going over deposition notes when she looked up and found Damien standing much closer than she expected—his arm brushing hers as he set down a file.

She jumped slightly. "Oh—thanks."

His smile was easy. "Sorry, didn't mean to startle you."

She gave a small, polite laugh. "No worries."

"You've been killing it lately," Damien said, his tone warm, his gaze lingering just a beat too long. "I don't know how you do it."

Violet shifted back in her chair, the sudden closeness making her throat go dry. "Thanks. Just... staying on top of things."

"Let me help," he said, lowering his voice as if they were sharing a secret. "You don't have to do everything alone."

The way he said it sent a prickle down her spine. It wasn't overt, but something about the way he was looking at her—intent, expectant—felt... off.

She cleared her throat. "Actually, Damien… could I ask you for a favour?"

"Anything," he said quickly, a little too quickly.

"I was thinking it might make sense if you assisted one of the other attorneys for a while. Just to balance the workload."

He blinked, clearly thrown. "You want me reassigned?"

"No, not like that," she said, forcing a smile. "It's just been really hectic. You've been great, honestly—but I think it'd help everyone if we spread things out a little."

For a second, something shifted in his expression—like a mask slipping. But it was gone just as quickly.

"Of course," he said smoothly. "Whatever you need."

"Thanks," she said, watching him walk away.

She didn't know why her stomach twisted as the door closed behind him. He hadn't said or done anything overtly wrong. Just… stood too close. Smiled a little too long. Spoken like he knew her better than he should.

It wasn't enough to raise alarms.

But it was enough for her to head straight to HR and ask—casually, professionally—if Damien could be reassigned to another case.

"Just a temporary shift," she told them. "To ease up on the pressure."

They agreed without question.

Violet returned to her office, trying to shake the unease settling in her gut.

No, she wasn't suspicious.

But for the first time, she was starting to listen to the feeling she usually pushed aside.

Something was… off.

And Chad's absence wasn't helping.

All it had taken was a quiet conversation with HR—just a single meeting behind closed doors—and Damien was gone.

Reassigned at her request. No questions. No pushback. Just a brief, professional email confirming the change and a new name on her case file by Wednesday morning.

Violet had braced for some kind of reaction. A lingering look. A thinly veiled comment. One last passive-aggressive remark to let her know she'd gotten under his skin. But Damien hadn't said a word. He didn't even glance her way on his way out.

Somehow, that silence felt more ominous than anything he could've said.

Her new paralegal, Julia, was a revelation. Sharp, organised, unflinchingly kind. She anticipated Violet's needs before she voiced them, handled tasks with quiet confidence, and carried none of the strange tension that had plagued Violet's days with Damien.

For the first time in weeks, Violet didn't feel like she had to constantly look over her shoulder.

Still, she couldn't shake the feeling that the stillness around her wasn't safety.

Just the quiet before another storm.

She left the office a little after seven. Her heels clicked sharply in the underground garage, each step echoing off the concrete like a metronome in the empty stillness.

She glanced at her phone.

A missed call from Lance.

She smiled softly, thumbs tapping out a quick reply: Leaving the office now. Call you in ten?

She never hit send.

A low growl broke the silence—low, deliberate.

Her head snapped up.

A sedan—dark, unlit—wasn't parked. It was moving. Fast.

Headlights off. Engine roaring. Gaining speed.

Coming straight for her.

She froze. Her breath caught mid-inhale.

The phone slipped from her hand, hitting the concrete with a sharp crack.

Her body refused to move.

The car was coming straight for her.

There wasn't time to scream.

A shadow blurred into her peripheral vision—boots pounding the ground—and in the next second, a pair of arms crashed into her side, tackling her to the ground just as the vehicle whooshed past.

The heat of it. The sound of it. The sharp reek of rubber and oil as it missed her by inches, and hit a concrete pillar with a sickening crunch, reversed in a squeal of tyres, and sped off into the shadows.

Everything went still.

Violet lay on her back, winded, with the taste of metal in her mouth and her heart galloping in her chest.

The man above her rolled to his feet, scanning the garage like a hawk.

"Miss Miller," he said, breath controlled but tight. "Are you okay?"

She blinked up at him, dazed. "I—I think so."

"Can you move?"

He offered her his hand and helped her up carefully, keeping himself between her and the open garage as he pulled a small radio from his pocket.

"Black sedan," he barked. "Headed for east exit. Covered plates. Possible driver sighting—male, late twenties, black hoodie."

Static crackled in response, then another voice: "Copy. Cameras tracking now."

Violet clutched his arm, still shaking. "Who are you?"

"Sam. I'm with Mr. Morgan's security detail." He paused. "He asked me to shadow you in the garage until further notice."

"Until—" Her voice broke. "Until someone tries to kill me?"

"Until you're safe," he corrected gently, eyes never leaving the shadows.

She turned and looked at the pillar—scarred, cracked, concrete dust still drifting to the ground—and her knees nearly gave out.

If he hadn't tackled her when he did—

She wouldn't be here.

"Thank you," she whispered, her voice cracking.

Sam said nothing. Just handed her a bottle of water, scanned the area again, and kept himself between her and the darkness.

"Chad needs to know," she said after a moment, her voice barely a breath.

"He already does."

Chad stared out the floor-to-ceiling windows of his penthouse, the city lights glittering below him, meaningless in their beauty. Half past seven. She should be home by now.

Violet.

It had been five days since he'd seen her. Five days without the sound of her voice, without catching her gaze from across a room and feeling like the rest of the world could fall away.

It was killing him.

The updates helped—Frank was steady, reliable, gave him hourly check-ins—but they didn't soothe the ache in his chest. He missed her. Missed her laugh. Missed the way she tilted her head when she was thinking. Missed holding her like he never wanted to let go.

His phone buzzed.

Frank.

Chad's pulse kicked up. Probably just checking in to say she was home safe.

He answered on the first ring. "Frank."

There was no hesitation on the other end—but no comfort either.

"Morgan. It's Miss Miller."

Chad's entire body went still. "What about her?"

"She was just targeted. Someone tried to run her down in the parking garage. No accident. Headlights off. Full speed."

The blood drained from Chad's face. "Is she—"

"She's alive. Sam tackled her out of the way with half a second to spare."

He squeezed his eyes shut, a harsh breath breaking from him as rage and fear surged, sharp and choking. "Where is she?"

"We're taking her back to her apartment. She's shaken but physically okay. I'll see you there."

"I'm coming now." His voice was pure steel, edged with fire.

He didn't wait for a response.

The moment the call ended, Chad was already moving—jacket, keys, and the Glock that was never too far away, and was never left behind. His pulse roared in his ears, a war drum of panic barely restrained. His hands were steady, but only because rage held them still.

Someone had tried to kill her.

Not scare her. Not threaten.

Kill.

He couldn't breathe right until he saw her for himself. Until he could touch her, hold her, make sure with his own eyes that she was still whole.

That she was still his.

Whoever had made that attempt had just marked themselves. Because they hadn't gone after just anyone.

They'd come for Violet.

And that was their first mistake.

Because Chad Morgan didn't lose what he loved.

Not ever.

And God help him—he did love her. Fiercely. Completely. More than he'd ever let himself admit until now.

Chapter Twenty

Violet sat curled on her couch, a throw blanket clutched tightly around her shoulders, but the tremors wouldn't stop. Her body was unharmed—miraculously—but her mind hadn't caught up. It was still stuck in that moment: headlights, the roar of an engine, the sheer certainty that she wasn't going to make it out alive.

Frank and Sam had swept her apartment twice, checking locks, securing windows, moving with the kind of calm professionalism meant to reassure. She barely heard them. They were in the kitchen now, waiting for Chad.

She couldn't stop hearing it.

Someone had tried to kill her.

Not frighten. Not intimidate. Kill.

The word sat heavy in her chest like a stone, pressing the air from her lungs. Her arms curled tighter around her body, hands clenched in the blanket as if it could hold her together. She didn't know if she was going to cry, scream, or shatter into pieces.

The knock on the door was sharp. Urgent.

Sam moved fast, already halfway across the room before Violet had even lifted her head. He looked through the peephole and opened the door without a word.

Chad stepped inside like a storm front. His jaw was set, tension coiled tight in every line of his body. His eyes swept the room in one hard, practiced scan—until they landed on her.

Violet.

She was curled on the couch, pale, and trembling, but alive. Breathing. His whole world narrowed to that one fact.

He looked like he hadn't taken a full breath since the phone call—like something had been crushing his chest and only now, seeing her, could he breathe again.

"Thanks, guys," he said, his voice low and controlled, but not calm. Not even close. "I'll take it from here."

Sam gave a nod, and Frank clapped Chad's shoulder on the way past. Neither man said a word. They didn't need to. They moved quietly out the door, leaving behind only the echo of their presence and the crackling silence that followed.

Chad crossed the room slowly, as if afraid any sudden movement might shatter her.

"Violet," he breathed, voice rough with a thousand things he hadn't said. He knelt in front of her, reaching out—his hands hovering just inches from her arms. "Let me hold you."

She flinched, so subtly it was almost imperceptible—but he saw it. And he froze.

Her eyes lifted to his, wide and rimmed with unshed tears, but there was steel beneath the fear. A fresh wound. Deeper than anything the car could've done.

"No," she whispered. Her voice was raw. "I can't let you do that."

He went still. "Vi—"

"I'm not something you can just hold when it's convenient, Chad." Her breath hitched. "You made it pretty clear where we stand."

His hands dropped to his sides. Like they didn't belong to him anymore. Like they'd lost their purpose the moment she pulled away.

The silence that stretched between them was thick—alive—with everything they'd both left unsaid. It pulsed in the room like a second heartbeat, broken only by the faint tick of the clock on the wall and the sound of her shallow breaths.

"I was wrong, Violet," he said finally, his voice low, but no less intense.

Her gaze flicked up, tired, and guarded. "About what, Chad?"

He swallowed hard. "About everything. About pretending I could stay away. That I could protect you without wanting you. That I could walk away from you and not lose my damn mind."

She said nothing, but her arms tightened around herself like she was protecting herself.

He leaned forward slightly, his voice softening. "I don't want to run anymore. I don't want to pretend that what's between us isn't real. I want to be with you."

Violet blinked, her throat working around a lump she didn't dare let rise. "You don't get to say that now. Not after the way you left me standing there like I meant nothing."

"You meant everything," he said, pained. "That was the problem. I was scared. Of what I felt. Of what it could cost you. I thought pushing you away was protecting you."

She laughed, bitter and broken. "And how'd that work out for me, Chad? Someone just tried to run me over in a parking garage."

He flinched like she'd slapped him.

"I'm sorry," he said quietly, sincerely. "I'm so damn sorry. But I swear to you, I will never make that mistake again. You're not just someone I want to protect—you're someone I want to build a life with. Every breath I've taken without you these last five days has felt wrong."

Violet looked at him, eyes glassy, lips trembling. For a second, it seemed like she might fold into him, let him in.

But then she looked away, down at the floor.

"I want to believe you," she whispered.

"Then let me prove it," he said, desperate now. "Not with words. With actions. Day after day, as long as you'll let me."

Her eyes met his again, this time uncertain. Fragile.

He didn't touch her. Didn't push.

But God, he wanted to.

The silence swelled between them again, thick with the weight of all the wounds, all the longing.

Chad stayed perfectly still—chest heaving, eyes locked on hers, like any sudden move might scare her off. He looked wrecked. Raw. And real in a way Violet hadn't let herself imagine in days.

She hated how much she still loved him.

Her body ached with the memory of his arms. Her lips burned with the ghosts of kisses she'd tried to forget. And now, with him kneeling here—heart in his eyes, hands trembling at his sides—she couldn't breathe past the ache.

"You broke my heart," she said softly, like confession and accusation in one breath.

"I know," he rasped. "And I'll spend the rest of my life making it whole again if you let me."

Her jaw trembled. Her breath caught.

And then she moved.

She leaned into him.

Chad's eyes widened, but he didn't reach for her—didn't dare.

She reached up slowly, her fingers brushing the edge of his jaw. A single tear slipped down her cheek, and he caught it with his breath.

"Don't make me regret this," she whispered.

Then she kissed him.

It wasn't tentative. It wasn't soft.

It was desperate and deep and full of everything they hadn't said. All the love. All the anger. All the nights spent aching for each other and pretending they didn't.

Chad let out a broken sound against her mouth—half relief, half hunger—and then his arms were around her, holding her like a man starved. Like she was breath. Salvation. Home.

And Violet kissed him back like she'd finally found her home—with him, with herself, with the truth they couldn't deny anymore.

The moment deepened, the world outside falling away until there was only the two of them—locked in a kiss that tasted of sorrow and salvation. When he finally pulled back, it was only far enough to rest his forehead against hers, his chest rising and falling in uneven breaths.

Then he stood. Slowly. Gently.

He gathered her into his arms like she was something precious, fragile—his hands steady beneath her knees and across her back. Violet didn't resist. Her fingers curled into the collar of his shirt, and she leaned her cheek against his shoulder, closing her eyes as the steady beat of his heart thundered beneath her ear.

He carried her through the apartment without a word, the only sound the soft pad of his footsteps against the hardwood floor. Her bedroom door swung open with the lightest touch. Moonlight spilled through the window, silvering the shadows.

He set her down like she was something sacred, something breakable. His hands lingered at her waist, but he didn't rush, didn't demand.

Violet reached for him first.

Her fingers found the hem of his shirt, and he let her pull it over his head. Her hands ran over his chest, trembling, reverent—as if mapping each line, each scar, grounding herself in the reality of him.

His breath caught when she undid the first button on her blouse.

"Violet," he whispered, voice hoarse. "Are you sure?"

Her eyes met his—uncertain but open. "Yes."

That one word cracked something in him. He reached for her then, slow and aching, brushing the backs of his fingers along her cheek before easing her blouse from her shoulders. He kissed each inch of skin as it was revealed—soft, tender kisses that asked for permission and gave promises in return.

They undressed each other like a prayer.

No rush. No urgency. Just the quiet hum of need and reverence between them. Every kiss was a vow. Every touch a confession.

When she was down to nothing but her breath and the rise and fall of her chest, he paused, his hands cupping her face as he kissed her again, slower this time—deeper. She curled her hands around his neck, pulling him closer, and for a long, breathless moment, they just stood there, wrapped in each other, their bodies touching from shoulder to knee.

Then he laid her back gently onto the bed, following her down, bracing his weight on one arm as he hovered above her, his fingers brushing the hair from her face.

"I was so scared I was going to lose you," he said, his voice shaking with all the emotion he hadn't been able to speak aloud. "When I got that call when I heard what happened—I've never known fear like that. I thought I'd never see you again. Never hold you again. And it gutted me."

Violet reached up and touched his cheek, her thumb brushing along the line of his jaw.

"I'm here," she whispered. "I'm right here."

He kissed her then—slow, deep, reverent. A kiss that said thank you and I'm sorry and I love you all at once. A kiss that wasn't just about passion, but about presence. About healing.

When their bodies finally joined, it wasn't rushed or wild—it was slow and consuming, like two people relearning the feel of home. Every movement was careful, connected, like they were stitching themselves back together in the places they'd come undone.

Violet held on to him like he was the only thing tethering her to the earth.

And Chad moved with a tenderness that unravelled her completely, his forehead pressed to hers, his breath mingling with her own.

There were no walls between them anymore.

No fear. No pride. Just truth.

Just love.

And when they reached the edge together—clinging to each other, hearts pounding in rhythm—it wasn't just a release. It was a beginning.

A homecoming.

The bedroom was cloaked in shadows, the only light the faint silver wash of the moon spilling through the window. The world had gone still around them, hushed like it was holding its breath.

Violet lay curled against Chad's chest, her fingers idly tracing the faint line of a scar just above his heart. He held her like he never wanted to let go—one arm wrapped securely around her back, the other gently stroking her hair. His touch had softened since earlier, but the intensity in him hadn't faded. It had simply quieted, deepened.

Neither of them had spoken in a while.

There was no need.

The silence between them was warm. Full. Laced with all the words they hadn't yet dared say.

Chad shifted slightly, just enough to press a kiss to the crown of her head. She felt it like a tremor through her whole body—tender and unguarded.

"Vi," he murmured, his voice low and raw. "I need to tell you something. And I don't want to wait anymore."

She lifted her head, just enough to look up at him.

His eyes met hers in the dark—shadowed but clear, honest.

"I love you."

Her breath caught.

He swallowed, holding her gaze. "I think I've loved you for longer than I even realised. Maybe since that day at the VA hospital when you were yelling at me then collapsed into my arms. Maybe before that—maybe I was just waiting for you to walk into my life so I could finally feel something again."

Violet's chest tightened, her heart thudding hard against her ribs. "Chad…"

"I was scared," he said quietly. "Of what it meant. Of how much I needed you. But I'm not scared now. I love you. I love you so damn much it hurts to breathe without you."

She stared at him for a long moment, eyes glimmering in the dark. Then, slowly, she reached up and cradled his face in both hands.

"You idiot," she whispered, her voice breaking with something soft and fierce. "I love you too."

His eyes closed for half a second, like the words physically hit him. When he opened them again, there was something unguarded in his expression—vulnerable, almost boyish.

"I was afraid I'd lost my chance," he said hoarsely.

"You didn't," she whispered. "You scared me. You broke my heart a little. But you didn't lose me."

A quiet, ragged breath escaped him.

She leaned in and kissed him, slow and gentle, and it felt different this time. Not desperate. Not frantic. Just full of truth.

"I love you," she said again against his lips, as if saying it twice would make up for the time they'd lost.

Chad pulled her tighter into his arms, burying his face in her hair. "Say it again."

"I love you."

His arms tightened around her. "One more time."

She smiled against his chest, that aching, beautiful smile that only he ever got to see. "I love you, Chad Morgan."

And in the quiet after, when the night wrapped them in silence again, they held each other close—two hearts finally at rest. Two souls no longer wandering.

Home.

Together.

Chapter Twenty-One

Violet stirred beneath the soft weight of Chad's arm draped across her waist, sunlight beginning to filter through the bedroom curtains. She blinked slowly, still wrapped in the hazy warmth of dreams—and the lingering ache of last night. Of whispered confessions. Of skin, breath, and need.

Chad shifted behind her, brushing a kiss to the nape of her neck, his voice rough with sleep. "Good morning, beautiful."

She turned in his arms, a sleepy smile tugging at her lips. "Hi."

His eyes searched her face for a long moment. Then he kissed her—slow and deep, like a promise. One hand slipped to her hip, the other tangled in her hair. She melted into him, gasping softly as he rolled her gently onto her back.

There were no more walls between them. No barriers. Just the raw honesty of a love that had waited too long, and the craving that hadn't eased since the night before.

When they made love again, it was unhurried. Reverent. Each touch a memory, each kiss a vow. I'm here. I'm not going anywhere.

Later, they moved through the quiet rhythm of morning—Violet towelling her damp hair, Chad buttoning his shirt beside her, pausing now and then to tuck a strand behind her ear or steal a kiss.

Outside, Chad opened the passenger door of his black SUV and waited until she was seated before closing it gently and circling to the driver's side.

The drive was quiet but not strained. Companionable. Chad reached for her hand as they neared downtown, their fingers threading over the console.

"I won't be long," he said as he pulled up in front of the tall glass building that housed her law firm. "But I've got to check in with Jared this morning. Sam and Frank will be watching you until I get back, okay?"

Violet gave a soft laugh, amused but touched. "Chad, I'm fine."

His gaze darkened, serious. "Someone tried to run you down in a parking garage, Vi. You're not fine. And I'm not taking chances."

That edge of intensity made her heart skip—but it also sent warmth curling through her chest. He wasn't smothering her. He was protecting her. Because he loved her.

She leaned in and kissed him—soft, quick, but full of meaning. "Okay. Thank you. I love you."

"I love you too," he said, pressing his forehead to hers. "More than anything."

She got out and walked toward the entrance, throwing him a smile over her shoulder. Sam and Frank fell into place behind her with quiet precision.

When she reached her office and unlocked the door, she stopped short.

A large, dark grey suitcase sat in the middle of the floor.

Violet blinked. Frowned.

It hadn't been there last night.

She stepped forward cautiously. There were no tags. No note. Just a sleek, nondescript suitcase sitting like an intruder in the centre of her space.

She made a mental note to ask Julia about it.

Before she could reach for her phone, a knock sounded at the open door.

"Morning," Damien said brightly, stepping inside with a coffee. "Brought your usual—extra foam, no sugar. Like always."

Violet turned, still frowning at the suitcase, but managed a grateful smile. "Thanks, Damien. That's thoughtful."

He handed her the cup, expression warm and easy. "Also wanted to say thanks—for reassigning me to the Henderson case. It's a great opportunity. I really appreciate the trust."

She nodded, relaxing slightly. It was a relief that he wasn't upset. "You've earned it. I'm glad it's working out."

Damien gave a polite nod and turned toward the door. "Well, I'll let you get to it. Busy day, I'm sure."

"Always," she said lightly.

With a wave, he slipped out, leaving her alone again—with the coffee in her hand and the suitcase still silently looming across the room.

She watched the door close behind him. The warmth of his smile lingered—but so did the unease curling low in her gut.

Her gaze returned to the suitcase.

Still there. Still unexplained.

A chill prickled over her skin.

She set the coffee on her desk and hesitated, her fingers resting on the lid. Maybe it was nothing. Maybe she was overreacting—after the parking garage, after the sleepless night, after the weight of everything.

Get a grip, Vi.

Still, she didn't drink right away.

She reached down to power on her computer. The quiet hum was grounding, a slice of normal in the strange tension pressing against her ribs. The screen flickered to life.

She finally reached for the cup.

Warm. Familiar.

Just coffee.

She took a careful sip.

Bitterness. A trace of vanilla.

Normal.

And yet…

Her eyes flicked back to the suitcase.

That knot in her stomach pulled tighter.

Another sip. Her eyes didn't move.

A low hum bloomed in the back of her skull—barely noticeable at first.

She blinked. Rubbed her temples.

The hum grew. Her vision shimmered.

She reached for her mouse, but her fingers didn't cooperate. The cursor zigzagged. Her muscles felt… off.

A strange taste coated her tongue. Metallic. Wrong.

Her breath caught.

The coffee.

A jolt of panic struck her chest.

Her body reacted before her mind caught up. She turned sharply to her drawer, yanking it open.

Her Fitbit.

Still inside. Still fully charged.

Her hand closed around it like a lifeline. She didn't know why she grabbed it—only that she had to.

She slipped it into her bra, pressing it against her skin.

The room tilted.

She tried to stand. To call someone.

Her knees gave out.

Her hand slipped from the desk.

The carpet rushed up to meet her.

And then—nothing.

Chad had just finished scrubbing through the last of the surveillance footage from the parking garage. The frame froze on the moment that made his stomach lurch—Sam hurling himself at Violet, tackling her out of the way. If he'd been a second later—just one—she would've been crushed against the concrete pillar.

Chad's blood ran cold.

Behind him, Jared let out a low breath. "This guy's not playing around. She was inches from being killed."

"I know," Chad said, voice low and tight, eyes still locked on the screen.

Jared hesitated, then asked carefully, "Miss Miller… she's more than just a client, isn't she, boss?"

Chad thought about deflecting. Thought about keeping it professional. But instead, he looked Jared straight in the eye. "She's my future wife."

A slow grin spread across Jared's face. "Well. Good on you, boss."

Chad didn't smile back.

He checked his watch. Violet should still be at her office now. He hadn't heard from her since dropping her off—unusual, maybe, but not unheard of. Still, something gnawed at him.

He pulled out his phone and called her.

It rang. And rang. No answer.

He tried again. Same result.

Chad's gut twisted. He hit speed dial.

"Boss," Sam answered, his voice easy, casual—and that alone eased some of the tightness in Chad's chest.

"Where is she?"

A beat of silence.

"She's in her office," Sam said. "Told us to wait downstairs. We figured it was fine."

"You figured?" Chad's voice dropped, low and lethal.

"I—I'm going in now. I'll check her office."

"Do it. And call me the minute you lay eyes on her."

Chad was already moving, striding toward the exit with Jared on his heels.

"You think something's wrong?" Jared asked.

Chad didn't look at him. "I know something is."

His fingers tightened around his phone as it rang again—Violet's number. Straight to voicemail.

No answer.

His chest tightened, dread coiling like a vice around his ribs.

Something was wrong.

Terribly, unmistakably wrong.

Chad stood in the middle of Violet's empty office, his eyes scanning every corner like he could will her back into the space. Jared, Sam, and Frank flanked him, tense and silent. Julia stood near the door, her expression drawn and confused.

"You didn't see Violet at all this morning?" Chad asked, voice clipped.

Julia shook her head. "No. I usually get in later than she does."

Chad's jaw clenched. "What about Damien? Have you seen him today?"

She frowned. "Now that you mention it… no. I haven't."

"Damn," Chad muttered under his breath, pacing once.

The silence stretched thick in the room, the weight of Violet's absence pressing down on them all.

Chad turned sharply to Jared. "Work with the security team. I want every second of footage pulled—lobby, elevators, parking garage. She didn't just vanish."

Jared nodded. "On it."

"She's somewhere in this building," Chad growled, his voice low and dangerous. "Or someone made damn sure we can't find her."

Chad stood frozen in Violet's office, the quiet hum of the building doing nothing to steady the pounding in his chest. Her phone lay on the desk, screen dark. Her purse sat beside the leg of her chair, like she'd set it down and simply forgotten to pick it back up.

The desk drawer was open, but otherwise, everything looked… untouched. No signs of a struggle. No overturned chair. No broken glass. Just eerie stillness.

Chad's eyes narrowed as they landed on the coffee cup.

It sat dead centre on the desk—half full, foam collapsed, lid slightly askew.

He stepped closer.

A smudge of soft pink gloss clung to the rim—Violet's. His chest tightened. He picked it up slowly, thumb grazing the trace of her mouth. Lifting the lid, he brought it to his nose.

His brow furrowed. Not just coffee.

He hit Frank's number. "Bring me a drink test kit. Now."

"You think she was drugged?" Frank's voice sharpened on the other end.

"Yes."

Minutes later, Frank entered, the kit in hand. Chad moved quickly, testing the liquid.

Positive.

"Shit," Frank muttered.

Chad's stomach dropped. Rohypnol—fast-acting, disorienting, near-impossible to detect in the moment. If she'd taken more than a sip, she wouldn't have made it out of the room.

He set the cup down with deliberate care, but fury coiled in his gut.

This wasn't careless. This wasn't random.

Someone had targeted her.

And they'd taken her.

His fists clenched.

Whoever did this had no idea what kind of hell was coming for them.

Jared and Sam stepped into Violet's office, tension written all over their faces. Jared looked grim.

"He left the building," Jared said, eyes locking with Chad's. "Damien. He walked out the front door with a large suitcase."

Chad's grip tightened around the test strip still in his hand. His jaw clenched. "He drugged her coffee."

Sam swore under his breath. "Bloody hell."

"Did he get into a vehicle?" Chad asked sharply.

Jared shook his head. "Not from what we can see. Just walked off like it was nothing. I'm heading to the main office to check the street security cams—see if we can trace his direction from there."

"Go," Chad ordered. "Take Frank with you."

Jared nodded and they both bolted.

Chad turned to Sam. "You're with me."

They were out the door and into the SUV a moment later, Chad behind the wheel, fury vibrating off him like static. Every muscle in his body was tight, like a spring coiled too tightly, ready to snap.

"Bloody hell," Chad muttered, running a hand through his hair. "Lance is gonna have my balls for this."

Sam didn't reply, the silence in the car heavy with tension. There was no denying it— something was horribly wrong, and it was spiralling faster than Chad could get a handle on. His thoughts raced, but his body moved on autopilot. His eyes flicked to the rearview mirror, checking the road for any sign of movement, any clue, any trace of Violet's disappearance.

Chad hit Lance's number on speed dial, one hand white-knuckled around the wheel, the other gripping the phone. The tension in his chest seemed to tighten with each ring. He barely heard the first two.

He picked up on the third ring.

"Hello?" Lance's voice cut through the static, laced with grogginess, still thick with sleep.

Chad didn't waste a second. His voice came out cold, clipped, controlled—despite the burning panic clawing at his insides. "Violet's missing."

Lance's voice shifted immediately, now wide awake and on alert. "What do you mean, missing?"

Chad gripped the wheel harder, knuckles turning white. "It looks like Damien drugged her coffee. Took her out of the building in a suitcase."

There was a long, awful pause on the other end. The seconds stretched, thick and suffocating. Then, Lance's voice came through, a raw edge of disbelief mixed with anger. "Fuck. Chad, you promised me."

The weight of Lance's words hit Chad like a punch to the gut. He knew. He knew the responsibility he had, the promise he made to keep Violet safe. And now—now, she was gone, and he was scrambling, failing.

"I know," Chad said, his voice a low growl. "I didn't plan for this. We're doing everything we can. I'm on my way to the office now, checking footage. I need you to stay calm, Lance. We'll find her."

But even as he said the words, a sickening thought twisted in his gut. What if they were already too late?

The sound of tyres screeching on the asphalt filled the silence in the car. Sam glanced at Chad, but Chad didn't return the look, his mind already racing ahead to the next steps, to what they needed to do.

"You can't just—" Lance started, the frustration in his voice rising. "You can't just sit around. You should've—"

"I'm doing everything I can!" Chad snapped, cutting him off. His eyes burned with frustration, but his heart was a mess of fear. "I've got Jared checking the cameras, but Damien's ahead of us. We'll find her, Lance. I swear to God, we will. Just don't—don't do anything reckless. You're not in this alone."

Another pause. Chad could practically hear Lance's teeth gritting. The silence between them was thick, loaded with unsaid words. Finally, Lance spoke, his voice steadier, but still tight with anger and worry.

"You'd better, Chad. You'd better find her. I can't lose her. She's all I've got."

"I will," Chad said, his voice hard with determination. "I'll call you as soon as we get a lead."

"Fuck that, I'm on my way to your office."

Lance hung up without waiting for a response.

The weight of the phone call sat heavy in the car, the silence now a cold, oppressive thing. He had promised Lance. And now Violet—*his Violet*—was missing. Drugged. Taken. God only knew where.

Sam's voice broke through the silence. "We'll get her back. We will."

Chad didn't reply. He couldn't. The rage was too thick, the guilt too loud. He just nodded once, eyes fixed on the road as the city blurred past, his entire being focused on one thing.

Find Violet.

Before it was too late.

Sam shifted in his seat, his jaw clenched tight but said nothing.

Chad's foot pressed harder on the gas, the SUV speeding down the road as the minutes seemed to drag on forever. His mind was already racing ahead, planning the next steps. He couldn't let Lance down. He couldn't let Violet down. Not when every instinct in him screamed that time was running out.

They needed answers—and fast.

Chapter Twenty-Two

The first thing Violet felt was pain—sharp and searing at the back of her head, like someone had split her skull open. Then came the confusion, a slow, sludgy awareness crawling through her mind like molasses.

She tried to move, but her limbs refused to obey. Her wrists stung. Her ankles too. Something coarse and tight bit into her skin.

Plastic ties.

Panic surged like a bolt of electricity through her chest.

Her eyes flew open.

A soft amber light glowed overhead, casting a golden warmth across the small cabin. The ceiling was low, the wooden beams exposed and recently polished. A scent of lavender hung in the air, cloying and sweet—too sweet. A small fireplace flickered in the corner, its fake flames humming gently. A plush area rug lay beneath the bed, and nearby, a table was set for two with mismatched but carefully arranged dishes. A kettle sat on the stove, as if he'd just made tea. Everything was tidy. Intentionally so.

She lay on a bed covered with a faded quilt, the kind you'd find in a cozy mountain inn. But the plushness beneath her was a lie. Her limbs throbbed where the zip ties dug in, the plastic slicing into already raw skin. A gag filled her mouth—rough fabric knotted at the nape of her neck, sour with her own panic.

She twisted her head—and froze.

Damien sat beside the bed in a cushioned chair, as if he were simply keeping her company after a long nap. His hands were folded in his lap. His expression was peaceful. Dreamy, even. That same unnerving calm she'd once brushed off as introversion.

But here, surrounded by carefully curated comfort, his serenity felt warped. Wrong.

He'd tried to make this place feel like home. Their home. But everything about it made her skin crawl.

And the way he looked at her—like she was already his, like she belonged in this cabin with him—was far more terrifying than any scream she couldn't let out.

"You're awake," he said, like they were colleagues meeting for coffee. "I was starting to worry. You hit your head pretty hard when you fainted."

Violet's breathing quickened, sharp and panicked. She yanked at the zip ties, the plastic biting into her raw, trembling wrists. Pain flared, hot and searing, but she didn't stop. Her muffled cries fought against the gag, desperation rising with every frantic tug. She lifted her hands to pull the gag out of her mouth. But he put a hand on hers and stopped her.

He watched her for a long moment, then sighed. "I didn't want to do this, Violet. I really didn't. But you didn't leave me much choice."

She thrashed harder, fury rising. Her heart thundered, each beat an explosion of fear.

"You kept pushing me away," Damien continued, tilting his head like a curious child. "Flirting with Chad Morgan. Letting him put his hands on you like he owned you."

His jaw tightened, just briefly. "I was patient. I gave you space. I waited. But you just kept ignoring the signs. The flowers. The messages. That perfume you liked. I thought you understood."

Violet whimpered against the gag, her breath coming in shallow bursts. Her eyes were wide, frantic, scanning the room for anything—anything—she could use. Her mind fought to stay rational, clinging to every piece of advice she'd ever given a client: stay calm, assess, survive. But her body betrayed her, trembling so violently she could barely think.

Damien leaned in, and she flinched.

He didn't seem to notice. Or maybe he did—and liked it.

With a sickening gentleness, he brushed a strand of hair from her damp forehead. "I'm sorry about yesterday," he murmured, his tone calm, almost tender. "I was angry. I'm just... so glad I didn't kill you."

Her heart seized.

He tried to kill me.

Her eyes widened, and his smile deepened as if they were sharing a sweet memory instead of a nightmare. "You'll see," he continued softly, "once the dust settles, this will be better. Quieter. Just you and me. Safe."

She twisted away from his touch, every muscle screaming to recoil. But there was nowhere to go. The zip ties dug deeper into her skin. Damien's smile faltered, a flicker of wounded disappointment in his eyes.

"You're scared," he said, nodding to himself. "I get it. You don't see the full picture yet. But you will. I did this for us."

He rose, moving around the room with the slow, deliberate pace of someone lost in a daydream. "They'll look for you, of course. But I've planned for that. Working in law, dealing with criminals—you learn where they mess up. I didn't."

He turned to her, proud. "No digital trail. No witnesses. And Chad?" His voice dipped into something darker. "He won't find you."

At the mention of Chad, something inside her stopped trembling. Something hardened.

Not fear.

Resolve.

He'll come. He always does.

She clung to that truth like a lifeline.

Damien turned back toward her, eyes shining with a glassy conviction that chilled her to the bone. "This—" he swept his hand in a wide, reverent arc, encompassing the cabin, the bed, the flickering firelight dancing on the walls, and finally, the space between them— "this is where it all begins, Violet. Our new life."

She didn't move. Couldn't. Her wrists were raw from the zip ties, her ankles throbbed. But her gaze stayed locked on his—unblinking, cold, razor-sharp despite the storm of panic building in her chest. He wanted a reaction. Wanted fear. Wanted her to crumble.

She wouldn't give it to him.

"I've made everything perfect," Damien went on, his voice soft, almost dreamy. "This place—it's safe. It's peaceful. Just for us. I know it doesn't look like much now, but once you're settled, you'll see."

He crouched beside the bed again, reaching out with slow reverence to tuck a piece of hair behind her ear. The tenderness of it made her stomach turn.

"We're far out," he murmured. "No neighbours. Patching cell service. No one can hear if you scream. But I don't want you gagged. I want to hear your voice. I want to be able to kiss your lips. So, I'm going to take it off now." His head tilted, that soft, unhinged smile twitching at the corners of his mouth. "Don't scream, Violet. Don't ruin this."

She held his gaze and gave the smallest, slowest nod. Not submission—control.

He loosened the gag with aching care, as though unwrapping a gift he'd waited too long to open. When the fabric fell away, she drew in a shallow breath, the air thick with woodsmoke and madness.

"Damien," she said, her voice hoarse but steady. "Why are you doing this?"

His smile deepened, but his eyes—those eerily calm, lifeless eyes—never changed. "Why?" he echoed, almost amused. "Because I love you. Because the world out there didn't deserve you. They poisoned you against me. But here? Here, no one can interfere. No one can steal you away."

Violet stared at him, her voice low and even. "This isn't love."

He blinked, confused for a beat, like she'd just spoken a foreign language. Then he laughed—quiet, breathy, unhinged. "You don't mean that. You're scared. I get it. But love is sacrifice. And I gave up everything for this. For you."

As he stood and began pacing, lost in the fog of his own fantasy, Violet's mind snapped into sharp, strategic focus. There would be no waiting for miracles. No helpless damsel in distress.

Chad would come for her.

He always did.

But until then—she would endure. She would outlast this.

Damien's voice broke through her thoughts, soft and reverent, as if speaking a sacred vow. "I've dreamed about you for months. About holding you. About what it would feel like to finally be inside the woman I love."

He moved closer, eyes shining with a feverish devotion that made her stomach lurch. She flinched instinctively, recoiling against the mattress as he bent over her.

"I love you, Violet," he whispered, and before she could turn her head away, his mouth pressed against hers—uninvited, insistent. He moaned softly, like he was savouring the first bite of something forbidden, his touch reverent in all the wrong ways.

She went still beneath him, her skin crawling, heart slamming against her ribs. Then he pulled back, smiling, as if they'd shared something intimate and true.

"You taste like heaven," he breathed.

Her jaw clenched. Her eyes burned—not from tears, but with white-hot fury. He thought he was winning. That her silence was surrender.

He couldn't have been more wrong.

"I want to take the zip ties off," he said, voice low with anticipation. "Because I want to feel your arms around me."

She stared at him, steady and cold. "Damien, this isn't love. This is wrong. You need help. You're confused."

"I'm not confused," he snapped, his voice cracking. "You are. Everything was fine— until that smug bastard showed up. That oaf looked at me like I was dirt beneath his expensive shoes."

"He's my friend," she said firmly. "He was protecting me."

Damien laughed, sharp and bitter. "Protecting you? You didn't need protecting. I was watching over you—always. At work, at your building, on your morning runs. I kept you safe when you didn't even know you were in danger."

He stepped closer, eyes glazed with manic devotion. "But now... now we're finally alone. There's nothing in our way. You'll see, Violet. You'll understand when I touch you. I'll make sure you enjoy it. I want to hear you moan my name when I'm inside you."

A sick shiver ran down her spine, but she didn't flinch.

Instead, she met his gaze with icy defiance. You'll never break me, her eyes said. No matter what you do.

Because Chad was coming.

And she was going to survive.

Violet forced her breathing to steady, every instinct in her screaming to recoil, to fight— but she didn't. Not yet. She needed him calm. Predictable.

"You've… always looked out for me," she said softly, her voice trembling just enough to sound sincere, not frightened. "I didn't realise it. Not until now."

Damien froze, his head tilting slightly. A spark lit in his eyes, like a child receiving long-awaited praise.

"You mean that?" he whispered.

She nodded, eyes flicking toward the window, gauging the angle of the sun, the distance to the door. She couldn't see much—just trees. Endless woods. But it didn't matter. All she needed was one chance.

"I was overwhelmed," she murmured. "Chad confused me. But here… it's quiet. I can think. About us."

Damien smiled like a man hearing wedding vows.

He moved then, slowly, crawling onto the bed behind her. She stiffened, every muscle screaming as she felt the mattress dip. His arms slid around her, possessive, and trembling. One hand settled at her waist. The other, dangerously high near her ribs, started to move.

"You feel so right in my arms," he breathed, nuzzling into her hair. "Like you were made to be here. With me."

Violet pressed her lips together, willing herself not to flinch. Stay still. Play along. Think. Wait.

She needed him to believe her—just enough.

"If you cut my wrists loose," she said softly, infusing her voice with a mix of longing and hesitation, "I could touch you too."

Damien's eyes lit up with something fragile and desperate. Hope.

Chad stormed into headquarters, his jaw clenched, his footsteps sharp and deliberate against the concrete floor. The air shifted with his arrival—tight with tension. Sam followed close behind, silent, and grim. At the far desk, Jared and Frank were hunched over a laptop, the screen casting flickers of light on their furrowed faces.

"Jared," Chad barked without slowing. "Anything?"

Jared looked up, dark circles under his eyes. "Still combing through CCTV. No hits yet. The guy that took her knew how to stay off the grid."

Chad gave a curt nod. "Keep digging. I'll be in my office. I need a minute."

Without waiting for a reply, he strode toward the door and slammed it shut behind him, the sound echoing like a gunshot.

Sam let out a low breath and glanced at the others. "He's not just pissed. He's wrecked."

Jared kept his eyes on the screen, voice quiet. "He told me this morning… he's going to marry her."

Frank blinked. "No shit?"

"Oh, hell," Sam muttered, rubbing a hand down his face. "No wonder he looks like he's ready to kill someone."

They all turned toward Chad's closed office door, the silence stretching between them.

"Then we better find her," Jared said, his fingers flying over the keyboard. "Before he tears the city apart."

Chapter Twenty-Three

Chad closed the door behind him and leaned back against it, the silence of his office pressing in like a vice. His chest ached—tight and hollow all at once. He dragged a hand down his face, then crossed to the desk, staring blindly at the photos and reports strewn across it.

How could he have let her out of his sight?

How the hell did this happen?

He clenched his fists, the memory of her laugh, her voice, her smile—everything about Violet—flashing through his mind like blades. She had trusted him. He'd sworn to protect her. And now… now she was gone.

He gripped the edge of the desk, his knuckles white. The weight of failure crashed over him in waves. His knees buckled slightly, and he bent over, bracing himself as if the desk was the only thing keeping him upright. His breaths came hard, shallow. If he let go—if he allowed himself to fall—he wasn't sure he'd get back up.

Please be okay, he thought, squeezing his eyes shut. Please hold on.

The door banged open behind him.

"What the hell are you doing in here when my sister's missing?" Lance's voice cut through the air like a gunshot.

Chad didn't move. Not right away.

Lance wheeled in, fury in his voice—but then he stopped. He'd never seen Chad like this. Not in war. Not in loss. Not ever.

"Cap… what's wrong?"

Chad turned slowly, his face a storm of pain and devastation. He looked stripped raw, barely holding it together.

And before he could stop himself, before he could pull the words back…

"I love her, Lance."

Silence.

The admission hung there, thick with emotion. And in that moment, Chad didn't look like the cold, controlled commander Lance had followed into hell. He looked like a man utterly broken.

"She's not just someone I was protecting. She's… everything." Chad's voice cracked. "And if I lose her—I don't know how the hell I'm supposed to live with that."

"Hell…" Lance exhaled, voice softer now, the fire in his tone replaced by stunned realisation. "Does she know?"

Chad looked up, eyes bloodshot, jaw tight. "Yeah. She knows." His voice was rough, barely steady. "She loves me too. We finally admitted it to each other last night."

Lance leaned back in his chair, dragging a hand through his hair. "Fuck, Chad. I had no idea. I thought she hated you."

Chad gave a bitter huff, somewhere between a laugh and a sigh. "She did. For a long time."

"What happened?"

"I rejected her," Chad said quietly. "Five years ago. She came to me… opened up… and I pushed her away." His voice faltered. "Told myself it was for her own good. That I couldn't offer her a future. But the truth? I was scared. And she never forgave me."

It hit Lance all at once, like puzzle pieces finally snapping into place. He blinked, stunned. "That explains a lot."

"Yeah," Chad said, voice hoarse. "It explains everything."

The room fell silent. Just the sound of Jared's fingers flying across keys in the next room, muffled by the door. Then Lance looked up, his face more serious than Chad had seen it in months.

"Then we better get her back, brother. Because if you love her, and she loves you— you fight like hell to make sure this doesn't end here."

Chad's eyes locked on his, and for the first time in what felt like hours, he nodded with purpose. "I'm going to. Even if it kills me."

Chad and Lance burst out of the office together, tension radiating off them in waves. Jared barely looked up from his screen, already sensing the storm brewing.

"I found him," Jared said quickly, pointing to the footage. "Street cams picked him up outside Violet's office. But then he goes out of shot… and after that, nothing."

Lance leaned in, his face twisted in disbelief. "Is my sister in that suitcase?"

Chad answered, his voice low and grim. "Yes. We're certain she is."

Jared clicked the next clip. "Look—this is him taking coffee into her office just after nine. Then—" he jumped ahead on the timeline, "—he goes back in ten minutes later. Comes out with the suitcase. Heavy, like he's struggling with the weight."

"For fuck's sake," Lance growled, fists clenching. "This guy's a bloody psycho."

Chad's eyes were locked on the screen, jaw clenched so hard it looked like he might shatter his teeth. "We're going to find her."

Jared looked between them. "I've got teams working on traffic cams, toll booths, anything we can scrape. He planned this—he's off grid now. But we'll catch up."

Chad turned to Jared, his voice like steel. "Pull every favour. Call in every contact. I want every square mile of this city crawling with eyes."

Lance wheeled around to face Chad, his voice low and razor-edged. "And when we find him?"

Chad didn't blink. "We end it."

Lance's jaw clenched, but his voice stayed steady. "Does she have her Fitbit on?"

Chad turned to him, confused. "What?"

"Her Fitbit," Lance repeated. "She wears it almost every day—even at work. If it's still on her, we might be able to trace it."

Chad's eyes snapped into focus. "I didn't notice this morning."

"It's worth checking," Jared said quickly. "If it's on and syncing, we might get a location."

They all turned to Jared and watched him type furiously on the keyboard.

Jared said, hands flying across the keyboard. "Give me a second... I'm in. Her dashboard's up."

Everyone leaned in.

"No new steps since yesterday. No heart rate either. She's must not have it on."

Chad swore under his breath, eyes burning. His fists clenched.

"But—wait—" Jared's voice shifted. "The device pinged twenty minutes ago just outside the city."

Chad froze mid-step. "Where?"

"She must have it on her, just not on her wrist," Lance said with a grim sort of pride. "Smart."

Jared tapped furiously, the map blinking to life on his screen. "Looks rural. Northeast—Wurtsboro. It's patchy, but I've got coordinates."

"Wurtsboro?" Chad echoed, already shrugging into his jacket. "That's nearly two hours out."

"I'm sending the coordinates to your phone now," Jared said. "Looks like deep woods. Maybe a cabin."

Sam and Frank were already on their feet behind him, loading gear.

"Then we don't waste a second," Chad said, striding toward the door.

Lance wheeled after him, jaw tight. "Bring her home, Cap."

Chad turned, his eyes blazing. "I will."

Violet's voice came out soft, but deliberate. "Yes, Damien... I want to touch you too."

He didn't move for a second. Just stared at her like he was trying to read her mind.

"I want to believe you," he murmured, voice thick with emotion. "I really do, Violet."

Slowly, he reached down and began pulling her shirt free from the waistband of her skirt. She fought every instinct not to recoil—not to scream. Her pulse thundered in her ears, but she made herself breathe evenly, made herself stay soft. Believable.

His hand splayed across her bare stomach.

Her head turned to look back at him. She could feel him getting aroused his body flush up against her backside.

She forced a sigh. "Mmm, that feels good… having your hands on me, really on me, finally."

He stilled, eyes flicking up to hers. Searching. Hungry for validation.

"You mean that?" he whispered.

She nodded gently, even managed a tremulous smile. "Of course. I was just scared before. It's a lot, being here… with you. Like this."

He blinked, eyes glistening with fragile, desperate hope. "I knew you'd come around," he murmured, almost like a prayer. "You just needed time."

Slowly, with unsettling care, his fingers skimmed over the raw, reddened welts around her wrists. The zip ties bit into her skin, but his touch was featherlight—mocking gentleness wrapped around something vile.

"Let me take these off," he whispered, reverent as a worshiper before an altar. "I want to feel you… really feel you."

Violet's breath hitched—caught somewhere between dread and a sliver of hope.

"Please," she said, her voice low, coaxing. "I want to touch you too."

He paused, eyes studying her as if she were a fragile artifact in a museum. Then he reached into his back pocket, fumbling slightly before producing a small pocketknife. The metal glinted under the soft cabin lights as he leaned over her, the blade moving toward the plastic binding her hands.

Just a little longer. Just a little closer to freedom, she told herself, her pulse thundering in her ears.

But he froze. His expression changed—something darker clouding his features.

"You're not lying to me, are you, Violet?" His voice dropped, low and dangerous.

Her heart slammed against her ribs. "No, of course not," she said, soft and sweet as honey. "I wouldn't lie to you."

"Prove it."

She blinked. "How?"

He shifted, sliding her gently onto her side to face him, his gaze devouring her with longing. "Put your arms around me," he murmured, his voice trembling with need. "And kiss me like you mean it."

Violet's stomach churned. Oh, hell—how was she supposed to do this when everything in her screamed to recoil? Every inch of her skin crawled just being this close to him.

But then came the voice in her head—clear, cold, and ruthless. This is the only way out. You have to convince him.

She shut her eyes, summoning an image of Chad—his warmth, his steadiness, the way he looked at her like she was his whole world. Pretend it's him. It has to be him.

Swallowing down the rising bile, she slowly lifted her bound arms and looped them around Damien's neck. He shuddered at her touch, a soft gasp escaping him like a man starved.

And then she kissed him.

The moment their lips met, nausea surged through her. His taste, his scent, the sheer wrongness of it made her want to scream. But she didn't. She forced herself to kiss him like her life depended on it.

Because it did.

Damien groaned into her mouth, his hands gripping her waist as he deepened the kiss. His tongue pressed against hers, invading, possessive. She fought the urge to gag, her stomach twisting violently.

"Violet," he breathed against her lips, trembling. "Oh, Violet… I've waited so long for this."

She forced a small whimper—something soft, something encouraging. Her mind raced behind the mask of submission.

Just a little longer. Just a little closer to the knife.

Damien's hands slid down to her hips, then lower, grabbing her backside and pulling her tightly against him. She felt the hard press of his arousal through their clothes, and bile rose in her throat.

"God, I want you," he groaned, grinding against her. His breath was ragged, desperate. "I've waited so long."

Violet closed her eyes for half a second and summoned the image of Chad—his hands, his voice, his warmth. Anything to ground her. To help her pretend.

"I need to touch you," she whispered, her voice soft and trembling—masking revulsion with need.

And in her mind, she saw the pocketknife. Inches away. Just a little closer.

Damien's breath was hot against her cheek, his voice unsteady. "Then touch me, baby… show me."

Before she could reach for it, he moved—quick, almost frantic—as if afraid she might vanish. He pulled her arms from around his neck, cradling them like something fragile. Then, reaching behind him, he grabbed the pocketknife and flicked it open.

"Hold still," he murmured, as if this were some tender moment between lovers. Carefully, he slid the blade beneath the zip tie and sliced through.

Her wrists sprang free, raw, and trembling.

"There," he breathed, watching her closely. "Now you can really touch me."

Violet swallowed hard, nodding once. Her fingers curled slightly—she had to act natural. Had to play it just right. Her eyes flicked to the knife still resting by his thigh.

Just a little closer.

She forced a trembling smile. "Lie back," she said softly. "Let me."

He grinned, euphoric. "Just like my dreams."

Violet's hands were free, but her ankles were still bound. The zip ties dug into her skin, cruel restraints that mocked her. So close—yet still caged.

But not for long.

Damien leaned back against the pillows, his eyes glazed with lust and delusion, like he was admiring something he believed he owned. He yanked his pants off in one rough motion, leaving only his shirt—unbuttoned, hanging loose—and his boxers.

"Come here," he murmured, voice thick. "Let me see you."

She forced herself to move, slow and deliberate, straddling him with every ounce of fake submission she could muster. Her hands shook as they slid over his chest—not with want, but with raw, controlled panic. She dipped lower, toward the knife near his thigh, her stomach twisting.

His hands moved to her blouse, unbuttoning it clumsily, pushing it aside until he could cup her bra-clad breasts.

"God, Violet," he groaned. "You're perfect. Just like I imagined."

She forced a breathy laugh, bile rising in her throat. Her fingers brushed the cool metal handle.

Closer.

Then—swiftly, with all the force of desperation—she snatched the knife.

He blinked in surprise, lips parting.

"Violet—what are you—"

Too late.

She threw herself off the bed, landing hard on the floor, the breath knocked from her lungs. Her fingers worked fast, sawing at the zip ties around her ankles, heart thundering like a drum in her ears.

"Violet!"

The ties snapped.

She was on her feet in an instant—just as Damien's expression shifted, the fog of desire clearing from his eyes, replaced by confusion… then rage.

"Violet—!"

She didn't wait.

She ran.

Chapter Twenty-Four

Chad's knuckles were white on the steering wheel, the engine of the black SUV roaring as they sped down the highway. Sam sat beside him, eyes fixed on the road ahead, his jaw clenched tight. Frank, in the back seat, was scanning the dark, wooded landscape that blurred past the windows, his hand resting on the door as if he could will the vehicle to go faster.

"It's only ten more minutes," Chad muttered, barely able to focus on the road. His mind was a swirl of images: Violet's face, her smile, her fear, her voice pleading for help. Each thought was like a knife twisting in his chest. The clock was ticking, and every second that passed felt like an eternity.

"Yeah, but ten minutes could feel like ten hours right now," Sam said, his voice low but steady. "We're gonna find her. You're gonna bring her home."

Chad nodded but didn't say anything. There was nothing left to say. His mind raced through every possible scenario—every worst-case possibility—each one darker than the last. He had to believe they were going to get there in time. He couldn't let himself think otherwise. If he did, if he allowed that kind of doubt to creep in, he wouldn't be able to move. And that was something he couldn't afford.

His phone buzzed. Chad hit the hands-free button without taking his eyes off the road.

"Chad?" Jared's voice came through, tight with urgency. "Her Fitbit's pinging every ten minutes. The signal's steady—she hasn't moved. She's still in the area."

"I'm going as fast as I can," Chad growled, his foot pressing harder on the gas. "We're almost there."

"You'll find her," Jared said. "We're with you. We won't stop until we do."

The words were meant to reassure, but they landed like lead in Chad's chest. He gripped the wheel tighter, his knuckles pale against the leather. Every second that ticked by stretched thinner than the last. Violet was out there—alone, terrified, and in danger—and he was still too damn far away.

"Stay in contact," Chad said, voice clipped. "Let me know the moment anything changes."

He cut the call with a hard press of the button. The silence that followed was deafening.

From the back seat, Frank leaned forward, catching Chad's eyes in the rearview mirror. "You need to hold it together, boss," he said quietly. "We all know what she means to you."

Chad's jaw flexed, his mouth a grim line. He didn't respond—he couldn't. There wasn't time to process emotions, not now. But Frank was right. This wasn't just another protection detail. This was Violet.

The SUV tore through the shaded woodland road, its engine growling as the tyres chewed up gravel and pine needles. Headlights slashed through the thickening dark, casting ghostlike shadows across the dense undergrowth. Sunlight couldn't touch this stretch of forest; the thick canopy overhead devoured it whole, turning the afternoon into a dim, oppressive twilight.

Inside the vehicle, the atmosphere was electric—coiled tension ready to snap.

As they approached a fork in the road, the GPS gave a sharp ping.

"There," Sam said, stabbing a finger toward the left turn. "This is it. We're close."

Chad didn't hesitate. He yanked the wheel hard, the SUV fishtailing as it careened onto a narrow dirt path. The trees immediately pressed in, branches arching overhead like bony fingers closing into a tunnel. It was the kind of road people didn't just stumble across—it had been chosen, hidden. A perfect place to disappear.

The road curved sharply. The dense woods swallowed everything beyond the twin beams of light. Tension twisted in Chad's gut, a suffocating knot of dread and urgency. His hands were tight on the wheel, jaw clenched, breath shallow.

Then the speaker buzzed again. Jared's voice crackled through the static, urgent.

"There should be a cabin at the end of that road," he said. "Signal's locked in. She's right there, Chad. You're almost on top of her."

Before Chad could answer, Sam suddenly leaned forward, squinting through the windshield.

"Oh God—there! There she is!"

Chad's breath caught like a punch to the chest.

Violet.

She was running straight toward them, bursting from the tree line like a shot—barefoot, blouse wide open and flapping around her. Her hair was wild; face streaked with sweat and desperation. Her eyes were wide, unblinking, locked on the SUV like it was her only lifeline.

She didn't scream.

She didn't cry.

She just ran.

Everything she was had narrowed to one final burst of survival.

Chad barely processed her image before he saw him.

Damien.

He exploded from the shadow's seconds later—barefoot, shirt hanging open, clad only in boxer shorts, looking feral and unhinged. His chest heaved as he sprinted after her, and in one hand, gleaming in the headlights—

A knife.

Rage detonated in Chad's chest like a landmine.

He slammed the brakes so hard the SUV shrieked in protest, tyres spitting gravel like shrapnel into the woods. The vehicle skidded sideways, jarring against the uneven dirt path, but Chad didn't wait. He was out before the car had even stopped moving, the driver's door flying open as he exploded into the open, boots pounding the forest floor.

"Violet!" he bellowed, sprinting forward, adrenaline burning like jet fuel in his veins. "Run to Sam! Go—*now!*"

Her head snapped toward him at the sound of his voice. Recognition sparked in her eyes. Then—relief. And finally—hope.

She didn't hesitate. Violet bolted straight for Sam, who had already thrown open the passenger door and was running toward her, arms wide, ready to catch her and shield her from the chaos behind.

But Chad wasn't looking at Violet anymore.

His entire focus tunnelled in on Damien.

The bastard had stopped for a beat, startled by the sudden confrontation. But it wasn't fear in his eyes.

It was obsession. Twisted, delusional rage.

"She's mine!" Damien shrieked, wild and panting, the knife flashing in his grip like a serpent's fang. "She doesn't belong to you!"

Chad's lip curled, voice dropping to a lethal growl. "You're done, Damien. You'll never lay a hand on her again."

And then Damien lunged.

The blade tore through the air, aimed at Chad's chest, but Chad had already moved. His combat instincts surged to the surface—sharp, honed, unflinching. He sidestepped, grabbed Damien's wrist mid-strike, and twisted hard with the force of a breaking tide.

A sickening crack echoed through the trees. Damien screamed, the knife flying from his hand and thudding into the dirt.

But Chad wasn't finished.

Not even close.

He slammed Damien backward, his momentum crashing them against a thick tree trunk. Bark splintered beneath the impact. Chad pinned him there, one powerful forearm crushing into Damien's throat, the other fist clenched and cocked, trembling with restraint.

"You terrorised her," Chad spat, voice like gravel. "You hunted her like she was prey."

Damien writhed, choking out something that might've been a protest—but Chad didn't care. His vision had gone red. His entire body trembled with the force of holding back the full brunt of his rage.

"She was never yours," Chad hissed, pressing harder, voice raw with fury. "She never will be."

"Chad!" Frank's voice cracked like a whip through the haze. "We've got her—she's safe! You need to let go!"

Chad's gaze snapped toward them.

Violet was in Sam's arms, sobbing, her whole body trembling as she clung to him like she was drowning. She was alive. She was breathing. And she was safe.

That was all that mattered.

Chad stepped back and let Damien collapse to the forest floor like discarded trash, gasping and clutching his shattered wrist. Frank was already there, cuffing him with brutal efficiency, zip ties cinching tight. Damien wouldn't get far this time.

He was finished.

Chad didn't wait.

He turned and ran—straight for Violet.

Her eyes met his as he approached, and in that moment, her whole body sagged toward him. She stumbled from Sam's arms, and Chad caught her. Held her. Wrapped her up in his arms like she was the most fragile, precious thing in the world.

"I've got you," he whispered fiercely into her hair. "You're safe now, baby. I've got you."

And he wasn't letting go.

Not ever again.

The sterile lights of the emergency room were almost too bright after the dim chaos of the forest.

Violet sat hunched on the gurney, wrapped in a hospital blanket, her legs dangling, bare feet still streaked with dirt. A nurse had cleaned the cuts on her knees, patched a shallow wound on her shoulder, and offered her a cup of water she hadn't yet touched. Her blouse had been replaced by a pale-blue hospital top, the open collar revealing bruises beginning to bloom along her collarbone.

Chad stood by the door, arms folded, watching her like he was afraid she might vanish again.

The doctors had assured them she was physically okay—no internal injuries, no signs of a concussion—but the trauma lingered like smoke, thick in the air between them.

"Want me to give you space?" Chad asked quietly.

Violet looked up, and for a second, her eyes were glassy, distant. Then she shook her head and extended a hand toward him.

He was at her side in an instant, taking her hand, sitting on the edge of the bed. He didn't speak. Just held her fingers in his, his thumb tracing small circles into her skin.

"Is he gone?" Violet's voice was hoarse, brittle.

"Damien's in custody," Chad said, his voice low, steady. "Frank and Sam handed him over to the local sheriff. He's not getting out anytime soon."

Violet nodded, but the movement was small—tight and mechanical, like her body had forgotten how to respond naturally. Her bottom lip quivered as her eyes filled again. "He was going to… to hurt me." Her throat bobbed as she swallowed. "He—he wasn't going to stop."

Chad's stomach turned to ice. The words landed like blades.

He couldn't think about what might've happened if they'd been a minute later—if she hadn't broken away and run—if he hadn't seen her in time. A dark roar pressed against the back of his skull. He swallowed it down.

"I know," he said, his voice rasping. "But you got away. You ran, Violet. You fought."

Her hand trembled in his.

"I was so scared," she whispered. "But I knew you would come."

Chad leaned in, gently pressing his forehead to hers. "Always."

Suddenly, the door to the hospital room opened with a soft knock, and the sound of wheels on tile echoed in. Chad looked up, relief breaking through the storm.

Lance.

"Hey," Lance said, wheeling himself into the room, his voice thick with emotion. "I had to see for myself."

Violet's eyes filled again, but this time with something warmer. She gave a small, broken laugh and held out an arm.

Lance rolled forward and grabbed her hand with his, squeezing it tight. "Jesus, Vi. When Chad called and said they had you safe—I swear, I've never been more grateful in my life."

"I'm okay," she whispered, though her voice cracked. "I'm really okay now."

Lance glanced at Chad, then back at his sister, his jaw tight, eyes glossed with a sheen he didn't bother hiding. "You're safe now, Vi. That's all that matters. And you don't have to talk about any of it until you're ready. You just focus on breathing… on healing."

Violet nodded slowly, her expression distant for a moment as she stared at the soft folds of the blanket pooled in her lap. Her voice, when it came, was small. Fragile.

"When I started feeling… funny in the head," she said, pressing two fingers to her temple as if to make sense of it, "like things weren't real, like I was floating out of my body—I don't know how, but something told me I needed to get my Fitbit."

Chad leaned in closer, his brow furrowed. "You mean when he drugged you?"

She nodded, her gaze flicking to his. "I think so. My thoughts were all jumbled, and I couldn't walk right, but this voice in my head—maybe it was Mum's, maybe it was mine—I just kept thinking, if you can get the Fitbit, someone will find you."

"Thank God you did," Lance said, his voice cracking. He reached over and squeezed her hand. "That little thing… that little act might've saved your life."

Violet let out a trembling breath, her voice raw. "I grabbed it out of my drawer. I could barely think straight, but I kept telling myself I needed to hide it. I couldn't let him see it." Her fingers curled around the blanket, her knuckles white. "So, I shoved it into my bra. I was so scared, Chad. My whole body was shaking. But I knew… if I didn't get that thing on me…" Her voice cracked, tears sliding silently down her cheeks. "No one would know where I was."

Chad's throat closed. He hadn't realised he was holding his breath until it released on a ragged exhale. He brushed his thumb over the back of her hand, grounding himself in the feel of her skin. Warm. Alive.

"You were brilliant," he said quietly. "Even drugged, terrified—you still fought. That signal gave us the lead we needed. You saved yourself."

A long silence stretched between them, heavy with everything unspoken. Then Violet gave a small, exhausted smile, tears shining in her eyes.

"I just wanted to come home."

Chad leaned in, kissing her temple. "You are home now. And you're not going anywhere."

Lance met Chad's eyes again—this time with unspoken gratitude. Trust. Brotherhood. They were a unit now. Violet's protectors. Her family.

Chapter Twenty-Five

The sliding doors of the emergency room hissed open, and the late afternoon sun spilled across the hospital floor. Chad walked just a step behind Violet, his hand hovering at her lower back in quiet protection. Lance followed on her other side, manoeuvring his wheelchair with practiced ease.

Waiting outside were Sam, Frank, and Jared—three men who'd dropped everything the moment Chad called. Their postures were loose, but their eyes tracked Violet like hawks, cataloguing every bruise, every stitch, every shadow beneath her eyes.

Violet paused when she saw them, heart swelling with something fierce and warm. These weren't just Chad's men—they were hers now too. Family by fire.

She stepped forward without hesitation.

"Thank you," she whispered, voice still soft from the trauma but full of meaning.

Before any of them could reply, she pulled Sam into a hug. He froze like he'd never been hugged in his life, then awkwardly patted her back. Violet kissed his cheek. His ears turned red.

Next was Frank, who muttered something about not being good with emotions even as she wrapped her arms around his solid middle. He grunted, then gently squeezed her shoulder. She kissed his cheek too.

Jared tried to play it cool, arms crossed—until Violet's hug cracked his posture. He gave in with a half-smile, accepting the cheek kiss with a murmur of "You're welcome," his voice rougher than usual.

"Stop looking like I just proposed to you," Violet teased gently, eyes shining with unshed tears. "It was a thank you, not a marriage proposal."

Sam coughed, looking away. "Yeah, well… any time."

Chad stood off to the side, watching the quiet exchange with something warm settling behind his ribs. These men—his brothers-in-arms—hadn't just protected Violet.

They'd shown up for her. And for him.

Lance wheeled up beside him and nudged Chad's leg. "You gonna get all misty-eyed on me, Captain?"

"Shut up," Chad muttered.

But his hand found Violet's again anyway.

And he didn't let go.

Chad helped Violet into his SUV, his large hands surprisingly gentle as he guided her into the passenger seat. He adjusted the seatbelt across her body with deliberate care.

She didn't protest, just watched him in silence, her eyes shadowed with everything she wasn't ready to say.

He closed her door and rounded the hood with purposeful strides, slipping into the driver's seat and starting the engine. The cabin filled with the soft hum of the motor and the low thrum of tyres on asphalt as they pulled away from the curb.

They didn't speak. Words felt too fragile, too small for the heaviness hanging between them. But as they merged onto the quiet road leading into the city, Chad reached across the console and laced his fingers through hers.

His grip was steady, warm. Protective.

Violet looked down at their joined hands and exhaled slowly, the tension in her shoulders easing just a little. Her fingers curled around his instinctively, like her body trusted him even if her mind was still catching up.

The city lights spilled across the windshield in golden ribbons as they drove in silence, their connection humming louder than any conversation.

Chad's thumb stroked lightly over the back of her hand, and he glanced at her briefly, his jaw tight with unspoken emotion.

He hated that someone had taken away her peace, her confidence, her sense of safety. And he swore, silently and fiercely, that he would do whatever it took to get it back for her.

By the time they pulled into the underground garage of his penthouse building, the silence between them had shifted. It was no longer heavy. It felt like understanding. Like comfort.

Chad parked in his private spot and cut the engine. The silence lingered for a beat before he turned to her, his fingers still entwined with hers.

"You're safe now," he said softly. His voice was low, sure, and Violet believed him—because when Chad Morgan said something, it wasn't a promise. It was a certainty.

She nodded, not trusting her voice, and let him help her out again. The garage was cool and quiet, their footsteps echoing off concrete as he guided her to the private elevator with a hand on the small of her back. The contact was light, respectful—but grounding. She didn't realise until that moment just how much she needed to feel anchored.

The elevator doors slid open, and they stepped inside. Chad pressed his thumb to the biometric scanner, and the system beeped softly in response.

Violet glanced up at him as the elevator began to ascend. "You really don't take chances, do you?"

His mouth quirked at one corner, not quite a smile. "Not when it comes to people I care about."

The elevator opened directly into his penthouse, and warm, recessed lighting flickered to life as they entered. The space was quiet, polished, expansive—floor-to-ceiling windows looked out over the city skyline, and the scent of leather, clean wood, and something distinctly him filled the air.

Chad closed the door behind them and turned to her. "You want something to drink? Food? I can have something brought up."

Violet shook her head. "No, thank you." She hesitated, then looked up at him, her voice softer now. "But I do need to talk to you. About what happened."

His expression shifted, the easy calm giving way to something more focused. He nodded once and stepped closer, brushing a hand lightly along her back. "Come sit," he said, guiding her toward the couch.

She followed without protest, sinking down into the deep cushions as he sat beside her. Not too close, but not distant either. Just enough space to breathe but not feel alone.

Chad turned toward her, one arm resting along the back of the sofa, his body open, attentive. "I'm listening, Violet. Whatever it is, I'm here."

She looked at him for a long moment, as if weighing how much she could say—how much of herself she could hand over without unravelling completely.

Her lips parted, then pressed shut again. She exhaled slowly, like forcing the truth out of her lungs would hurt less than keeping it inside.

She stared at a fixed spot on the floor, where the grain in the hardwood blurred from the heat behind her eyes. Her fingers twisted the edge of her sleeve, tugging, releasing, then tugging again.

"I had to kiss him…" she said, her voice barely above a whisper.

The words falling like stones between them. Chad's entire body went still, a flicker of something dark flashing in his eyes.

"To escape," she added, her gaze locked on her trembling hands. "I had to make him believe I wanted him."

"Violet…" His voice was rough, straining to contain the fury beneath it.

"No," she said quickly, lifting her eyes to his. "I need you to hear this. All of it." Her voice shook, but she pushed forward. "It was the only way I could get him to cut my hands loose. He thought I wanted to be with him. That I was… willing."

Chad said nothing. He didn't interrupt. He didn't move. He just listened, giving her the space to bleed out the truth.

"I'm sorry, Chad," she whispered, shame creeping into her voice.

His brow furrowed, confusion flickering across his face. "Sorry?" he echoed. "What the hell are you sorry for?"

She looked away. "Because I let him think—"

"No." He leaned forward, his voice firm but tender. "Don't. Don't blame yourself for surviving."

She swallowed hard.

"You did what you had to do to stay alive," he said, his tone low, intense. "You fought in the only way you could. And I thank God you did. I thank God you came back to me."

Tears welled in her eyes, her breath catching in her throat.

"You hear me?" Chad said softly, reaching for her hand, his thumb brushing gently across her knuckles. "You don't owe me an apology. You owe yourself compassion."

He sighed, the sound heavy with emotion. "Listen to me, Violet. Five years ago, when you came to me and said you wanted us to try—really try—as a couple… I wanted nothing more than to take you in my arms and never let you go. I wanted you so much it hurt."

Her lips parted, confusion and heartache flooding her features. "Then why…"

"I rejected you," he said, voice low and raw, "because I didn't think I was good enough for you. I thought I was too damaged. That I was broken because of the things I had to do when I was deployed. The things I've seen… the things I've done. I thought if you really knew the weight I carried, you'd see me differently. That you'd stop loving me."

"Chad," she whispered, emotion thick in her throat, "I would never have judged you. Not for doing what you needed to do to survive. To protect the men beside you."

He nodded slowly, his eyes searching hers. "And that's exactly how I feel about what you're telling me. What you had to do to survive—that doesn't change how I see you. It doesn't stain your worth or make you less of the woman I love."

She gasped softly at the intensity, blinking as if she wasn't sure she'd heard him right.

"I love you, Violet," he said again, firmer this time. "And I thank my lucky stars that you're here, safe with me now. That I get another chance to protect you. To love you the way I should've all those years ago."

Tears streamed down her face, unchecked and silent, as she whispered, "I love you, Chad Morgan."

Chad's smile was tender, reverent—like the words were something sacred. He leaned in, kissed her forehead, then pressed his against hers. "Tell me what you need, baby."

She drew in a shaky breath. "I need to wash him off me."

He nodded without hesitation and stood, guiding her gently by the hand down the hallway to his bedroom. The space was warm, minimal, masculine—shades of charcoal and navy, clean lines, soft lighting. He didn't say a word as he led her into the ensuite bathroom, flipping on the dim overhead lights and turning on the rain shower.

Steam began to fill the space as he turned back to her, his eyes full of quiet strength.

"I'll give you a minute," he murmured, starting to back away.

"No." Her voice was small but firm. She reached for his wrist. "Don't go. I don't want to be alone right now."

Chad stilled, his eyes locking with hers. "Okay," he said softly. "I'll stay."

They moved in unison then, slowly, carefully. Violet's fingers trembled as she peeled off her blouse, Chad stepping in only when she faltered. He undid the buttons with quiet reverence, like handling something fragile, never rushing her. She unhooked her bra, stepped out of her skirt, her underwear. He followed her lead, discarding his shirt, his pants, everything that separated his skin from hers.

No hunger. No heat. Just closeness.

When they stepped into the shower, the warm water cascaded over them, a gentle rhythm muffling the world outside. Violet stood beneath the stream, eyes closed, breathing deep, like she was trying to exhale the memory of fear and reclaim her body.

Chad reached for the soap and lathered it in his palms.

"May I?" he asked, voice barely audible over the water.

She nodded.

He started with her shoulders, his hands moving slowly, reverently. He washed her arms, her back, her neck—every inch touched with quiet tenderness. He didn't linger, didn't stray. Just gave her care, gave her peace.

When his hands reached her stomach, a soft sob escaped her lips, her body trembling beneath his gentle touch. Chad leaned in without hesitation, pressing a tender kiss to her damp temple. His voice was a low murmur against her skin.

"You're safe. You're here. You're mine."

Violet turned in his arms, burying her face against his chest, her breath coming in soft, uneven bursts. He held her tighter, letting the silence wrap around them, broken only by the rhythm of the water falling over their bodies.

She tilted her head and kissed the centre of his chest, just over his heart. Her hands roamed across the strong planes of him—warm, solid, familiar. Slowly, she rose on her toes, her fingers finding his face, cupping it with aching tenderness. Her eyes searched his, and then she kissed him.

It was soft at first—hesitant, searching—but when he responded, it deepened, turned hungry. Every shared breath, every touch carried the weight of all the time they'd lost… and all the love they still had left to give.

The heat built between them swiftly, beautifully, layered with need and trust.

"Make love to me, Chad," she whispered, her voice full of yearning. "Please."

He didn't hesitate. He lifted her into his arms with effortless strength, and she wrapped her legs around him, her hands clutching his shoulders, her mouth seeking his again.

Steam wrapped around them like a veil as Chad pressed her gently against the warm tile, his hands firm at her hips, grounding her, steadying her. Violet clung to him, her fingers threading into the wet strands of his hair, her mouth moving hungrily over his.

There was nothing tentative about this. Nothing hesitant.

Only years of longing, buried feelings now breaking through the surface like waves crashing onto shore.

Chad's mouth trailed from her lips to her jaw, down the delicate curve of her neck. Each kiss was reverent, an unspoken apology for the time they'd lost, the pain she'd endured. He let his hands roam with careful grace, cupping her breasts, brushing his thumbs gently over her nipples until she arched against him, a soft gasp escaping her throat.

"You're so beautiful," he murmured, voice hoarse with emotion. "So damn beautiful."

Violet cupped his face again, pulling him back to her for a kiss that was all fire and need. Her legs tightened around him, and he groaned into her mouth, the sound vibrating through her. She felt him hard and ready against her, and her body responded with an ache so deep it made her dizzy.

"I need you," she whispered against his lips. "Now. I don't want to feel anything else but you."

He looked into her eyes then, a flicker of hesitation in the depths of his gaze—not from doubt, but from the weight of what she'd been through.

"Are you sure?" he asked, his voice like gravel. "I need you to be sure, Violet."

She nodded, her hand pressing over his heart. "You make me feel safe. I want you, Chad. No one else. Only you."

That was all it took.

He shifted, adjusting her in his arms, guiding himself to her entrance. With slow, aching precision, he pushed into her—inch by inch—until he was buried deep, their bodies joined completely.

They both stilled, breathless. Violet clutched at his shoulders; her forehead pressed to his. The moment pulsed between them—hot, sacred, raw.

Chad began to move, slow and measured at first, his hands holding her as if she were something precious. The slick heat of the water pouring over them only heightened the sensations—the contrast of strength and gentleness, the way he filled her perfectly.

She moaned softly, her mouth trailing along his jaw, her teeth grazing lightly at his throat. "God, Chad…"

His rhythm deepened, powerful and unrelenting now, but never rough. Their bodies moved in harmony; a slow dance built on years of denied desire and emotion.

"I love you," he whispered into her ear. "I love you so damn much."

Tears mingled with the shower water on her cheeks as she kissed him again, everything inside her unravelling at once. Her climax built from the centre of her being, curling outward like flame, until she shattered with a cry against his mouth, her body pulsing around him.

Chad wasn't far behind. His breath grew ragged, his thrusts erratic, and then he groaned her name like a prayer, releasing with a force that shook him to his core.

For a long moment, they just held each other, tangled in the mist and warmth, their bodies trembling, their hearts racing.

No words were needed.

She was his.

He was hers.

And the world, for now, had narrowed to just the two of them.

Epilogue

Twelve months later…

The elevator doors slid open on the executive floor of Morgan Global Security. Violet stepped out, the soft click of her heels echoing against the polished floors. She inhaled deeply—the familiar scent of leather, wood polish, and faint cologne filling her senses. A warm sense of belonging wrapped around her, steadying her heart as she made her way toward Chad's office.

At his usual post outside the door, Jared sat behind his desk, absorbed in his laptop. He looked up as soon as he heard her, his face breaking into a wide, genuine grin. Pushing his chair back, he rose to greet her.

"Hello, counsellor," he said warmly. "Heard you won your big case yesterday."

Before she could respond, Jared pulled her into a quick, brotherly hug, pressing a light kiss to her cheek.

"I did," Violet said with a proud smile, feeling lighter than she had in weeks. She nodded toward Chad's office. "Is he in?

"Yep. Go right in," Jared said, winking. "He's always happy to see you."

"Thanks, Jared." Violet leaned in and kissed his cheek, grateful for the easy affection that had grown between all of them.

Gathering her courage, Violet crossed the room and knocked lightly before pushing open the office door.

Chad looked up—and in that instant, the whole world seemed to stop. His blue eyes lit with a heat and tenderness that never failed to undo her. Without hesitation, he stood, moving around his desk with that powerful, purposeful stride she loved.

The moment he reached her; he opened his arms. She stepped into them without a second thought, feeling the weight of the world lift from her shoulders as he closed her in his embrace.

"Hello, Mrs. Morgan," Chad murmured, his voice thick with affection. "To what do I owe this pleasure?"

As she melted into his arms, a memory came rushing back—the day they said, "I do," six months ago.

She had stood at the top of the aisle in delicate lace and flowing satin, her dark hair swept back, her eyes bright with unshed tears. She wasn't nervous. She wasn't afraid. She was simply ready.

Beside her, Lance adjusted the wheels of his chair and offered his arm with a proud, steady smile. His suit was crisp, his posture proud, and his expression—so full of fierce love and bittersweet pride—that Violet had to blink hard to hold it together.

The music swelled, and together they made their way down the aisle.

At the end of it, waiting like an anchor in the storm, stood Chad.

He wore a black tuxedo cut to perfection, but it wasn't the tailoring she noticed—it was the way he looked at her. Like she was the first, last, and only thing he would ever want.

Jared stood beside him, grinning broadly, amusement and pride in his expression. In the front pews, Sam and Frank stood tall, eyes suspiciously glassy, pride etched on their faces.

Jared elbowed Chad lightly. "You're the luckiest son of a bitch alive, you know that?"

Chad didn't take his eyes off Violet. His smile was slow and sure, steeped in certainty. "Believe me," he said softly. "I know."

Now, in his office, Violet returned to the present, her heart full to bursting as she looked up at the man who had been her anchor through every storm.

She smiled, brushing her hand against his chest, feeling the steady thud of his heart. "I have news for you," she said, voice barely above a whisper.

Chad's brow furrowed, protective instincts rising fast. "Are you okay?"

"I'm fine. Actually… better than fine."

His head tilted slightly, impatience laced beneath concern. "Vi," he said gruffly. "Tell me."

She took a steadying breath, the moment swelling between them, heavy with hope and possibility.

"You're going to be a daddy."

For a heartbeat, Chad froze—muscles taut, breath suspended. And then—he laughed. A raw, stunned sound of pure, unfiltered joy.

"A daddy…" he echoed, testing the word on his tongue, tasting it like a miracle he never quite dared to believe.

Before Violet could respond, his mouth found hers—urgent, grateful, reverent. His arms wrapped tight around her as he lifted her clean off the floor, twirling her in a circle as she laughed breathlessly against his lips.

He set her down gently but didn't let go. Cupping her face in his hands, his gaze burned into hers.

"You're sure?" His voice was rough, thick with emotion.

"Positive," Violet whispered, laughter trembling with happy tears. "Chad, I'm so happy."

"You've made me the happiest man in the world," he said, pressing his forehead to hers, his voice shaking.

Still holding her close, he couldn't stop smiling. He kissed her forehead once more, then laced their fingers together.

"Come with me," he said, voice husky with excitement. "They need to hear this from us."

Violet laughed softly as he led her toward the outer office. Jared looked up, brows rising at Chad's unguarded smile—rare, genuine, and unmistakable.

Sam and Frank, just stepping out of a nearby conference room, stopped mid-sentence at the sight of them. They exchanged a look, eyebrows raised.

Lance rolled out from his office, curiosity in his eyes. Now a strategic consultant for Morgan Global Security, he still kept close tabs on everything—especially where his sister was concerned.

Chad didn't hesitate.

He stepped into the centre of the room, Violet tucked proudly against his side, and said, "I'm going to be a dad."

For a beat, silence. And then—

"Are you serious?" Jared practically shouted, springing to his feet.

"No way!" Sam barked, clapping Chad on the shoulder so hard he nearly stumbled.

Frank grinned, stepping forward to shake Chad's hand, then pulled him into a fierce hug. "About damn time."

Lance rolled forward, emotion shining in his eyes. "Vi..." he said thickly. "You're gonna be a mum."

Violet knelt in front of him, taking his hand. "And you're going to be the best uncle," she whispered, her voice trembling.

Lance squeezed her fingers, just breathing for a moment, soaking it all in.

"You guys..." Jared shook his head, still half-laughing, half-choking up. "You made this whole damn place a family."

Sam grinned. "Guess we'd better start baby-proofing the office."

Chad tightened his arm around Violet, heart full to the brim. He looked around at each of them—Jared, Sam, Frank, Lance—and knew, without question, he wouldn't want to start this chapter of his life with anyone else by his side.

"Thank you," Chad said quietly. "For being here. For being family."

Jared, voice steady and sure, answered first. "Always."

And in that sunlit office high above the chaos of the city, surrounded by the people who had stood by him through every trial and triumph, Chad Morgan realised something simple and true:

He wasn't just building a future.

He was building a legacy—with the woman he loved and the family he'd found.

And it was only just beginning.

The End

Forever Yours

Alison Reid

A complete standalone romance
Previously published individually

Chapter One

Celeste Beaumont stood before the full-length mirror in her spacious Sydney apartment—a lavish twenty-first birthday gift from her parents—and smoothed her hands over the fitted navy-blue skirt of her suit. The soft fabric hugged her curves in all the right places, the epitome of refined elegance with just a whisper of sensuality. The woman staring back at her was poised, powerful, and undeniably beautiful—someone who commanded attention without ever demanding it.

At nearly twenty-five, she had come into her own. Gone were the awkward teenage years when her tall, lanky frame had felt more like a burden than an asset. Now, she moved with effortless grace, every step purposeful, every gesture poised. She had learned to embrace her height rather than shrink from it. There was strength in the way she carried herself, a quiet confidence that spoke of a woman who knew exactly who she was.

Years of discipline had shaped her svelte figure—Pilates, morning runs along the harbour, balanced meals that never veered into obsession. She had cultivated a body that was strong yet feminine, one that fit seamlessly into the world of polished professionals she moved in.

Her chestnut-brown hair cascaded in soft waves down her back, catching the golden morning light that filtered through the large bedroom windows. Thick and luxurious, it was the kind of hair people instinctively reached out to touch. Sun-kissed strands of auburn and gold framed her high cheekbones and delicate jawline, adding warmth to her already striking features. She ran a brush through it before deciding to leave it down.

Then there were her eyes. Almond-shaped and hazel with flecks of gold, they were her most revealing feature. Too expressive at times. Too easy to read when she let her guard slip. They had once belonged to a girl who had dreamed, who had waited, who had wasted years hoping for something that would never be.

Now, they belonged to a woman who had learned that waiting was a waste of time.

Her full lips, naturally plump and effortlessly kissable, were enhanced with a subtle rose-coloured gloss. They curled into a small, knowing smile—one of quiet self-assurance.

She reached for her navy heels, slipping them on with ease. The buttery-soft leather moulded perfectly to her feet, adding a few more inches to her already impressive height. With them, she was statuesque. Unshakable.

Confidence surged through her veins as she took one last glance at her reflection.

This was the woman she had become. A woman who was successful, independent, desired.

And it was time to take the next step.

She had spent far too long holding onto something that no longer held value. Waiting for the right moment. The right person. The right spark.

She was done waiting.

Celeste Beaumont was ready to lose her virginity.

Celeste had never been the type to rush into things. Raised by two exceptionally successful parents, she had learned patience, discipline, and control from an early age. Her father, Jonas Beaumont, was one of the most sought-after wealth managers in the country, handling fortunes that spanned continents with a level of precision that rivalled the sharpest minds in finance. Her mother, Hope Beaumont, was a renowned surgeon, her hands saving lives with the same unshakable confidence she had instilled in her daughter.

Excellence wasn't a choice in the Beaumont household—it was the standard.

From the moment Celeste could walk, she had been expected to excel. Her parents had given her the best of everything—education at the finest schools, access to opportunities most could only dream of, and, most importantly, unwavering love and support. They had raised her to be strong, self-sufficient, and relentless in her ambitions.

They were proud of her. She had never once doubted that.

But they had also set the bar impossibly high.

Failure was not an option.

Neither was settling.

And for years, that mindset had dictated every aspect of her life. It was why she had climbed the corporate ladder with precision, landing a coveted position as an assistant manager at one of Sydney's most prestigious banks before the age of twenty-five. It was why she held herself to impossibly high standards, ensuring she was always composed, polished, and in control.

And it was why she had never given herself to a man.

Her best friend, Kathleen Carter, had always been the one person who truly understood her. They had been inseparable since childhood—two girls navigating the world of privilege with laughter, secrets, and the kind of loyalty that withstood everything.

Everything, that was, except Andrew Carter.

Kathleen's older brother. The golden boy.

For years, Celeste had harboured a ridiculous, all-consuming crush on him.

He was the kind of man fairy tales were written about—charming, ambitious, devastatingly handsome. The kind of man who could walk into a room and command attention without trying. And the kind of man who had never seen her as anything more than his little sister's best friend.

She had adored him.

Perhaps, in some quiet, foolish part of her heart, she had even loved him.

But Andrew had never been hers to love.

Then he had married Sarah.

Celeste and Kathleen had never liked Sarah. There was something off about her, something too polished, too perfect. She had the kind of beauty that belonged on magazine covers, the kind of presence that made other women feel like they were standing in the shadow of something untouchable. But beneath the poised smiles and sugar-coated words, Celeste had always sensed something disingenuous.

She had never been able to prove it.

Not that it mattered now.

Andrew was in New York, living the life he had built with his wife, and Celeste was here, in Sydney, staring at herself in the mirror, realising just how much time she had wasted on a man who had never been hers.

Gone was the timid girl who had once hidden in the background, waiting, hoping.

Gone was the girl who had spent years comparing every man to Andrew Carter, searching for the impossible, the unattainable.

A pang of old longing tightened in her chest, but she shoved it aside.

She had spent too many years waiting—waiting to be noticed, waiting to be wanted, waiting for a man who had never once thought of her the way she had thought of him.

That girl no longer existed.

This was her time.

And she was done waiting.

It was time to move on. Time to find someone worthy. Someone she could trust enough to share the one thing she had been holding onto for far too long.

For years, every man she had met had been held up to an impossible standard—the shadow of Andrew looming over every date, every touch, every almost-lover. No one had ever measured up.

But as she stared at herself now, she realised how foolish that had been.

Andrew wasn't the ideal.

He was just the past.

And she was ready for something more.

She had been wined and dined by powerful men, danced in candlelit ballrooms, sipped champagne on yachts, and kissed strangers under the glow of city lights. But none of them had ever made her feel that deep, undeniable pull. That intoxicating spark that would push her to take that final step.

But waiting for some grand, earth-shattering passion was starting to feel foolish.

Waiting, in general, was foolish.

Being a twenty-five-year-old virgin was unacceptable.

Celeste prided herself on being a woman in control, a woman who made decisions with precision and purpose.

And she had finally made this one.

It was time.

Chapter Two

Andrew Carter strode through the bustling terminal of JFK Airport, his long, purposeful strides carrying him toward the departure gate without hesitation. Years of confidence and discipline had moulded him into a man who commanded attention wherever he went and today was no different.

He barely noticed the way people glanced at him—some with admiration, others with curiosity. At six-foot-three, with broad shoulders that filled out his tailored navy blazer, he was hard to miss. His dirty-blond hair, always neatly styled, was just long enough to run a hand through when deep in thought. His piercing blue eyes, sharp and assessing, had once been filled with ambition and drive. Now, they carried something else.

Resolve.

The flight attendant stationed at the entrance to first class flashed him a sultry smile, her red lips curving in invitation as she welcomed him aboard.

He barely spared her a glance.

You're wasting your time, lady.

He wasn't interested in beautiful women—not anymore. Not after Sarah.

The betrayal still gnawed at him. Not because his heart was broken, but because of how blind he had been. Eight years of marriage, eight years of excuses, empty apologies, and outright lies. She had cheated on him multiple times, and every single time, he had been stupid enough to believe her. To forgive her.

Until he didn't.

Until he saw her for what she truly was—a selfish, manipulative woman who had used him for his success, his name, and the prestige that came with being Mrs. Andrew Carter.

But that was over now. The divorce was final.

He was done with the lies.

Done with Sarah.

And done with the kind of women who only saw him as a prize to be won.

As he reached his first-class seat, he unbuttoned his blazer and sat down, stretching out his long legs. The soft leather moulded to his body, but comfort wasn't what he was after.

He was after a fresh start.

Sydney.

Home.

After years of chasing his career in New York, he was finally going back to the people who actually mattered—his parents, his sister Kathleen. He had landed a position at one of Sydney's most prestigious law firms, a career-defining move for a man who had built his reputation as one of the top criminal lawyers in New York.

But this wasn't just about work.

This was about reclaiming his life.

The plane began to taxi down the runway, and Andrew leaned back in his seat, exhaling slowly.

Goodbye, New York.

Goodbye, Sarah.

Goodbye to the past that had held him back for far too long.

Sydney was waiting.

And this time, he wasn't looking back.

He had once thought his life would look entirely different by now. That he would be a father, coming home from work to a house filled with laughter, tiny feet running across hardwood floors, and a woman who loved him—not for his success or status, but for the man he was.

Sarah had told him she wanted children too. She had painted a perfect picture of their future—weekends at the park, family vacations, bedtime stories. But that, like everything else about their marriage, had been a lie.

Every time he had brought up the subject, she had an excuse. It wasn't the right time. Her career was taking off. They needed to travel more, enjoy their freedom. Then it became about the apartment being too small. Then the house in the Hamptons wasn't ready. There was always something.

It had taken him years to see the truth.

She had never wanted children with him. Maybe she had never wanted them at all.

And now, standing on the other side of it all, he was grateful.

If they had kids, it would have tied him to her forever. It would have made the mess of his life even bigger, tangled him in obligations with a woman he had spent far too long trying to please.

The divorce had been finalised over six months ago, the last of their shared assets divided, their high-society friends forced to pick sides. He had left New York's elite behind without a second thought.

He didn't belong there.

Sydney had always been home.

But he had been young, dumb, and so in love with the idea of Sarah that he had followed her across the world, leaving behind his family, his friends, everything familiar.

She had wanted New York—wanted the high life, the galas, the social circles that made and broke reputations with whispered secrets over champagne.

And he had wanted to make her happy.

So, he had done what any lovesick fool would do. He had packed up his life and followed her, convinced that love meant sacrifice, that if he gave enough of himself, she would give back in return.

Looking back, he couldn't believe how blind he had been.

He had gone back to Sydney over the years, of course. His parents, his sister Kathleen— he had missed them more than he had ever let on. But every time he visited, he had been alone.

Sarah had always had an excuse.

Too busy with work. Too many social obligations.

There was always something—an important gala, a last-minute client meeting, a networking event she simply couldn't miss. And when she wasn't busy with work, she was too exhausted to travel. The long-haul flight would be a nightmare, she'd complain. Jet lag was brutal, and she had a delicate system.

But she had no problem jetting off to the Hamptons, no trouble finding time for exclusive ski trips with her so-called friends—trips he later found out had included more than just friends.

She had never cared about his family.

Never cared about him.

That should have been a red flag. A glaring, neon warning sign that their marriage wasn't what he thought it was.

But the biggest warning sign?

The sex.

Or rather, the lack of it.

For him, at least. Not for her. She had been getting plenty—from all the lovers she had taken over the years.

At first, he had blamed himself. He was a criminal lawyer, working gruelling hours, sometimes pulling all-nighters to prepare for cases that could make or break his career. He had thought maybe he was too distracted, too unavailable. Maybe she resented that.

But then he had tried. He had taken her on romantic getaways, made reservations at the most exclusive restaurants, surprised her with gifts, kissed her in that way he knew used to drive her crazy.

And still, she had pulled away.

Excuses. Always excuses.

"I have an early morning."

"I'm exhausted."

"Not tonight, Andrew. I'm just not in the mood."

For years, he had accepted it. Had told himself that marriages had rough patches, that passion ebbed and flowed. That she still loved him.

But it hadn't been a rough patch.

It had been a goddamn lie.

Because while she was avoiding his bed, she had no trouble warming someone else's.

And the worst part? He had known. Deep down, he had always known. The long business dinners, the phone calls she had taken in hushed tones, the way she had started dressing up for other people but not for him.

He had just been too much of a fool to admit it.

Andrew exhaled slowly, rolling his shoulders back against the plush seat.

Not anymore.

The engines roared as the plane lifted into the sky, leaving New York behind.

He wasn't that man anymore.

The man who made excuses for his wife's infidelity.

The man who clung to a marriage that had been over long before he signed the divorce papers.

The man who loved a woman who had never truly loved him back.

No. That Andrew Carter was gone.

And good riddance.

The plane jolted slightly as it climbed higher, breaking through the thick clouds over New York.

Andrew closed his eyes, letting the weight of the last decade slip from his shoulders.

Sydney was ahead.

His family. His career. His future.

And this time, he was getting it right.

Chapter Three

The sun was still low in the sky as Celeste Beaumont made her way through the quiet apartment complex's underground car park. The early morning light filtered through the tall buildings, casting long shadows on the ground.

She walked briskly, the soft hum of the city just beginning to stir around her. Her steps were confident, each one filled with purpose. She had a full day ahead—another day of proving to herself that she wasn't just the girl who once thought ambition alone would be enough. She was a woman who'd built a life on her own terms.

Sliding into the sleek, black BMW convertible, Celeste gripped the wheel, letting her fingers curl around the leather. With a smooth motion, she started the engine, the low growl of the car waking her up more fully. The wind hit her face as she lowered the roof, the cool morning air whipping through her hair. She loved the feeling of freedom the convertible gave her—the sense that, no matter what the day brought, she was in control.

The drive to work was quick, the streets still relatively clear as the city slowly came to life. As she neared the bank, she found a spot in the underground parking lot and manoeuvred her car into the space with ease. Celeste enjoyed the quiet solitude of the early mornings before the bustle of the office truly began. She parked and took a moment, hands still resting on the wheel as she caught her breath.

Her reflection in the rearview mirror caught her attention, and she smiled at the woman staring back. Confident. In control. Independent. It had taken years to get here, to shed the shy, unsure girl who had once lingered in the shadows. Now, she stood firmly in the light—ready for whatever life had in store.

After taking a final glance around, Celeste grabbed her bag and stepped out of the car, walking briskly toward the entrance of the bank. The familiar clink of her heels echoed through the parking structure as she headed inside, passing the security desk with a quick nod to the guard.

"Morning, Celeste," Karen, the receptionist, called out as she passed the front desk. "Looking fabulous as always."

"Thanks, Karen. You too," Celeste replied with a bright smile, a hint of pride in her voice. She always tried to be kind to the people she passed, whether they were colleagues or just people in the building. It was part of her charm—a way to spread a little positivity wherever she went.

As she walked through the hallways toward her office, Celeste greeted her co-workers, who nodded or waved as she passed. She had worked hard to build a reputation in the office—not just as a competent assistant manager, but as someone who was approachable, professional, and, most importantly, reliable. People respected her, and she'd earned that respect through years of determination.

Stopping at the door to Richard's office, Celeste gave a quick knock before peeking her head inside.

"Morning, Celeste," Richard, the bank manager, greeted with a nod, his eyes still focused on the stack of papers on his desk. "Ready for another busy day?"

"You know it," she replied with a playful wink. "I live for the chaos."

He chuckled, the corners of his mouth twitching upward as he glanced up briefly. "I'll never understand how you thrive in it."

Celeste shrugged with a grin, her confidence unwavering. "It's all part of the fun. Keeps me sharp."

Richard chuckled again and returned to his work, clearly not bothered by her light-heartedness. The banking world wasn't always glamorous—filled with deadlines, forms, and a fair amount of tedium—but Celeste took pride in every task, whether it was handling a difficult client or ensuring every report was spot on. For her, each challenge was just another chance to prove her worth.

As she walked away, she felt a brief sense of satisfaction—today would be no different. She was ready for whatever came her way.

Reaching her office, she stepped inside, closing the door behind her. The room was just as she left it—clean, organised, everything in its place. The walls were decorated with a few framed photos of her family and friends, reminders of the life she'd built away from home. As she sat down at her desk and switched on her computer, she reached for her phone, quickly glancing at the notifications.

One new message—Kathleen.

She unlocked her phone and smiled as she saw her best friend's name on the screen. They hadn't caught up in a while, and Celeste always looked forward to their time together.

Hey, you! Fancy some drinks on Friday night? I'm dying for a catch-up!

Celeste tapped out a quick response, her fingers flying across the screen.

You bet. I could use a drink after this month! Where are we going?

A few seconds later, Kathleen's reply came through.

I know the perfect spot. I'll text you the details later. Can't wait to see you!

Celeste felt a wave of excitement wash over her. It had been too long since she'd let loose and spent some quality time with Kathleen. They'd been friends for years, ever since primary school, and though life had gotten busy, their bond remained unshakeable.

She put the phone down with a contented sigh, knowing the weekend was going to be something to look forward to. As she got settled into her workday, her mind occasionally wandered to the thought of Friday night—of laughing with Kathleen, having a few drinks, and letting her hair down for a change.

For now, though, there were emails to respond to, meetings to attend, and a busy day ahead.

But Friday night, there would be a little freedom. And Celeste was ready for it.

The long flight had drained him, but Andrew Carter couldn't shake the quiet relief that settled over him as the plane touched down in Sydney. After twenty-three hours of cramped seats, stale air, and the hum of the engines, he was finally home.

He moved through the airport with the practiced efficiency of someone accustomed to business travel—quick steps, calm demeanour, and the determined focus of a man who had lived in airports more than he cared to admit. The weight of the past few years seemed to lift with every step, the endless cycle of work and disillusionment fading into the background.

New York, with its relentless energy and endless opportunities, had once been his whole world. Now, it felt like a place he had outgrown. The life he had built there was unravelling in ways he hadn't expected, but Sydney—his true home—was calling him back, steady, and unyielding.

Outside the terminal, his chauffeur stood by the limousine, holding the door open with professional grace. Andrew slid into the plush leather seats, letting the familiar luxury of the car settle him. The city sprawled outside, bright, and full of life, but there was a distance between him and the landscape. It was Sydney, yes, but it didn't quite feel like home just yet.

The last time he'd been back, everything had been different—he had been different. A younger man, still wrapped in the idealism that had driven him to New York in the first place. Now, there was a change in him. A resolve, perhaps—a quiet anticipation for what was to come.

His penthouse wouldn't be ready for another fortnight, so he would be staying at his parents' house in the meantime. The thought of it was comforting, even if it was temporary. After everything that had happened, the idea of being surrounded by family, by familiar faces, was a balm he didn't realise he needed.

He had missed them more than he cared to admit—his parents, especially, who had always been there for him, even during his lowest points. His sister, Kathleen, too. She had been a constant throughout the chaos of the past few years. They'd kept in touch over phone calls and texts, but it wasn't the same as sharing the same space. It had been too long.

The limousine cruised down the long driveway of the Beaumont's' estate in Vaucluse, the grandeur of the multimillion-dollar home sprawling before him. The house sat perched on the cliffs, overlooking Sydney Harbour, a location that offered both privacy and luxury in equal measure.

The sprawling property had always been a sanctuary for him, even as a child. The house, with its sprawling lawns and sea views, had been a place to retreat from the hustle of the world. And now, as an adult, it still held the same quiet comfort.

Andrew's gaze moved to the porch, where his parents stood waiting, their smiles wide as they saw the car approach. His mother, Judy Carter, a statuesque woman with an easy warmth, waved excitedly. His father, John Carter, a former high-powered lawyer with an air of authority, stood beside her with his characteristic proud smile.

The car came to a gentle stop, and Andrew stepped out, stretching his long legs, muscles stiff from the hours of sitting. He walked toward the porch, the soft crunch of gravel underfoot breaking the quiet. His mother was the first to greet him, her arms wrapping around him in an embrace that was both strong and comforting.

"Andrew! You're finally home! It's so good to see you!" she exclaimed, pulling back to look at him with glistening eyes.

"Good to be home, Mum," he replied, his voice thick with emotion, the rawness of the moment catching him off guard.

His father gave him a firm handshake and a hearty slap on the back. "Glad to see you back in one piece. I know that flight can be a killer."

Andrew managed a smile, his father's no-nonsense demeanour always grounding him. "It wasn't fun, but I'm here now."

As his mother stepped aside, his sister Kathleen emerged from behind them, her smile bright as she caught sight of him. She was exactly as he remembered—effortlessly beautiful, poised, and welcoming. But there was a change in her too, one that was harder to define. Maybe it was just the years that had passed, or maybe it was the way she seemed more self-assured, more at ease in her own skin.

"Look at you, Andrew. It's been way too long," Kathleen said, wrapping her arms around him in a hug that felt like home. When she pulled back, her eyes searched his face—assessing, remembering. "You look... different. Lighter, maybe."

He laughed softly; the sound almost unfamiliar after so much time spent in the controlled, business-like environment of New York. "I feel different. It's good to be home, Kath."

The family gathered in the kitchen, the scent of freshly brewed coffee filling the air as they settled in to catch up. The conversation flowed easily—stories of old family friends, updates on the latest happenings with their parents' business ventures, and the familiar teasing that only siblings could get away with.

Despite the time and distance, it all felt effortlessly normal, as if no time had passed at all. And as Andrew listened to them, his heart softened, realising how much he had missed this—the simple joy of being around the people who knew him best.

It was two in the afternoon, a warm Monday in Sydney, and the sun hung lazily in the sky. The warmth of the day mirrored the warmth in his chest, but there was something else there, too—a stirring, a quiet anticipation that had been growing ever since he'd received the call about his new job, which would begin next Monday.

This return, he realised, was more than just about escaping the ghosts of New York or running from the disillusionment that had consumed him there. It was about reconnecting with the things that truly mattered. Family. Roots. Sydney. The city, the people, the life he had once known but somehow drifted away from.

As the sun began to dip lower in the sky, casting a golden glow over the lawn, Andrew felt a sense of peace settle in. For the first time in a long while, he felt like he was exactly where he needed to be.

Chapter Four

Celeste froze at the entrance of the bar, her grip tightening on her purse strap as her gaze locked onto the last person she ever wanted to see—Andrew Carter.

Kathleen had said she had a surprise for her. Celeste just hadn't expected it to be him.

Her pulse kicked up, and for a brief moment, she considered turning around and walking right back out. But she wasn't a coward, and she wouldn't let Andrew—of all people—rattle her.

Still, the sight of him hit her like a tidal wave—unexpected, overwhelming, and impossible to ignore. It had been years since she'd last seen him, but time had done nothing to dull the effect he had on her. The boy she had once crushed on was now a man—taller, broader, exuding a quiet confidence that only made him more infuriatingly attractive.

Kathleen had sworn to never mention Andrew to her. It had been an unspoken agreement after Celeste confessed her teenage infatuation, an embarrassing admission she had made in a moment of weakness. Kathleen had never betrayed her trust, had never uttered a single word about him after that… but she could have warned her about this.

Of all nights.

Celeste took a slow breath, pushing down the ridiculous flutter in her chest. This was supposed to be the week she finally put the past behind her, the week she found someone—anyone—to help her shed the one thing tying her to her old, naive self. Her virginity had become a burden, something that made her feel like a relic in a world of experience. She was ready to change that.

And now, here he was.

Where was Sarah?

Her gaze flicked toward him, searching for the wife he had once adored, the woman he had left for New York with all those years ago. But there was no sign of her. Just Andrew, standing with Kathleen and two men who looked vaguely familiar, laughing easily, completely unaware of the turmoil she was in.

She clenched her jaw.

The past had no place in her life now. She had come here for a fun night out—not to get sucked back into feelings she had long since buried.

So, she lifted her chin, smoothed her dress, and took a step forward.

If Andrew Carter was back in town, he would have to deal with her presence. Not the other way around.

Andrew and Kathleen stood in the bustling bar area of an exclusive club, the hum of conversation and clinking glasses creating an ambient buzz around them. Andrew couldn't help but feel slightly out of place. It wasn't that he didn't enjoy the scene; it was just that after years of high-powered meetings and corporate dinners in New York, the laid-back atmosphere of Sydney's nightlife felt like a distant memory.

His attention flickered back to his old schoolmates, George and Bryan, who were leaning against the bar, chatting animatedly. Kathleen had insisted on this reunion, bringing him to the same club where she was meeting her friend for drinks. Andrew couldn't remember the last time he'd had a night out with these guys, and honestly, the thought of catching up with old friends made the evening feel more nostalgic than thrilling.

George suddenly let out a low whistle, breaking Andrew's thoughts. "Whoa, look at that woman who just walked in. What a bloody stunner."

Kathleen didn't even turn around. She rolled her eyes and smirked, clearly used to George's over-the-top commentary. Andrew, however, couldn't help but look. Along with Bryan, he turned his head to follow George's gaze.

Striding toward them was a tall, drop-dead gorgeous woman. Her long legs were accentuated by a sleek green silk dress that hugged her curves in all the right places, but it wasn't overly tight—just the perfect fit. The dress swished as she moved, her confidence radiating through every step.

Bryan let out a low whistle. "I wouldn't mind getting to know that. What do you think, Andrew?"

Andrew raised an eyebrow, glancing at Bryan before responding, "No thanks, I'm over beautiful women."

Kathleen shot him a worried look. "You can't think all beautiful women are like Sarah, Andrew," she said softly.

Andrew's expression hardened at the mention of Sarah. That chapter of his life—the one he had left behind in New York—felt like a distant memory now, one he had no intention of revisiting. Not tonight. Not ever.

Instead, his focus shifted to the woman making her way toward them, her confident stride impossible to ignore. There was something about her—something that made his pulse quicken. A strange familiarity nagged at the edges of his mind, but he couldn't quite place it.

"Oh great," George muttered under his breath, grinning. "She's coming this way."

Kathleen turned with an amused laugh, nudging George playfully. "Down, boy," she said. "That's my friend Celeste."

Andrew blinked, his brow furrowing as he did a double take. Celeste?

"That's Celeste?" he asked, disbelief creeping into his voice.

Kathleen chuckled at his reaction. "Yes, Andrew. She's no longer a lanky teenager." She waved enthusiastically toward Celeste, who lifted her hand in return—graceful yet composed, a picture of quiet confidence.

Andrew's gaze lingered on her as she neared them, his mind struggling to reconcile the memory of the awkward fifteen-year-old with the woman standing before him now. The years had reshaped her in ways he hadn't anticipated. Gone was the lanky teenager he barely remembered. In her place stood a woman who radiated confidence, elegance, and a quiet kind of power that was impossible to ignore.

A sudden, unwelcome realisation settled in his chest. He was attracted to her.

And he didn't like it.

Beautiful women were trouble. He knew that better than anyone. They came with expectations, demands, and the ability to destroy a man's life if given the chance.

And Celeste? She was stunning. Which meant she was dangerous.

Bryan, unable to contain himself, murmured, "Oh, I think I'm in love."

Kathleen laughed, shaking her head. "That's what all men say when they meet Celeste."

Andrew barely heard them. He was still trying to reconcile the woman approaching them with the distant memory of the lanky teenager she used to be. She carried herself with effortless grace, her confidence evident in every step. And when she smiled— warm, genuine, dazzling—it was impossible to look away.

"Well, well, well," Celeste said, amusement lacing her tone as she stopped in front of him. "Look who it is. Andrew Carter, back in Sydney after all these years."

Before he could react, she leaned in—just close enough for him to catch the faintest trace of her perfume—then pressed a quick kiss to his cheek. A fleeting touch, barely there, yet it sent an unexpected jolt through him.

Andrew blinked, momentarily thrown off balance. The faint warmth lingered where she had kissed him, and for a second, he had no idea what to do with the unexpected sensation.

It had been ten years. When he left, she was just a kid—barely fifteen, awkward, forgettable. Now, she was anything but forgettable. The transformation was startling. She was self-assured, striking, and something else he couldn't quite put his finger on.

Finally, he managed, "Celeste. It's been a long time."

She arched a perfectly shaped eyebrow, clearly amused by his lacklustre response. "A long time?" she echoed. "Andrew, it's been ten years! You've been off living it up in New York, haven't you?" Her gaze flicked over him before she casually added, "So… where's Sarah?"

The question hit like a slap. Andrew's body tensed, his jaw tightening as he cast a glance at Kathleen.

His sister, looking completely unbothered, simply shrugged. "What?" she said innocently. "We do have better things to talk about than you, you know." Then she turned to Celeste and added, "Sarah and Andrew are divorced now."

Celeste's eyes widened, a flicker of surprise crossing her face before it was replaced with something else—something pleased. "Oh," she said, drawing out the word, her tone just shy of apologetic. "Sorry to hear that."

Kathleen snorted. "No, you're not. You liked her about as much as I did."

Celeste's lips curved into a knowing smile. "Guilty," she admitted.

Andrew let out a dry, sarcastic laugh. "Did no one like my wife?"

All four of them answered in perfect unison. "No."

He stared at them, one by one, and found nothing but unwavering honesty in their faces. They had all seen something in Sarah that he hadn't—or maybe, something he had refused to see. The realisation left a bitter taste in his mouth.

"Well," he said flatly, forcing aside the irritation clawing at him. "She's in New York, and hopefully, she stays there."

Kathleen, ever the peacekeeper, shot him a knowing look before flashing a playful smile. "That's ancient history now, Andrew. We've all changed." She nudged Celeste with a smirk. "Some more than others."

Celeste chuckled, the sound smooth and effortless, as if she hadn't just walked into an unexpected reunion with the one man she never wanted to see again. The tension in the air dissolved with the warmth of her laughter, but Andrew felt something else linger—something unspoken, something he wasn't quite ready to name.

"Well," she said, crossing her arms, amusement flickering in her dark eyes. She leaned against the bar, her hips tilting in a way that made Andrew's gaze momentarily drop before he forced himself to look back up. "It's good to see you, Andrew. How long are you visiting for?"

"I'm back for good."

Her eyebrows lifted slightly. "Oh, I see." A pause. Her gaze flickered toward George and Bryan, who were watching her with open admiration. Her lips curled into a knowing, mischievous grin.

"Hello, I'm Celeste," she said, extending a hand toward George.

He took her hand smoothly and pressed a kiss to the back of it. "George Dawsett. Lovely to meet you."

Bryan, ever the showman, grabbed her hand next and kissed it with an exaggerated flourish. "I'm Bryan Harris... marry me."

Celeste laughed, a soft, melodic sound that sent an unexpected warmth through Andrew's chest. "You never know your luck, Bryan," she teased, her eyes glinting with amusement.

Kathleen rolled her eyes, though her smirk betrayed her amusement. "Trust me, Bryan, you're not the first to ask."

Andrew watched the exchange, his focus narrowing in on Celeste. The way George and Bryan interacted with her—so familiar, so easy—shouldn't have bothered him. It didn't bother him.

Except... it did.

He wasn't jealous. Of course not. He wasn't interested.

But as Celeste turned her attention back to him, her smile lingering, Andrew couldn't shake the feeling that maybe—just maybe—he should be.

Chapter Five

The group settled around a large round table, the dim lighting of the exclusive club casting a golden glow over their drinks as they placed their orders. Before Celeste could even sit properly, George and Bryan manoeuvred themselves to either side of her, a synchronised move that made Kathleen stifle a laugh behind her cocktail glass.

Bryan, ever the bold one, leaned in with a hopeful smile. "Please tell me you're single?"

Celeste arched a perfectly shaped brow, amusement flickering in her gold-flecked hazel eyes. "As a matter of fact, yes, I am." She smirked, taking a slow sip of her wine.

Bryan let out an exaggerated sigh of relief. "Finally, some good news."

Kathleen, shaking her head, decided to intervene. "Don't get your hopes up, Bry. Celeste only dates men for a short time."

Celeste gasped in mock offence, pressing a hand to her chest. "Kath! That's so unfair." Then, with a playful pout, she added, "You have to kiss a few frogs before you find your prince."

George grinned, swirling the whiskey in his glass. "So that's what you're looking for then? A prince?"

Celeste tilted her head, considering the question as she traced the rim of her glass with her fingertip. Then, with a slow, knowing smile, she met his gaze. "Isn't every girl?"

Andrew, who had been quiet up until now, found himself watching her more closely than he intended. Celeste was flirtatious, confident, and undeniably beautiful, but when George asked if she was looking for a prince, she hesitated—just for a second. A flicker of something unreadable crossed her face before she flashed her signature smirk.

That hesitation stuck with him.

He took a sip of his drink, forcing himself to look away.

He wasn't interested. Not in Celeste. Not in anyone.

Or at least, that's what he kept telling himself.

As the conversation flowed, Kathleen leaned toward Celeste with a knowing smile. "You know, Bry's a doctor, and George here is a police detective. Quite the dynamic duo, don't you think?"

Celeste arched a brow, her lips twitching into a smirk. "A doctor, a lawyer, and a detective all at the same table? I feel very safe."

George chuckled. "And what about you, Celeste? What do you do?"

Before Celeste could answer, Kathleen beamed with pride. "She's the youngest assistant manager at one of the most prestigious banks in Sydney."

Celeste rolled her eyes, but her smile was playful. "Stop, Kath, you'll make me blush."

Turning to Bryan, she tilted her head slightly. "Oh, Bryan, you might know my mother—Hope Beaumont?"

Bryan's eyes widened in recognition. "Hope Beaumont is your mother? She's a brilliant surgeon!"

Celeste's features softened with pride. "That she is."

Bryan leaned back, appraising her with newfound admiration. "Well, if she's your mother, then it makes sense why you're already so successful."

Kathleen chimed in, grinning. "And her father is one of the most sought-after wealth managers in the country."

George frowned slightly, curiosity flickering in his eyes. "So, with brains, beauty, and a background like that… why are you single?"

A wistful look crossed Celeste's face. "Haven't found the right one yet."

Her voice was light, but there was an undeniable undercurrent of something else—a quiet sadness that didn't go unnoticed.

Andrew, who had been observing the conversation intently, felt a sudden, inexplicable urge to know more. "How are your parents?" he asked softly, his voice betraying a hint of curiosity.

Celeste met his gaze, her eyes briefly clouded by something unreadable. She answered, her tone neutral but with a quiet strength. "Very well, thank you."

For a moment, their eyes locked, the silence between them heavy with unspoken words. The air seemed to thicken, a tension crackling in the space between them. But just as quickly as it had appeared, it faded as Celeste returned her attention to her drink, her smile returning as if the moment had never happened.

The rest of the evening flowed smoothly, filled with laughter, teasing, and light-hearted banter. There was a warmth to the group, a sense of familiarity that made the night feel almost effortless.

As the evening wore on, Kathleen, ever the social butterfly, casually mentioned, "You're all coming to Andrew's homecoming party tomorrow night, right?" She grinned. "My parents insisted on throwing something to welcome the prodigal son back home."

George and Bryan quickly agreed, both clearly eager to spend more time with the group. But when Celeste hesitated, Andrew couldn't help but notice the slight pause in her response. He couldn't place it, but something about her reluctance bothered him.

Kathleen, ever the persuasive one, shot Celeste a playful look. "Come on, Celeste, bring your date if you have one."

All three men turned their attention to her, clearly hoping she didn't have one. The possibility that Celeste might be seeing someone seemed to hang in the air, unspoken but palpable.

Celeste paused, her lips curling into a playful smile as she met their gazes. "No date, I'll be there," she said with a light, almost dismissive tone, though there was a flicker in her eyes that suggested she wasn't entirely comfortable with the attention.

Andrew felt an unexpected surge of relief wash over him at her response, though he couldn't quite place why it bothered him. He quickly pushed the feeling aside, not wanting to overthink it.

Once Celeste and Kathleen had excused themselves to the ladies' room, George was the first to break the silence. He leaned in, lowering his voice. "Just so we're clear, I'm pursuing Celeste. Do you two have a problem with that?"

Bryan grinned. "Absolutely."

Andrew's response was sharper. "Yes."

George raised an eyebrow, clearly surprised—especially by Andrew's response. "I thought you said you weren't interested in beautiful women?"

"I'm not," Andrew replied quickly, though the words came out a bit too sharp. "I just think it's a bad idea."

"Why?" George and Bryan both pressed in unison.

Andrew hesitated for a moment, looking away. He wasn't sure why he was suddenly so defensive. "You heard Kathleen. She's... not the type to stick around. A few dates and she's done. She probably breaks hearts along the way," he added, hoping his words would deter his friends from pursuing Celeste. But even as he said it, he wondered why it mattered so much.

Bryan chuckled. "She can break my heart any day."

George nodded, his grin widening. "Mine too."

Andrew let out a dry laugh, shaking his head. "She doesn't seem like the type to get too attached. I'd bet most of her relationships don't make it past a few dates."

Bryan raised an eyebrow. "That's a hell of an assumption to make."

George crossed his arms. "You sound like you've already decided she's trouble."

Bryan, however, wasn't letting him off the hook so easily. "That witch of a wife really did a number on you, didn't she?" he said, his voice laced with a wry edge.

George, who had been listening intently, furrowed his brow. "Sarah cheated, did she?" he asked, his tone a mix of disbelief and curiosity.

Andrew let out a sharp, bitter laugh. "Multiple times," he said, the words tumbling out with more force than he meant. There was no use in sugar-coating it; the truth was ugly, and it was a weight he'd carried far too long.

George's expression softened, sympathy flickering across his face. Bryan, however, gave a slow nod, his expression unsettlingly calm as he processed the information. "Jesus, mate," Bryan muttered, his voice low. "No wonder you're so messed up about everything."

Andrew's gaze fell to the table, his fingers gripping his glass a little too tightly. "Yeah, well, trusting women after something like that isn't easy," he said quietly, his voice almost lost in the weight of the words. The betrayals, the lies, the constant feeling of being deceived— it all hung around him like a cloud he couldn't escape.

The silence between them thickened before George spoke again, his voice steady, but with an edge of concern. "You need to deal with all that before you start making assumptions about people, Andrew," he said, his tone leaving no room for argument. "Celeste seems like a genuinely good person, and I don't think Kathleen would keep her around if she was anything like what you just said."

Andrew looked up, meeting George's eyes. There was a brief moment where he saw the truth in his words. He exhaled slowly, frustration simmering beneath his skin. "I know," he muttered, his voice tinged with regret. "I just… haven't figured out how to trust again, not after everything."

As Celeste and Kathleen stood at the sink, washing their hands and adjusting their makeup in the powder room, Kathleen shot Celeste a mischievous grin.

"You still have a big crush on him, don't you?" she asked, her voice light but teasing.

Celeste's fingers trembled slightly as she reapplied her lipstick. She kept her gaze fixed on the mirror, but she wasn't really seeing her own reflection—just the memory of Andrew's eyes on her, the way he had watched her so intently at the table.

"Is it that obvious?" she murmured, hating how vulnerable she sounded.

"Only to me," Kathleen replied, a knowing smile tugging at her lips. "Go for it, Celeste."

Celeste blinked, her breath catching. "What!? He's your brother!"

Kathleen shrugged, her grin widening. "Yeah, so?" She turned to Celeste, her expression softening. "Look, my brother's been through hell, and he doesn't trust easily. But I've never seen him react to anyone the way he reacts to you."

Celeste swallowed, her heart skipping a beat. "He barely reacted at all."

Kathleen smirked. "Exactly."

Celeste's face flushed, and she looked down, trying to gather her thoughts. "I don't know… It just feels… complicated."

"Complicated, schmomplicated," Kathleen said, waving her hand dismissively. "Life's too short for that. You've got to take your chances when you get them."

Celeste hesitated, her reflection in the mirror offering no answers, only a reminder of the tangled feelings she was trying to ignore.

Celeste's fingers trembled slightly as she reapplied her lipstick. She hesitated, watching the colour glide over her lips, as if searching for certainty in its perfect, unbroken line. "If I do… what if it doesn't work out?"

Kathleen shrugged casually, not missing a beat. "It's not going to change how I feel about either of you," she said with a reassuring smile. "But I'd be thrilled if it did work out."

Celeste looked at her, studying her friend's expression in the mirror. There was no judgment, no hesitation—just a quiet confidence that only Kathleen could exude. It made Celeste pause, her thoughts settling for a moment.

"I guess I just don't want to mess things up," Celeste murmured.

Kathleen's eyes softened, her smile warm and supportive. "You won't know until you try," she said gently. "And if it's meant to be, it'll work out. You deserve to be happy, Celeste. Don't let fear stop you."

Chapter Six

Celeste sank into the cool leather seat of the Uber, the quiet hum of the engine filling the silence as the city lights blurred past the window. She leaned her head against the glass, her thoughts drifting back to her conversation with Kathleen.

'You deserve to be happy, Celeste. Don't let fear stop you.'

The words had stayed with her, lingering in her mind like an echo she couldn't ignore. Maybe Kathleen was right. Maybe it was time to stop overthinking, stop second-guessing, and just go for what she wanted.

And what she wanted… was Andrew.

Celeste exhaled slowly, pressing her lips together in thought. She wasn't naïve—Andrew had his walls, and she understood why. His ex-wife had shattered his trust, leaving him wary of women, of relationships, of anything that required emotional vulnerability. But that didn't mean she had to be afraid, too.

She liked Andrew. More than that, she was attracted to him in a way she had never felt for anyone else. And if she was honest with herself, there was something undeniably thrilling about the idea of being with him, about finally experiencing what she had spent years waiting for—with a man she trusted.

Would he reject her? Maybe.

Would it hurt? Probably.

But Celeste wasn't the type to let fear dictate her choices. Rejection was a possibility, but it wasn't the end of the world. If she didn't take the chance, she'd never know what could have been.

She shifted slightly in her seat, her fingers brushing the hem of her dress as she considered her next move. It wasn't just about attraction—it was about choice. About taking control of her desires instead of letting uncertainty hold her back.

Her pulse quickened at the thought. If Andrew said no, she'd move on. But if he said yes…

A shiver ran through her.

The Uber pulled up outside her apartment, and Celeste thanked the driver before stepping out onto the quiet street. The night air was crisp, but she barely felt it as she unlocked the door and stepped inside.

Tomorrow.

She'd take a chance.

She'd see if Andrew was ready for her… or if she'd have to walk away.

Either way, she wasn't afraid anymore.

She tapped her fingers against her chin, considering her options. If Andrew truly wasn't interested, she knew George and Bryan definitely were. They were both attractive, successful men, and either of them would be more than happy to sweep her off her feet.

But deep down, she knew they weren't who she wanted.

Andrew was the one who made her heart race, the one who had lingered in her thoughts for far too long. She wasn't naive—she knew he was guarded, that whatever had happened to him had left scars. But she wasn't looking for forever.

She just wanted… an experience.

Her experience.

She sighed, leaning her back against the inside of her apartment door. Six weeks until her twenty-fifth birthday.

Surely, she could get this done before then.

Andrew gripped the steering wheel a little tighter than necessary as he drove through the quiet streets, his jaw set in irritation. The night had gone well enough—until George and Bryan started falling over themselves to take Celeste home.

They were too eager, too obvious.

And it annoyed the hell out of him.

He hadn't planned to offer her a ride, but when the other two had jumped at the chance, something in him had snapped. Before he could think better of it, he'd made the offer himself. But Celeste had declined, and that was when he'd learned something unexpected—she no longer lived with her parents.

For years, her family's house had been just up the street from his parents'. She had always been around—the girl with the sharp wit and that teasing smirk, the one who never let anything rattle her. But now? She was on her own. Independent.

That realisation unsettled him more than he cared to admit.

Kathleen shifted in the passenger seat, watching him closely. The silence stretched between them until she finally spoke, her tone casual but laced with meaning.

"So… Celeste has changed since you last saw her."

Andrew kept his eyes on the road, though he felt Kathleen studying him. "People change," he replied, his voice deliberately neutral.

Kathleen hummed, clearly unimpressed with his non-answer. "That's not what I meant, and you know it."

Andrew sighed, rolling his shoulders as if that could shake off the strange tension coiling in his chest. "Yeah, she's different," he admitted, his grip tightening slightly on the wheel. "More… confident."

Kathleen let out a small laugh. "Celeste has always been confident."

Andrew frowned. Yes, she had. But it was different now. Before, her confidence had been playful, almost reckless. Now, it was… assured. Steady. As if she knew exactly who she was and didn't need validation from anyone.

And that? That made her even more dangerous.

Dangerous to him.

Because he'd already felt it—that pull, the quiet way she got to him without even trying. He didn't like it.

Didn't want it.

Kathleen smirked, clearly reading his thoughts. "George and Bryan are both interested," she mused, her voice laced with amusement.

Andrew clenched his jaw. He knew that. He'd seen it. And the worst part? Celeste hadn't seemed bothered by their attention.

"She can date whoever she wants," he said flatly, keeping his gaze straight ahead.

Kathleen arched a brow. "Uh-huh."

He shot her a quick glare. "What?"

She grinned. "Nothing. You're just brooding a little harder than usual."

Andrew exhaled sharply, shaking his head. "I'm not brooding."

Kathleen laughed. "Sure. And Bryan and George totally don't have competition."

Andrew ignored that.

But the thought lingered.

And he hated how much he cared.

Andrew's hands tightened around the steering wheel as he turned onto their street. His jaw clenched so hard it ached.

Kathleen, ever the instigator, smirked as she glanced at him. "They both asked me for her phone number." She picked up her phone from her lap, her fingers hovering over the screen. "I should just text it to them now."

"Don't."

The word came out sharper than he intended, laced with something that made Kathleen pause.

Slowly, she turned her head, studying him with growing amusement. "Wow." She let out a low whistle. "You really are brooding."

Andrew exhaled through his nose, gripping the wheel tighter. "I just don't think she'd appreciate you handing out her number like that."

Kathleen grinned, leaning back in her seat. "Uh-huh. So, this is about her privacy and not at all about you not wanting them to have it?"

He shot her a look. "Drop it, Kath."

But she only laughed. "You know, if you want her number so badly, all you have to do is ask."

Andrew scowled. "I don't want her number."

Kathleen didn't even try to hide her amusement. "Sure, you don't."

Andrew didn't respond. Because the truth was, he did want it.

And that irritated him more than anything.

His grip on the wheel tightened. Damn it.

Celeste stood in front of her full-length mirror, eyes scanning her reflection as she tugged at the hem of the dress she had chosen. It was deep red, simple yet elegant, hugging her curves in all the right places without being too revealing. She had always preferred understated elegance, and tonight, she wanted to look just that—elegant, confident, and… *irresistible.*

A deep breath escaped her as she smoothed down the fabric, her fingers brushing over the delicate lace trim at the neckline. She didn't need to second-guess herself. Tonight wasn't about impressing anyone. It wasn't even about Andrew—well, it sort of was, but she wasn't going to admit that. It was about her.

She was ready. Ready to take control of her life, ready to stop worrying about what-ifs, ready to see what would happen next.

She adjusted her hair, sweeping it to one side in loose, soft waves. She hadn't done much with it—just enough to look polished. The last thing she wanted was to seem like she was trying too hard.

With a glance at the clock, she saw that she still had time. She picked up her phone and checked the message from Kathleen.

Don't overthink it, Celeste. Go for it. It's his party, but it's your night too.

She smiled, slipping her phone back into her purse. Kathleen had been a voice of reason, encouraging her to just go for what she wanted. And what she wanted was simple—to have a good time and maybe, just maybe, make Andrew see her in a different light.

Celeste looked at herself one more time, her reflection staring back at her. The girl in the mirror was someone who had finally accepted her own worth. She wasn't a little girl anymore, afraid of her desires and too unsure of herself to take chances.

Tonight, that girl was gone.

With a final glance around her apartment, she grabbed her keys, checked her purse for her essentials—lip gloss, phone, ID—and headed out the door.

Chapter Seven

Celeste arrived five minutes after seven, and as she stepped out of the car, she was immediately struck by how Andrew's parents' home shimmered in the evening light. The entire place was bathed in a soft glow, both inside and out, with the lights spilling across the manicured lawn. The air hummed with the quiet pulse of music, and a dance floor had been set up beneath the stars, string lights crisscrossing above in a delicate web of twinkling brilliance, making the night feel like something out of a dream.

As soon as she entered the grand foyer, she spotted Bryan near the door, a warm smile spreading across his face as he saw her approach.

"You look stunning, Celeste," he said, his eyes scanning her with appreciative attention, lingering on her as though she were the only person in the room.

Celeste felt her cheeks warm under his gaze, her heart fluttering just slightly. "Thank you, Bryan," she replied, offering a polite yet grateful smile. Despite the compliment, she couldn't shake the feeling that all eyes in the room were on her, so she quickly turned her attention to her parents, who were standing across the room near the far wall.

"Come on, Bryan, I'll introduce you to my parents," Celeste offered, extending her hand to him. Bryan took it, and as they walked through the crowd, she felt a faint unease. She couldn't quite place it, but there was no spark with him, no electric connection like she had hoped for. He was charming, yes, but Celeste knew deep down that her heart wasn't in it.

As they made their way through the lively party, her eyes scanned the room, searching for a certain presence. She spotted George and Andrew standing near the bar, deep in conversation with two other men. Their laughter rose above the hum of the crowd, and Celeste found herself drawn to the sound, her pulse quickening the moment she saw Andrew's face.

His back was to her, but even from this distance, Celeste could tell it was him. The way he held himself, the slight tension in his shoulders, the way he laughed with his friends—it was all so unmistakably Andrew.

Her heart skipped a beat as her thoughts shifted to him, and for a moment, everything else in the room blurred away. But before she could linger too long in her thoughts, her father's voice broke through the haze.

"Sweetheart!" he called out, his face lighting up when he saw her. His arms opened wide, welcoming her as though she had been away for years.

Without hesitation, Celeste practically flew into his embrace, her laughter spilling from her as he swung her around in his strong arms, just as he had when she was a little girl. She buried her face in his shoulder for a moment, feeling that comforting sense of being home.

"You look beautiful as usual," he said, his voice filled with pride, his hand smoothing over her hair.

Celeste laughed, pulling away from the embrace and swatting at his chest playfully. "Daddy, stop! I'm not a little girl anymore."

Her father grinned, brushing a hand through her hair affectionately. "You'll always be my little girl, sweetheart."

Celeste couldn't help the smile that tugged at her lips. It was the way he always made her feel—special, important, loved—and it never got old. She turned to her mother, who was standing nearby, watching the interaction with a soft, knowing smile.

"Hello, sweetheart," her mother said, embracing her with a warm hug. "You look lovely as always."

Celeste kissed her mother's cheek and smiled. "Thanks, Mum."

Bryan, who had been standing off to the side, watching the family reunion with a smile, cleared his throat softly, drawing Celeste's attention.

She turned back to him, feeling a slight awkwardness now that the introduction moment was about to come. "Mum, Dad, this is Dr. Bryan Harris," she began, her voice steady despite the slight flutter in her chest. "Bryan, these are my parents, Jonas and Hope Beaumont."

Her father chuckled softly and extended his hand to Bryan. "Well, you must be someone special," he said, his grin wide. "You're the first male friend Celeste has introduced us to."

Bryan accepted the handshake with a confident smile, glancing at Celeste for just a moment before returning his attention to her father. "I hope so," he said smoothly, his gaze shifting between Jonas and Celeste. "It's nice to meet you."

Hope, ever the professional, reached out to shake Bryan's hand with a calm smile. "Dr. Harris, I've seen you in the ER," she said, her tone warm but slightly formal. "It's nice to finally meet you outside of the hospital."

Bryan's smile remained easy, his tone just as polite. "It's lovely to meet you too, Dr. Beaumont."

Celeste couldn't help but feel the quiet tension rising in the back of her mind. There was nothing about Bryan that made her heart race, no undeniable pull like she felt when she thought of Andrew. Yet she forced a smile, choosing to focus on the moment with her parents and push aside the thoughts that clouded her mind.

Bryan, oblivious to Celeste's internal turmoil, continued chatting amiably with her parents, seamlessly weaving in compliments and pleasantries. But Celeste's gaze, almost against her will, flickered once again toward Andrew. This time, he had turned slightly, his posture stiff, and she caught the familiar outline of his face—his jaw clenched tightly, and his eyes seemed to burn with an intensity that told her he was annoyed.

For a moment, it felt as though the entire room slowed, the hum of conversation fading into the background as her heart thudded in her chest. Celeste's eyes locked with Andrew's for the briefest of seconds, and that electric connection made her pulse race. It was as if time had stopped between them, the energy palpable, charged, and undeniably magnetic.

But just as quickly as it had come, the moment was gone.

Bryan's voice broke through her thoughts, pulling her back into the present. "Shall we grab a drink?" he asked with a grin, offering her his arm.

Celeste nodded, trying to shake the lingering sensation of Andrew's gaze from her mind. She forced a smile and allowed Bryan to lead her toward the bar, even though her thoughts were still miles away.

At the bar, Bryan ordered a whiskey, and Celeste chose a glass of champagne, the bubbly liquid a distraction she hoped would steady her nerves. They were standing near Andrew, George, and the other two men now, their laughter still ringing in the air. George spotted her and, with a wide grin, walked over to her.

"Celeste, you look breathtaking," George said, leaning in to plant a kiss on her cheek.

Celeste felt a flicker of discomfort at the touch but smiled and gave him a polite nod. Bryan, meanwhile, took a step back, giving them space.

Andrew's jaw tightened even further, the muscles in his face visibly clenching as he watched the exchange. Celeste caught the shift in his expression out of the corner of her eye, and it didn't escape her that he seemed less than pleased. But before she could dwell on it, George began introducing her to the other two men standing with him.

"This is Harrison and William," George said, gesturing to the men. Harrison, tall with an easy smile, and William, more reserved but with a warm handshake, both extended their hands to Celeste.

"Nice to meet you," Harrison said, his voice smooth and confident.

"Pleasure," William added, his tone polite with a smile.

Celeste smiled and shook both their hands, but as she turned to face Andrew, her heart gave a little flutter.

"Hello, Andrew," she said softly, her voice more uncertain than she had intended. She leaned in, brushing a quick kiss against his cheek.

To her surprise, Andrew froze. His entire body went rigid, and Celeste, along with the four other men standing there, could feel the tension hanging in the air. The moment stretched longer than it should have, a sharp stillness hanging between them all. His reaction didn't go unnoticed by anyone, and for a heartbeat, no one spoke.

But before anyone could make a comment or break the awkward silence, they were interrupted by a voice from across the room.

"Celeste, there you are!" Kathleen's cheerful voice rang out, her presence as vibrant as ever. "I want you to meet my friend Adam."

Celeste turned, grateful for the distraction, and allowed herself to be pulled into the crowd. The eyes of the men she had just been speaking with seemed to fall away, and she felt the weight of the tense moment with Andrew slowly lift. Kathleen's arm linked with hers, and before Celeste could respond, she was being swept toward a new part of the party.

As they made their way through the guests, Kathleen leaned in close, her voice dropping to a conspiratorial whisper. "He's playing hard to get. You need to do the same."

Celeste's heart skipped a beat, uncertainty flickering in her chest. "Maybe this is a bad idea?" she murmured, her voice tinged with hesitation. She had felt the charge between her and Andrew, but it was hard to ignore the distance that lingered between them.

Kathleen's expression softened, her eyes glinting with a mixture of playfulness and sincerity. "No, trust me. He's got it bad for you. He just doesn't want to admit it yet."

Celeste couldn't quite suppress the feeling that her emotions were tangled in a web of uncertainty, but something in Kathleen's conviction made her pause. She had always trusted her friend's instincts, and part of her wanted to believe that, maybe, just maybe, what Kathleen was saying was true.

As Celeste and Kathleen disappeared into the crowd, the group of men was left standing in an uneasy silence, the air thick with the aftereffects of Celeste's brief interaction with Andrew. George, still with a playful smirk on his face, watched her retreating figure, before turning his attention back to Andrew.

"You really aren't interested in Celeste, are you?" George asked, his voice light, yet carrying a trace of genuine curiosity. "You practically froze when she kissed you. That wasn't just a little awkwardness, mate."

Andrew stiffened, an uncomfortable knot tightening in his chest. He took a long sip of his drink, trying to steady himself against the rising tide of unease. He didn't want to dive into any personal revelations, least of all with George. "I'm just not interested in women right now," he replied, his voice sharper than he'd intended. The words tasted bitter on his tongue. He wasn't interested in anyone right now—not like this.

George raised an eyebrow, clearly sceptical. "Right," he said, his tone dripping with disbelief. "If you say so."

William, who had been quietly watching the exchange, finally chimed in. His voice was low, smooth, carrying a hint of admiration. "Why? She's smoking." He grinned, his gaze lingering on Celeste's retreating form. "Wouldn't mind getting to know her better myself."

Harrison, eager to join the conversation, added, "Same here. She's hot as hell."

Andrew shot them both a glance but didn't respond. There was a tightness in his chest whenever he thought about Celeste, but it wasn't just her beauty—it was something deeper, something tangled and complicated that he couldn't bring himself to unravel, not yet.

Bryan, who had been standing off to the side, sipping his whiskey, spoke up. His tone was confident, almost cocky. "Well, I'm glad you're not interested, Andrew. Because I want her."

The words hung in the air, and a strange tension descended upon the group. George's eyes narrowed, a sly grin curling at the corners of his mouth. "Bullshit, mate," he said, amusement mixing with a hint of challenge. "I'm asking her out tonight."

Andrew watched the exchange between Bryan and George with growing discomfort. He didn't know why, but the thought of either of them getting too close to Celeste left a sour taste in his mouth. He didn't like it, not one bit. But what could he do? He couldn't exactly throw down a claim on her. Not that he wanted to.

Did he?

No, he's not interested.

Bryan's grin widened, clearly unruffled. "You can try," he said smoothly. "But she just introduced me to her parents."

George laughed, a dismissive sound. "So? What's that supposed to mean? I don't see a ring on her finger."

Bryan's smile didn't falter. His voice was cool, steady. "Her father told me I must be special," he said, his gaze never leaving George's. "I'm the first man she's introduced to them. Not many can say that."

There was a pause, a beat of silence, as the weight of Bryan's words sank in. George exchanged a look with William, who shrugged slightly, sensing the subtle shift in the atmosphere.

"You think that means something?" George asked, half-amused, half-impressed.

Harrison spoke up, his voice thoughtful. "Could be. If her father's making a point of noting the lack of male friends, that's telling."

"I think it means she's already seeing something in me," Bryan said smoothly, his tone quieter now, but still dripping with confidence.

"I agree with Harrison," William added, his voice laced with a touch of intrigue. "It probably is significant."

George rolled his eyes, clearly unconvinced. "You guys are really reading into this, huh?"

Andrew, however, didn't respond to the banter. His thoughts were elsewhere, tangled in a mix of confusion and frustration. He knew this wasn't just about competition—this was about something deeper, something inside him he wasn't yet ready to face. He wanted to step forward, to do something about it, but he couldn't bring himself to. Not yet.

"Let the games begin, mate," George finally said, breaking the silence, his voice light but laced with challenge. He looked at Bryan, his expression a mixture of amusement and challenge. "May the best man win."

Bryan's smile was tight, but there was a gleam in his eyes, a competitive fire. "I'm not in the habit of losing," he said simply.

Andrew shook his head, a bitter laugh escaping him. "You two think you've got it all figured out, huh?" His eyes flickered to Celeste, now standing a few feet away, laughing with Kathleen. The sight of her eased some of the tension in his chest, but it also deepened the ache. "But you haven't got a clue."

The words hung in the air like a heavy fog. Andrew wasn't just wrestling with the idea of competition—he was wrestling with himself. His feelings, his doubts, his confusion— it was all too much, too soon. He wasn't ready to confront it. Not yet.

For now, he would stand back, watch, and let the game play out.

The stakes were higher than ever.

Chapter Eight

Celeste had always prided herself on being a good listener, and tonight, she was determined to follow Kathleen's advice to the letter. The evening was unfolding exactly as her friend had suggested: ignore Andrew, enjoy herself, drink, dance, and charm every other man in the room. It was an unconventional approach, but at that moment, it felt like the only option left.

Kathleen's parting words echoed in her mind as they'd parted ways to mingle with the crowd: "Just have fun, Celeste. I'll keep an eye on Andrew and let you know how much he hates this."

Celeste couldn't have asked for better advice. The growing tension between her and Andrew had become almost unbearable, but tonight, she wasn't about to let it ruin her. Tonight, she was going to enjoy herself—no matter how hard Andrew tried to make her feel guilty about it.

She could already feel it. From the moment she'd stopped by the bar, raising her glass of champagne to her lips, she could sense Andrew's gaze on her like a physical force. Even though she didn't turn to acknowledge him, she felt his eyes boring into her, his expression a mixture of disbelief and frustration. Each time she laughed with George or danced with Bryan, she could see the muscles in Andrew's jaw tighten, his posture stiffening further. The more fun she had, the more agitated he became.

George, ever the flirt, spun her around the dance floor with ease, his hand resting possessively on her waist. His grin was wide, his banter light-hearted, and before long, Celeste found herself laughing freely, the tension of the evening slipping away with each step. She hadn't realised how much she needed this—how much she needed to stop thinking about Andrew for once and just be in the moment.

"You're a fantastic dancer, Celeste," George said, his eyes sparkling with approval as he spun her again. "How did I not know this about you?"

Celeste grinned, her heart light. "I like to surprise people," she replied, her voice playful, teasing.

Kathleen had been right—this was exactly what she needed. For the first time that night, she felt herself starting to enjoy the evening. No more obsessing over Andrew or what he might be feeling. She was going to have fun, and if that meant charming every man in the room, then so be it.

After a few songs with George, Celeste found herself swept into Harrison's arms for a slow dance. He was charming in a quieter, more reserved way, his smile easy and disarming. He had a subtle warmth to him that made her feel at ease. As they swayed together, Harrison leaned in closer, his breath warm against her ear.

"I've got to admit," he murmured softly, "I'm a little surprised you're still single."

Celeste laughed lightly, shaking her head. "Maybe I'm just waiting for the right guy," she teased, her voice light but sincere.

Harrison raised an eyebrow, a teasing glint in his eyes. "Well, you certainly have every guy in this room captivated tonight," he said, his tone playful but warm.

Kathleen's voice broke through her thoughts, a little while later, as she approached, her grin wide and mischievous. "Update: Andrew's pacing by the bar. He's practically seething over there," she said, her voice full of amusement. "I've never seen a man so tortured by a woman just having fun."

Celeste's heart fluttered unexpectedly at the thought of Andrew's frustration, but she refused to let it show. She forced a smile, her gaze briefly flicking over to him. He wasn't even looking at her anymore—he was staring down at the floor, his hands clenched into fists, his posture rigid. But she knew, without a doubt, that his irritation was directed at her.

"Good," Celeste murmured, though her words felt hollow in her own ears. "Let him stew."

Kathleen nudged her with her elbow, a playful glint in her eyes. "Keep going, Celeste. He'll crack. I can see it already."

The next hour passed in a blur of laughter, dancing, and light conversation. Bryan was next—quick to lead her back onto the floor for a slow waltz. His easy confidence and smooth words kept her engaged, and Celeste had to admit, he was good at making her feel the attention of every man in the room. As they danced, Bryan leaned in, his lips brushing her ear.

"You're amazing, Celeste," he murmured, his voice low and sincere.

Celeste froze for a moment, surprised by the intensity in his words. But she quickly recovered, her lips curling into a soft smile. "Thank you, Bryan," she said, her voice light.

Bryan's smile deepened, his eyes warm with admiration. "I'd love to get to know you better," he said, his tone almost a whisper as they glided across the floor.

Celeste turned her head slightly, meeting his gaze with a slow smile. "I suppose that could be arranged," she said, her voice teasing but genuinely interested.

Bryan chuckled softly. "I hope so," he replied, his eyes never leaving hers.

Celeste found herself intrigued by Bryan. If Andrew wasn't going to make a move, maybe it was time to pursue someone else. Bryan was handsome, charming, and seemed to be genuinely interested in getting to know her. The idea of starting something with him was tantalising, but a part of her hesitated. She didn't like to hurt people, and she wasn't sure how Bryan would react if things didn't work out between them. Still, the attraction was undeniable, and she couldn't help but wonder where it could lead.

The music shifted again, and soon, Celeste was back on the dance floor, this time with Adam, another one of Kathleen's friends who seemed just as eager to spend time with her. The more she danced, the more she felt the undercurrent of tension building—each man vying for her attention, but it was Andrew who couldn't seem to tear his eyes away.

Celeste wasn't sure how much longer she could keep up this charade. Her heart raced—not because of the dancing or the attention, but because of Andrew. She was playing a game, and it felt wrong. Yet, there was something intoxicating about the way he seemed so desperate to control his emotions. Every time she glanced in his direction, he was staring at her, his jaw tight, his hands balled into fists. It was as if he was on the verge of snapping.

Kathleen appeared again, her grin wide and knowing. "He's about to explode," she whispered. "I think it's time for you to go upstairs to freshen up. I think he'll follow."

Celeste hesitated, her pulse quickening. Her heart was torn between wanting to keep playing the game and needing to know if Andrew would finally make a move. She had planned to stay the night at the house, so going upstairs was the perfect excuse. She glanced at Andrew again—his posture tense, his gaze never leaving her. He was holding back, she could see that now. But the signs were unmistakable.

Kathleen, sensing her hesitation, squeezed her hand, urging her forward. "Trust me, he won't be able to resist following you."

Celeste nodded slowly, her heart racing. She turned, stepping away from the dance floor, moving toward the stairs. As she ascended, she tried to reason with herself: If he doesn't follow, I'm done trying to attract him. I'll pursue Bryan for what I really want.

She paused at the top of the stairs, her breath coming in shallow bursts. This was it—the moment of truth. Would Andrew follow her, or would he continue to keep his distance? Either way, Celeste was ready for whatever came next.

Celeste entered the guest suite, closing the door behind her with a soft click. She moved toward the ensuite, feeling the weight of the night pressing down on her. The evening had been a blur of laughter, music, and moments with every man in the room but one. And that one, of course, was the only one who really mattered. She needed a break from the tension that had been building between her and Andrew.

After freshening up, Celeste gazed at her reflection in the mirror. Her thoughts were a whirlwind, but she knew one thing for certain: she had done exactly what Kathleen suggested. She had ignored Andrew, enjoyed herself, and danced with every man who looked her way. It had worked—Andrew was annoyed, which was precisely what she wanted. But why did it feel like a small victory with a price tag attached?

When she stepped out of the ensuite, she wasn't prepared to see Andrew standing at the bedroom door. He was a statue of frustration, his presence so commanding it practically filled the room. Her heart skipped a beat.

"What the hell are you playing at?" His voice was low, tight with tension, as his eyes locked onto hers.

Celeste blinked, momentarily taken off guard by the sudden confrontation. But then she quickly masked her surprise with an innocent look, tilting her head slightly. "What do you mean?"

He pushed off the doorframe, his anger simmering just beneath the surface. "You with every man downstairs drooling over you," he snapped, eyes narrowing. "What is this game, Celeste?"

A playful smile tugged at her lips, a little too composed to be innocent. "I'm having fun," she said, her tone almost too light.

"That's not having fun," he shot back, his gaze darkening. "You're up to something."

Celeste's smile wavered for just a moment, but she quickly regained her composure. "No, I'm not," she answered, her voice cool, though part of her knew she was lying. She was up to something—but he didn't need to know that just yet.

His frustration intensified; his body coiled with tension. "Yes, you are. And you're not leaving here until you tell me exactly what it is." His jaw clenched as he moved a step closer, the space between them now charged with an undeniable intensity.

She stood her ground, meeting his eyes, even though the air felt heavier with every passing second. He was close enough now that she could almost feel the heat of his anger. He was waiting. Demanding.

Celeste swallowed, the weight of the moment pressing down on her. She'd been avoiding the truth for too long, and now, maybe it was time to just be honest. She wasn't sure what would happen afterward, but she couldn't keep playing games. Not anymore.

"If you must know…" she started, her voice steady but carrying a weight she hadn't expected to reveal. "I'm trying to find a worthy man to help me lose my virginity."

The words hung in the air like a punch to the gut. She could feel the impact of them the second they left her lips, but it was out there now, and there was no taking it back.

For what felt like an eternity, Andrew didn't speak. He was frozen, his eyes wide with shock as he processed what she'd said. She didn't look away, didn't flinch under the intensity of his gaze. This was her truth, whether he accepted it or not.

"You…" He finally found his voice, his tone ragged, like he was struggling to make sense of it. "You're serious?"

Celeste nodded, her pulse quickening. She couldn't take it back now, and despite the vulnerability flooding her chest, she didn't regret saying it. "Yes," she said, her voice unwavering. "I am."

The silence between them stretched, unbearable and thick with unspoken words. Celeste held his gaze, watching as his hands balled into fists, as if he were fighting with himself to keep from reacting.

"You're not serious," he muttered, shaking his head, disbelief still evident in his voice. "You can't still be a virgin."

Her eyes softened, but she didn't look away. "I am," she said quietly. "And it's time I lost it. I'm twenty-five soon. I've waited long enough."

The words echoed in the space between them, raw and honest. Celeste let the truth settle, the weight of it pressing against both of them.

But then she added, her tone cutting through the tension, "But if you're going to stand there and judge me, then you can go to hell."

Andrew froze, his expression unreadable for a moment. He was a man used to control, to being able to dictate situations, but this… this was beyond him. His mind raced. His chest tightened. This wasn't how he'd imagined this conversation would go. But this— this was something else.

"You're serious?" he asked again, his voice barely above a whisper, his gaze narrowing as he took a step forward, as though the truth of her words was a bitter pill he couldn't quite swallow. "You want to lose your virginity to one of the men downstairs?"

Celeste's heart pounded in her chest, but she didn't move, didn't flinch. She met his gaze head-on, and for the first time tonight, she allowed herself to feel what she was about to say.

"To be honest," she said, voice steady despite the vulnerability rushing through her, "you would be my first choice."

Chapter Nine

The silence that followed was suffocating.

Andrew stood frozen, his breath shallow, his mind a whirlwind of conflicting emotions he couldn't quite untangle. The weight of her words pressed down on him, thick and inescapable.

How could this stunning, captivating woman still be untouched by a man?

The thought of her with someone else—another man's hands on her, another man's kiss—stung in a way he hadn't prepared for. It wasn't about control. It wasn't about possession. It was something deeper, something primal. The intensity of his feelings crashed into him like a wave he hadn't seen coming.

And the worst part? It wasn't just the thought of losing her to another man that set his teeth on edge—it was the idea that she was offering herself to him, and he didn't know if he had it in him to take that step.

A gnawing ache settled in the pit of his stomach. The thought of being the man she trusted with something so intimate sent a rush of protectiveness through him.

What if I hurt her? What if I can't be what she needs?

But then doubt crept in. Could he trust her? Was this just a fleeting impulse? Or was this the start of something neither of them was ready for?

Andrew took a step closer, his body tense, his eyes dark with an unfiltered emotion he couldn't name.

"Celeste," he murmured, his voice barely above a whisper, cracking under the weight of his feelings. "You can't—"

But the words dissolved on his tongue. What could he possibly say? What could he do?

Celeste met his gaze, her expression unreadable. She hadn't expected him to accept her confession easily—she was prepared for rejection. Ready to face it without flinching. But she wouldn't let him off easy.

"You don't have to say anything," she said, her voice calm, though there was an unmistakable steel beneath it. "I'll just go ask my second choice."

His composure snapped.

"Who?" His voice was sharper than he intended, his eyes flashing with a mix of anger and something far more complicated.

"Bryan." Her tone was steady, but her heart skipped a beat at the fire in his eyes.

Silence stretched between them, heavy with unspoken words, thick with tension.

"Don't." His voice was raw; a quiet command laced with something almost desperate. His hands curled into fists at his sides.

Celeste arched an eyebrow, surprised by the force of his response. "Don't what?"

"Don't ask him," Andrew said, his voice rough, as if he was fighting to keep himself in check.

She tilted her head, trying to mask the sting his hesitation caused. "Why? You're obviously not interested in me. I know Bryan is."

His jaw clenched, his expression tight. He exhaled slowly, his gaze flicking away before locking back onto hers with an intensity that made her breath hitch.

"What's the rush?" he asked, his voice quieter now, but no less urgent.

She felt a pang of something she couldn't quite name in her chest—a mix of frustration and vulnerability. "I'll be twenty-five in six weeks," she said, her voice firm but edged with something softer. "I don't intend to still be a virgin by then."

Her admission hung in the air like a challenge, a question, an unspoken invitation all at once.

Andrew felt the words like a punch to the gut. Twenty-five in six weeks. Still a virgin.

It shouldn't matter. It's not my concern. But it did matter. More than he wanted to admit.

His chest tightened, his mind a battlefield of emotions. The thought of being her first; of being the man to introduce her to something so intimate, sent a surge of possessiveness through him that both alarmed and unsettled him. But it wasn't just about that. It was the knowledge that if he said no, she would turn to someone else. Someone like Bryan.

The idea was unbearable.

His hands clenched at his sides as he battled the war raging inside him. He couldn't let her go. But could he trust himself to take that step with her?

He had never been anyone's first before. Not even Sarah's. His past was messy—riddled with trust issues, betrayal, regrets he preferred not to revisit. After Sarah, he had sworn off complications. And Celeste… she was the kind of complication that could bring a man to his knees.

But Celeste wasn't just beautiful. She was effortlessly beautiful. Unlike Sarah, who had been carefully polished—flawless makeup, designer clothes, curated perfection— Celeste was natural. She didn't need embellishments. She didn't need to try. She was breathtaking just as she was.

That only made it harder.

He had spent years avoiding entanglements that could leave him vulnerable again. But Celeste wasn't just asking for a night—she was offering him something deeper. And that terrified him.

Because if he had her, even once, he wasn't sure he could ever let her go.

His voice was rough when he finally spoke, low and strained. "Will you give me time to think about it?"

It wasn't a rejection. It wasn't an agreement. It was the only thing he could offer her in this moment—caught between the sharp edge of his desire and the weight of his hesitation.

Celeste studied him, searching his face for something—doubt, reluctance, anything—but whatever she saw seemed to satisfy her.

After a long moment, she nodded.

"Okay," she said, her voice steady, though the flicker of uncertainty in her eyes betrayed her. "I'll give you time to think about it."

Then she took a step closer.

Her chin tilted up slightly, her gaze locked with his—intense, challenging, yet filled with something dangerously close to hope.

"But first," she continued, her voice soft but unyielding, "I want you to kiss me. Really kiss me. I need to know we'll be compatible if you say yes."

Andrew froze.

Every fibre of his being screamed that this was a bad idea, a mistake—but the words had already left her lips, and the magnetic pull between them was undeniable.

He should walk away.

He needed to walk away.

But she was too close. Too warm. Too much.

Her breath, soft and uneven, mingled with his, carrying the unspoken invitation between them. It wrapped around him, luring him in, breaking down every last shred of resistance he had left.

And then, without another thought, he kissed her.

At first, his lips barely brushed hers—a whisper of contact, a test, a moment suspended in fragile uncertainty. But the second she responded, the moment she pushed up on her toes and pressed against him with quiet, unmistakable urgency, something inside him shattered.

His restraint. His hesitation. His control.

A deep, guttural sound rumbled from his chest as his hands found the curve of her waist, dragging her closer, anchoring her to him as the kiss deepened, grew hotter, more demanding.

Celeste gasped against his lips, her fingers fisting in his shirt as she clung to him, as though she needed him as much as he needed her. Heat unfurled inside her, sharp and dizzying, making her ache in places she had never known could ache. This wasn't just a kiss—it was a collision, a consuming force that stole the very air from her lungs.

His hands slid lower, mapping the curve of her spine, his grip possessive, desperate. Every inch of her body was on fire, every nerve alive under his touch. He was everywhere—his warmth, his scent, the quiet, needy sounds escaping his throat, like he was fighting and losing the same battle she was.

She was unravelling. And she wanted him to come undone with her.

Andrew's heart pounded so hard he could hear it, feel it in the way his body responded to hers, in the way he couldn't stop, couldn't slow down. She tasted like temptation, like something he'd never allowed himself to crave, and yet, here he was, sinking deeper, starving for more.

His fingers slid into her hair, tangling at the nape of her neck as he tilted her head back, devouring her. His tongue swept against hers, coaxing a breathy moan from her lips, a sound so intoxicating it sent a raw surge of need through him.

Damn it.

This was dangerous.

And yet, he couldn't stop.

Celeste felt the moment hesitation flickered through him, the moment a sliver of reality tried to break through the intensity of the kiss. She refused to let it.

Not yet.

Her hands skimmed up his chest, feeling the rapid thud of his heartbeat beneath her fingertips. He was just as lost as she was, just as consumed. That knowledge gave her boldness, made her press closer, arching into him, deepening the kiss until there was no space left between them.

Andrew groaned, his grip tightening on her, his body warring between holding her tighter and pulling away.

He had to stop this. He had to—

With sheer, agonising effort, he tore his lips from hers, sucking in a ragged breath as he rested his forehead against hers.

Silence crackled between them, thick and electric, filled with the echoes of everything they had just shared.

He squeezed his eyes shut, his hands still gripping her waist, unable to let go, unable to think past the rush of blood in his veins and the fire still burning beneath his skin.

What the hell had he just done?

Celeste didn't move. She could feel his breath on her lips, uneven, unsteady, and she knew—he was struggling just as much as she was. Her heart slammed against her ribs as she swallowed, her voice barely a whisper.

"I think that proved we're compatible, don't you?"

Andrew's fingers flexed against her hips, his grip involuntary, like he couldn't quite bring himself to let go. His jaw tightened, his silence stretching between them—not empty, but weighted, thick with everything he wasn't saying.

Celeste's gaze locked onto his, searching, demanding. Her voice was soft, but there was no mistaking the edge of vulnerability beneath it. "Tell me you felt it too."

His throat worked as he swallowed hard. He opened his mouth, but the words refused to come.

Because he had felt it.

Felt it deep in his bones. Felt it in the way his body still burned, in the way his heart still thundered, in the way his hands refused to loosen their hold on her.

It wasn't just a kiss. It had been a collision. A surrender.

And that terrified him.

Celeste's breath hitched as she searched his face, her own emotions tangled between exhilaration and uncertainty. "Is it always like that?" she whispered. She had been kissed before, but nothing—nothing—had ever felt like this. Like being completely unravelled and put back together all at once.

Andrew's jaw tensed. His pulse hammered. His voice was rough, stripped bare when he finally spoke.

"No. It's not."

The confession hung between them, stark and undeniable.

Celeste's heart pounded against his chest, a frantic rhythm he could feel as though it were his own. He had nothing left to hide behind—no logic, no excuses. Just the raw, electric reality of what had just happened.

His voice was barely a whisper. "What now?"

She inhaled shakily, her hands still resting on his chest. "You have two weeks to decide," she murmured, her breath uneven, her lips still parted from their kiss.

Andrew's grip on her tightened instinctively. Decide?

The word echoed in his mind, rattling through the chaos she had unleashed inside him.

Celeste tilted her head, watching him, her expression unreadable—except for her eyes. Her eyes told a different story. A storm of emotions swirled there, flickering between hope, defiance, and something dangerously close to longing.

"After that…" she exhaled, her voice steady, but the slight tremor in her breath betrayed her.

"If you say no…" she hesitated just long enough for the words to sink in, then finished with quiet finality.

"I make another choice."

The air between them thickened, charged with something unspoken, something that tasted like an ultimatum wrapped in heartbreak.

Chapter Ten

After the party, Kathleen breezed into Celeste's guest suite, practically glowing with mischief.

"I knew it," she said, arms crossed smugly as she leaned against the doorframe. "You've been acting all kinds of weird tonight. Something definitely happened."

Celeste hesitated for a moment, feeling her heart race as she tried to figure out how to explain it. Then, with a deep, steadying breath, she let it slip. "He kissed me."

Kathleen's eyes went wide, her jaw dropping. "Andrew?"

Celeste nodded, not trusting her voice to do more than that.

Kathleen didn't wait another second. She practically launched herself onto the bed, crossing her legs like they were teenage girls gossiping at a sleepover. "And?"

Celeste's breath caught, her pulse racing just at the thought of the kiss. She swallowed hard, trying to hold it together. "It was… amazing."

Kathleen's grin was practically contagious. "Like, fireworks in your chest, heart-melting kind of amazing? Or the kind of kiss that ruins you for every other man on the planet?"

Celeste groaned, sinking back onto the bed, her hands running through her hair in a mix of frustration and disbelief. "I don't even know how to describe it. It was… intense. Like, he was trying not to kiss me, but then… he couldn't stop."

Kathleen gasped, her eyes sparkling with excitement. "Oh my God. That's the kind of kiss that changes everything. Everything."

Celeste let out a shaky laugh, her hands covering her face as she tried to process the overwhelming feelings swirling inside her. "I don't know what to do, Kath. I've never felt anything like that."

Her best friend nudged her playfully. "Simple. You make him realise that life's not complete without kissing you again."

Celeste bit her lip. "He asked for time to think."

Kathleen rolled her eyes dramatically, flopping back onto the bed beside her. "Oh please. Don't overthink it. He's already made up his mind. He just doesn't know how to admit it yet."

Celeste turned her head, studying Kathleen's face, searching for any sign of doubt. "You really think so?"

Kathleen gave a sly smirk. "Celeste, men are simple. If a guy kisses you like that and then spends the whole night glaring at anyone who dares come near you, like he wants to throw them into a lake… trust me, he's already hooked."

Celeste's heart stuttered in her chest, her breath catching.

She wanted to believe it.

God, she needed to believe it.

The party was over. The guests had long since departed, the music had faded, and the house had settled into silence. Yet Andrew lay in bed, wide awake, staring at the ceiling as the weight of the night pressed down on him.

Celeste.

His fingers twitched at the memory of her in his arms, the way she had melted against him, the way her breath had hitched when he kissed her. He had kissed plenty of women before—some fleeting, some meaningful—but never had it felt like this. Never had a single touch left him completely wrecked.

Not even Sarah.

His ex-wife had been his first love, the woman he thought he would spend forever with. And yet, as much as he had loved her once, he couldn't recall ever feeling this kind of raw, unrelenting need. That kiss with Celeste had changed something— unlocked something inside him that he wasn't sure he was ready to face.

And so, he had left. He had pulled away, excused himself, and disappeared to his room, desperate for distance, desperate to clear his head.

But she had come back down. A few minutes later, he had seen her through his bedroom window, stepping onto the terrace as if nothing had happened. She had smoothed her dress, tossed her hair over one shoulder, and rejoined the party, a smile on her lips that didn't quite reach her eyes.

She hadn't looked for him. Hadn't chased after him.

That should have been a relief.

It wasn't.

Instead, after he returned to the party, he had spent the rest of the night watching her.

She had been radiant, effortlessly drawing attention as she laughed and danced, as if the kiss they had shared hadn't left her completely undone. As if it hadn't mattered.

But he knew better. He had felt it in the way she had clung to him. In the way she had challenged him with her eyes, daring him to feel, daring him to want her.

And then there was Bryan.

Andrew's stomach tightened as he remembered the way Bryan had hovered near her, the way he had touched her arm, leaned in too close, whispered something in her ear that made her laugh.

Second choice.

The words echoed like a curse in his mind, sour and unwelcome. He had no right to feel this way—no right to want to put a fist through a wall just because Bryan looked at her like she was something he could claim.

She wasn't his to claim.

And yet, the idea of Bryan touching her, kissing her—being with her—made something dark and possessive coil inside him.

He turned onto his side, pressing a hand to his face, exhaling sharply.

He needed to stop this.

Celeste had given him two weeks to decide.

But the truth was, he already knew.

The thought of her moving on, choosing someone else…

It was unbearable.

Celeste couldn't sleep.

She had spent hours tossing and turning, her body still humming from that kiss. It had unravelled her. She had never imagined a single moment could leave her so shaken, so breathless.

She had tried to play it cool afterward, forcing herself to return to the party as if nothing had happened. She had laughed, danced, made polite conversation. But the entire time, she had been painfully aware of Andrew's presence. She had felt his eyes on her, the tension in his jaw every time Bryan came near.

He wanted her—but he wasn't ready to admit it.

Now, as the night stretched on and exhaustion refused to come, she found herself pacing in her bedroom, unable to shake the memory of his lips on hers, his hands gripping her like he couldn't bear to let go.

With a frustrated sigh, she collapsed onto the bed, staring up at the ceiling. The room was silent, but her mind was anything but. Every time she closed her eyes, she felt it all over again—Andrew's lips on hers, the way he'd held her, the way he'd hesitated as if fighting something he didn't want to admit.

It had been more than a kiss.

At least, for her.

She hadn't told Kathleen the whole truth—that she had offered Andrew one night to let go of the weight of her inexperience.

The truth was, she wanted more. She ached for more.

But if one night was all Andrew could give her, then she would take it.

She would take whatever pieces of him he was willing to offer, even if it meant shattering in the end.

The next morning, Jonas and Hope Beaumont had arranged a lunch at the Sydney Yacht Club, inviting Judy and John Carter, along with Andrew, Kathleen, and, of course, Celeste. It was a meeting of old friends—one that Celeste wasn't entirely sure she was ready for.

After the long, restless night, she needed to freshen up and change. She had planned to take an Uber back to her apartment, but Kathleen had other ideas.

"You're not calling an Uber," Kathleen announced, looping an arm through Celeste's as they stepped onto the sun-drenched terrace. "Andrew can take us."

Celeste stiffened. "That's not necessary. I don't want to be a bother."

Andrew, who had been nursing a coffee at the outdoor bar, looked up at the sound of his name. He arched a brow, setting his mug down. "Take you where?"

"Celeste's place," Kathleen said breezily, ignoring Celeste's pointed glare. "She needs to change before lunch, and since you're going too, it just makes sense."

Celeste opened her mouth to protest, but Kathleen squeezed her arm in warning. With a sigh, she conceded. It wasn't worth the argument.

Andrew studied her for a beat before giving a small nod. "Fine. Let's go."

As they made their way to his sleek black car, Celeste could feel the tension simmering between them. Last night still lingered in the air—unspoken but undeniable.

Andrew kept his gaze forward as he drove, his jaw tight, his grip firm on the wheel. Celeste sat beside him, her hands folded in her lap, staring out the window, willing her racing thoughts to settle. Kathleen, oblivious or simply determined to ignore the tension, chatted about the yacht club, the weather, anything to keep the silence at bay.

When they arrived at Celeste's apartment—a lavish high-rise overlooking Sydney Harbour—Kathleen wasted no time.

"Come on, Andrew," she said, grabbing his arm. "You've never seen Celeste's place, have you? Let me give you the grand tour."

Celeste shot her a look, but Kathleen just grinned before tugging Andrew inside, leaving Celeste no choice but to let it happen.

With a sigh, she headed straight to her bedroom, eager for a moment to herself. She stepped into the shower, letting the warm water wash away the tension clinging to her. But even as she stood beneath the steady stream, last night replayed in her mind— Andrew's lips on hers, the way he had held her like he couldn't bear to let go, and then, just as suddenly, the way he had pulled away.

By the time she stepped out, towelling off, she forced herself to push it aside. She had to focus. Today wasn't about last night—it was about their families, the lunch, keeping up appearances.

She slipped into a flowing yellow sundress, the fabric light and airy against her skin. It complemented her sun-kissed complexion, the colour bright and cheerful—perfect for the afternoon ahead.

Pulling her hair up into a high ponytail, she studied her reflection.

She looked… fine. Collected. Like a woman who had spent a restful night dreaming instead of lying awake, replaying a single kiss that had unravelled her entire world.

She smoothed her hands over the dress, exhaling slowly. It didn't matter how she felt. What mattered was control—holding herself together, pretending last night hadn't changed everything.

Because if she let herself believe, even for a second, that it had meant as much to him as it had to her… she wasn't sure she'd survive it.

Andrew followed Kathleen around Celeste's apartment, taking in the space. It was elegant yet warm, a reflection of her—sophisticated but inviting.

Family photos lined the hallway wall, capturing moments of Celeste's life: childhood memories, holidays, glimpses of a life he had never been part of. A few pictures with Kathleen were mixed in, their years of friendship evident in their wide smiles and carefree laughter.

"She loves this place," Kathleen said, gesturing around. "It's her sanctuary."

Andrew nodded, his attention lingering on a particular photo—Celeste on a beach, wind in her hair, her smile radiant. She looked happy, free.

And then, as if summoned by his thoughts, she appeared.

She stepped into the room in a bright yellow sundress, her golden skin glowing, her long legs effortless in their grace. Her high ponytail gave her an air of casual elegance, and for a moment, he couldn't breathe.

She looked good enough to eat.

And now, he had to sit across from her at lunch, keeping his hands to himself when all he wanted was to erase the space between them. Pretend that last night hadn't happened.

Because touching her was all he wanted to do. And it was the one thing he couldn't allow himself…yet.

Chapter Eleven

As Celeste, Kathleen, and Andrew stepped into the Sydney Yacht Club, the crisp ocean breeze carried the scent of salt and freshly prepared seafood. The elegant space was filled with the low hum of conversation and the occasional clink of glasses.

Andrew's sharp gaze swept the room, immediately landing on their parents, already seated at a prime table near the water. But they weren't alone.

Bryan stood with them, engaged in what appeared to be a lively conversation with Celeste's father.

Andrew's jaw tightened. "What the hell is he doing here?"

Celeste's stomach dropped at the irritation in his voice. She had been so preoccupied with her own thoughts that she hadn't even noticed Bryan's presence until now.

"I have no idea," she murmured, more to herself than to him.

Kathleen, however, smirked knowingly. "He was invited by Celeste's parents."

Andrew let out a short, humourless laugh, his lips curling in disdain. "Well, it must mean something when you introduce a male friend to your parents."

Celeste snapped her gaze to him, her heart skipping a beat. His tone was casual, almost indifferent, but the tightness in his jaw and the way his fingers flexed at his sides betrayed something much deeper.

She had introduced Bryan to her parents, though she couldn't quite explain why. It had been a spur-of-the-moment decision, something she hadn't fully thought through last night. Now, in the light of Andrew's reaction, it felt like a mistake.

He was jealous.

And as much as part of her wanted to feel annoyed by his possessiveness, another part of her was inexplicably thrilled by it.

Bryan spotted Celeste across the room and excused himself from her father's conversation. With a confident stride, he made his way toward her, his smile widening as he reached her. Without hesitation, he pulled her into a hug and kissed her cheek.

"Hi, Celeste," he said, his voice smooth. "Your parents invited me this afternoon. I hope you don't mind."

She smiled, trying to keep her tone light. "No, not at all."

Bryan's gaze flickered to Kathleen and Andrew as he greeted them with a smile. Then, with a subtle but possessive move, he took Celeste's hand in his, his fingers tightening around hers. The gesture was casual enough to seem harmless, but to Andrew, it felt like a silent claim.

Celeste felt the warmth of Bryan's touch, but it didn't send a thrill through her the way Andrew's gaze did. Bryan was kind, charming, and undeniably attractive—on paper, he was everything a woman should want. And yet, standing between the two men, she was acutely aware of the way her pulse quickened under Andrew's stare, not Bryan's touch.

Andrew's jaw tightened, and Celeste could feel the shift in the air. Kathleen, ever the observant one, grinned mischievously, clearly enjoying the tension between them.

Bryan, oblivious or perhaps purposefully ignoring the undercurrent of discomfort, gently pulled Celeste by the hand toward the table, pulling out a chair for her with a casual ease. She greeted both sets of parents with a kiss on the cheek, her mind distracted by the subtle but undeniable presence of Andrew's stare burning into her back.

Lunch was cheerful and relaxed, but every so often, Celeste caught the constant flicker of tense looks from Andrew, his gaze sharp, his posture rigid. She couldn't help but feel the weight of his unspoken thoughts pressing against her as the meal went on.

Afterward, needing a moment of escape, Celeste excused herself and made her way toward the powder room. But just before she reached the door, she was startled when Bryan gently grabbed her hand from behind. His touch was warm, his fingers wrapping around hers with an unexpected firmness.

Before she could react, he gently pushed her back against the wall, his body a breath away from hers, caging her in with his arms on either side. She was taken aback by the sudden closeness, her heart thumping in her chest.

Bryan bent his head, his lips hovering just above hers, his voice soft. "Go out with me, Celeste?"

Celeste opened her mouth to respond, but before she could get a word out, a voice rang out from behind her, cool and commanding.

"Is there a problem here?" Andrew's voice was laced with something darker, a hint of jealousy that Celeste couldn't ignore.

The tension between the three of them thickened instantly. Celeste's breath caught in her throat, her pulse hammering in her ears. She was caught in the middle of something she hadn't anticipated, and the weight of it pressed down on her. Without a word, she ducked under Bryan's arms and quickly stepped into the powder room, her heart racing as the door clicked shut behind her.

Bryan stood still for a moment, his expression a mix of disbelief and irritation. He shot a quick glance at the door where Celeste had disappeared, then turned to Andrew. "What the hell, Andrew?"

Andrew's posture was rigid, his jaw clenched tight, eyes locked onto Bryan with a cold, unwavering intensity. "What was that, Bryan?"

Bryan took a step forward, frustration clear in his stance. "Can't you tell? I told you I was interested in Celeste. I've made no secret of it."

Andrew didn't flinch. His gaze remained sharp, his voice low and dangerous. "Well, I might have a problem with that."

Bryan's expression darkened, his anger rising as the words spilled from him. "You said you had no interest in her. What's changed?"

The tension in the air crackled, thick, and charged with unresolved emotions.

Andrew paused, his eyes narrowing as he turned slightly, his gaze lingering on the door to the powder room where Celeste had vanished. Then, with a quiet, finality, he replied, "I've changed my mind."

Without another word, he turned and walked back to the table, leaving Bryan standing there, frustration simmering just below the surface. The unspoken weight of Andrew's words hung heavy in the air.

Celeste took her time in the powder room, splashing cold water on her face in an attempt to calm the whirlwind of emotions racing through her. The confrontation between Andrew and Bryan had left her reeling, unsure of what to make of it all. She stared at her reflection in the mirror, trying to steady her breath.

By the time she was ready to leave, the door creaked open, and Kathleen's voice sliced through the quiet.

"What on earth happened between Bryan and Andrew? They look like they're about to kill each other." Amusement danced in her eyes, but there was a thread of genuine curiosity beneath it.

Celeste exhaled shakily, drying her damp hands on a paper towel. She hesitated, struggling to put into words the tension she had just witnessed. "I… I'm not sure. They just… had a moment."

Kathleen arched a sceptical brow. "A moment? Celeste, they were practically throwing daggers at each other with their eyes. That wasn't just a moment."

Celeste sighed, pressing her fingertips against the cool marble countertop, her mind still tangled in the events of the afternoon. "I don't know, Kath."

Kathleen folded her arms, her expression shifting to one of smug satisfaction. "Well, Andrew must have figured something out because he told me to go home with Mum and Dad. He wants to talk to you—and he's taking you home."

Celeste's pulse quickened. She didn't respond immediately, letting Kathleen's words sink in. Andrew's sudden shift unsettled her, the weight of unspoken things pressing against her chest. The tension between them had always been there, but now it was different—undeniable.

She met Kathleen's gaze, her lips curving into a small, nervous smile. "Well… I guess I'm about to find out what's going on."

Lunch wrapped up soon after. Bryan insisted on driving her home, but before he could push the issue, Andrew cut in with a firm, unquestionable, "She's coming with me."

No room for argument.

Bryan left shortly after, and once goodbyes were exchanged, Andrew drove Celeste back to her apartment in silence. The air between them was thick, humming with unspoken words.

When they reached her apartment parking lot, Andrew finally broke the quiet. "We need to talk."

Celeste nodded, her stomach twisting with anticipation. "Okay."

Inside, she turned to face him, her heart pounding. "What do you want to talk about?"

Andrew's gaze locked onto hers, intense and unwavering. "I think you know."

She knew exactly what he wanted to talk about—her initiation to sex.

Celeste took a steadying breath and gestured to the couch. "Okay. Sit down."

Andrew lowered himself onto one end of the sofa, and she took the opposite, the space between them charged with an unspoken tension.

His gaze was serious, searching. "Are you sure this is what you want?"

"Yes," she said firmly, meeting his eyes without hesitation. "I'm not changing my mind."

A muscle in his jaw tightened, but he nodded. "Okay… what are you expecting?"

She frowned slightly. "What do you mean?"

His voice was steady, measured. "Are you expecting just one night, or do you want more?"

Celeste considered his question carefully. She had thought about this for a long time, weighed the risks and rewards. Finally, she said, "If the first time is… good, I'd like to learn how to please a man. If more than one lesson is required…" She trailed off, letting the implication hang between them.

Andrew exhaled slowly, rubbing a hand along his jaw. He couldn't believe they were actually having this conversation, but if they were going to do this, there had to be clear rules. "Okay… what about contraception?"

"I'm on the pill," she said, her voice calm. "I take it for my cycles."

He nodded, considering. "Do you want me to wear a condom? I haven't been with anyone since my last test screening. I'm clean, but if you want me to, I will."

Celeste held his gaze, her answer immediate. "No. I trust you."

Andrew studied her for a long moment, trying to wrap his head around everything they had just discussed. Finally, he exhaled, rubbing a hand over his jaw. "Okay," he said slowly. "I'll… help you. But I have some expectations."

Celeste sat up straighter, meeting his gaze. "Okay."

His expression was serious, unwavering. "If we do this, for however long it lasts, you can't be with anyone else."

Celeste blinked, clearly taken aback. "Of course not," she said, as if the thought had never even crossed her mind. Then she arched a brow. "Same goes for you."

Andrew's lips quirked slightly, the barest hint of a smirk before he nodded. "Of course."

Celeste smiled. "Okay… when?"

Andrew considered for a moment. "I start a new job this week, and next weekend I'll be moving into my new apartment. So, is the weekend after next okay with you?"

She nodded. "Yes."

He stood. "Alright, I'll take you out to dinner Friday week."

Celeste stood as well, tilting her head. "You don't need to do that."

Andrew's gaze locked onto hers, unwavering. "If we're doing this, we do it properly."

Something about the way he said it sent a shiver down her spine. "Okay," she murmured.

She walked him to the door, but before leaving, he turned and handed her his phone. "I need your number."

She took it, quickly typing in her number. A second later, her phone vibrated in her pocket.

Andrew smirked as he put his phone away. "Now you have mine too."

They stood there for a beat, the air between them thick with something unspoken.

Celeste hesitated, then met his gaze. "Should we seal the deal?"

Something flickered in Andrew's eyes—heat, possession, something she wasn't sure she was ready to name.

Without another word, he pulled her into his arms, his lips claiming hers in a kiss that stole her breath and sent a rush of heat through her veins. It was slow, deliberate, yet undeniably powerful. By the time he pulled away, she was lightheaded, her heart hammering against her ribs.

Andrew's thumb grazed her jaw, his voice low and controlled. "Goodnight, Celeste."

Then he turned and walked away, leaving her standing in the doorway, still breathless, still reeling.

Chapter Twelve

The next two weeks dragged on with excruciating slowness for Celeste. She had barely heard from Andrew since that night. He had decided that he would be her first lover. But after that momentous night, silence fell between them. She tried to distract herself with work at the bank, but her mind often wandered to thoughts of Andrew.

Then, finally, on the second Wednesday, her phone buzzed. It was a message from him.

I'll pick you up for dinner at six on Friday. Get ready for something special. I've been thinking about you.

Her heart skipped a beat. It was as though a switch had been flipped inside her, and suddenly, the world around her felt sharper, more vibrant. She felt a strange mixture of anticipation, hope, and the remnants of doubt. It had been a long wait. But now, the clock was ticking toward Friday, and she couldn't help but count the hours.

Friday afternoon arrived, and with it, a surge of nerves that was hard to shake. The bank closed early on Fridays, and Celeste had the afternoon free. She decided to take her time and prepare for the evening ahead. She called ahead to her favourite salon, asking for the full treatment.

When she walked into the sleek, modern salon, the familiar smell of lavender and citrus greeted her. The technician at the wash station massaged her scalp as they washed and conditioned her hair. She let herself relax into the process, closing her eyes as the tension melted from her body.

She was a woman who rarely spent time on herself, but tonight, she was determined to look and feel her best. After the shampoo, she sat down for a manicure and pedicure. Her nails were painted a soft, blush pink. Then came the waxing, the buffing, and the soft scrubbing that left her skin silky and smooth.

When the technician was finally finished, Celeste glanced at her reflection, taking in the woman staring back at her in the mirror. The person she saw was beautiful, confident, and ready. Ready for tonight. For Andrew.

Across town, Andrew had spent the past two weeks navigating his new role at the prestigious law firm. His colleagues were hardworking and sharp, pushing him to prove his worth. He'd thrown himself into his work, trying to bury any thoughts of Celeste beneath piles of case files and deadlines. But, despite his best efforts, Celeste lingered in his mind.

He'd moved into his new penthouse apartment the previous weekend, and now, as Friday night approached, he was determined to make the evening unforgettable for her.

Andrew had always been a man who believed in giving his best. Tonight was no different. He'd thought long and hard about how to make Celeste's first experience special. After all, he knew the weight of the moment.

He'd hired a private chef to prepare a gourmet meal in his apartment, and as the chef worked in the kitchen, Andrew set about creating an atmosphere that would be romantic, intimate, and personal.

He placed candles strategically around the living room, the bedroom, and even the ensuite bathroom. Soft, flickering light illuminated the space, casting a glow that felt like a dream. He arranged flowers—delicate white roses—on the dining table and scattered them across the room. He wanted everything to be perfect.

As he adjusted the final candle on the dining table, he stepped back and surveyed the room. It was exactly how he imagined it. Perfect. Just for her.

Every moment with Celeste felt like a gift he hadn't expected, and yet now that it was happening, it was as if everything had led him to this point. He had spent the past two weeks fighting the growing pull between them, telling himself that he should focus on his new career, on everything else that demanded his attention. But even as the days went by, her image lingered in his mind—her laugh, her smile, the way her eyes softened when she looked at him.

He hadn't planned to want her. He hadn't planned to be so attracted to her. Especially when he swore he would avoid beautiful women at all costs. But Celeste, she was different. The pull he felt was undeniable, a force he couldn't fight. And it wasn't just physical—there was something about her, something deeper that called to him, something that told him this wasn't just a fleeting attraction.

He didn't know what the future held, but as he glanced around the room one last time, he realised that right now, everything felt right. Perfect, just as it should be. For her.

At six pm, Celeste stood in front of her bathroom mirror, one last look at herself before the evening began. She had chosen a soft, silky dress in a deep burgundy colour, one that clung to her curves in a way that felt just right. She had kept her makeup simple— smoky eyes, a hint of blush, and just a touch of lip gloss that made her look natural yet alluring. Her hair framed her face in soft waves, and the finishing touch was delicate gold earrings.

She felt beautiful.

Her doorbell buzzed, and Celeste's heart skipped a beat. She hurried to the door, opening it to find Andrew standing there with a warm smile, looking every bit as handsome as she remembered.

"You ready for tonight?" he asked, his eyes sparkling with something she couldn't quite name.

"I'm ready," she replied, her voice steady despite the fluttering in her chest. She grabbed her small clutch, feeling the slight weight of it in her hand as she stepped out the door and into the night with him.

The city streets were alive with the hum of Friday evening traffic, the sound of distant chatter, the flashing lights of neon signs. But for Celeste, everything else blurred into the background. Her mind was focused solely on Andrew, on the anticipation of what lay ahead, on how perfectly this evening had been set up for them.

When they arrived at Andrew's penthouse, he guided her through the sleek, modern building, and as the elevator doors opened, Celeste stepped into a world that took her breath away. Soft ambient lighting filled the space, creating a warm and intimate atmosphere, and the delicate scent of fresh flowers wafted through the air. Every detail was perfectly arranged, and her heart raced as she took it all in.

"Everything looks beautiful," she said, her voice tinged with awe.

Andrew's gaze softened, his eyes locking onto hers with a depth of emotion that made her stomach flip. "You're beautiful," he whispered, his voice low and sincere.

Celeste's cheeks flushed, her nerves bubbling to the surface. "Thank you," she said, her voice barely above a whisper. She could feel her heart beating faster, her anticipation building.

Andrew stepped closer, his hands reaching out to take hers. His thumbs brushed across her skin gently, as if he was savouring the moment. "You look incredible," he murmured, his voice rough with emotion, and for a brief moment, Celeste felt as if the world outside had faded entirely, leaving just the two of them in this intimate space.

She smiled, feeling the warmth of his touch spreading through her. "Thank you," she whispered back, her voice full of sincerity.

Andrew smiled, his eyes twinkling with an emotion she couldn't quite name. Without saying another word, he led her to the dining table where a gourmet meal awaited them, the chef having outdone himself. The table was set perfectly, with delicate silverware and soft candlelight flickering in the background.

"Shall we eat?" Andrew asked, his voice playful yet full of sincerity.

Celeste nodded, feeling as if she were floating. They sat down to enjoy the meal, and the outside world seemed to dissolve around them. There were no distractions, no pressures, just the two of them, savouring each bite and each moment. The conversation flowed easily, their laughter mixing with the soft music playing in the background.

As the evening unfolded, Celeste found herself feeling more at ease, the nervousness she had arrived with slowly slipping away. She wasn't just preparing for her first time with Andrew; she was embracing something deeper, something more meaningful. She was ready to take this step with someone she had come to trust, someone who truly cared about her. For the first time, she allowed herself to fully embrace that feeling, knowing that this night was the beginning of something new, something beautiful.

After dinner and dessert, the chef had left, and the apartment seemed quieter now. The soft glow of candlelight illuminated the space, casting a warm, romantic glow. Andrew, his eyes still holding that tender look, took a step toward her.

"Would you like to dance?" he asked, his voice soft, yet full of invitation.

Celeste's heart stilled. There was something in the way he spoke, in the way he looked at her, that made her pulse race. Without thinking, she stepped into his arms, her body instinctively moulding to his as they swayed to the slow rhythm of the music.

The world outside ceased to exist, and in that moment, it was just the two of them. The warmth of his embrace, the tenderness in his touch, the quietness of the night— they all combined to create a sense of peace she hadn't known she'd been longing for.

Andrew's hand gently rested at the small of her back, his other hand holding hers as they moved together. Celeste's breath hitched slightly as he lowered his face, brushing his lips gently against her ear.

"I haven't stopped thinking about you, Celeste," Andrew whispered, his voice soft and full of meaning, like a confession meant only for her ears. The words hung in the air between them, heavy with emotion, and Celeste's heart fluttered in her chest as she met his gaze. There was something in his eyes, something tender, almost vulnerable, that made her breath catch.

She pulled back just enough to look up at him, her lips parting slightly as she let the words settle in her mind. "I haven't thought of anything else either," she murmured, her voice quiet but full of the same emotion that echoed in his. In that moment, it was as if time itself had slowed, and all that mattered was the connection between them.

They continued to dance, their bodies swaying in perfect harmony. The music, a soft and romantic melody, wrapped around them like a warm embrace, and everything outside the two of them faded away. There was no past, no future—just the present, just this moment, as they held each other in the intimacy of the dance.

As the music slowed even further, Andrew drew her more firmly into his arms. His body pressed gently against hers, the heat of his touch seeping into her skin, making her pulse race. His hand moved to her chin, his fingers gentle as he cupped it, tilting her face slightly so she was looking directly at him. His touch was tender, almost reverent, as if he was savouring every second of this closeness.

"If you want me to stop at any time, you just have to tell me, okay?" he whispered, his voice low, laden with sincerity. His eyes searched hers, waiting for a response, for some kind of confirmation that she felt the same.

Celeste's heart raced as she looked into his eyes. His words, the care, and the respect in them, made her feel seen, made her feel cherished. She knew he wasn't just thinking of the physical act, but of the emotional journey they were about to take together. She could feel the weight of his question, and she realised, with a sudden clarity, that she was ready. She had trusted him to this point—now she was ready to trust him with her body.

She whispered, barely audible, her voice trembling with the intensity of the moment, "Okay."

And then, without another word, his lips met hers.

Chapter Thirteen

It began softly, a gentle brush of his lips against hers, as though he was testing the waters, making sure she was truly ready. But the moment their lips touched, Celeste felt a rush of warmth flood through her—longing, affection, a connection that swept over her completely. Her body responded instinctively, her hands finding their way to his shoulders, pulling herself closer, as if she couldn't get close enough.

The kiss deepened, their mouths moving together with a hunger that had been building between them for so long. Andrew's hand slid from her chin to the back of her neck, his fingers threading through her hair, pulling her closer. Celeste's breath hitched as the kiss became more urgent, each of them trying to express everything they'd been feeling in that one perfect moment.

She could taste his desire, feel it in every touch, every movement. But beyond that, there was care—his respect for her, the way he held back just enough, letting her guide the pace, letting her decide when to take the final step. It wasn't just passion. It was trust.

Her hands slid down to his chest, feeling the steady beat of his heart beneath her fingertips. This was the moment—everything they'd been waiting for, the moment where everything would change.

When they finally broke apart, both breathless, Andrew's eyes burned with dark desire. His forehead pressed gently against hers, their breaths mingling in the stillness between them.

"I've wanted this… wanted you, since I saw you walking toward me at the club that first night," he whispered, his voice raw, filled with longing.

Celeste's lips curled into a small, knowing smile, her fingers tracing slow circles over his chest. "I think I've always wanted you," she whispered back, her heart full of a warmth that made the outside world feel irrelevant.

For a long moment, they stood there, holding each other, as if time had paused, waiting for them to make the next move. The weight of the moment hung in the air, thick with anticipation.

Without a word, Andrew scooped Celeste into his arms, his grip tender but urgent, carrying her to the bedroom with focused intensity. His eyes never left hers as he moved with deliberate steps. The soft glow from the flickering candles cast a warm light, making the air feel heavier, more intimate.

As he set her down beside the bed, he gazed at her, his fingers brushing the zipper of her dress. His touch was slow, almost reverent, savouring every inch of skin that came into view as his eyes remained locked on hers.

As the dress slipped from her body, pooling at her feet, revealing the delicate lace of her panties and the height of her heels, Andrew couldn't contain the quiet breath that escaped him. He stared, taking in every inch of her—vulnerable, yet strong in her openness. She kicked off her heels with effortless grace, casting the dress aside as if it were nothing more than a barrier between them.

There she stood—a vision of beauty, unapologetically herself—everything he had longed for and more. His heart pounded in his chest, a mix of desire and admiration stirring deep within him. She was more than just a woman before him. She was a revelation.

In the dim light, his gaze lingered on her soft, velvety skin. "You're so beautiful," he murmured, his voice thick with awe and something deeper.

Celeste's cheeks flushed, but she didn't look away. There was no embarrassment, only a connection, an intimacy that made her feel seen in a way she hadn't before.

"Undress me," he commanded, his voice low, filled with quiet urgency.

Her hands moved with purpose, fingers grazing over the smooth buttons of his shirt. Slowly, she worked them free, the fabric sliding off his broad shoulders to reveal his muscular chest, dusted with a light sprinkling of curls. His body was powerful, yet there was a vulnerability in the way he allowed her to undress him—each movement a silent invitation, drawing them closer in a dance neither could resist.

Her fingers traced over his chest, exploring, feeling the warmth of his skin beneath her touch. A deep moan rumbled in his throat, his eyes closing. "You're so beautiful... so strong," she whispered, awe in her voice, her heart racing with each breath.

With quiet resolve, she reached for his belt, undoing it with practiced ease. Her fingers worked at the buttons of his trousers, the sound of fabric shifting filling the space between them. She slid the zipper down, her hands moving lower, pulling the trousers down his long, sculpted legs.

He stood before her, the only barrier between them his underpants, which failed to hide the evidence of his desire. The intensity of the moment stretched between them, each second pulsing with anticipation.

Andrew slid his hand into her hair, his fingers tangling in the soft waves as he tilted her head back, exposing the delicate curve of her throat. His lips found her skin, trailing a path of warm, hungry kisses down her neck. His other hand cupped her breast, teasing and tantalising, drawing breathless gasps from her.

Slowly, his lips moved lower, dipping into the valley between her breasts. A groan of satisfaction escaped him as he reached one rosy, tight nipple. His mouth closed over it with heat that sent pleasure spiralling through her. She gasped, her body arching instinctively against him. Every brush of his tongue over her sensitive skin felt like a caress that robbed her of her sanity.

She writhed against him, her body aching for more, her breath coming in quick, shallow bursts. Sensing her need, Andrew lifted her into his arms, his tenderness surprising her. He gently lowered her onto the bed, each movement deliberate, matching the intensity that burned between them.

His eyes never left hers as he removed his underwear, settling next to her. He stroked her stomach with slow, deliberate movements, sending shivers of anticipation through her. He let his fingers trail lower, brushing the waistband of her panties before his lips found hers in a kiss—sweet, slow, utterly captivating.

His fingers slipped lower, teasing the soft skin of her inner thighs, moving toward the apex of her desire. Celeste's breath hitched, and then a low moan escaped her lips. His mouth took hers deeply, his fingers exploring the soft, yielding folds of her flesh.

With expert ease, his fingers slid through the tender, moist folds of her most sensitive centre. Celeste gasped, her body writhing in ecstasy, her hips moving instinctively. The pressure between her legs built, searching for something elusive but necessary. Then pleasure exploded through her like a blinding light. "Andrew!" she screamed, her body arching as the waves of pleasure took over.

He released her lips, kissing his way down her neck, his mouth moving lower as he kissed and sucked his way to her breast, taking her nipple into his hot, wet mouth. Celeste sobbed with ecstasy as he moved to the other nipple, giving it the same attention. His hand never stopped teasing, stroking her folds with an intensity that matched the heat between them.

His mouth moved lower, kissing her stomach, as one hand kneaded her breast, pinching her nipple softly. He slid her panties off slowly, replacing them with his mouth. His tongue traced the wet folds, and Celeste arched against him, her body aching for more.

"Andrew… please!" she cried, her body trembling.

He continued to suck and lick, building the pressure inside her, until she couldn't think—only feel. Waves of pleasure crashed over her again. "Andrew!" she cried out once more.

He continued, until her convulsions subsided, then slowly moved back up her body, capturing her breast in his mouth before moving to the other. His body settled between her legs, his arousal pressing against her soft thighs.

"Celeste," he whispered, kissing her neck. "You're so beautiful. Are you sure this is what you want?"

"Yes… please, Andrew, teach me," she begged.

With slow, deliberate movements, Andrew slid into her, inch by inch, savouring the exquisite heat of her. She was tight, her body trembling beneath him, every inch of her responding to his touch. Their breaths mingled, the rhythm between them building in waves of anticipation and need.

Then, with one deep, claiming thrust, he breached the last of her innocence.

Celeste cried out—a soft gasp torn from her lips—pleasure and pain colliding in a breathless moment.

Andrew froze, his gaze searching hers, his body taut with restraint. "You're mine," he whispered, voice thick with emotion. Then, slowly, reverently, he began to move again—each motion a vow, each breath a promise, unable to control the intensity of his feelings.

She clung to him as he kissed her deeply, their bodies moving together in a rhythm that swept them both into a whirlwind of sensation. The tension mounted until, at last, Celeste cried out in ecstasy, her body writhing as waves of pleasure washed over her. Andrew stiffened, a low growl escaping him as he climaxed with her.

Afterward, Andrew reluctantly pulled away, rolling onto his back and drawing Celeste into his embrace. She nestled against him, feeling the steady rhythm of his heartbeat and the warmth of his skin.

"That was… incredible," Celeste whispered, her voice filled with awe and gratitude.

Andrew pressed a gentle kiss to her forehead, his lips lingering for a moment. "It was, thank you, Celeste," he murmured, his voice low and sincere.

Chapter Fourteen

A little while later, Andrew rose from the bed and made his way to the ensuite. Celeste heard the sound of water running, but her body was too relaxed to move. She smiled to herself, savouring the warmth that still lingered from their shared moment. But then, Andrew reappeared, sweeping her up into his arms without a word.

"Andrew?" she murmured, blinking up at him.

"Trust me," he said, his gaze steady and comforting. "A bath will help."

Before she could protest, he carried her effortlessly to the tub, which was already filled with warm water, the steam rising gently into the air. He lowered her slowly into the soothing embrace of the water.

Celeste sighed deeply as the warmth enveloped her. "Ahhh," she breathed, closing her eyes and letting the tension melt away.

Andrew slid in behind her, his strong frame pressing lightly against hers as he settled into the water. With careful hands, he took a washcloth and lathered it with soap, the gentle scent of lavender filling the air. He began to wash her, his touch tender, but with a hint of something deeper—something that made her feel cherished. The sensation of the soft cloth moving over her skin, the warmth of the water, and the closeness of his body all combined to create a sense of bliss she never wanted to end.

It felt like heaven. The warm water wrapped around her like a cocoon, easing away every trace of tension, while the gentle pressure of Andrew's body behind her added a layer of comfort she hadn't known she needed.

She glanced over her shoulder, her lips curling into a playful smile. "You know how to make a girl feel special," she teased, her voice soft and relaxed, the words slipping out like a secret shared between them.

Andrew chuckled, the sound deep and low, as he leaned in and pressed a tender kiss to the tip of her nose. "I try," he said with a hint of modesty, but the gleam in his eyes told her that he was savouring the moment just as much as she was.

"Well, you're succeeding," she replied, her voice tinged with affection. She shifted slightly, sinking further into the warmth of the bath, and relaxed completely against his chest. His arms came around her instinctively, pulling her closer as she nestled into him. The steady rhythm of his heartbeat beneath her ear was grounding, reassuring—like nothing could touch them here.

Andrew sat in the bath with Celeste, holding her close, his arms wrapped securely around her. The warmth of the water was nothing compared to the heat still lingering between them. Making love to her had been incredible—unlike anything he had ever experienced.

He had never felt emotions this intense, not even with his ex-wife, Sarah. What he felt for Celeste went beyond passion—it was something deeper, something raw and undeniable. She awakened something in him, something he hadn't even realised he was missing. She was so open, so responsive, so achingly honest in the way she gave herself to him.

They sat in silence for a while, neither needing words. The world outside the bathroom ceased to exist, leaving only the quiet intimacy between them. The only sounds were the soft ripple of water as their bodies shifted slightly, the steady rhythm of their breathing, and the occasional contented sigh escaping between them.

Andrew rested his chin lightly on the top of her head, inhaling the faint, lingering scent of her skin. He tightened his hold on her, as if anchoring himself to this moment, to her. There was a peace in this, a quiet certainty that she was meant to be in his arms.

Celeste let out a soft, blissful sigh, her fingers tracing idle patterns along Andrew's arm where it rested protectively across her stomach. Neither of them spoke, yet in the quiet intimacy of the moment, an unspoken understanding passed between them. The way their bodies fit together so naturally, the warmth of his embrace—it was more than just passion.

This felt... real.

A slow, tender ache spread through her chest, a longing that had nothing to do with desire and everything to do with the man holding her. She turned in his arms, straddling him, the water sloshing softly around them. Her hands slid up his shoulders, fingers threading into his damp hair as she gazed into his dark, smouldering eyes.

Andrew didn't speak, but the way he looked at her—his gaze heavy with emotion, with want—made her pulse flutter. Slowly, she lowered her head and pressed her lips to his.

The kiss started soft, almost reverent, but as soon as their lips met, a spark ignited between them. Andrew's hands slid up her back, pulling her closer as he deepened the kiss, his tongue sweeping against hers in a slow, tantalising dance.

A shiver of pleasure ran through Celeste as she moaned into his mouth, her body melting into him. The heat of the water was nothing compared to the heat building between them once again. Andrew groaned low in his throat, his hands sliding down to grip her hips, holding her in place as the kiss grew hungrier, more urgent.

The bath had been meant to relax them, to soothe their bodies after the intensity of their passion. But as their lips moved together, their breaths mingling in the steamy air, it became clear—they were nowhere near finished with each other yet.

Andrew's hands roamed over Celeste's wet skin, tracing the curve of her back, down to her hips, gripping them possessively. His mouth left hers only for a moment, his lips travelling along the line of her jaw, down the slender column of her throat, tasting the droplets of water that clung to her flushed skin.

He murmured against her lips, his voice thick with need. "I want you again."

Celeste's breath hitched, her heart pounding at the raw hunger in his voice. She had never felt so desired, so completely consumed by another person.

"Yes," she whispered, her voice a trembling sigh of surrender.

Andrew didn't hesitate. With a deep, guttural moan, he gripped her hips and lifted her, aligning their bodies before slowly, deliberately lowering her onto him.

Celeste gasped, her fingers digging into his shoulders as he stretched and filled her. "Oh… yes."

Andrew groaned, his head falling back against the edge of the tub, his hands guiding her movements as they adjusted to the delicious, aching rhythm between them.

"You feel incredible," he rasped, his voice edged with reverence and restraint.

Celeste braced her hands against his chest, rolling her hips in slow, teasing circles, watching as his jaw tensed, his muscles flexing beneath her fingertips. The warm water rippled around them, adding to the sensual embrace of their bodies.

Their eyes locked, a silent conversation passing between them—one filled with longing, surrender, and something deeper neither dared to name. The flickering candlelight danced over their wet skin, casting golden reflections on the rippling water, making everything feel almost dreamlike.

Celeste gasped as Andrew's hands gripped her hips with a firm yet reverent touch, guiding her movements as their bodies found a perfect rhythm. The pleasure coiling deep inside her built with every slow, deliberate thrust, every stroke of his hands across her back, down her sides, anchoring her to him as he lost himself in her.

"Celeste," he breathed, his voice raw with emotion, with need.

She leaned forward, pressing her forehead against his, her breath mingling with his in the steamy air, her heart racing in time with his. His name trembled on her lips, a whisper, a plea, as he filled her completely, body and soul.

The world outside this moment no longer existed. There was no past, no future—only now.

The tension coiled tighter, higher, until she could no longer hold back. The heat, the pressure, the exquisite ache of him moving inside her—everything shattered into blissful release.

A cry escaped her lips as the waves of pleasure crashed over her, pulling her under, drowning her in sensation. Andrew followed a heartbeat later, groaning her name as he thrust deep, holding her against him as his own release overtook him.

They clung to each other as their bodies trembled, their hearts pounding in unison. The water rippled around them, their breath coming in ragged gasps as they slowly came back down from the dizzying heights of passion.

Celeste buried her face in the crook of his neck, pressing soft, lingering kisses against his damp skin. Andrew's hands slid up her back, holding her close, as if he couldn't bear to let her go.

"That was…" she murmured, still breathless.

"Incredible," he finished for her, tilting her chin up to claim her lips in a slow, reverent kiss.

For a long moment, they simply held each other in the warm water, the night stretching endlessly around them, cocooning them in the quiet intimacy of their mutual attraction. The candlelight flickered across their damp skin, casting golden reflections over the rippling surface. Neither of them spoke; words felt unnecessary. Instead, they let their bodies remain entwined, their breathing slow and steady, matching the gentle rise and fall of the water around them.

As the warmth of the bath began to fade, Andrew shifted, pressing a lingering kiss to Celeste's bare shoulder. "Come on, beautiful," he murmured.

He stood and stepped out of the tub, droplets glistening as they trailed down the hard lines of his body. Grabbing a thick, plush towel, he quickly dried himself before turning back to Celeste, his gaze filled with tenderness.

Without a word, he reached for her, lifting her effortlessly from the water. She let out a small, surprised laugh, but it quickly faded into a sigh as he wrapped her in the towel, his hands smoothing it over her curves with slow, deliberate strokes. He took his time, drying every inch of her with reverence, pressing soft kisses against her damp skin as he worked.

"You're taking such good care of me," she whispered, tilting her head to look up at him.

Andrew's lips curled into a smile. "I intend to keep doing so."

Once she was dry, he scooped her into his arms again, carrying her back to bed as though she weighed nothing. He laid her down gently, slipping in behind her, his chest moulding perfectly against her back. His arms wrapped around her, his lips brushing one last kiss against the nape of her neck.

They drifted into sleep, the scent of each other, the warmth of their shared embrace, lulling them into a deep, contented slumber.

Chapter Fifteen

The first rays of dawn crept through the curtains, casting a soft golden glow across the room. Celeste stirred, stretching slightly, feeling the warmth of Andrew's body still wrapped around her.

His arms tightened instinctively, pulling her closer.

A slow, playful smile curved her lips. Pressing back against him, she felt the unmistakable hardness of his arousal pressing against her bottom. A shiver of anticipation ran through her, heat pooling deep in her core.

Andrew let out a low groan, his breath warm against her ear. His hands, large and strong, slid up her body, cupping her breasts, his thumbs brushing over her sensitive peaks.

"Celeste," he rasped, his voice thick with sleep and desire.

She arched into his touch, her breath hitching as he kneaded her breasts with slow, languid strokes.

"Good morning," she whispered teasingly, pressing herself more firmly against him.

Andrew chuckled, the sound deep and husky. "It's about to be."

Andrew's mouth lingered at the delicate curve of Celeste's neck, his lips pressing hot, open-mouthed kisses along her skin. His breath was warm and ragged, his need for her evident in the way his hands moved over her body—possessive, reverent, and slow, as if savouring every inch of her.

Celeste let out a soft, breathy moan as his fingers traced down her stomach, teasing the sensitive skin just above the place she ached for him most. She pushed back against him instinctively, her body already craving more.

Andrew groaned, his hands gripping her hips as he positioned himself behind her, his arousal pressing against her warmth. "You're so damn sexy," he murmured against her ear, his voice husky with desire.

He teased her, sliding the head of his length against her slick folds, drawing another gasp from her lips. He moved torturously slow, coaxing whimpers from her until she was trembling in his arms.

"Andrew," she pleaded, her fingers gripping the sheets. "Please."

That one word undid him.

With a deep, guttural groan, he guided himself inside her, inch by inch, stretching her, filling her completely. Celeste let out a shuddering moan, her head tilting back against his shoulder as her body welcomed him.

He started slow, savouring the way she felt around him, the intoxicating tightness of her warmth gripping him like a vice. He kissed her shoulder, her neck, the curve of her jaw, his breath ragged as he fought for control.

But Celeste wanted more.

She rolled her hips against him, meeting his thrusts, urging him deeper. A growl rumbled in his chest as he tightened his grip on her waist, his movements growing more urgent.

The rhythm between them became faster, more intense, their bodies moving in perfect sync. The soft sounds of their lovemaking filled the room—the rustle of sheets, the slick slide of skin against skin, the breathless moans, and whispered names.

Celeste felt herself spiralling, pleasure coiling tighter and tighter within her, her body shaking with need. Andrew reached between her legs, his fingers finding the sensitive bundle of nerves at her core, circling it with expert precision.

Her moans turned into desperate cries as the pressure inside her built to an unbearable peak.

"That's it, baby," Andrew groaned, his own restraint slipping as he drove into her harder, deeper, the intensity of his movements pushing them both to the edge.

Celeste gasped, her body tensing as the first wave of release crashed over her, pleasure blinding and overwhelming. She cried out his name as her walls clenched around him, pulling him deeper into her ecstasy.

With a final, shuddering thrust, Andrew followed, his body tensing as he found his own release, a deep, guttural moan escaping his lips as he poured himself into her.

For a long moment, they remained tangled together, their bodies slick with sweat, their hearts pounding in perfect harmony. Andrew pressed a tender kiss to her shoulder before gently rolling her onto her side to face him, keeping her close.

Breathless and spent, Celeste nestled into his embrace, his arms wrapping securely around her.

"That was…" she trailed off, her voice still shaky from the aftershocks of pleasure.

Andrew chuckled, kissing the top of her head. "Incredible."

She smiled, pressing a lingering kiss to his chest, right over his heartbeat. "Mmm. Best wake-up call ever."

Andrew chuckled, his arms tightening around her, holding her close. His voice was warm with promise as he murmured, "Just wait until tomorrow morning."

A soft, contented sigh escaped her lips as she nestled against him, their bodies still entwined. The steady rhythm of his heartbeat, the warmth of his skin against hers—it was all so easy, so natural.

Sleep pulled them both under once more, Celeste's lips still resting against his chest, as if even in dreams, she never wanted to let go.

Their brief slumber did little to quell the hunger simmering between them. When Celeste stirred again, her lips still resting against Andrew's chest, she felt his strong arms tighten around her instinctively, as if he couldn't bear to let her go.

She smiled against his skin, placing a soft kiss over his heartbeat. "Morning again."

Andrew chuckled, pressing a kiss to the top of her head. "Seems we can't get enough sleep… or each other."

With effortless strength, he shifted, sliding out of bed and scooping her up into his arms.

"Shower," he murmured.

She wrapped her arms around his neck, laughing softly as he carried her into the bathroom. The steam from the warm water already filled the space, the scent of lavender and musk curling in the air.

He set her down under the gentle spray, reaching for a bar of soap and lathering his hands before gliding them over her skin. At first, his touch was innocent, his large hands moving with slow, soothing strokes across her shoulders, down her arms, across her back.

But as he reached her stomach, his fingers splayed, tracing the dip of her waist before sliding lower. His ministrations became less about cleansing and more about exploring.

Celeste shivered despite the warmth, tilting her head back as his touch ignited a familiar ache. "Andrew…"

His lips found the spot just beneath her ear, his breath hot against her damp skin. "I know," he whispered, his voice raw with need. "I can't stop touching you."

She turned in his arms, her hands sliding up his wet, muscled chest, fingers tracing the hard planes of his body. She kissed him with fervour, her lips moulding to his, their mouths moving together in a sensual dance.

"I can't seem to stop wanting you," she murmured between kisses, pressing herself against him, feeling the rigid evidence of his desire against her belly.

Andrew groaned, his grip tightening around her waist. "I feel the same." His voice was thick with desperation. "I need to be inside you again."

Without another word, he grasped the backs of her thighs and lifted her effortlessly. Celeste gasped, her arms winding around his neck as she instinctively wrapped her legs around his waist.

She felt him, thick and ready, pressing against her entrance. Their eyes met, raw emotion passing between them, and then—with one smooth, powerful thrust—he claimed her once more.

A cry escaped her lips as he filled her completely, stretching her, consuming her.

Andrew buried his face in her neck, groaning as he began to move, each thrust deep and deliberate, rocking her against the tiled wall. The warm water cascaded over them, but neither noticed, lost in the heat of each other.

Celeste clung to him, her nails digging into his shoulders, her breath coming in ragged gasps as pleasure built between them once more.

Their bodies moved in perfect sync, the rhythm of their lovemaking as natural as breathing. The slick slide of wet skin, the intoxicating press of lips, teeth, and tongues—it was overwhelming, all-consuming.

"Celeste," Andrew rasped, his pace growing erratic, his control slipping as he neared the edge.

She was right there with him, her body trembling, her head falling back against the tiles as wave after wave of pleasure coiled tight inside her.

And then, in a blinding rush, they shattered together.

Celeste cried out his name as her release crashed over her, her walls clenching around him, milking his own pleasure from him. Andrew groaned, his body tensing, his grip on her tightening as he followed her over the edge.

For a long moment, they simply held each other, their bodies trembling in the aftermath, their hearts pounding in unison.

Then, slowly, Andrew lowered her back onto her feet, pressing a tender kiss to her lips.

"That," she panted, pressing her forehead against his, "was the best shower I've ever had."

He grinned, brushing a wet strand of hair from her cheek. "We might have to make it a morning tradition."

She laughed, resting her hands against his chest, her fingers tracing lazy circles over his skin. "I don't think I'd survive."

Andrew smirked, his eyes dark with amusement and something deeper. He caught her lips in a slow, teasing kiss, his breath warm as he murmured against her mouth, "Oh, sweetheart, you underestimate me."

She shivered at the promise in his voice, but before she could respond, he wrapped her in a soft, fluffy towel and dried her off with a gentleness that sent warmth pooling in her chest. Once she was warm and dry, he scooped her up effortlessly and carried her back to bed.

Celeste barely had time to sigh in contentment before exhaustion tugged at her once more. Her body melted into the mattress, the scent of Andrew still lingering on her skin as she drifted into a deep, dreamless sleep.

Meanwhile, Andrew pulled on a pair of track pants and padded to the kitchen, the morning sun casting golden streaks across the floor. He moved with quiet efficiency, cracking eggs into a pan, the sizzle of bacon filling the air. He toasted some bread, sliced a ripe tomato, and arranged everything neatly on two plates.

Satisfied, he set the table, taking a moment to admire his work. A small smile played on his lips. He wasn't a chef by any means, but he wanted to take care of Celeste—to show her, in little ways, just how much she was beginning to mean to him.

Once everything was ready, he returned to the bedroom, leaning down to brush a few strands of hair from her face.

"Sweetheart," he whispered, nudging her gently.

She stirred slightly, a sleepy hum escaping her lips. "Mm…"

Andrew chuckled softly, pressing a kiss to her temple. "Breakfast is ready."

At the mention of food, Celeste cracked one eye open, her lips curving into a drowsy smile. "You cooked?"

"Of course. I figured after the night we had; you'd need some fuel." His voice was full of playful arrogance, and Celeste laughed, stretching lazily beneath the sheets.

"Mmm. Now that's what I call a perfect man."

Andrew smirked, offering her his hand. "Come on, gorgeous. Let's eat before it gets cold."

Chapter Sixteen

Celeste stretched again, her movements slow and unhurried, a soft hum escaping her lips as she finally slid out of bed. The morning sunlight poured through the windows, bathing the room in a golden glow, casting a halo around her tousled hair. She padded toward the bathroom, completely unaware of the way Andrew's eyes followed her every step, his gaze darkening with quiet admiration.

He stood by the doorway, one of his oversized T-shirts dangling from his fingers, his expression unreadable as he watched her. The shirt would drape perfectly over her tall, graceful frame, and for a brief moment, he imagined her curled up in it, lost in his scent, as if she belonged to him in every possible way.

Before she could disappear into the bathroom, he stepped forward, slipping the shirt over her head in one smooth motion. The soft fabric fell just to the tops of her thighs, skimming her skin in a way that made something tighten in his chest.

"Much better," he murmured, his voice huskier than before. His fingers brushed her bare arms as he adjusted the hem, but his touch lingered, as if savouring the effortless beauty she exuded—even in something as simple as his clothes.

Celeste tilted her head up, her lips curving in amusement. "Possessive much?"

Andrew smirked, his hands settling at her waist. "Just making sure you're properly dressed," he said, though the heat in his gaze suggested something else entirely.

Celeste let out a soft, teasing laugh, rising onto her toes to brush a kiss against his jaw. "Come on, perfect man. You promised me breakfast."

With a low chuckle, Andrew laced his fingers through hers and led her toward the kitchen—though in that moment, food was the last thing on his mind.

They made their way to the dining table, their plates piled high with the hearty breakfast Andrew had prepared. The conversation flowed easily between bites of crispy bacon and fresh coffee, but there was something deeper in the air. The connection between them wasn't just physical—it was something more, something that had been growing with every shared smile and stolen touch.

They ate, laughed, and teased each other about their movie preferences, but beneath the light-hearted banter, there was a quiet understanding—a bond that was steadily becoming unbreakable.

The hours passed in a quiet, golden blur, each moment slipping seamlessly into the next. They made love twice more, each time different—Andrew guiding her gently, showing her how many ways mutual pleasure could be shared, how connection could be felt in every sigh, every touch, every whispered word.

By the time the sun began to dip below the horizon, casting the sky in a wash of amber and rose, they were still curled up together on the couch. Their bodies were tangled, their fingers intertwined, the silence between them rich with meaning. Andrew's hand never strayed far from hers—his thumb brushing against her skin now and then—and every subtle touch sent a tender warmth spiralling through her, a reminder that she was desired, wanted and his.

As the night settled, they shared a quiet dinner, the intimacy between them more pronounced. It wasn't just the closeness of their bodies but the quiet, knowing glances exchanged across the table, the unspoken words filling the space between them. Their connection was something deep, something that felt like it could change everything.

Later, as they cleared the plates, Celeste stood hesitantly, her fingers nervously twisting together. Her energy had shifted, and Andrew noticed it immediately. He set his glass down and watched her carefully, sensing that something was on her mind.

"What's on your mind, sweetheart?" he asked, his voice gentle, inviting her to share whatever was troubling her.

Celeste took a deep breath, her heart pounding in her chest. She had never felt this way before—vulnerable, but safe at the same time. She met his gaze, and for the first time, the words came easily, even though they felt like a leap.

"I… I want to learn how to please you with my mouth," she confessed, her voice soft but steady, a quiet honesty in the words.

Andrew's breath caught in his throat, his heart racing at the vulnerability in her confession. He hadn't expected it, but his desire flared at the sincerity in her eyes. His hand tightened around the edge of the table, trying to steady himself.

"Are you sure?" His voice was rougher now, the deep, restrained desire in his tone unmistakable.

Celeste nodded, her body leaning closer to his. "Yes. I want to make you feel as good as you make me feel," she whispered, her words filled with determination.

Andrew's smile deepened, and the intensity in his eyes only grew. "Then let me teach you," he murmured, pulling her gently onto his lap, his voice low and filled with promise.

Celeste's heart raced. There was something about the way he said those words, the way they made her feel both vulnerable and powerful at the same time. With Andrew, she didn't have to be afraid of her own desires. He welcomed them, nurtured them, and made her feel like her pleasure mattered just as much as his.

She was a quick learner, her focus entirely on him as she explored, each movement more confident than the last. With each gentle touch, each careful adjustment, she could see the pleasure in his eyes growing, the tension in his body increasing. She was determined to make him feel as incredible as he had made her feel, and with every breathless murmur of encouragement from him, she found herself lost in the rhythm of their shared experience.

Everything Celeste did seemed to send him into a heightened state of bliss. His breath quickened, his fingers tangled in her hair, and his thighs tensed beneath her. She revelled in the control she had over him; in the way she could bring him to the brink of madness with a single, well-placed touch. Her own pleasure mirrored his, the connection between them intoxicating, almost overwhelming.

When Andrew could finally move again, his chest rising and falling in quick, ragged breaths, he pulled her back into his arms. His hands slid down her body, tracing the curve of her spine, before he kissed her deeply, passionately, as if he couldn't get enough of her.

"You're incredible," he whispered, his voice hoarse, filled with awe. "Absolutely incredible."

Celeste smiled against his lips, the warmth of his words wrapping around her like a blanket. "I'm just getting started," she teased softly, her fingers threading through his hair.

Andrew chuckled, but it was a sound laced with satisfaction, his eyes dark with a mix of adoration and desire. He had never experienced anything like this before.

As he caught his breath, he found himself thinking about how perfect she was. Not just in her beauty, but in the way they fit together. Physically, emotionally—they were a perfect match, something rare, something special.

Her intelligence, her humour, the way she responded to him—he was more certain than ever that Celeste was the one. He didn't want to be with anyone else.

"I don't want this weekend to end," he said softly, his voice filled with a quiet intensity that made her gaze up at him, her eyes mirroring his emotions.

Her smile was gentle but full of understanding. "I don't either," she replied, her hand resting over his heart, the connection between them deepening with the simplicity of the gesture.

But eventually, the weekend did have to end. As Andrew drove Celeste home Sunday afternoon, the reality of their separation loomed closer. He walked her to her door, his steps slow as he tried to prolong their time together.

When they reached her front door, Andrew pulled her into his arms, kissing her slowly, deeply, a kiss filled with all the things he hadn't said. When they finally pulled apart, he rested his forehead against hers.

"Have a good week," he murmured softly, his voice warm, a promise lingering in his words.

Celeste paused, her lips curving into a soft, knowing smile, though her eyes held something deeper, a flicker of vulnerability that she hadn't shared with anyone before. She let out a small sigh, as though bracing herself before speaking the words that had been on her mind all week. "I will," she replied, her voice a little softer than usual, a quiet sincerity laced with longing. Her gaze softened as she glanced up at him, her lips parting slightly as she added, "I'll miss you."

Andrew's heart swelled with something unspoken, a rush of emotion he couldn't quite name. In that simple confession, Celeste had given him a glimpse into her own feelings—feelings he had hoped were there but hearing them made them all the more real. He leaned in for one last kiss, his lips brushing hers in a tender, lingering touch that seemed to hold all the emotions they hadn't fully expressed. When they pulled away, he stepped back reluctantly, watching her disappear into her home, knowing that the week ahead would stretch out endlessly, far too long for his liking.

The days that followed seemed to move in slow motion. Celeste and Andrew both felt the weight of their separation in different ways. The hours felt longer, the minutes stretching out as if time itself was determined to make them both wait. By Friday afternoon, Andrew was a bundle of restless energy. He could hardly focus on anything other than the ache in his chest, the urgent need to see Celeste again. He had been patient all week, but now the feeling of longing had become a physical ache. He needed to see her, to feel the warmth of her presence again.

Unable to keep it inside any longer, he reached for his phone. His fingers hovered over the screen for a moment before he typed out a simple, direct message.

Please tell me I can see you tonight.

It only took a few moments for her reply to come through, and Andrew's breath hitched as he read the words.

Wild horse couldn't keep me away.

A smile broke across his face as he read her message, the anticipation flooding through him. Without wasting another second, he texted her back:

Can't wait to see you.

Celeste was already on her way by the time Andrew finished his message. The drive was quick for her, the streets humming under the wheels of her car as she thought of nothing but being with him again. She arrived at his apartment building, her heart pounding as she stepped out of the car and made her way up the elevator to his door.

As soon as she arrived, the door swung open before she could even knock. Andrew stood there, looking just as restless as she had imagined. Without a word, he pulled her into his arms, his lips capturing hers in a kiss that was desperate and hungry, as though he had been starved for her touch all week. The kiss was intense, filled with a yearning that neither of them could contain, and it left her breathless as he gently tugged her inside, the door clicking shut behind them.

The weekend passed in a whirlwind of closeness. They fell into their rhythm again, spending hours wrapped up in each other's company, the outside world nothing but a distant memory. They shared quiet moments of tenderness, stealing kisses when their lips met, and spent the nights tangled up together in a blissful haze. Time felt like it was theirs again, and it was as if the world outside their bubble ceased to exist.

As the following weekend rolled around, things shifted slightly. They were no longer just two people sneaking around, savouring the moments they had together. Now, they were becoming part of a larger world, and that world included their friends. Andrew had arranged for a group outing with Celeste and a few of their close friends: Kathleen, George, Bryan, William, and Harrison.

The evening was full of laughter and conversation, and Andrew found himself enjoying the company of his friends, but there was an underlying tension he couldn't quite shake. He and Celeste had been so wrapped up in their own bubble that the idea of other people knowing about their relationship hadn't seemed necessary—until now. They talked, laughed, and shared stories, but every now and then, Andrew's gaze would flicker toward Celeste, catching her eye across the table. A silent understanding passed between them, and he could sense that she, too, was wondering about the same thing.

Later that evening, after everyone else had left and the laughter of their friends had faded into the night, Celeste and Andrew found themselves alone once again. They sat together on the couch, the silence between them a comfortable one, yet still heavy with unspoken thoughts. Andrew leaned back against the cushions, glancing over at Celeste, his expression thoughtful.

"So," he began, his voice casual but with an undercurrent of something deeper, "what do you think? Should we tell people about us?"

Celeste looked at him for a moment, her fingers toying with the edge of her glass. She took a deep breath, a small sigh escaping her lips as she considered his question. Her eyes met his with a thoughtful expression, as though weighing the decision carefully.

"I don't know…" she began, her voice hesitant but clear. "It feels right when we're together, you know? But the moment we tell people, things might change. There are always expectations, assumptions… I don't think we're ready for that yet."

Andrew nodded, his eyes softening as he understood her perspective. He had been thinking the same thing. The magic of their relationship was in the quiet moments they shared, free of judgment or pressure. They were still finding their footing, and they both knew that the world outside could complicate things in ways they weren't ready for.

"I agree," he said softly, his hand reaching for hers. "I don't want anyone else's opinions clouding what we have. Not yet. I think we'll know when the time is right."

Celeste squeezed his hand gently, a reassuring smile crossing her lips. "Exactly. When we're ready, we'll tell them. But for now…" She leaned in, pressing a soft kiss to his lips. "Let's just enjoy this."

Andrew smiled against her lips, feeling a wave of relief wash over him. They were on the same page, and that made everything feel more secure. There was no rush, no need to label things prematurely. What they had was theirs, and that was enough—for now.

Chapter Seventeen

The weekend of Celeste's twenty-fifth birthday had finally arrived, bringing with it the promise of a night filled with excitement, laughter, and celebration. Her parents had spared no expense, throwing her a lavish party that gathered friends, family, and familiar faces from every corner of her life.

The anticipation was almost too much to bear.

Tonight wasn't just about marking another year—it was the night she and Andrew would finally go public with their relationship. No more stolen moments, no more keeping their feelings a secret. She was ready for everyone to know, ready to celebrate her birthday with the man who set her heart racing.

But was she ready for everything that came with it?

She knew Andrew cared for her—deeply. She could see it in his eyes, feel it in the way he touched her, the way he always seemed to be near. But love? The kind that consumed; that left no room for doubt. She wasn't sure. Not yet.

She knew she loved him.

A flicker of uncertainty tightened her chest.

Shaking the thought away, she glanced at the clock, then at the front door.

Where is he?

The chatter of guests spilled in from the terrace and backyard, their laughter weaving through the elegant ambiance of the softly lit house. Golden fairy lights twinkled against the evening sky, casting a warm glow over the space. Celeste smoothed the sleeve of her dress, the silky fabric cool against her skin. She imagined Andrew stepping through the door, his eyes lighting up the moment he saw her, and the thought brought a small, excited smile to her lips.

But the door opened—and it wasn't Andrew.

George stepped inside, his signature confident grin in place. His eyes swept the room before locking onto her.

"Hey there, birthday girl," he drawled, his voice effortlessly smooth, laced with a flirtation that Celeste had long learned to brush off.

She smiled politely. "Hey, George."

Her focus shifted toward the door again, her excitement undeterred. She was still waiting, still expecting him.

George, however, had other plans.

He moved closer, closing the space between them with a casual ease, his presence suddenly more intense than usual. Celeste felt a shift in the air—a subtle tension creeping in. His hand came to rest on the back of the couch beside her, his body angled toward hers in a way that made it impossible to ignore.

"You look stunning tonight," he murmured, his gaze flickering down her dress before returning to her face.

Celeste offered a polite nod, trying not to stiffen. "Thanks. Just having a quiet moment before things really get going."

"I get that. Big night. Twenty-five." He grinned.

She laughed, momentarily relaxing. "Getting old, huh?"

"Never." His voice was lower now, his body shifting even closer.

The air thickened. Celeste's heart picked up, but not in the way it did with Andrew. This was different. Uneasy.

"You know," George whispered, his breath brushing her ear, "I've always thought you were… special."

Something in his tone sent a shiver down her spine—not the pleasant kind.

"George, I—"

Before she could finish, his lips were on hers.

The kiss was sudden. Unwanted.

Shock paralysed her.

Her body went rigid, her mind racing to catch up with what was happening. There was no warmth, no spark, nothing but the overwhelming realisation that this was wrong. She wasn't kissing him back. She wasn't even moving—just frozen in disbelief.

She only wanted Andrew.

They had agreed tonight would be their night. Their moment.

And now—

Celeste wrenched herself free, stepping back as though burned. Her chest heaved, the sting of betrayal and fury bubbling to the surface.

"What the hell was that?" she snapped, her voice sharp with anger.

George took a step back, looking sheepish, his confidence faltering. "I—I thought—"

"No." The word was final, cutting through his stammering like a blade. "You thought what, exactly? That because I've been nice to you, it meant this?" She motioned between them, disgust tightening her throat.

"I didn't mean to—"

"Didn't mean to?" she echoed, her voice rising. "I never encouraged this, George. I told you I wasn't interested. And you still—" She swallowed hard, fury and hurt warring inside her. "You completely disregarded my feelings. That was wrong."

George ran a hand through his hair; his face clouded with regret. "I'm sorry, Celeste. I misread—"

"No, you didn't." She shook her head; arms crossed tightly over her chest. "You wanted what you wanted, and you took it. That's not a mistake. That's a choice."

He exhaled heavily, nodding. "You're right." His voice was softer now, laced with genuine remorse. "I messed up. I'm sorry."

Celeste held his gaze for a beat longer before shaking her head. "Just… go."

She didn't wait to see if he listened.

Her legs felt unsteady as she turned away, the weight of the moment crashing down on her. Her stomach twisted into knots.

Where was Andrew?

Her heart pounded with urgency. She had to tell him—there was no question about it.

The moment he arrived, she would. No hesitation. No second-guessing.

She just needed him to walk through that door.

Andrew gripped the steering wheel so tightly his knuckles turned white. His pulse thundered in his ears, his chest aching with a pain so sharp it nearly stole his breath.

Celeste.

He had let his guard down for her. He had believed in her.

The image of her in George's arms burned in his mind, searing through him like a brand. The way they stood so close, the way George leaned in—it was enough to make his stomach twist with betrayal. And the worst part? She hadn't pushed him away.

He had thought they were building something real, something different from the love he had lost before. After two years of shielding his heart, of convincing himself that he didn't need love, Celeste had slipped past his defences. He had trusted her, let himself imagine a future with her. But in the end, she was no different from Sarah.

Sarah—his ex-wife, the woman who had shattered his faith in love with a cruel, unforgivable truth.

The memory of her betrayal clung to him like a shadow, refusing to fade. It hadn't been just one mistake, one moment of weakness. No, Sarah had been unfaithful multiple times throughout their eight-year marriage, each deception cutting deeper than the last. By the time he had uncovered the full extent of her lies, his trust had already been chipped away, piece by piece, until there was nothing left to salvage.

It had destroyed the life he had built, forced him to start over, to rebuild himself from the ruins of a love that had never truly been his. And in the aftermath, he had sworn— never again. Never again would he allow himself to be that vulnerable, that blind.

And yet, here he was, sitting behind the wheel of his car, drowning in the same gut-wrenching pain.

Only this time… this time, it was worse.

Because with Sarah, the cracks had been there all along. Their marriage had been unravelling long before the final betrayal. A part of him had known, even if he hadn't wanted to admit it. But Celeste? Celeste? He hadn't seen this coming. He had believed in her. Believed in them.

He had trusted her.

And now, that trust lay in pieces at his feet.

A bitter laugh escaped his lips, sharp and hollow in the stillness of the car. Fool me once, shame on you. Fool me twice…

His grip tightened on the steering wheel, his knuckles white from the pressure. His pulse pounded at his temples, a dull, insistent ache that only fuelled the storm raging inside him. He swallowed against the knot in his throat, but the pain remained, thick and suffocating. His chest burned—not from anger, not even from betrayal, but from the bitter sting of hope that had been ripped away.

He had let his guard down. For her.

And she had shattered him.

He clenched his jaw and started the engine. He wasn't going to stay here, wasn't going to put on a fake smile and pretend everything was fine while his heart was breaking.

No, he was leaving.

His fingers trembled as he reached for the ignition, hesitating for just a second—just long enough for doubt to creep in. What if he had misunderstood? What if there was an explanation?

But then he saw it again, clear as day. George leaning in, his hand too familiar on Celeste's back, the way she hadn't immediately pulled away.

A bitter laugh scraped his throat. Explanations didn't matter. Trust did.

And his had just been shattered.

The engine roared to life, drowning out the sound of his heart breaking.

Because if he stayed, he might just make the mistake of hoping she'd explain. That there was some logical reason for what he saw. That she hadn't betrayed him.

But hope was for fools. And Andrew had been a fool for the last time.

Celeste spent the rest of the night in a fog of confusion, her heart heavy with unease. She tried to lose herself in the celebration—the hum of conversation, the clinking of glasses, the bursts of laughter that should have felt warm and familiar.

But everything was muted, distant, as if she were watching her own birthday party from behind glass. The laughter sounded hollow, the music a dull thrum against her skin. Someone called her name, and she forced a smile, nodding at whatever was said. But her mind was elsewhere, fixated on a single, unshakable thought.

Where was Andrew? Her eyes kept flicking toward the door, searching for Andrew. But he never came.

The party continued around her, a blur of voices and clinking glasses, but her mind was elsewhere. Every laugh that left her lips felt hollow; every smile forced. She checked her phone again and again, hoping—praying—for a message from him. But there was nothing.

Where was he?

A knot tightened in her stomach. Something was wrong. She could feel it.

She kept telling herself she had to tell him everything—had to explain what happened with George. She valued honesty, and with Andrew, it mattered even more. She knew what his ex-wife had done to him, how deeply betrayal had scarred him. The last thing she wanted was for him to hear about George's mistake from someone else. He needed to hear it from her.

But how could she explain when he wasn't here? When he wasn't answering.

With every unanswered call, every unread message, the sick feeling in her gut deepened.

Had something happened? Was he okay? Had he chosen to ignore her?

Or… had he chosen not to come at all?

By the time the party wound down and the last guest had left, Celeste was exhausted—physically, emotionally—but there was no relief, no escape from the turmoil twisting inside her.

Alone in her old bedroom in her parents' home, she kicked off her heels and sank onto the edge of the bed, staring at her phone. Still nothing.

With a restless sigh, she pushed to her feet and crossed the room, pulling back the curtain to peer out into the dark night. Her gaze swept over the quiet street, searching.

Andrew's car was nowhere to be seen.

Her fingers curled around the curtain as a lump formed in her throat.

She had waited for him.

And he hadn't come.

Why?

The thought sent a chill through her. Andrew wasn't the type to disappear without a word. He was reliable, steady, the kind of man who showed up. So why hadn't he?

She grabbed her phone and called him—again. Her breath hitched as the call rang and rang, each unanswered tone tightening the knot in her stomach.

She tried a text instead. Her hands trembled as she typed the message.

Andrew, where are you? I need to talk to you. Please call me.

She sent it, then stared at the screen, willing it to light up with a reply.

Seconds passed. Then minutes. Nothing.

An uneasy weight pressed down on her chest.

Something wasn't just wrong.

Something was very wrong.

Chapter Eighteen

Celeste barely slept. Every hour that passed without hearing from Andrew deepened the sick feeling in her stomach. She had called, texted—over and over—but there was nothing. No reply. No missed calls. No indication that he had even seen her messages.

Something had to be wrong.

By the time the sun rose, exhaustion clung to her but worry overpowered it. Andrew wasn't the type to disappear like this. Even if he was upset, even if something had happened—he would have said something. Unless… he couldn't.

The thought chilled her. Maybe he was sick. Maybe he was hurt. Maybe he needed her.

Determined, she threw on a sweater over her tank top, slid into sneakers, and grabbed her keys. She wasn't going to sit around waiting for a response that might never come. If Andrew wouldn't answer, she would go to him.

The elevator ride to Andrew's penthouse felt like forever. Celeste's stomach churned with nerves as she stepped into the quiet hallway, the hum of the city muffled by the luxury of the high-rise.

She knocked. Then knocked again.

No answer.

Her pulse pounded in her ears. Was he even home?

She lifted her hand to knock once more when—finally—she heard movement inside. The lock clicked. A moment later, the door swung open.

Andrew stood there.

Dishevelled. Exhausted.

And colder than she had ever seen him.

Relief flooded through her first. He was okay. Whatever had kept him from answering, it wasn't because he was lying in a hospital bed somewhere. Without hesitation, she stepped forward, wrapping her arms around him, pressing herself against his chest.

"Thank God you're okay," she murmured against him. "I've been worried sick."

But his arms didn't come around her.

He didn't melt into her embrace.

Instead, he stood stiffly, rigid, his body like stone beneath her hands.

Something was wrong.

Celeste pulled back slightly, tilting her head up to meet his gaze.

"Andrew?"

His face was unreadable—cold, detached, nothing like the man who had kissed her senseless just days ago, the man who had looked at her like she was his whole world.

Now, there was nothing.

No warmth. No softness.

Just ice.

"What are you doing here?" His voice was flat, emotionless.

Celeste blinked, startled by his tone.

"What do you mean? You weren't answering your phone. I thought something happened to you."

His expression didn't change. If anything, his jaw tightened, his blue eyes darkening into something unfamiliar.

"I'm fine."

The words were clipped, dismissive.

She studied him, trying to make sense of it.

"Then why didn't you answer me?"

Andrew let out a bitter laugh, but there was no humour in it. He turned away, running a hand through his hair before pacing a few steps into the room.

Celeste hesitated for only a second before stepping inside, closing the door behind her. She didn't wait for an invitation—she had never needed one before.

"I was at my birthday party, waiting for you," she reminded him softly. "You never came. And now you're—" She gestured toward him, toward the ice in his voice. "What's going on?"

Andrew scoffed, shaking his head.

"What's going on?" he echoed, voice tight with barely restrained emotion. His lips twisted into a smirk, but it held no warmth.

"You wanted to lose your virginity before your twenty-fifth birthday. Mission accomplished."

The words sliced through her, leaving her breathless.

Celeste took a step back, as if physical distance could protect her from the venom in his voice.

"Andrew, I don't—"

Her voice caught.

He was shutting her out.

On purpose.

And then he said the words that shattered her.

"You were just a hookup. There was never a future for us."

The world tilted.

Celeste inhaled sharply as if he had struck her.

Her stomach twisted, bile rising in her throat.

"What?"

Andrew still wouldn't look at her.

She searched his face, desperate for any sign that this was some cruel joke, that he didn't mean it. But there was nothing.

No hesitation. No regret.

Just a wall so high she could barely see the man she had fallen for on the other side.

"You don't mean that," she whispered, her voice cracking.

His expression didn't change. He finally met her eyes, but his gaze was empty, hollow.

"I do."

Tears burned the backs of her eyes.

"Andrew, please—"

"You should go," he said flatly.

"You got what you wanted."

The finality in his tone was like a slap.

Celeste swallowed against the lump in her throat. Her hands trembled at her sides, but she forced herself to straighten her spine.

She had come here to find him, to make sure he was okay.

But now, standing in front of him, she realised she had made a terrible mistake.

He didn't want her here.

Didn't want her, period.

She waited. Just for a second.

Just to see if he would stop her.

If he would take it back.

But he didn't.

So, with her heart shattering in her chest, Celeste turned and walked out the door.

Each step felt heavier than the last, like she was dragging the weight of her broken heart behind her.

And when the door clicked shut behind her, she let the first tear fall.

As soon as the door clicked shut behind Celeste, Andrew stood frozen, staring at the spot where she had just been. The weight of the silence that followed felt suffocating, thick, and oppressive, pressing down on him with an intensity he couldn't escape. For a fleeting moment, he wanted to run after her, to stop her, to pull her back into his arms and apologise, tell her that he didn't mean a word of what he'd just said.

No, she kissed George.

His pulse quickened. His chest tightened as if the breath had been knocked out of him. He could still feel the warmth of her against him, the softness of her body, the gentle way she had leaned into him. And then he saw her face. The pain, the shock, the absolute devastation reflected in her eyes. The same eyes that had once looked at him with so much hope, so much trust. Now they were empty, vacant, as if she had been hollowed out by his words.

God, what have I done?

You protected your heart, that's what you did.

You protected yourself from another cheating female.

The thought came to him like a harsh whisper, an insidious justification that didn't sit right. It didn't matter that it had been him who had decided to push her away, to make her feel like she was just another conquest. He had felt the sharp sting of betrayal just imagining her with George, even though it wasn't like that, even though he hadn't bothered to ask her to explain.

Why didn't I ask her to explain?

He clenched his fists at his sides, the knot in his stomach twisting. It was true. He had jumped to conclusions. He had seen her kiss George at that party, and he hadn't given her a chance to clarify. Instead, he had let his fears drive him, blinding him to the reality of the situation. Why hadn't he taken the time to listen to her side, to ask what had really happened? She had been waiting for him. She had wanted him there.

He could feel the ache in his chest—a dull throb that had nothing to do with his heart physically breaking and everything to do with how badly he had hurt her. The warmth of their time together, the softness in her voice, it all seemed so far away now. He had wanted to shout after her, to beg her to stop, to explain himself, to tell her that none of this was real—that he never wanted to hurt her. But the words had already come out, cold and cutting, and now they hung in the air like an insurmountable barrier between them.

Why did I say that?

But maybe it was for the best. Maybe it was better to protect himself than to keep putting his heart on the line. It had been easier to let her think she meant nothing to him than to admit the truth to himself. She doesn't need me to complicate her life, he thought bitterly. I don't need her to complicate mine.

The truth was, he was terrified. Terrified of feeling too much, of letting his guard down, of falling into something real when he didn't trust it. When he didn't trust himself. His heart ached, but it was a self-inflicted wound. He could feel his pride clawing at him, telling him to stand firm, to leave things as they were. It was easier this way. If he chased after her now, what would he do when the next thing went wrong? What if she pulled away again? What if he ended up disappointed? No, it was better to protect his heart, even if it meant hurting her in the process.

His hand ran through his dishevelled hair, the tightness in his chest intensifying. He had done the unthinkable—pushed her away, told her she meant nothing when every fibre of his being screamed the opposite. He cared. He cared more than he had ever cared about anything. He had wanted to be with her, to hold her, to make her feel safe and cherished. But then the thought of George kissing her—the kiss—had been too much to bear. He had let his insecurities and doubts consume him.

As he stood there, the silence swallowing the space, his legs trembled, and for the first time, he felt the weight of his own vulnerability. He wasn't just hurting from seeing her walk away. He was hurting because he had pushed her away. He had built the wall, not her. And now she was gone, walking away with pieces of his heart.

His mind replayed the moment—her voice, cracking, pleading with him. "You don't mean that." The agony in her tone had been like a knife to his chest. But it had been too late. The damage had already been done, and now he was standing there, in the quiet of his penthouse, with the suffocating silence pressing in on him.

She looked shattered. Her face was pale, her eyes red from unshed tears. The way she had looked at him—so broken, so confused—was etched into his mind. He had wanted to comfort her, to tell her that he was sorry, that it wasn't her, it was him. But he had let the fear take over, had built the walls around his own heart instead of letting her in.

I can't lose her.

He took a few shaky steps toward the door, his hand reaching for the handle, but he froze. His pulse thudded in his ears. The temptation to chase after her—to make it right—was unbearable. But what if she didn't want him to come after her? What if she never wanted to see him again after everything he had said?

I've ruined it.

His chest tightened again, and the tears he had been holding back for so long burned at the back of his eyes. He felt like an idiot. He had let his own demons tear apart something beautiful, something that could have been real. And now she was gone. And maybe she was never coming back.

The seconds stretched into what felt like eternity, his body frozen in indecision, his heart pounding in his chest.

He turned away from the door, dragging a hand down his face. It was the worst feeling, the kind of hollow emptiness that only came from knowing you had broken something so fragile—and that it might never be fixed. And it was all his fault.

This felt ten times worse than losing his marriage, the pain was all-consuming.

He sank onto the couch, his hands trembling as they gripped the armrest. His mind raced with images of Celeste—her smile, the way her hair cascaded over her shoulders, the softness in her voice when she spoke to him. And now, all of that was gone.

He was the one who had let his fear destroy it. And now he had to live with the consequences. But how could he live with the idea that the one person he had cared for, the one person who had gotten under his skin, might be gone forever?

The thought of never seeing her again, of never holding her in his arms, was more than he could bear.

"I love Celeste," he whispered to the empty room. "I messed up badly."

And for the first time in a long time, Andrew felt the weight of his own mistakes pressing down on him.

Chapter Nineteen

It was Wednesday morning, three days after Andrew had shattered her heart. She still didn't understand. She had thought he cared, thought he loved her, but she had been wrong. So wrong.

She knew from the start that getting involved with Andrew meant risking her heart, but he had made her feel special, cared for... even loved. Now, that feeling seemed like a cruel illusion, and she was left to pick up the pieces.

But she had to move on. So, she threw herself into work, burying her pain beneath spreadsheets and reports. Anything to keep her mind off the hurt.

The morning had been busy, just like every other at the bank. Celeste sat at her desk, tapping away at her computer, finishing the last notes from a meeting with a long-time client. The fluorescent lights hummed overhead, and the constant murmur of coworkers discussing loan approvals, account balances, and the occasional gossip provided the soundtrack to her day. Routine. Predictable. Safe.

Her last task was a simple one: double-check some figures and send them off to Richard, her manager. She was wrapping up the report when the sudden bang of the front doors opening echoed across the room.

Celeste looked up, brow furrowed, as hurried footsteps followed. But it wasn't until she noticed movement at the far end of the room that her blood froze.

Masked figures. Four of them, all in black, their faces hidden beneath balaclavas, each gripping a gun.

Time seemed to slow.

Celeste's breath caught as the full weight of the situation sank in. Her mind raced, but her body remained frozen. The bank, for one brief moment, fell silent before chaos erupted. Screams tore through the air as customers scrambled to their feet, stumbling over each other in a frantic attempt to escape. Employees shouted commands, urging everyone to stay down, to remain calm, but their voices only fed the panic.

A voice, sharp and commanding, cut through the noise. "Everyone on the floor! Now!"

Celeste's heart pounded in her chest, but her body wouldn't obey. She had to stay calm. She had to stay invisible.

A manager near the vault, eyes wide with terror, was shoved forward. "Open it," one of the robbers barked.

He hesitated, shaking, before stumbling toward the vault. Celeste's hands trembled, her pulse roaring in her ears. She saw the fear on Richard's face, the way his hands slicked with sweat as he fumbled with the vault's combination.

The door creaked open, but before Richard could access the money, the robbers grew impatient.

Bang!

The gunshot rang out with terrifying clarity, splintering the air. Richard jerked, then collapsed to the floor, lifeless, blood pooling around him.

Celeste's stomach twisted in horror. She tried to suppress the rising panic, forcing herself to focus. Her eyes darted to the floor as she kept her head down, but the knot of dread in her chest tightened with every passing second.

"Stay down! Stay down!" someone yelled, and Celeste instinctively ducked lower into her chair, hoping to remain unnoticed.

But it was too late.

One of the robbers, taller than the rest, moved through the bank with chilling calm. His eyes scanned the room, each deliberate flick of his gaze making Celeste's pulse spike.

Then, his eyes locked on hers.

"You. Get up."

Celeste's blood turned to ice.

Her mind screamed at her to stay still, to disappear into the background, but her body betrayed her. Her heart hammered in her chest, drowning out everything else. She froze, her breath coming in shallow gasps.

The man's gun was trained on her.

Bang!

A shot rang out, too close, too fast. The bullet ricocheted off the ceiling above her, leaving a jagged hole. The room held its breath, the dust settling in the eerie silence that followed.

Celeste had no choice. No time to think. A rough hand grabbed her arm, yanking her from her chair with a terrifying force. She stumbled to her feet, disoriented, the world spinning around her in a blur.

"She's coming with us," the man growled, his voice low and commanding.

Her mind screamed for her to break free, but his grip was like iron. His fingers dug into her arm, dragging her forward. The chaos of the room seemed to fade into the background, muffled, as though she were hearing it underwater.

The doors burst open. Cold air hit her face like a slap. She squinted against the harsh daylight, the street outside a blur of frantic people running in every direction.

A van—black and ominous—was waiting by the curb. The back door swung open, and the man shoved her inside, tossing her onto the floor as though she were nothing more than an object.

Before she could process what had just happened, the door slammed shut. The van's engine roared to life, and the vehicle lurched forward, speeding away from the bank.

Celeste's breath caught in her throat. Her hands trembled uncontrollably in her lap, but she knew she had to stay calm. She had to think. The fear was overwhelming, but she was good at hiding it. She couldn't afford to fall apart now.

The van swerved through the streets, the city blurring by as her pulse hammered in her ears. She sat as still as possible, trying not to draw attention to herself.

Her thoughts flashed to Andrew. Would she ever see him again? Would she survive this?

She glanced out the window, watching the tall buildings, the bustling traffic, the pedestrians going about their day—unaware of the nightmare unfolding just a few metres away.

Her world had been upended in an instant. The terror, the violence—it was too much to process.

But it wasn't over. Not yet. She wasn't dead. Not yet.

And that meant there was still hope. She just had to hold on long enough to find it.

The van came to a stop about an hour later. Her body ached from the hard floor, every bump and jolt sending pain through her limbs. But it wasn't just her body that hurt— it was her mind, struggling to make sense of the chaos, trying to understand the nightmare she found herself in.

She overheard fragments of conversation—two names that stood out. Reece, the leader by the sound of things, and Troy, the man sitting behind her in the van. Troy's gaze burned into her like a predator eyeing its prey, his grin making her skin crawl. He looked at her like she was nothing more than a piece of chocolate on Easter morning, ready to be devoured. The thought made her stomach turn.

When the van finally stopped, she was yanked roughly out of the back. Her knees scraped against the hard pavement as she stumbled, her arms still bound and her mind racing.

Reece, stepping out first, grabbed her arm and helped her to her feet with surprising gentleness, as if his earlier commands hadn't been laced with threat. Then, he turned on Troy, voice sharp and commanding. "Don't hurt her. She's worth a fortune."

That was when it hit her. Reece knew exactly who she was.

Her family's name carried weight. Jonas Beaumont, her father, was a prominent wealth manager—his clients included some of the wealthiest individuals across the globe. Her mother, Dr. Hope Beaumont, a renowned surgeon who had built a reputation in the medical world that commanded respect. Together, they were one of the city's most influential families, their wealth and connections woven into the very fabric of society.

And Celeste? She worked for one of the most prestigious investment banks in the world, managing accounts for clients whose portfolios spanned continents. She had always known that her family's fortune made her a target—a magnet for greed. But never, in her worst nightmares, had she imagined that she would become the very thing others might fight over.

She was yanked forward into an abandoned warehouse, its cold, decaying walls offering little comfort. The floor beneath her was as unforgiving as the rest of the world now felt. They bound her to a metal pillar with harsh ropes, the cold steel pressing against her back as she was forced to sit. Her eyes scanned the room, taking in the dim lighting and the crude lounge area where the four robbers had set up camp. They seemed oddly relaxed for men who had just committed such a violent crime, their voices low as they exchanged laughter, the sound clashing against the cold, silent reality that now surrounded Celeste.

She was just a pawn in their game, a piece to be held for ransom or perhaps used as leverage, but no matter what they intended, the terror of it all was overwhelming. Her thoughts screamed for clarity, but the knots in her stomach only tightened, and the weight of what was happening pressed down on her chest.

She had been a target for the world's greed. But now, Celeste realised, she had become something much darker—a symbol of what could be taken, held hostage, and manipulated. She wasn't sure how she would get out of this, but one thing was certain: she had to survive. She had to hold on.

Her family's name might have made her a target, but it was that same name, that same legacy, that she would cling to in the hope that someone would come looking for her.

Chapter Twenty

Late Wednesday afternoon, the sun streamed through the blinds of Andrew's office, casting long shadows across his desk. He sat there, lost in his thoughts, the weight of the week pressing heavily on his shoulders. His mind was elsewhere, wandering through memories he couldn't seem to escape. Celeste—he couldn't stop thinking about her. He had tried to tell himself that pushing her away was the right thing to do, that his harsh words had set them both free. But deep down, he knew the truth: he was a fool. And he missed her. More than he cared to admit.

A frantic knock on the door pulled him from his reverie, jolting him from the fog in his mind. Before he could even respond, the door swung open, and Kathleen stormed in, breath coming in quick, panicked bursts. Her face was streaked with tears, her eyes wide with fear.

"You need to see this," she said urgently, thrusting her phone into his hands. Her hands trembled as she spoke, her voice shaky and strained.

Andrew blinked, trying to make sense of the sudden shift in the room's energy. His heart began to race, the tension in the air palpable. Without thinking, he pressed play on the news alert flashing across the screen.

The familiar tones of a news anchor filled the room, but their words barely registered as Andrew's mind struggled to catch up with what he was hearing.

"Breaking news from Sydney," the anchor's voice echoed. "The most prominent investment bank has been robbed in broad daylight. Tragedy has struck. The manager, Richard Wright, was shot in the attack and is now fighting for his life. Meanwhile, the assistant manager, Celeste Beaumont, daughter of prominent Sydney family, has been taken hostage. Authorities are unsure of her whereabouts or whether she is still alive, but they are urging anyone with information to come forward. We now go to eyewitness reports."

The screen shifted to a woman, crying, her voice raw with emotion.

"They just shot the manager," she choked out. "He was doing everything they asked, and then they shot him."

The reporter asked, "What can you tell us about the woman who was taken?"

"Celeste," the woman gasped. "It was like they were looking for her. As soon as the leader saw her in her office, he grabbed her and threw her into the van."

"What was her demeanour like?" the reporter pressed.

"You could tell she was scared, but she was trying to remain calm. I saw how hard they shoved her into the van. They didn't care if they hurt her."

The news anchor returned with a grim update. "We now have footage of the bank robbery. Please be advised, some scenes may be confronting."

Andrew's pulse quickened as the footage of the chaotic scene flashed across the screen. People running in panic, the manager collapsing, blood spreading across his shirt. Then, another shot. Celeste, being yanked by one of the attackers through the bank's foyer, the scene shifting to police swarming the area.

But it wasn't until the camera focused on the image of the kidnapped woman that Andrew's heart truly stopped. His breath caught in his throat as he stared at the screen.

Celeste.

His chest constricted, and a sharp pain bloomed in his chest. No. Not Celeste.

The image of her, so helpless, so terrified, was burned into his mind.

"They took her!" Kathleen's voice, frantic and raw, sliced through the fog in his mind. Her words barely registered as Andrew's vision blurred. The reality of what was happening crashed down on him like a tidal wave.

Celeste. His Celeste. The woman he had foolishly dismissed. The one he had pushed away with lies. Taken. And now, he didn't know if he would ever get the chance to make things right.

The room seemed to close in on him. The air was thick, suffocating. A crushing wave of guilt and terror slammed into him, sending him reeling backward in his chair. His hand gripped the phone, his only tether to reality, his body shaking with panic.

How could he have done this? Just days ago, he had told her—what? That she meant nothing to him. That there was no future for them? Those words, those brutal, callous words, replayed in his mind over and over, like a sickening loop.

'You were just a hookup. There was never a future for us.'

The cruel dismissal felt like a jagged knife in his gut now. How could he have been so heartless when every part of him had known the truth—that he did want her? That there could have been something real between them?

But now, it might be too late. She could be gone forever, and all he had left were the consequences of the lies he'd spoken.

His hands trembled, clenched into fists. His breath came in uneven gasps. He had never felt more powerless, more helpless.

"Andrew…" Kathleen's voice was softer now, her hand resting gently on his arm. "What can we do?"

"We can't do anything, Kath," he said, desperation creeping into his voice. "The police have to find her. Alive."

The words hung in the air between them, heavy and hopeless. The weight of them crushed him. Celeste could be out there, terrified, not knowing if she would ever see another day. And he had let her go. Pushed her away when he should have fought for her.

The guilt and fear weighed on him, crushing him. She didn't deserve this. She didn't deserve to be caught up in the mess of his mistakes.

And now, all he could do was wait. Pray. Hope against hope that someone—anyone—would find her before it was too late.

The city was still reeling. The streets felt eerily quiet, as though the air itself had thickened with the weight of what had happened. Celeste's disappearance had consumed the city, and whispers in cafés and frantic news reports on every channel kept her name on everyone's lips. No one could escape it. Not even Celeste's parents, Hope and Jonas, who clung to whatever shred of hope they could find, praying for her safe return.

Kathleen, unwilling to leave their side, had moved in with them. She offered what little comfort she could, though nothing seemed to fill the gaping void left by Celeste's absence. The days blurred together, each one longer than the last, but they refused to give up. Celeste couldn't be gone forever.

The police had set up a tap on their phone line in case the kidnappers contacted them, but it was Friday morning, and there had still been no ransom call.

Andrew had just arrived at the Beaumont home when George pulled up with his partner, Detective Julie Ebejer.

Kathleen stepped into the foyer as George greeted Andrew. Julie moved into the living room to join Hope and Jonas, while the two detectives they were replacing exited the house, exchanging nods with George as they left.

George ran a hand down his face, looking defeated. "What a bloody mess. Still no ransom call, and we've got no leads. It's all just so frustrating."

Andrew and Kathleen exchanged a look of disbelief, the weight of the situation sinking in. Andrew couldn't hold back. "Surely you know something, anything?"

George's shoulders slumped in exhaustion. "The only lead we've got is Troy Summers. He's a real piece of work. Robbery, assault, and rape—his rap sheet's a mile long."

"Rape?!" Kathleen gasped, her voice barely above a whisper, her face pale with shock.

Andrew's blood ran cold. His concern for Celeste's life had already been consuming, but now it was twisted with an even darker fear for her well-being. "He wouldn't… would he?"

George shook his head; frustration etched across his face. "I'm sorry, guys, but we just don't know for sure. Not yet."

He let out a long, heavy sigh. "I feel terrible about the way Celeste and I argued at her birthday party… I didn't realise how much it would haunt me until now."

Andrew's eyes snapped to George, a flash of suspicion and something darker creeping into his chest. "Argued?"

George lowered his head, regret washing over his face. "Yeah. I kissed her, and… well, she was pissed. I didn't know what came over me."

Kathleen's eyes widened in shock. "You kissed her? Why?"

Andrew's blood boiled with a mix of anger and disbelief. Without thinking, he shoved George hard, the force of it catching him off guard. "You bloody bastard."

George, still taken aback, stumbled back a few steps. "Andrew?"

"We broke up because of you!" Andrew's voice cracked with raw emotion. She was innocent, damn it.

What have I done? She cared for me so much; after not turning up to her birthday party, she came to my apartment thinking I was sick or hurt… and I treated her like… like Sarah.

His hands clenched into fists, trembling with pent-up rage. He pushed George again, harder this time. "What the hell were you thinking?"

"I didn't know you two were together," George shot back defensively, his voice rising. "Celeste would've told you it was my fault!"

Kathleen's face twisted in disgust as she looked at Andrew. "You didn't let her, did you? You thought she was like Sarah, didn't you?"

Andrew met her gaze but said nothing. His eyes betrayed everything he couldn't put into words.

The weight of what he had done settled over him like a suffocating blanket, relentless and heavy, pressing down on his chest until he could barely breathe.

"Andrew!" George's voice was sharp, but his expression softened with a mixture of regret and guilt. "I swear, I never would've kissed her if I knew you two were together. I had no idea."

Before Andrew could respond, the shrill ring of the phone sliced through the heavy silence.

George's demeanour shifted immediately. He straightened, his professional mask slipping back into place as he walked briskly into the living room. Hope and Jonas sat together, their bodies intertwined in a fragile show of support, holding on to each other as though they were clinging to the last vestiges of hope.

The room was suffocating, the weight of the moment pressing down on everyone. The air felt thick with the anticipation of what might be on the other end of the line.

This could be the call they were waiting for.

Chapter Twenty-One

Jonas sat in the living room, his eyes bloodshot from sleepless nights, staring at the phone as it rang. Each passing second felt like an eternity, a relentless reminder of the pain they were enduring. Hope sat beside him, her hand gripping his tightly, her heart breaking for the daughter they might never see again. Yet, in the midst of their anguish, they still clung to a fragile thread of hope. Maybe—just maybe—they could bring Celeste home.

George stood nearby, his voice calm but urgent. "Okay, just try to stay calm and keep them talking for as long as you can."

Jonas nodded, his face a mask of controlled desperation. He tried to steady his breathing, but the weight of the situation pressed heavily on his chest. George pressed the speaker button on the phone, then pointed at Jonas, signalling for him to speak.

"Hello, this is Jonas Beaumont," Jonas said, his voice steady but laced with a faint tremor.

Andrew sat rigid in an armchair; his breath held as though he could change the course of events with sheer will. His eyes locked on Jonas, his heart pounding in his chest. Every person in the room hung on the first word from the voice on the other end— the person holding Celeste hostage.

A cold, sinister voice finally broke the silence, sending an icy chill down Jonas's spine. "Mr. Beaumont, I must say, you have a lovely daughter. You must be very proud?"

Jonas's grip on Hope's hand tightened, his throat dry. "Is she okay?" he managed to choke out, fear and love intertwining in his voice.

The voice on the other end seemed to savour the moment, relishing the control. "She is... for now."

Jonas's pulse hammered in his ears, but he forced his voice to remain steady. "I want to hear her voice."

A pause, then the voice returned, cold and calculating. "In due time. But first, I'll tell you what I want."

Jonas's jaw tightened, his grip on Hope's hand a vice, but he kept his voice controlled, demanding, "What do you want?"

The voice answered, its words hanging heavy with intent. "Four million dollars."

Kathleen gasped, her face draining of colour. Four million dollars—the price of their daughter's life. It was the grim reality they had feared.

Jonas's hand trembled, but his expression remained stoic. He glanced at Hope, her face twisted in anguish but locked onto him, silently pleading for him to stay strong.

His voice was calm, unwavering. "Okay. But first, I want to hear her voice."

"Okay," came the cold reply.

Then, the voice they'd been waiting for—her voice—crackled through the phone, fragile but unmistakable. "Daddy?"

Jonas's breath hitched. Tears welled in his eyes. "Sweetheart," he whispered, heart breaking.

"I love you, Daddy," Celeste's voice trembled. "Tell Mum I love her too."

Andrew's throat tightened. He wanted to say something, to reassure her, but the words would feel hollow. He had hurt her, failed to trust her.

Hope's voice broke through, trembling but strong. "We both love you too, sweetheart." She squeezed Jonas's hand, her words the only comfort they had to offer.

The phone went silent, and the tension in the room became suffocating. Then the cold voice returned. "That's enough. She's fine, as long as you do what you're told."

Jonas's heart sank, but he forced himself to stay focused. "Okay. How? Where?" His voice was steady, despite the storm raging inside him.

The voice chuckled, sending a shiver down everyone's spine. "We'll be in touch. Make sure you're ready."

The line went dead with a click. Silence. The weight of what had just happened crashed down on them.

After the phone was hung up, the room fell into an oppressive silence, each person processing the horror of the conversation they had just witnessed. The weight of what was unfolding crushed them, but in that moment, George's voice cut through the tension, sharp and practical.

"Do you have access to that amount of money?" George asked, his tone steady, though the gravity of the situation was evident in his eyes.

Jonas didn't hesitate. There was no second-guessing, no wavering. "Yes, the money's not a problem." His voice was firm, a testament to his resolve to do anything to bring Celeste back. But then, as if he couldn't bear the uncertainty that still lingered in the air, he added, "Will they give her back when we pay?" His eyes flicked to George, a silent plea for reassurance. He needed something concrete, something to hold onto as the darkness of the situation loomed over them.

George looked at him directly, his expression grim but honest. "It's rare that they don't. Typically, they honour the exchange, but..." His voice trailed off, and he took a moment before continuing, the weight of his words hanging heavy in the room. "We can't be one hundred percent sure. There's always a risk that they could do something… stupid."

The unsaid words lingered in the air like smoke. They could kill her anyway.

Andrew's blood ran cold, the chilling realisation settling deep within him. His hand, still gripping the armrest of the chair, went white-knuckled with tension. The terrible truth hit him harder than a physical blow—there was no guarantee. None.

Celeste was still trapped in the hands of people who viewed human life as a mere pawn in their twisted game. The sinister voice on the other end of the phone had made it abundantly clear—this wasn't about money alone. This was about control, power, and the sadistic pleasure of toying with those who loved her. They weren't dealing with ordinary criminals; these were people who existed beyond any moral compass, whose actions were driven by a ruthless desire to break others, to see them suffer. There were no limits to what they might do, and that realisation hit like a hammer to Andrew's chest.

As a criminal lawyer, Andrew had spent his career studying the darkest corners of human nature. He knew what people were capable of when they were backed into a corner, what they could do when their only goal was to inflict pain, chaos, and fear. He knew that the kind of person on the other end of that call was capable of anything, and it terrified him. He wanted to scream, to lash out, to demand more answers, to force the situation into some kind of resolution. But he couldn't. He was paralysed by the weight of his own helplessness. Every rational thought seemed to shatter in the face of his fear.

His mind raced with dark possibilities. What if they don't give her back? What if this is just the beginning of something far worse than they're prepared for? The questions gnawed at him, each one more suffocating than the last. There was no guarantee that the money would bring Celeste home. There was no guarantee that the criminals would keep their word, that they wouldn't decide to take something even more precious. And in the back of his mind, a far darker thought simmered—what if they had something far worse planned for her?

The terror of it all overwhelmed him, and for a moment, he felt utterly powerless, like a spectator in a nightmare he couldn't wake up from. He had always been able to navigate the murky waters of criminal law, to predict the moves of the dangerous minds he had faced. But this... this was different. This was personal. This was Celeste. The woman he loved. And the stakes were far higher than anything he had ever encountered in a courtroom.

Andrew tried to focus, to think rationally, but the fear clawed at him. What if he failed her? What if they were already too late?

Hope, still clutching Jonas's hand, seemed to shrink inward, her shoulders slumping as the weight of the words hit her, too. She had been silent for so long, her face a mask of composed devastation, but now her vulnerability broke through. "What if they don't...?" she whispered, her voice trembling. The question hung between them, the nightmare they all feared made real.

Jonas squeezed her hand tighter, trying to offer her the strength he was barely holding on to himself. His eyes locked onto George's, the unspoken pain in his gaze clear.

"What can we do to ensure she comes back? What if we give them the money and they just disappear?"

George ran a hand through his hair, frustration and helplessness etched into his features. "We can't guarantee anything, but we'll do everything we can to track them, to catch them. We're monitoring the situation closely." He paused, his gaze flicking from Jonas to Andrew. "We'll have to make the exchange as clean as possible. No cops, no interference, but we'll have a team ready to move as soon as we get the signal."

Andrew stood up abruptly, the tension in his body like a coiled spring ready to snap. His fists clenched at his sides, his mind spinning with a hundred different possibilities, all of them horrifying. "We can't just stand by and hope they follow through," he said, his voice tight with barely contained rage. "We need a plan. A real one."

George nodded, his face set with grim determination. "I know. But we need to be careful. We don't want to risk her life. One wrong move, and this whole thing could spiral out of control."

Jonas was silent, his eyes fixed on the floor, but the depth of his pain and frustration was clear. His daughter was out there, somewhere, at the mercy of a monster, and all he had to rely on was a slim hope that the criminals would stick to their word. A hope that felt more fragile by the second.

In that moment, the room felt colder, darker, as if the very walls were closing in on them. The day stretched ahead, filled with uncertainty, and the dreadful thought of what could happen if the exchange didn't go as planned gnawed at each of them.

The worst part wasn't the money—money could be found. It wasn't even the time—it could slip by too quickly, but time could be manipulated. The worst part was the lingering unknown. They were all just sitting ducks in a game that had no rules, no guarantees. Their daughter's life was in the hands of someone who might very well decide to make a deadly statement, to take away the one thing that meant everything to them.

Jonas finally spoke, his voice raw with emotion, but steady. "We'll pay them. Whatever it takes. We'll get her back." He turned to Hope, and though the words were meant for her, they rang out for all of them. "We will get her back."

Andrew nodded slowly, though his mind was filled with turmoil. He wasn't sure if he could believe it, but he had no choice. This was the path they were on. The game had begun, and they could only pray that they wouldn't lose.

Chapter Twenty-Two

Celeste's eyes snapped open to the faint light creeping through the slats of the boarded-up windows. The dim glow barely pierced the gloom, leaving the warehouse cold and suffocating. Her body felt like a heavy weight, each muscle aching with tension, frozen in place. Every inch of her was taut, primed for flight or fight, but there was nowhere to run. The silence was deafening, broken only by the distant clinking of chains and the oppressive sound of her own rapid, shallow breathing.

She was in an abandoned warehouse, somewhere far outside the city, and the sheer isolation of it sank deep into her chest, like a vice. Her mind spun, racing through every possible scenario, none of them offering any hope. How did I end up here? The question echoed in her mind, but it was one without an answer. The only thing that was real, the only thing that mattered, was that she was trapped.

Her hands were bound behind her with rough rope, the fibres digging into her skin, each tug of her wrists sending a flare of pain up her arms. Her legs were bound to a rusted chair, each movement she tried to make only serving to dig the rope deeper into her flesh. The cold air bit at her exposed skin, sending a shiver through her, but she kept herself still, holding her breath. Stay calm, Celeste. Don't show them you're afraid.

Her fingers trembled slightly, betraying the tight coil of panic in her chest, but she willed herself not to give in. The slightest show of fear would give them power over her, and she couldn't let that happen. Not now. Not when she was so close to losing everything.

She swallowed hard, blinking back the dizziness that clouded her vision. Her pulse thudded in her ears, a frantic drumbeat that seemed to echo through the empty, stagnant air. The ache in her head was a constant companion, a dull pressure that reminded her of the brutal knock she'd taken earlier. She could still feel the tightness in her throat, a painful reminder of the emotions she had been forced to swallow—fear, sadness, regret.

She'd heard her parents' voices this morning, on the phone. The raw desperation in their words had been impossible to ignore, like a constant echo in her mind. Maybe this is the last time I'll ever hear them. She had told them she loved them, but there was so much more she wanted to say. She wanted them to tell Andrew that she loved him too, that despite everything, she had always cared. She wanted to ask them to pass on the message, but what would be the point? He didn't care about her—not the way she had hoped, not the way she needed. To him, she was just a fleeting distraction, a hookup in a string of many. The harsh truth stung like salt in a wound.

Tears welled in her eyes, but she quickly blinked them away. Crying wouldn't change anything. It wouldn't bring her back to the safety of her parents, and it certainly wouldn't make Andrew see her as anything more than a momentary lapse in his otherwise detached life. So, she shut it all down—her emotions, her heart—and steeled herself for whatever came next.

Four million dollars. That was what Reece had asked for.

Celeste wasn't stupid. She knew exactly what they wanted from her. She was leverage. A pawn in their twisted game. She wasn't a person to them—she was a price tag, a bargaining chip, an object to be traded.

The sound of a door creaking open interrupted her thoughts, pulling her back into the present. Heavy footsteps echoed across the concrete floor, slow but deliberate, as if the man approaching her enjoyed the sound of his own power.

Her heart skipped a beat. It was him. Troy. The one who had fired the shot at the bank manager—tossing a cruel, vicious reminder into her mind that these people weren't to be underestimated. They were dangerous. All of them. But Troy... Troy was different. He was the one she feared the most.

Troy's footsteps stopped directly in front of her. She could smell his presence before she even saw him fully, the acrid stench of cigarette smoke and stale sweat hanging in the air. He loomed over her, his dark eyes glinting with something predatory as he looked her up and down, a cruel smirk spreading across his face.

"Well, well," he said, his voice low and dark, tinged with amusement. "What do we have here? All on your lonesome."

Celeste kept her gaze lowered, unwilling to meet his eyes, afraid of what he might see in her. But Troy didn't care about that. He was already too far gone. He reached down, his fingers brushing against her calf, the touch sending a sickening chill down her spine. Slowly, deliberately, he ran his hand up her leg, pushing the fabric of her dress higher as he moved.

"You're a prime female, you are," he purred. "Strong, healthy... you'd be one hell of a good lay. You'd put up a good fight."

Celeste's stomach churned with revulsion, her body instinctively trying to shrink away, but the ropes held her tight, trapping her in place. She gritted her teeth, trying to focus on the space inside her head, on anything that could keep her from breaking under his touch.

His hand moved higher, his fingers brushing the edge of her thigh, and Celeste flinched, her pulse racing. The heat of his breath on her skin made her stomach twist in disgust. She tried to pull away, but the ropes held her firm. She felt his lips against her neck, soft at first, then pressing harder, his tongue tracing the line of her jaw. A shudder of revulsion ran through her, her body freezing in place.

Don't let him win. Don't let him take you.

But just as Troy's hand inched further, his grip tightening around her, a voice cut through the oppressive tension.

"What the hell do you think you're doing, Troy?"

Reece's voice was sharp, filled with fury. He stormed into the room, his broad form filling the doorway, his eyes blazing with anger. He was the one in charge. And his tone was a command, not a suggestion.

Troy jerked back, his hand falling away from Celeste's leg as he turned toward Reece, a momentary flash of defiance crossing his features. "I was just having a little fun," he said, his voice dripping with sarcasm.

Reece's eyes flashed dangerously. He was on Troy in an instant, his hand connecting with a sharp slap that rang through the room.

"I told you, unharmed," Reece snarled, his voice cold with menace. "She's worth more to me alive and untouched, you fool."

Troy staggered back, stunned by the blow, but Reece was already turning away, his expression shifting to something colder. He focused on Celeste, his eyes softening for a moment, but only for a moment.

"We're getting the ransom, Celeste. Hold on just a little longer. It'll be over soon."

But Celeste couldn't shake the lingering feeling in her chest—the sense that even if they met Reece's demands, everything she had ever known may be lost forever anyway.

It was Saturday morning—at least, Celeste thought it was. Time had lost all meaning in the cold, damp warehouse where she sat bound to a chair. The hours stretched endlessly, blurring together in a haze of exhaustion, fear, and the dull ache of her stiff limbs. She had tried to keep track of the days, but sleep had been fitful, stolen in brief, uneasy intervals.

Last night, she had overheard the kidnappers talking. They had been in high spirits, laughing and cheering over the news that her father was going to pay the ransom—four million dollars. A million each. They had spoken about it so casually, as if her life was nothing more than a business transaction. The thought made her sick.

They had left to retrieve the money, but before they did, Reece had come to her.

He had crouched down in front of her, his expression unreadable in the dim light. For a moment, she thought she saw something resembling guilt in his eyes, but she refused to believe it. He had played his part in this, and no amount of regret would change that.

"I'm sorry about all this, Celeste," he had said, his voice quieter than usual. "But it'll be over today. Your father is paying the ransom, and when we're far enough away…" He hesitated, his gaze flickering over her bound form. "I'll let them know where you are."

Celeste had stared at him, searching for any sign of sincerity. Did he really mean that? Or was this just another manipulation, another lie to keep her quiet?

"Why should I believe you?" she had whispered, her throat dry from hours of silence.

Reece had sighed, running a hand through his dishevelled hair. "You don't have to," he admitted. "But I swear, I never wanted this to happen."

Then he had stood up and walked away, leaving her alone in the suffocating silence of the warehouse.

Andrew stood in the Beaumont living room, his fists clenched at his sides as he stared at the black duffel bag sitting on the coffee table. Four million dollars. That's what those bastards thought Celeste's life was worth. As if she could be measured in numbers. As if she was just another transaction.

His chest burned. Four million dollars. That's what they thought she was worth? She was priceless. And he would do whatever it took to get her back.

Jonas paced by the window; his expression grim. "I still don't like this," he muttered. "We should be the ones making the drop."

George shook his head. "Hope insisted. She's the least threatening option. If they sense anything's off, they'll kill Celeste before we even get close." His voice was steady, but Andrew could hear the tension behind it. The unspoken fear.

Andrew hated this plan, but they had no choice. The police were standing by, ready to follow the kidnappers once they had the money. If all went well, Celeste would be safe before the day was over.

But Andrew had a sinking feeling that nothing about this was going to go smoothly.

Chapter Twenty-Three

Dr. Hope Beaumont stood alone in the empty parking lot, her heart hammering against her ribs. The weight of the duffel bag in her hands felt unbearably heavy, not because of the money inside, but because of what it represented—her daughter's life, hanging in the balance.

She had followed the kidnappers' instructions to the letter. No police visible. No trackers in the bag. No last-minute tricks. Just her and the ransom.

The night air was thick with tension, the dim glow of a flickering streetlamp casting long shadows across the cracked pavement. Silence pressed in around her, broken only by the distant hum of traffic.

Then, the sound of an approaching engine.

A black SUV rolled into the lot, its headlights off, moving with slow, predatory purpose. Hope's breath caught in her throat as the vehicle came to a stop inches from her. The back door swung open, and a man stepped out. His face was hidden beneath a baseball cap, his posture radiating cold authority. He didn't speak. He didn't hesitate. He just reached forward and ripped the bag from her grasp.

Hope barely had time to take a step back before the SUV's tyres screeched against the pavement. The vehicle sped off, disappearing into the night.

For a split second, there was only silence.

Then—movement.

The police were in motion.

Unmarked cars that had been lying in wait slipped into traffic, shadowing the kidnappers at a distance. Everything was going according to plan. The ransom had been exchanged, and soon, they would track the men back to Celeste.

Then the gunfire started.

A sharp crack split the air, followed by another, then another. Bullets tore through the night, shattering windshields, slamming into metal. Tyres screeched as cars swerved to avoid the chaos. Sirens erupted, the wail of police cruisers blending with the deafening roar of the firefight.

The kidnappers had realised they were being followed. And they weren't going down without a fight.

The chase turned deadly in an instant.

Officers returned fire, ducking behind their vehicles as rounds ricocheted off the pavement. Civilians screamed in the distance, fleeing for cover as the standoff escalated.

One of the kidnappers went down—a bullet to the chest ending his escape attempt instantly. Another was wounded, collapsing against the hood of a stolen car. A third was dragged from the driver's seat, his hands wrenched behind his back as he was arrested.

Detective George Dawsett snapped the cuffs around Reece Maddox's wrists, tightening them just enough to make a point. His voice was clipped, measured as he began reading him his rights.

"You have the right to remain silent. Anything you say can and will be used against you in a court of law. You have the right to an attorney—"

Reece barely seemed to hear him. His chest rose and fell rapidly, his face pale beneath streetlights.

But one got away.

Troy Summers.

While the others had been caught in the shootout, Troy had slipped into the shadows, vanishing into the chaos of the city.

George watched Reece carefully. The kidnapper was sweating, his hands flexing behind his back. Not with fear. Not with guilt. With urgency. This was different.

"Things will go a lot easier if you tell us where she is," George said, his voice hard.

Reece's lips parted. His jaw clenched. Then, he spoke.

"She's in an abandoned warehouse outside of town," he said, his words coming fast, his voice tight. "That's where we've been keeping her."

George leaned in, every muscle in his body coiled with tension. "Where exactly?"

Reece rattled off an address, then hesitated. A flicker of something crossed his face—guilt? Fear? Then he swallowed hard and met George's gaze head-on.

"You need to hurry," he said, his voice dropping to a whisper. "Troy knows we lost the money. He's going back there."

George's blood ran cold.

"And… listen to me." Reece inhaled sharply, his jaw tightening. "He's tried to touch her before."

George's spine went rigid.

"I stopped him," Reece said quickly. His hands curled into fists behind his back. "I swear I stopped him. But… she doesn't deserve that." His eyes were dark, haunted. "You have to hurry."

George didn't hesitate.

He shoved away from Reece, barking orders for another officer to take Reece away then he was in his car his partner Julie next to him.

"We need back up! Now!"

They didn't have time to waste.

Because if they were too late—Celeste wouldn't just be a hostage anymore.

The darkness inside the warehouse was suffocating. The air was thick with dampness, the stench of rust and mildew clinging to her nostrils. Celeste sat bound to a chair, her wrists raw from the unforgiving ropes that dug deep into her flesh. Her body ached from hours of captivity—muscles stiff, skin chilled, a dull throb pulsing in her temple where she had been struck.

She had tried to stay strong, to keep herself from sinking into despair, but as the minutes stretched into eternity, her hope began to fray, unravelling thread by fragile thread.

Then—

Footsteps.

Heavy. Purposeful.

Each step echoed ominously, sending tremors of dread through her spine.

The rusted metal door groaned open, spilling a sliver of moonlight into the suffocating darkness. The silver glow barely illuminated the damp concrete, but it was enough for her to see the silhouette of a monster.

Troy stepped inside.

His presence swallowed the room, his broad frame casting long shadows against the walls. His movements were unhurried, deliberate—as if savouring the moment. Predatory eyes locked onto hers, gleaming with something dark, something twisted.

A slow grin curved his lips.

"We lost the money," he murmured, stepping closer. His voice was low, edged with something cruel. "So now, I'll have you instead."

Celeste's stomach twisted violently. No. No, no, no.

Troy crouched in front of her, his fingers trailing over the ropes binding her wrists. Teasing. Toying. She could smell him—whiskey, sweat, and the faint trace of cologne. The scent of a man who had already crossed every line imaginable.

His fingers curled at the neckline of her dress.

And then—he yanked.

The fabric tore straight down the front, the violent rip echoing like a gunshot in the empty space. Cold air rushed against her exposed skin, goosebumps rising over her flesh. Celeste gasped, her chest heaving, her heartbeat a frantic drum in her ears.

Troy let out a low whistle, his gaze dragging over her body with slow, deliberate satisfaction.

"I knew you'd look amazing naked," he breathed, reaching for her, his fingers aiming for the lacy fabric of her bra.

Celeste screamed.

Not just in fear—but in raw, primal survival.

The sound startled him. Just for a second.

Then—he laughed.

"No one's coming for you, sweetheart." His voice was thick with anticipation, his fingers grasping her chin, forcing her to look at him. His thumb brushed over her trembling lips, savouring the fear that quivered beneath his touch. "You're mine. And I'm going to enjoy every second of you."

He leaned in, his breath hot against her skin, lips ghosting over her collarbone, trailing downward—

Bang!

The warehouse door exploded open, slamming against the wall with a deafening crash.

A burst of light cut through the darkness.

Gunfire flared.

Troy jerked back, his hands flying up as a furious shout tore from his throat.

"Freeze! Hands in the air!"

George stood in the doorway; his gun drawn, steady, deadly. Behind him, a squad of officers flooded inside, weapons trained, the air electric with the promise of justice.

Celeste gasped, relief crashing over her like a tidal wave. They found me.

Troy snarled. His hand darted to his waist—a gun.

He raised it.

George didn't hesitate.

One shot.

The bullet slammed into Troy's chest. He staggered backward, his face twisting in pain. But before he fell—

His gun went off.

Celeste felt it before she even heard the shot.

A searing pain tore through her upper chest, hot, blinding.

Her breath hitched—shallow, ragged. The world around her tilted, spun, and then…

Darkness.

Andrew, Kathleen, and Celeste's parents sat in tense silence in their living room, their hands clenched, their faces pale. The clock on the wall ticked mercilessly, each second stretching into eternity. Every time the phone rang, every distant sound in the hallway, their hearts leapt with hope—and fear.

Then—a knock at the door.

The room went still.

Andrew was the first to his feet. Kathleen clutched Celeste's mother's hand tightly, while her father stood rigid, bracing himself.

The door swung open.

George stood there.

His face was grim, lined with exhaustion. His usually steady gaze was shadowed, and that alone made Andrew's stomach clench with dread.

"We found her."

Celeste's mother let out a choked sob, pressing her hands over her mouth. Her father exhaled sharply, his knees nearly buckling before he caught himself. Kathleen whispered a shaky prayer under her breath, gripping her rosary so tightly her knuckles turned white.

Andrew saw the way George's jaw tightened.

There was more.

His throat went dry. "Where is she?"

A terrible feeling coiled in his gut, squeezing tighter with every second George hesitated.

Finally, George met his gaze. "She's been shot."

The words felt like a fist to his chest.

"She was rushed to St. Vincent's Hospital."

Andrew didn't hear anything else. His vision blurred, adrenaline surging through his veins. He turned, bolting out the door before anyone could stop him.

Chapter Twenty-Four

The drive to the hospital was a blur. Andrew barely remembered running red lights, the sound of honking horns, his foot pressing down harder and harder on the accelerator.

He screeched to a halt in front of St. Vincent's, throwing the door open before the engine had fully died.

He ran.

Bursting through the doors of the emergency department, he searched desperately. The harsh fluorescent lights stung his eyes, the antiseptic smell filling his lungs, but he didn't care.

Then—

"Andrew."

He turned sharply.

Bryan was there, standing near the nurses' station, his face drawn with exhaustion.

Andrew rushed to him.

"Please." His voice was hoarse, raw. He grabbed Bryan's arms, barely able to contain the tremble in his fingers. "Tell me she's okay."

Bryan exhaled, steadying him. "She was shot in the upper left chest. It missed vital organs."

Andrew sagged against him, a strangled sound escaping his throat.

"She's unconscious," Bryan continued, his tone gentle but firm. "She's severely dehydrated. They've put her on fluids. The doctors are monitoring her condition, but she's stable for now."

Andrew swallowed hard, nodding. But it wasn't enough.

"I need to see her."

Bryan didn't argue.

He turned, leading Andrew through the corridor.

With each step, Andrew felt his pulse hammering, his body moving on pure instinct. The walls seemed to close in, the fluorescent lights casting everything in a sterile glow. Machines beeped in the distance. Nurses moved in and out of rooms, their voices hushed.

Finally, Bryan stopped in front of a door.

"She's in here."

Andrew hesitated only a second before stepping inside.

The sight of her stole the breath from his lungs.

Celeste lay in the hospital bed, pale, motionless. Wires and monitors surrounded her, the steady beeping of a heart monitor filling the silent room. An IV drip was attached to her arm, the fluid slowly dripping into her veins. A thick bandage covered her left shoulder, stark against her fragile skin.

Andrew's throat tightened.

"Celeste…"

He stepped forward, his knees nearly buckling as he reached her bedside.

Carefully, he took her hand.

Her fingers were cold.

Too cold.

He swallowed hard, pressing her hand between his own, trying to warm her.

"I'm here," he whispered. "I'm right here."

No response.

His grip tightened. "You have to wake up, Celeste. You fought so hard. You can't give up now."

His voice cracked.

"Please."

Silence.

He bowed his head, resting his forehead against her hand. A single tear slipped down his cheek.

She had to come back to him.

She had to.

Celeste drifted between the edges of consciousness, caught in the hazy space between sleep and wakefulness. The first thing she became aware of was the sound. A soft, steady beep… beep… beep… Somewhere nearby, a machine counted each fragile beat of her heart.

A strange weight pressed down on her, like she was floating yet sinking at the same time. Her body felt foreign, sluggish. Something beeped in the distance, steady and relentless.

Then—pain.

A deep, aching throb radiated from her left shoulder, a fiery reminder of everything that had happened.

She tried to shift, but even the smallest movement sent sharp stabs of agony through her body. A soft groan escaped her lips.

Then—warmth.

Someone was holding her hand. A firm but gentle grasp, fingers wrapped protectively around hers.

She forced her heavy eyelids to lift.

The bright hospital lights were disorienting at first, making her blink rapidly. The world slowly came into focus—white sheets, IV lines, the pale blue of a hospital gown. Then, as her vision cleared, her gaze landed on the two people beside her bed.

"Mum… Dad?"

Her voice was hoarse, barely more than a whisper.

Her mother let out a strangled sob, her hands tightening around Celeste's fingers as tears spilled freely down her cheeks. "Oh, sweetheart."

Her father's face was tight with emotion, his strong hands trembling as he clung to hers. "You're awake," he murmured, voice thick with relief.

Celeste swallowed, her throat raw. A thousand questions swirled in her mind, but she didn't ask them.

Because in that moment—seeing them, feeling them there, knowing she was alive— that was all that mattered.

The next time Celeste woke, the world was still a blur of sterile white walls and beeping monitors. But this time, she wasn't alone.

Bryan stood at her bedside, flipping through her chart with a concentrated frown. His presence was calm, familiar—a small comfort in the chaos of pain and confusion.

She swallowed against the dryness in her throat. "Bryan."

His head snapped up. At first, there was surprise in his eyes, then warmth. "Hello, sleepyhead." He smiled, stepping closer. "Good to see you awake. Your parents just left to get some rest. Andrew will be back soon."

No.

A cold dread settled in her chest.

She didn't want Andrew here. Didn't want to see the pity in his eyes, or worse—the guilt. She wasn't strong enough to let him break her heart all over again.

"No."

Bryan frowned, confused. "No?"

Celeste shifted painfully, wincing as she forced herself to sit up a little. "I don't want him here." Her voice was thin but firm.

The words had barely left her lips when a familiar voice called from the doorway.

"Celeste?"

Her breath caught.

Andrew.

He stood there, looking like a man on the edge of breaking. His hair was a mess, his clothes wrinkled as if he hadn't changed in days. The dark circles beneath his eyes told her he hadn't slept much either.

But none of it mattered.

She clenched her jaw, her heart twisting painfully in her chest. "No! Go away!"

Andrew flinched as if she had struck him.

"Celeste…" His voice was raw. "I'm sorry."

She turned desperately to Bryan, her eyes burning with unshed tears. "Make him go away."

Bryan hesitated, glancing between them.

But Celeste couldn't do this.

Celeste's breathing grew rapid, her chest rising in uneven, painful gasps. The monitors beside her bed beeped in protest, her elevated heart rate drawing Bryan's attention.

"Celeste, you need to calm down." His voice was gentle but firm, his hand hovering near her wrist as if debating whether to take her pulse.

But she couldn't calm down. Not with Andrew standing there, looking at her like she was something fragile—something broken.

She wasn't broken.

She refused to be.

"Make him go away." Her voice cracked, but her resolve did not. "Please."

Andrew took a step forward, desperation flickering in his eyes. "Celeste, don't do this."

"I don't want to see you!" she shouted, her voice trembling.

The pain in her chest flared, sharp and burning, but she didn't care. Anything was better than facing him—than letting him see her like this, weak and vulnerable.

Bryan glanced between them, hesitation clear in his expression. Then he exhaled heavily and turned to Andrew.

"You need to leave."

Andrew's face twisted with anguish. "Bryan, please—"

Bryan shook his head. "Not now." His voice was quiet but unyielding.

A long, heavy silence stretched between them.

Andrew swallowed hard, his hands clenching into fists at his sides. His lips parted, as if he wanted to say something—one last plea, one last attempt to make her see that he was here, that he still cared.

But Celeste didn't look at him.

She turned her face away, squeezing her eyes shut.

A moment later, she heard the quiet shuffle of footsteps retreating.

The door clicked shut.

Only then did the tightness in her chest ease, but the ache in her heart remained.

Andrew reluctantly stepped out of Celeste's hospital room, the weight of her rejection pressing down on him like an unbearable force. The sterile scent of antiseptic clung to the air, but all he could breathe in was regret.

The door clicked shut behind him, sealing the space between them—sealing his fate, perhaps. His heart clenched as he replayed her words in his mind, the sheer force of her anger, her pain. No! Go away! She had screamed at him like he was the worst kind of intruder.

And maybe he was.

He scrubbed a hand down his face, exhaustion sinking deep into his bones. He had barely slept, barely eaten since she had been taken. The past few days had been nothing but a blur of fear, desperation, and gut-wrenching guilt. And now? Now that she was safe—now that she was awake—he wasn't allowed to be by her side.

But could he blame her?

After everything… after how he had hurt her?

No.

He had broken her heart once. And in doing so, he had lost the right to stand beside her now.

Bryan stepped out of the room a moment later, closing the door softly behind him. He levelled Andrew with a hard stare; arms crossed over his chest. There was sympathy in his eyes, but it was overshadowed by something sharper—disappointment.

"What the hell did you do?" he asked quietly, his voice low but edged with accusation.

Andrew let out a bitter laugh, running a hand through his already dishevelled hair. "I screwed up," he admitted, his voice rough with self-loathing. "I didn't trust her. Accused her of something she didn't do." He exhaled sharply, looking away. "Then, like an absolute idiot, I told her she was just a hookup."

Bryan's eyes widened in disbelief. "You what?"

Andrew shook his head, a hollow chuckle escaping his lips. "Yeah. I know. I completely stuffed up."

Bryan was silent for a moment, his expression unreadable. Then, he sighed, pinching the bridge of his nose. "You hurt her, Andrew," he said, his tone quieter now but no less firm. "More than you probably even realise."

Andrew swallowed hard, his jaw clenching. "I know," he murmured.

The silence between them stretched, thick with things unsaid.

Finally, Bryan exhaled and looked back at him, his stance relaxing just slightly. "She's been through hell, Andrew. She needs to focus on recovering—not on old wounds."

Andrew nodded, but the agreement felt like a weight pressing down on his chest. "Yeah," he said, his voice hollow. "I get it."

But knowing it didn't make walking away any easier.

He turned, forcing himself to take a step, then another. But with every step down that sterile, fluorescent-lit hallway, the ache inside him grew.

With one last glance at the closed door—the barrier between him and the woman he loved—Andrew walked away, his heart heavier than ever.

Every step felt heavier than the last.

And with each one, he wondered if she would ever forgive him.

Or if he had truly lost her forever.

Chapter Twenty-Five

Celeste was released to her parents' home the Wednesday after her rescue. Though she was weak, her mother took careful charge of her recovery, ensuring her bandages were changed regularly and that she had everything she needed. The routine was exhausting, but she was grateful for the quiet, the comfort of home, and the steady presence of her loved ones.

She had many visitors.

Kathleen and George were by her side almost daily, their familiar presence a lifeline. Bryan checked in often, fussing over her as only he could. She found herself reassured by their company, even as exhaustion pulled at her constantly.

She was relieved to hear that her manager, Richard, had survived his gunshot wound. The knowledge lifted a weight off her chest—one less life lost in the nightmare she had endured.

And then, there was Andrew.

Or rather, the attempts he made to see her.

Kathleen was the first to bring it up. "He's been trying to come by," she said carefully, one afternoon as they sat in the living room. Celeste had been flipping through an old magazine, pretending she wasn't still thinking about the way Andrew had looked at her that day in the hospital—like he was breaking apart.

She stiffened, turning the page too quickly. "I don't want to see him."

Kathleen hesitated. "I think you should."

Celeste shook her head. "I can't."

Her best friend sighed but didn't press further. "Just… think about it, okay?"

Celeste promised she would. And she did.

Then Bryan visited a few days later, and something in his expression made her wary.

"You know, he was a mess when you were brought into the hospital," Bryan said casually, watching her reaction.

Celeste frowned. "What do you mean?"

Bryan exhaled, rubbing the back of his neck. "I mean, I've seen Andrew angry. I've seen him cocky. Hell, I've even seen him completely exhausted after a case. But that night? I've never seen him like that before."

Celeste swallowed, unsettled.

"He lost it when you were taken. And when he found out you'd survive? I swear, I thought he was going to collapse right there in the hospital." Bryan studied her closely, lowering his voice. "He loves you, Celeste."

Her chest tightened, but she said nothing.

It wasn't until George visited that everything finally clicked into place.

He sat beside her on the couch, his hands clasped as he hesitated. "Andrew was wrong," he admitted. "There's no excuse for the way he treated you. But he didn't say those things because he didn't care—he said them because he saw me kissing you on your birthday and he thought you cheated on him."

Celeste stiffened. "What?"

George nodded. "He saw us—saw me kissing you that made him believe the worst. And instead of asking you, instead of trusting you, he let his own fears get the better of him." He sighed. "Doesn't make it right. But it explains why he acted the way he did."

The pieces of the puzzle finally fit together.

Andrew had thought she had betrayed him. He had lashed out, pushed her away—not because she didn't matter, but because she did.

The realisation didn't erase the pain. It didn't undo the damage.

But it did make her wonder if she could forgive him.

It took another week and a half before she found the strength to do something about it.

On a chilly Friday night, she booked an Uber to Andrew's apartment, her heart hammering the entire ride.

By the time she stood in front of his door, she wasn't sure if she had made a mistake.

But then, before she could second-guess herself, she lifted her hand—

And knocked.

Andrew's week had been hell.

Every morning, he woke up reaching for someone who wasn't there. Every night, he lay in bed staring at the ceiling, haunted by the memory of Celeste's voice—her fury, her heartbreak.

And the worst part?

She still wouldn't see him.

Kathleen had kept him updated, relaying the barest details of Celeste's recovery. She's getting stronger every day. Her wound will take two months to fully heal, but she's making progress.

It was supposed to be good news. But all he could think about was how those two months would pass without him by her side.

It had been two weeks since she was shot. Two weeks since she was rescued. Two weeks since she had looked at him like he was nothing.

The weight of it was suffocating.

He had thrown himself into work, drowning in late nights and empty takeout containers, but nothing filled the void. Every case, every hour spent at his desk, only reminded him of the one thing he couldn't fix.

And it was his own damn fault.

Tonight was no different.

He sat slumped on his couch, a half-empty beer bottle dangling from his fingers, the TV playing something he wasn't even watching. His apartment was a mess—dishes in the sink, unopened mail scattered on the counter, evidence of a man who didn't have the energy to care.

Then—

A knock.

Andrew tensed. He wasn't in the mood for company. Probably Bryan checking in. Or worse—Kathleen, ready to lecture him again.

He ignored it.

Another knock.

His jaw clenched. Go away.

A third knock.

With a frustrated sigh, he shoved the beer bottle onto the coffee table and pushed himself off the couch. His patience was running on fumes as he stalked to the door, his movements tense and irritated.

If this was Bryan, he was going to tell him to shove his concern where the sun didn't shine.

He swung the door open with too much force, scowling. "What—"

And then he froze.

Celeste stood in front of him.

His breath caught.

For a second, he thought he was imagining her. She was the last person he expected to see—especially at his doorstep, especially after she had all but told him she never wanted to lay eyes on him again.

She looked… different.

She was thinner, her skin still pale, but there was strength in the way she stood. Her hair was pulled back in a loose ponytail, a soft hoodie draped over her frame, but his eyes immediately zeroed in on her left shoulder. The fabric of her sleeve did little to hide the bandages beneath.

His throat tightened.

She shouldn't have come here. She should have been resting.

She shifted, her expression unreadable. "Are you going to let me in?"

Andrew swallowed hard.

His pride, his guilt, his fear—none of it mattered.

Without a word, he stepped aside.

Celeste walked past him, into his apartment, into his space, and for the first time in two weeks—

Andrew could breathe again.

Celeste walked past Andrew, stepping into his apartment for the first time in what felt like a lifetime.

The place was a disaster.

Dishes piled up in the sink. Empty takeout containers littered the coffee table. A half-empty beer bottle sat next to a stack of unopened mail. The curtains were drawn, casting the space in a dim, suffocating gloom.

It smelled like stale coffee and exhaustion.

She turned to look at him.

Andrew stood frozen by the door; his eyes locked on her like he was afraid she might disappear if he blinked. He looked awful.

His hair was a mess, longer than she remembered, as if he hadn't bothered to cut it. His usual sharp jawline was shadowed with stubble, and the dark circles under his eyes told her he hadn't been sleeping—at least not well.

She clenched her hands into fists, trying to steady herself.

He was suffering.

A part of her wanted to hold on to her anger, to remind herself why she had stayed away. But seeing him like this, so visibly wrecked, made it harder to ignore the ache in her chest.

She cleared her throat, her voice coming out softer than she intended. "When was the last time you cleaned in here?"

Andrew blinked, as if the question caught him off guard. He glanced around as if just noticing the state of his apartment for the first time.

"I don't know," he admitted, rubbing a hand over the back of his neck. "Does it matter?"

Celeste sighed, stepping further into the room.

She wasn't sure what she had expected when she came here. Maybe for him to look the same—strong, composed, unshaken. Maybe for him to throw out an arrogant remark, some cocky comment about how she couldn't stay away.

But this?

This wasn't the Andrew she knew.

This was a man who had been unravelling piece by piece.

She turned back to him. "Yes, it matters," she said quietly.

His jaw tensed. "Why are you here, Celeste?"

Her heart thumped painfully.

For two weeks, she had thought about this moment. Rehearsed all the things she wanted to say. But now, standing in front of him, her carefully planned words scattered like dust.

"I—" She hesitated, swallowing hard.

Andrew took a slow step toward her. "Are you here to tell me you forgive me?"

Celeste searched his face.

The raw vulnerability in his eyes nearly broke her.

She exhaled shakily. "I don't know," she admitted.

Andrew flinched, just barely. He nodded, his gaze dropping. "Fair enough."

The silence between them stretched, thick and weighted, pressing down on both of them like a heavy fog.

Then, finally, Celeste spoke. "I know why you said what you did."

Andrew's head snapped up, something flickering in his expression—hope? Regret? Fear? "George."

She nodded. "He told me you saw him kissing me."

Andrew let out a bitter laugh, shaking his head. "And I didn't trust you enough to confront you." He ran a hand through his hair, the frustration evident in the tense set of his jaw. His gaze flickered to hers, hesitant. "And? Does knowing why change anything?"

Celeste inhaled deeply, steadying herself. "I'm not Sarah."

Andrew stiffened. His Adam's apple bobbed as he swallowed hard. "I know you're not."

"Do you?" she challenged, her voice sharper now. "Because you treated me like her. You thought I was just like her." She took a step closer, anger simmering beneath her skin. "I was going to tell you what George did as soon as I saw you, but you didn't give me a chance. You didn't even ask."

Andrew squeezed his eyes shut for a brief moment, as if the weight of her words physically hurt him. When he opened them again, they were raw with guilt. "I know," he admitted, voice low, hoarse.

Celeste's chest tightened.

She had wanted him to fight her on this, to defend himself, to give her an excuse to hold onto the anger she had been nursing for weeks. But there was no excuse. No justification. He wasn't trying to deny it.

He had simply… given up.

She stared at him, really stared at him, and for the first time, she saw just how much this had broken him, too.

It didn't erase what he had done.

But it made her wonder if he had been punishing himself just as much as she had been punishing him.

She folded her arms, her voice softer now. "Why, Andrew?"

He exhaled sharply, dragging a hand down his face before meeting her gaze. "Because I was scared," he admitted, his voice raw. "Scared of how much I needed you. Scared that if I let myself love you, you'd destroy me more than Sarah did." His voice dropped to a whisper, thick with emotion. "Because you mean more to me than she ever did. And I still managed to destroy us."

Celeste's breath caught.

She had expected defensiveness. Justifications. Anything but this.

Not his vulnerability laid bare. Not the quiet agony in his voice.

Her arms slowly dropped to her sides, her fingers twitching with the urge to reach for him. "Andrew…"

He shook his head. "You don't owe me anything, Celeste. Not your forgiveness, not your time, not even this conversation." His lips twisted into something resembling a smile, but it was hollow, full of self-recrimination. "But you showing up here tonight? It has to mean something. And I need to know… does it mean you're willing to try to forgive me?"

Her heart pounded.

She had thought she came for closure. That she would hear him out, say her piece, and walk away.

But the truth was, she could never stop loving him.

"I love you, Andrew."

Chapter Twenty-Six

Andrew's breath hitched. His hands clenched at his sides, as if afraid to reach for something that might slip through his fingers. His eyes, full of remorse and longing, searched hers for any trace of hesitation.

"You—" His voice cracked. He swallowed hard, his throat working. "Celeste, say it again."

She stepped closer, closing the space between them. "I love you, Andrew." This time, she said it with certainty, with quiet strength. Because despite everything—the hurt, the betrayal, the pain—her love for him would never truly fade.

A sound escaped him, something between a laugh and a sob. His restraint shattered as he reached for her, his hands trembling as they cupped her face, his thumbs skimming her cheeks as if trying to memorise every inch of her.

"You love me," he whispered, his forehead pressing against hers.

She closed her eyes, leaning into his touch. "I do. But if you don't feel the same, tell me now—because I refuse to be second choice."

Andrew let out a ragged breath, his grip tightening like he was terrified she'd slip away. He pulled back just enough to look into her eyes, his expression one of pure disbelief.

"I love you more than life."

A single tear slid down her cheek. Andrew caught it with his thumb, his touch lingering, reverent.

"I'll spend forever making it up to you," he murmured. "If you'll let me."

Celeste exhaled shakily, her heart warring between fear and hope. Then, finally, she nodded. "Okay."

That was all he needed.

His lips found hers—not in desperation, not in possession, but in devotion. He kissed her like she was his redemption, like every lost moment between them had led to this one. A kiss that held the echoes of their past and the unspoken promise of their future.

When they finally pulled apart, breathless and trembling, Celeste let her fingers brush against his jaw, feeling the roughness of stubble that hadn't been there before. She searched his face, seeing the exhaustion in his eyes, the shadows of guilt and regret still lingering.

She exhaled softly. "Can I sit down? I get very tired."

Andrew didn't hesitate. Without a word, he scooped her up, careful to avoid touching her injured left shoulder. Celeste gasped, but before she could protest, he carried her across the room as if she weighed nothing, his hold protective yet gentle. He sat down on the sofa, settling her onto his lap like it was the most natural thing in the world.

His arms wrapped around her, anchoring her to him. And then, as if he couldn't help himself, he kissed her again.

This kiss was different—slower, deeper, carrying the weight of all the nights he had spent imagining this moment. It was an apology, a plea, and a vow all in one.

When he finally pulled back, his forehead rested against hers, his breath warm against her lips.

"When they took you, I thought I'd lost you forever," he whispered, his voice raw. "I've never known fear like that, Celeste. It swallowed me whole."

She swallowed, reaching up to thread her fingers through his hair, letting the soft strands slip through her touch. "I was scared too," she admitted. "But I tried to stay strong."

His grip on her tightened, like he was afraid she might disappear. "I should have protected you. I should have—"

"You couldn't have known." She placed a gentle hand against his chest, feeling the steady, reassuring beat of his heart. "No one can protect me all day every day, Andrew. Not even you."

His jaw tensed, but he nodded, as if trying to accept that she was right, but it didn't make it any easier.

They sat there in silence for a long moment, wrapped in each other, the weight of everything they had endured pressing down on them. But for the first time in weeks, the burden felt lighter.

Andrew kissed her temple, his lips lingering. "Stay," he murmured against her skin. "Stay with me tonight."

Celeste hesitated, not because she didn't want to—God, she wanted nothing more than to stay in his arms—but because there was still so much to say, so much to heal.

Still, she found herself whispering, "Okay."

Because despite everything, despite the pain and the past, this—this—was where she belonged.

They spent the rest of the night talking and kissing—soft, unhurried kisses that spoke of longing and healing. Andrew held her close, his arms a shield around her, as if by simply keeping her near, he could erase every wound, every ache. Celeste was still too fragile for anything more, but that was fine with him. He didn't need more. He just needed her.

At some point, she rested her head against his chest, her fingers tracing idle patterns over his shirt. The steady rhythm of his heartbeat calmed her, made her feel safe in a way she hadn't in weeks.

"I believed you," she murmured, breaking the quiet.

Andrew's fingers, which had been running gently through her hair, stilled. "Believed what?"

"When you told me I was just a hookup." Her voice was barely above a whisper, but the words carried the weight of all the pain they had caused.

Andrew inhaled sharply, his entire body stiffening beneath her. He looked away for a brief moment, as if ashamed, before forcing himself to meet her eyes. His voice cracked under the weight of his own guilt. "Celeste... I hated myself the moment I said those words. I don't think I'll ever forgive myself for how I made you feel. But I was so caught up in my own perceived hurt, my own insecurities, that I didn't think. I lashed out, and I broke the one thing I never wanted to lose."

She swallowed, her throat tight, emotions thick in her chest.

"I'm so sorry," he whispered, cupping her face with gentle hands. His thumbs brushed away a tear she hadn't even realised had fallen. "I love you so much. I have since the day I saw you walking toward me in the club. Maybe even before that. I was just too damn scared to admit it."

Celeste closed her eyes, letting his words sink in, letting them soothe the wounds he had left behind. When she opened them again, she saw the truth written all over his face—the fear, the regret, the love.

"I love you too," she whispered, leaning in to press her lips to his—lightly, tenderly. A silent promise.

Andrew exhaled against her mouth, his breath unsteady, as if the weight of losing her had finally lifted from his chest. His voice was hoarse, raw with conviction. "Then let me spend the rest of my life proving it to you. Every single day."

Celeste hesitated for only a moment before she admitted softly, "You know, I fell in love with you when I was fifteen."

Andrew froze, pulling back just enough to search her face. "What?" His voice was thick with disbelief.

She smiled, a touch of shyness in her expression. "It's true. I was madly in love with you before you even married Sarah."

His gaze softened, something wistful passing over his features before he let out a quiet, almost pained chuckle. "If only I had my eyes open back then."

Celeste laughed, shaking her head. "You were too old for me."

He grinned against her lips, brushing a kiss over them. "I would have waited."

Her heart squeezed at his words, at the thought of how different their story could have been. But maybe this was how it was always meant to unfold. Maybe they had to lose each other to truly understand what they had.

And for the first time in a long time, Celeste let herself believe that maybe, just maybe, they could still have their forever.

Andrew suddenly stilled, his breath catching. Then, as if a thought had struck him, he pulled away, his eyes burning with something unreadable. "Wait. There's something I need to give you."

Celeste watched in confusion as he got up and strode toward his bedside table. He pulled open the drawer, retrieving a small, wrapped package before turning back to her. His expression was almost shy as he handed it over.

"I know it's late," he said, rubbing the back of his neck, "but I hope you like it."

Curious, Celeste took the gift from him and carefully peeled away the wrapping. Inside was a velvet box, smooth beneath her fingertips. She lifted the lid—and gasped.

Nestled inside was a stunning diamond bracelet. A single row of brilliant diamonds glittered under the dim light, and in the centre, an outline of a heart was delicately set in white gold.

Her breath caught. "Andrew… it's beautiful." She looked up at him, her eyes shining. "Thank you."

His lips curved into a soft smile as he reached for her hand. "Happy birthday, sweetheart."

Celeste swallowed against the sudden lump in her throat. She had spent her birthday waiting for him, believing that he had forgotten. But he hadn't.

Tears burned her eyes as she brushed her fingers over the delicate piece of jewellery, feeling the weight of what it meant.

She looked up at him, her heart full. "Put it on me?"

Andrew took the bracelet, his fingers gentle as he fastened it around her wrist. His touch lingered, and when he looked at her, there was something unspoken in his gaze— something deep and unshakable.

Celeste lifted her wrist, admiring the way the diamonds caught the light. "I love it," she whispered.

Andrew cupped her cheek, his thumb tracing the curve of her jaw. "I love you."

She leaned into him, their foreheads touching. "I know," she murmured. And she did.

Chapter Twenty-Seven

Over the next six weeks, Celeste slowly healed. Not just from the bullet wound that had nearly taken her life, but from the emotional wounds that had cut even deeper. The scars left by Andrew's past mistakes, by her own fears, by the pain of nearly losing everything—they weren't erased, but they had finally begun to heal.

Andrew had been patient, careful, and unwavering in his devotion. Every day, he proved that he was here to stay, not just with words but with actions. He took care of her without making her feel weak. He let her lean on him without making her feel dependent. And most of all, he never once made her doubt how much he loved her.

She had moved back from her parents' home to her apartment four weeks ago, reclaiming a part of herself that had felt lost in the chaos. Andrew had been there as often as work allowed, and Celeste—despite pretending to roll her eyes at his constant hovering—had secretly loved every second of it.

They had grown stronger than ever, their bond reforged not from blind passion, but from understanding, forgiveness, and an undeniable love that had survived everything thrown at it.

Though they had shared a bed, they hadn't made love—not because the desire wasn't there, but because Celeste's shoulder was still healing, and Andrew refused to let her feel even a flicker of unnecessary pain. He was content to simply hold her at night, to run his fingers through her hair, to press the softest of kisses against her temple. There would be time—plenty of time—when she was fully healed. For now, he was happy just having her close, keeping her safe.

Celeste was planning to return to work in the next few days, a decision that left Andrew both proud and nervous. He trusted her strength, but the thought of her out in the world again, beyond his immediate protection, unsettled him more than he cared to admit.

It was the Saturday before she was set to return, and she was spending the night at Andrew's penthouse, something that had become routine. But tonight was different.

Tonight, Andrew had a surprise for her.

He was going to propose.

It was something he had never imagined himself doing again. After the disaster of his first marriage, he had sworn off the idea of ever putting a ring on another woman's finger. Marriage had felt like a cage; a contract built on false promises and inevitable disappointment.

But then there was Celeste.

Celeste, who had turned his world upside down. Who had taught him what love was supposed to feel like. Who had made him realise that real love—true, enduring love— wasn't a burden. It was a gift.

He could not, would not, imagine a life without her in it.

And tonight, he would ask her to be his forever.

Celeste was at Andrew's apartment after he had finished work, a familiar and comforting routine they had fallen into. But tonight felt different.

Andrew had taken her to dinner at one of Sydney's most romantic restaurants. She looked breathtaking—elegant yet effortlessly beautiful. But more than that, she looked healthy, vibrant, and whole again. Seeing her like this, after everything they had been through, filled him with immeasurable relief and gratitude.

The evening had been perfect—soft candlelight, good wine, laughter, stolen glances. It was the kind of dinner that made the world shrink to just the two of them.

She was still smiling when they reached his apartment, still wrapped in the warmth of the evening. But the moment she stepped inside, her breath caught. The entire living room was bathed in the warm flicker of candlelight. Hundreds of candles, glowing softly, casting golden reflections across the floor-to-ceiling windows. The air smelled faintly of roses, a delicate floral fragrance that blended with the crisp scent of the night air drifting through the open balcony doors.

It was intimate. Romantic. Perfect.

Andrew took Celeste's hands in his, rubbing his thumbs over her knuckles as he stared at her, his expression suddenly serious.

She looked a little confused, tilting her head. "Andrew?"

He exhaled, steadying himself. This was it.

"Celeste," he started, his voice thick with emotion. "I arrived back in Sydney only four months ago, and I had no intentions of getting involved with any woman. I wasn't looking for love. Hell, I didn't even think I wanted it. But then I saw you." His lips curved slightly, his eyes softening. "You took my breath away."

She let out a small, shaky laugh.

He continued, his grip on her hands tightening. "I fought it at first. Told myself it didn't mean anything, that I was just drawn to you in some fleeting, meaningless way. But then Bryan and George started pursuing you, and I realised I couldn't stand the thought of another man touching you, kissing you." He let out a breath. "And then you told me about your ridiculous plan to lose your innocence before your twenty-fifth birthday, and Celeste—" He shook his head. "I couldn't even contemplate you being with Bryan. The thought of it drove me insane."

Her eyes shimmered in the candlelight.

"And then we made love," he went on, his voice turning rough with emotion. "And my mind was blown. I've never felt for a woman what I felt for you that night. What I still feel for you. You were so open, so giving, so incredibly honest that it brought me to my knees." He swallowed, his eyes darkening with regret. "And then I ruined it. I let my own fears, my own past, blind me. I let jealousy and stupidity convince me you wanted someone else, and I said things that should never have left my mouth."

Celeste squeezed his hands, as if telling him she forgave him.

"Even before you were taken, I knew I had made a mistake," he admitted. "I knew you would never have betrayed me. I wanted to fix things, to make things right. But before I could, you were gone." His voice cracked slightly. "I will never forget the terror I felt in those four days. Not just the fear of losing you, but the crushing agony of knowing that if something happened to you, I might never get the chance to make it right. I might never hold you in my arms again."

Celeste bit her lip, tears welling in her eyes.

"When you wouldn't let me see you afterward," he continued, his tone raw, "I thought I'd lost you for good. And for the first time in my life, I didn't care about anything else. Nothing mattered. Not work. Not my past. Not my future. Nothing." He exhaled, shaking his head slightly. "I was married to Sarah for eight years, and I never felt the kind of despair I felt at the thought of losing you. That was when I knew—what I felt for her was nothing compared to what I feel for you."

Her breath hitched.

"I never thought I'd love like this," Andrew admitted. "I never thought I'd find someone who could break down every wall I put up, who could make me want more, need more." He swallowed hard. "You have opened my eyes, Celeste. You've opened my heart. I can't imagine my life—any part of it—without you. And I don't want to."

She let out a quiet sob, her lips trembling.

"I love you with every fibre of my being," he whispered. "And I want you to be mine forever."

Then, slowly, he dropped to one knee.

Celeste let out a sharp breath, her hand flying to her mouth as she watched him pull a small velvet box from his pocket.

Andrew flicked it open, revealing a stunning diamond solitaire, the light catching on its flawless facets.

His voice was steady but filled with emotion as he asked, "Will you please marry me and make me the luckiest man on earth? Not because of fate. Not because of time. Not because of anything other than the fact that you love me. Be my wife, Celeste. Be my life. Because I'm forever yours."

Silent tears spilled down her cheeks. She tried to speak, but the lump in her throat wouldn't let her.

So, she nodded.

Frantically. Desperately.

Andrew let out a soft laugh of relief as he stood, slipping the ring onto her trembling finger before cupping her face in his hands.

"You're mine now, and I'm yours," he whispered, brushing his lips over hers in the gentlest of kisses. "Forever."

And Celeste, overwhelmed, overjoyed, wrapped her arms around him, pressing her face into his chest.

Because she knew—she had always known.

Andrew was hers.

And she was his.

Because love—real love—wasn't a burden. It was a gift. And it was theirs.

Forever.

Epilogue

18 months later…

Celeste stood in front of the full-length mirror, smoothing down the sleek satin of her dress. The deep emerald-green fabric hugged her curves in all the right places, the thigh-high slit revealing just a tantalising glimpse of her smooth skin as she moved. Her chestnut-brown hair was swept up into an elegant chignon, with a few loose tendrils framing her face, softening her sharp cheekbones. A pair of delicate diamond earrings—Andrew's gift from their wedding day—twinkled against her skin, and her makeup was subtle but striking, emphasising her full lips and the warmth in her gold-flecked hazel eyes.

She took a breath, steadying herself. Tonight wasn't just about celebrating their first year as husband and wife—it was about telling Andrew something that would change their lives forever.

As she stepped into the living room, her husband's gaze found her immediately.

Andrew Carter was already devastatingly handsome, but tonight, in his tailored black suit, the crisp white shirt unbuttoned just enough to hint at the strong chest beneath, he was breathtaking. His dark eyes raked over her slowly, appreciation and love shining in their depths.

A slow, knowing smile spread across his face. "You look stunning." He took both her hands, lifting them to his lips and pressing a lingering kiss to each. His touch was warm, reverent. "That dress is beautiful." Then, after a pause, his mouth curved into something far more wicked. "I can't wait to take it off you later tonight."

Celeste laughed, shaking her head. "You should be ashamed of yourself."

"Oh, I am," he murmured, his voice dropping into that deep, sinful tone that never failed to make her shiver. "I'm ashamed I can't do it right now."

Her heart fluttered, heat blooming beneath her skin. "Stop, or I will let you."

His eyes darkened at the challenge, but with a low chuckle, he offered his arm. "As tempting as that sounds, I made dinner reservations for us. And I fully intend to spoil my wife tonight."

They spent the evening wrapped in soft candlelight, savouring every bite of their meal, every stolen glance, every touch beneath the table. It was a night of quiet luxury and deep, unspoken love. They toasted to a year of marriage, to laughter, to all the moments that had brought them here.

But Celeste's heartbeat just a little faster with anticipation.

When they arrived home, Andrew stepped inside first, only to freeze in the doorway. His sharp intake of breath echoed in the quiet room.

The living room was bathed in the glow of hundreds of flickering candles, their golden light reflecting off the sleek hardwood floors, just like the night he had proposed eighteen months ago. The faint scent of roses lingered in the air; a soft, familiar fragrance that tugged at something deep in his chest.

He turned slowly, eyes locking onto hers. His voice was hushed, filled with emotion. "What's this, Mrs. Carter?"

Celeste stepped forward, taking both of his hands in hers.

"You know how much I love you?" she asked softly.

His grip tightened. "Yes. And I love you."

Her heart swelled. She took a steadying breath, then guided his hand to her flat stomach, pressing his palm against the warmth of her skin.

Andrew's body tensed. His blue eyes widened, filled with something close to awe, his breath catching as he looked from her stomach back up to her face. But he remained silent, waiting, almost as if he were afraid to hope.

Celeste swallowed past the lump in her throat, her voice trembling slightly as she whispered, "Mr. Carter, husband, the light of my life, my love… we are going to have a baby."

For a long moment, he just stared at her, as if the words hadn't quite registered. Then, slowly, his fingers curled against her stomach, his touch reverent, his expression filled with something raw and unfiltered—joy, disbelief, an overwhelming love that stole his voice.

"Celeste…" he finally breathed.

And then, without warning, he swept her into his arms, lifting her clear off the ground as he buried his face in her neck.

She laughed through her tears as he held her tightly, his body shaking with emotion.

"A baby?" he whispered, pulling back just enough to look into her eyes, as if he needed to see the truth in them.

She nodded, smiling so hard it hurt. "A baby."

Andrew let out a soft, disbelieving laugh before capturing her mouth in a kiss—one filled with wonder, with gratitude, with the kind of love that only grew stronger with time.

When he finally pulled away, his forehead rested against hers, his voice thick with emotion.

"You have no idea how happy you've just made me."

Celeste cupped his face, brushing her thumb over his cheek.

"I think I do," she whispered.

Wrapped in the golden glow of candlelight and the warmth of his embrace, Celeste knew their love had only deepened over the past eighteen months. They had come to understand that a love like theirs was rare and precious—something to be cherished, nurtured, and never taken for granted. And as she gazed into Andrew's eyes, filled with unwavering devotion, she knew with absolute certainty—this was only the beginning of their forever.

The End

The Playboy's Surrender

Alison Reid

A complete standalone romance
Previously published individually

Chapter One

Olivia Clifton was only twenty-three, and though she stood tall and carried herself with quiet strength, flying still made her uneasy. She wasn't terrified, exactly—but comfortable? Not even close.

To distract herself, she glanced down at her phone and reread the article she'd saved about the island she was headed to. The seaplane rattled gently beneath her, and she gripped the armrest tighter as her mother's voice echoed in her mind: "If God wanted us to fly, Livvie, He would've given us wings."

A soft smile touched Olivia's lips.

Her mother had always known how to make her laugh, even in the hardest moments. She was the kind of woman who had poured her entire heart into everything—into life, into love, and most of all, into being a mother. Taken too soon by cancer, she had died with grace and fierce tenderness, leaving Olivia with one final charge: "Live your life, baby. It's the only one you get. I don't regret mine—not a minute. I'm going to be with your father now."

He had died two years before in a tragic car accident, and her mother had never been the same afterward. They had been everything to each other—deeply in love, partners in every way. Olivia found peace in imagining them reunited, wrapped in the same kind of love she had always hoped to find for herself.

Blinking back the sting of tears, Olivia turned her focus to the glowing screen in her hand.

Tucked away in the crystal-clear waters of the South Pacific, Motukava is a secluded gem nestled among the lesser-known islets near Bora Bora. Encircled by a barrier reef and kissed by warm trade winds, this private island is a place untouched by time—wild, breathtaking, and heartbreakingly beautiful.

The shoreline is a sweeping crescent of sugar-white sand that melts into turquoise shallows. The water is so clear you can see the coral gardens below and the gentle movements of stingrays and reef fish gliding in and out of view. Palm trees sway lazily in the breeze, and vibrant bougainvillea spills over the pathways that wind through the resort's lush tropical gardens.

At the northern tip of the island, a row of ultra-luxury overwater bungalows stretch into the lagoon like a pearl necklace, each one outfitted with private decks, glass floors, and infinity-edge plunge pools. At the heart of the island stands the Alden Pavilion, a striking architectural centrepiece built with Polynesian-inspired design, housing the resort's fine dining restaurant, open-air lounge, and wine cellar.

Further inland, through a grove of hibiscus and frangipani trees, the kids' club is a magical hideaway—designed like a treehouse village—with hanging bridges, nature trails, and beachside learning huts. And soon, a holistic wellness retreat featuring yoga, spa treatments, and a meditation dome will be added to the impressive list of amenities.

Access to Motukava is by private seaplane or yacht only. There are no roads, no noise, and no distractions—just the symphony of the sea and the serenity of nature.

The island is completely self-sustained and eco-luxurious, with solar energy, desalination systems, and a strong focus on preserving its natural beauty.

Motukava is the crown jewel of billionaire playboy Jack Alden's empire—a sanctuary of indulgence and escape. More than just a resort, it's a world apart—where time slows, pretences vanish, and love stories are written beneath endless stars.

Olivia exhaled slowly, letting the words on her phone settle into her chest like the beginning of a promise. Motukava is not just a resort. It's a world apart—a place where time slows, masks fall, and love stories unfold under endless stars.

It sounded like paradise. And in just minutes, she'd be standing in the middle of it.

She glanced out the small oval window of the seaplane—and her breath caught.

There it was.

Rising from the sea like something out of a dream, Motukava shimmered in the late morning light. Lush green palms fringed the white sand shoreline, and the lagoon sparkled in impossible shades of turquoise and sapphire. From this height, the overwater bungalows stretched like pearls across the shallows, and the island's gentle curves gleamed like they'd been traced by a lover's hand.

A lump rose in her throat. This wasn't just beautiful—it was otherworldly. And beneath the fluttering nerves, a steady pulse of hope began to beat in her chest.

Maybe this was it.

Maybe this was where everything would finally change between her and Wyatt—the boy who had lived next door for as long as she could remember. The boy she had never stopped loving, no matter how many years had passed.

They'd grown up, side by side, in a sleepy suburb just north of Sydney, where the air always smelled faintly of salt and eucalyptus, and the sound of crashing waves was as familiar as birdsong. It felt like another lifetime now—like some faded chapter from a story she'd once told herself. The warmth of that old neighbourhood, the cul-de-sac cricket games, the smell of sausages on the barbecue—it all seemed a million miles away from this postcard-perfect island.

Wyatt had always been older. Wiser. Cooler. Five years separated them, but it may as well have been a decade when they were young. He was the golden boy—the one with the untouchable smile and a surfboard always leaning by his front door.

When she was little, he'd babysit her sometimes. Not that he was particularly attentive. He was usually distracted—half-watching cartoons with one eye, thumbing through texts with the other, surf wax tucked in his back pocket and his board already waiting by the door. But still, he was there. Present enough that she clung to those moments like treasures.

She'd sit at the front window after he left, chin resting on her knees, and watch as he jogged toward the beach—shirtless, bronzed, lit by the sinking sun like something out of a dream. Salt crystals sparkled in his tousled blond hair, his skin tanned by endless summers. He was effortless, free, a little wild. The boy every girl wanted.

And he had always been the one she waited for. Quietly. Constantly.

Even now, even here, on this impossibly beautiful island—part of her was still that girl at the window, hoping he'd turn around and really see her.

When he'd called out of the blue to say there was a vacancy on the island—a position in the resort's kids' club—her heart had leapt into her throat. He'd said, "You'd be perfect for it, Liv." And for a moment, it felt like the universe had cracked open and offered her a sliver of fate.

She applied that night.

And now, here she was—thousands of miles from home, flying over the Pacific, her whole life packed into a modest suitcase and the desperate hope that maybe... finally... he'd see her the way she saw him.

The plane touched down with a soft kiss against the lagoon, the floats skimming across glass-clear water. Olivia stepped off the seaplane and onto the sun-warmed dock, the heat wrapping around her like a welcome. The air smelled of salt and hibiscus, thick with tropical bloom and possibility. A soft breeze tugged at the hem of her cotton sundress as she adjusted her grip on her suitcase.

Her sneakers squeaked faintly against the polished wood.

And then she heard it.

"Liv!"

Her heart leapt.

She turned.

There he was.

Wyatt Boyd—taller than she remembered, bronzed, barefoot, and shirtless, his board shorts slung low on lean hips, a surfboard tucked under one arm. His smile stretched wide as he jogged toward her, waves crashing behind him like applause. He looked like a postcard—no, like every crush she'd ever had, distilled into a single breathtaking moment.

"Wyatt," she breathed, her voice catching in her throat.

He hugged her tightly, lifting her off her feet for a moment before setting her down with a grin and a quick kiss to her forehead. Her heart fluttered like a schoolgirl's diary.

"You look… exactly the same," he said, giving her ponytail a playful ruffle. "I'm so glad you made it."

"I'm glad too," she said, trying to keep her voice even. "It's beautiful here."

He nodded, already glancing toward the beach. "It is. The kids' club needs someone just like you. I told Julie you'd be a great fit."

Julie. The one who'd officially hired her. Olivia managed a smile, swallowing the urge to ask if he really meant it. Before she could say more, he shifted his board and took a step backward.

"Anyway, I've got a lesson starting in ten," he said, already in motion. "Let's catch up later, yeah?"

"Yeah," she murmured, watching him jog off, sand spraying behind him.

So that was the reunion.

Not exactly cinematic.

Not exactly anything, really. But then again, maybe the best stories didn't start with fireworks—they started with ordinary moments that refused to fade.

Before she could dwell too long on Wyatt's breezy departure, a smiling woman in a crisp white uniform approached with purposeful grace. A clipboard was tucked under one arm, and her sleek ponytail didn't have a single strand out of place.

"Miss Clifton?" the woman asked warmly. "Welcome to Motukava. I'm Kate Langdon—I'll be looking after you today. We're thrilled to have you with us."

"Thank you," Olivia replied, straightening instinctively. Her fingers fluttered to her sundress, smoothing the light cotton as her nerves caught up to her again.

Kate gave a reassuring nod. "We'll get you settled into your bungalow first, then this afternoon, I will give you your orientation which will include a tour of the kids' club. No pressure. It's mostly about getting your bearings today."

Olivia smiled, grateful for the kindness in her voice.

They climbed into a sleek white golf cart that hummed quietly as Kate steered it away from the dock. The path curved gently inland, winding beneath a canopy of palm trees that swayed lazily overhead. Bougainvillea spilled from trellises in bursts of pink and coral, and the air was filled with the scent of plumeria and salt.

As they rode, Olivia glimpsed flashes of the turquoise lagoon between the trees—so bright and crystalline it didn't seem real. It shimmered like a promise, like something only people with charmed lives got to experience. Not people like her, who had clawed their way through student debt and side jobs just to land this one chance.

The cart turned onto a smaller, shell-dusted path, leading them into a tucked-away grove of modest bungalows. Each one had a small porch, whitewashed walls, and a clay-tiled roof. Tropical plants framed every entrance, and the whole area felt peaceful, separate—like a little village nestled in paradise.

"This is the staff quarters," Kate explained as they pulled up to one of the bungalows. "Everyone working in hospitality stays in this section. It's a short walk to the main resort, and even shorter to the kids' club."

Olivia stepped out, her shoes crunching lightly on the gravel. The bungalow was simple but charming—one room, a tiny kitchenette, and a screened-in porch with a view of the jungle. Birds called out from somewhere above, and a soft breeze lifted the curtains through the open window.

"It's lovely," Olivia said, her voice soft with awe.

Kate smiled. "It's cozy, but the view makes up for the size. And you'll be amazed how quickly it feels like home. I'll leave your key on the table—you've got about an hour before we start the tour. Take a few moments to settle in."

As Kate turned to go, Olivia hesitated. "Um—do you know where Wyatt Boyd is staying?"

Kate paused, arching a brow. "Wyatt? He's one of the instructors at the water sports centre, right?"

Olivia nodded, trying to sound casual. "We grew up next door to each other. It's been a while since I've seen him."

"Oh, that's sweet. He's in the staff village too, just on the other side of the grove near the equipment shed. Probably out surfing or water skiing, knowing him."

"Right," Olivia said with a quick smile. "Thanks."

As the cart zipped away, she lingered on the porch for a moment, listening to the rustling leaves and the distant crash of waves. Her suitcase sat at her feet, dusty and travel-worn, but full of all the hopes she hadn't dared to say out loud.

She was here. Not just physically—but really here. On the island. With a job. With Wyatt.

It hadn't been the grand, romantic reunion she'd imagined. No fireworks. No lingering looks. Just a forehead kiss and a rushed goodbye.

Still… she was closer than she'd ever been.

Maybe the story wasn't unfolding the way she'd pictured it in her head, but stories had a funny way of twisting when you least expected it.

And maybe—just maybe—Motukava wasn't just a paradise for the rich and restless.

Maybe it was where her story finally began.

Chapter Two

The view from the Alden Pavilion's private terrace was spectacular—sunlight scattered across the lagoon like gold leaf on glass, the breeze rich with hibiscus and salt. Most people would kill for it. Jack Alden barely noticed.

He leaned against the stone balustrade, coffee cooling in one hand, eyes fixed on the horizon but mind miles away.

At thirty, Jack was the kind of man who turned heads without trying. Tall and broad-shouldered, he carried the lean, athletic build of someone who surfed when he could and trained when he couldn't. Dark hair curled slightly at his collar, tousled just enough to look expensive. His eyes—rich, espresso brown—were deep-set and intense, the kind that gave away nothing. His jaw was sharp, his skin sun-bronzed, and he had the quiet confidence of a man used to being listened to.

He wore linen and leather like armour, and his smile—when he chose to use it—could dismantle even the most sceptical woman. But lately, he hadn't been smiling much.

Not since Charlotte.

He took a slow sip of the coffee, more for something to do than out of need. The bitterness suited him. Lately, everything tasted a little like regret.

He'd met Charlotte at a charity gala in Monaco—flawless skin, champagne laughter, a diamond necklace that had clearly not been her first. She was beautiful, poised, and impeccably connected. She knew the difference between vintages without looking at the label and could navigate a social hierarchy faster than she could say "private equity."

He hadn't loved her. But he'd hoped he might learn to.

And after the steady parade of models, influencers, and heiresses who'd wanted his last name more than his heart, Charlotte had seemed… appropriate. Refined. Safe. At thirty, with five world-class resorts under his name and a media empire circling his every move, Jack had started to wonder if maybe love wasn't essential. Maybe a marriage of equals—mutual benefit, shared ambition, polite affection—was the grown-up choice.

Then came the prenup conversation.

He remembered it too vividly.

They'd been on his yacht in the Aegean, anchored off a private cove. The sky was velvet blue, the water crystalline. He'd poured her a glass of her favourite Chablis, and she'd curled against him in her silk robe, tan legs tucked beneath her like a cat in sunlight.

And then she'd said it. Lightly, as if it were just a thought.

"Jack, if we're going to do this properly, I think we need to talk about the prenup. I know your lawyers will want one, of course, but I'll need my own team to review it. And I think we both know a standard payout isn't exactly… reflective of what I'm bringing to the table."

He'd paused mid-sip, brows lifting slightly. "Reflective?" he repeated.

She smiled, slow and polished. "Darling, I'll be the wife of Jack Alden. That comes with expectations—appearances, hosting, travel. I'll be stepping into a role, not just marrying a man. You may not believe in fairy tales, but I didn't exactly sign up for a minimalist marriage."

The wool hadn't slipped from his eyes—it had been yanked.

Suddenly, every compliment, every laugh, every carefully timed appearance beside him at gala events came into focus. Charlotte had never loved him. She'd loved the idea of him. Of the lifestyle. Of the power and proximity.

He remembered setting his glass down on the polished teak table, hands steady even as his chest went tight.

"I see," he'd said.

"Don't be offended," she added quickly. "This is how people like us do things. It's practical."

But Jack had never been interested in practical. Not really. He'd built his empire from the ground up, yes—but not because he wanted to play the part. He wanted something real. Something rare. Something that couldn't be bought or bartered or negotiated with lawyers.

That night, after she'd fallen asleep, he'd sat alone at the bow of the yacht until dawn broke across the sea. And when the sun rose, so did his decision.

By noon, Charlotte was on his private jet back to London, with an extremely expensive diamond engagement ring and a platinum bracelet as a parting gift and a diplomatic goodbye.

It hadn't been messy. Jack didn't do messy. But the ache lingered. Not for her—but for what he'd nearly accepted. For the version of himself he'd almost become.

Now, a month later, he stood overlooking the island he loved most—Motukava. His crown jewel. His sanctuary. The one resort he didn't let investors touch.

Here, the air was cleaner. The silence deeper. The smiles more honest.

Here, no one cared about his money. At least, not as much.

He was still Jack Alden—billionaire, media fascination, international playboy—but on this island, he could forget all that. He could dig his heels into the sand and remember who he used to be.

And maybe, just maybe, remember what it felt like to want something real.

He set his coffee down and turned toward the glass doors leading into the Pavilion's executive lounge. The season was beginning. Guests were arriving. Staff were being briefed.

He was bored.

It crept in like humidity—clinging, heavy, impossible to shake. The sky was postcard blue. The palm trees swayed like dancers. Everything was perfect.

And yet, he felt absolutely nothing.

He was here to oversee the final stage of the newest addition to Motukava—a state-of-the-art holistic wellness retreat nestled into the northern cliffs of the island. A passion project. At least, it had started that way. A place for serenity. For stillness. For unplugging from the weight of the world.

The retreat itself was a masterpiece in progress—curved white architecture carved into the jungle like it had grown there, with floor-to-ceiling glass designed to blur the line between inside and out. It featured a meditation dome made from bamboo and quartz, suspended over a reflection pool. Spa suites hidden behind waterfalls. Open-air yoga platforms shaded by swaying vines. Every texture, every scent, every sound—calculated for peace.

Now the structure was complete. The finishing touches would begin next week: organic stone flooring, artisan copper soaking tubs, salt crystal lighting, eucalyptus walls in the aromatherapy rooms. It had to be flawless. This was Motukava. His pride. His escape.

Still… he was restless.

He wandered from the Pavilion's executive lounge, then out through the private corridor that led to the Alden Pavilion main reception room—a central hub of polished marble, rich timber, and tropical elegance that welcomed elite guests and hosted VIP briefings. He wasn't expected anywhere just yet. And he didn't particularly want to be. He just needed to move.

As he stepped into the air-conditioned hush of the Pavilion foyer, he paused, something—or other, someone—catching his eye.

She stood alone by the check-in desk, clutching a clipboard like a shield, nervously shifting from foot to foot. A woman. Young, maybe early twenties. Plain, if he was being honest, but not unpleasant to look at. Her dark blonde hair was pulled into a messy ponytail, frizz curling at the edges from the heat. He couldn't see her eyes from this distance, but she had an earnestness about her that made him look twice.

She wore the most unflattering sundress he'd seen in a decade—something shapeless and faded, with oversized sunflowers and wide straps that did nothing for her figure. Not the sort of attire you'd see on a Motukava guest, who paid thousands a night to exist in curated glamour.

And yet… there was something.

A grace that transcended the clothes. A posture not polished, but quietly self-possessed. She looked wildly out of place—but not in a way that called for fixing. More like a misplaced note in a symphony. Unexpected… yet somehow right.

He furrowed his brow and turned toward the front desk, where Kate, the Pavilion's guest liaison, was logging arrivals with her usual competence.

"Kate," he said quietly, his gaze lingering on the girl near the front desk. "Who's that?"

Kate looked up from her screen, then followed the angle of his nod. "Oh—Mr. Alden, that's our new hire for the kids' club. Olivia Clifton."

Olivia Clifton.

The name meant nothing to him.

"She's just waiting for me to give her orientation," Kate added, shifting her tablet to one side. "Arrived on the early flight this morning. Julie says she's got excellent credentials—degree in child development, summer camp director, experience nannying abroad. Really solid references."

Jack's brows lifted slightly. "I'm sure she does."

It wasn't her résumé that caught his attention.

It was the way she stood—uneasy, yes, as though trying to make herself smaller—but still somehow composed. Her arms were folded protectively over her clipboard, but her spine was straight, her chin lifted just enough to suggest quiet resilience. Like she'd learned to hold herself together in places where no one else would do it for her.

Definitely not a guest.

And not the usual hire either.

She was plainly dressed—too plainly for Motukava. The sun dress looked like it had been pulled from the back of a second-hand suitcase: shapeless, faded, yellow sunflowers on washed-out blue cotton. No makeup, no jewellery, not even sandals that matched. Most staff arrived with a sparkle of ambition in their eyes, hoping to climb their way into the glamorous side of resort life. Olivia Clifton didn't look like she had time for sparkle.

But she didn't look lost, either.

Jack studied her a moment longer. Her profile was gentle—delicate nose, soft mouth, a few strands of hair falling free from her ponytail to catch the light. He still couldn't see her eyes, and yet—he found himself curious. Not attracted, not in the way he usually was. Jack Alden had a type: leggy, poised, camera-ready. Women who looked like they belonged on the cover of a glossy travel magazine, draped across a yacht or sipping champagne at sunset.

This girl didn't fit the mould. Not even close.

But there was something there. A quietness that didn't feel weak. A stillness that suggested substance.

He wasn't drawn to her beauty—he wouldn't have even called her beautiful.

But he was… intrigued.

Something about her felt unscripted. Real. And in a world built on polish and performance, that was rarer than gold.

"Let me know how she does," he said quietly, turning away.

"I will," Kate replied, already stepping around the desk to greet Olivia with a warm smile.

Jack walked on, heading toward the northern path where the wellness retreat gleamed in the morning sun. Construction noise floated faintly on the breeze—hammers, drills, the occasional bark of a foreman's orders—but his mind wasn't on the build anymore.

He kept seeing her—her posture, her stillness. A woman trying not to be seen… and yet impossible to ignore.

He tried to put her out of his mind. He had work to do.

Chapter Three

Olivia Clifton adjusted the clipboard in her hands for the third time, trying to look like she belonged.

The lobby was unreal—open-air, cool with polished stone beneath her sandals and towering palms growing straight through the floor. Everything shimmered with quiet luxury. A water feature burbled somewhere behind her, and the air smelled like coconut, lime, and money.

She felt like she'd walked into a travel magazine by accident.

Her sundress was sticking to her back in the heat, and her hair—despite her best attempt at a ponytail—was already losing the battle against the island's humidity. She resisted the urge to smooth it again, instead locking her elbows and keeping her eyes fixed on the reception desk.

She had no idea where to look, where to stand, or what to do with her hands.

Don't fidget, she told herself. Just… breathe.

This wasn't the first time she'd started a new job, but it felt like the highest stakes. Motukava wasn't just a resort. It was the resort. A place so exclusive it didn't even advertise. Families with last names that opened doors flew halfway across the world to spend two weeks here, and Olivia was being trusted to help take care of their children.

You earned this, she reminded herself. Julie vouched for you. You've done this before. You are not an imposter.

But still, the little voice in the back of her head whispered that she didn't belong here. Not in this kind of place. Not with this kind of beauty. The guests walking past wore designer swimwear and had hair that didn't frizz. Their flip-flops probably cost more than her monthly rent back home.

She shifted her weight to one foot and accidentally made eye contact with a man across the foyer.

Tall. Barefoot. Linen shirt open at the throat. Skin bronzed like he'd never even heard of winter.

He was watching her.

Not in a creepy way. Not like some men used to—calculating, performative, always scanning for angles.

No. This man—whoever he was—looked at her like he was trying to solve a puzzle.

Their eyes didn't quite meet before he turned away, walking toward the far side of the Pavilion with the kind of relaxed authority that told her he belonged here more than anyone.

"Olivia?"

She startled slightly and turned toward Kate's voice. She had a tablet in hand and a practiced smile.

"You ready for your first look around the kids' club?"

Olivia smiled, her shoulders relaxing ever so slightly. "I am, thanks. I heard it's wonderful here."

"Oh, it's more than that," Kate said with a knowing grin, her tone laced with the kind of pride only someone who truly loved their job could carry. "Motukava is… special. Once it gets under your skin, you never want to leave."

She glanced down at her tablet. "Julie says you've got impeccable references. Camp director, child development major, international nanny experience… But what stood out most was this little note she wrote: 'She's magic with kids.'"

Olivia's smile turned shy. "I just… try to see them," she said softly, fingers brushing the edge of her clipboard. "That's usually the hard part, right? For grown-ups? Really seeing them."

Kate blinked, her smile warming. "I think you're going to do just fine here."

They turned toward a staff-only hallway, tucked discreetly behind a carved teak screen, and Olivia followed, her footsteps quieter now, steadier. Still, something tugged at her—an invisible thread pulling her glance over her shoulder one last time.

The barefoot man in the linen shirt was gone.

But his gaze stayed with her.

It hadn't been invasive. Or flirtatious. He hadn't smirked or sized her up. He'd simply looked—as if he were trying to figure out what he was seeing. Like she wasn't what he expected… but he hadn't written her off.

That alone made her chest ache a little.

Don't be ridiculous, she scolded herself. You're here to work.

Still, she tucked the thought away in the quiet pocket of her mind where she stored things that mattered.

Kate led her down a gently curving path bordered with lush foliage and pops of tropical colour—hibiscus, ginger lilies, even a few hanging vines with violet blooms. The hum of insects filled the air, along with distant laughter and the splash of water. Then, the trail opened up… and Olivia stopped.

"Oh," she whispered.

The kids' club wasn't just a building—it was a world of its own. A hidden village nestled in the jungle canopy, designed like something out of a child's most beautiful daydream.

Three interconnected treehouses stood on stilts, their thatched roofs shaped like oversized leaves, blending seamlessly into the branches above. Rope-and-wood suspension bridges swayed gently between them, and narrow spiral staircases wound around thick trunks. Below, winding trails led through miniature nature gardens, climbing walls shaped like coral reefs, and a shallow tide pool pond where kids could touch starfish and watch hermit crabs scuttle.

At the far edge of the clearing, two beachside learning huts sat open to the breeze, with painted driftwood signs reading Story time Shore and Art Cove. There were hammocks strung between palms, baskets of sand toys, and a shaded stage with curtains fashioned from colourful fabric scraps.

It was magical.

It was intentional.

Every corner had been designed not just for fun, but for wonder. For imagination.

Kate smiled at her silence. "We like to think of it as Neverland meets Montessori. A place where kids can be wild and safe all at once."

"It's incredible," Olivia said, still breathless. "It's… I've never seen anything like it."

She meant it.

She could already see it—muddy knees, salt-sticky fingers, seashell crowns and watercolour masterpieces. This place was freedom wrapped in joy. It was the kind of childhood space she wished she'd had.

A small group of women stood by the central platform, where a long curved table had been set for a staff welcome. As they turned toward her, Olivia braced herself—but their expressions were warm, curious, and kind.

"Ladies, this is Olivia Clifton," Kate said. "Newest member of your crew."

Margaret, the oldest, had silvery hair pulled into a no-nonsense bun and a twinkle in her eye that suggested she could build a sandcastle and discipline a sugar-crazed five-year-old at the same time. She reached out first with a firm handshake. "Welcome, love. We've been looking forward to meeting you."

Karen, tall and freckled, with sunburned shoulders and an easy laugh, gave her a wink. "You survived Kate's intro tour? That means you're already one of us."

Helen, petite with an artist's ink-stained fingers and a necklace made of sea glass, stepped forward last. "If you can read The Gruffalo five times in a row without losing your mind, you'll fit in just fine."

Olivia laughed, grateful for the warmth, the casual camaraderie, the absence of pretence. "I'm excited to be here," she said honestly. "And ready to help however I can."

Margaret nodded approvingly. "That's the spirit."

As they led her up the ramp toward the central treehouse, the sound of waves lapping the shore drifted in on the breeze. Olivia glanced out at the shimmering ocean through the trees.

She had no idea what her time on Motukava would bring—but for the first time in months, she felt like she'd landed somewhere she might actually belong.

The tour continued after the kids' club, winding Olivia deeper into the heart of Motukava. Kate was an excellent guide—cheerful, quick-witted, and clearly beloved by staff and guests alike. She seemed to know everyone by name, greeting landscapers, bartenders, and guests with the same effortless warmth.

They strolled through the spa nestled among ferns and trickling waterfalls, its open-air massage huts shaded by gauzy curtains. The main lodge rose like something out of a dream—stone and timber, with soaring ceilings and a view that framed the ocean like art. A few guests lounged on the wide deck, sipping cocktails served in coconut shells, the afternoon sun painting their skin gold.

"Staff eat here, too," Kate said as they passed a breezy dining hall. "Separate section in the back, but the food's the same. Trust me, the chef's a genius."

Olivia nodded, taking it all in. The entire resort was breathtaking, but more than that— it felt alive. Every corner whispered a story. Every space had been designed with intention and beauty. It was like living inside a secret, peaceful world untouched by everything she'd left behind.

By the time they circled back to the staff housing—a series of modern, minimalist bungalows tucked discreetly behind a lush wall of palms—Olivia was quietly in awe.

"Alright," Kate said, pulling up her tablet again. "You're officially off-duty until morning. Start tomorrow nine sharp. You'll be with Margaret shadowing the littles."

"Thanks," Olivia said, brushing windblown curls from her face. "This place is… incredible."

Kate smiled, eyes soft. "It grows on you. Get some rest—or go exploring. The beach is the best kind of therapy."

Olivia took the hint and headed down the narrow path that curved past the bungalows and spilled out onto the resort's private stretch of beach. The sand was warm and pale, the sea as clear as glass. She kicked off her shoes, carried them in one hand, and wandered down toward the waterline.

Far out beyond the break, a figure cut through the waves with athletic ease.

Wyatt.

She smiled despite herself, watching him surf—tanned and graceful, catching the curl of a wave and riding it effortlessly toward shore. He made it look so easy. So free.

A part of her—the hopeful, foolish part—wished he'd seen her on the tour. Wished he'd said something more when she'd told him she got the job.

She sank onto the sand leaning against driftwood log and wrapped her arms around her knees, watching as he paddled back out. When he finally emerged from the surf, dripping and radiant, board tucked under one arm, he jogged toward her with a grin.

"Hey, you made it," he said, brushing saltwater from his face.

"I did." She smiled up at him. "You were great out there."

He leaned down, pressing a kiss to her cheek. His lips were warm, still sun-heated. "Thanks, Liv."

The familiar thrill bloomed in her chest, but it fizzled just as fast.

"I'd love to hang out tonight, but I've got laundry to do," Wyatt added, slinging his surfboard under one arm with an effortless shrug. "Tomorrow, maybe?"

"Sure," Olivia said, forcing a smile. "No problem."

He pressed a quick kiss to her forehead—friendly, casual, like it meant nothing. Then he was gone, jogging barefoot up the sand toward the staff path, not even glancing back.

She watched him go, the imprint of his kiss still warm on her skin. It tingled—not because of what it was, but because of what it wasn't. Familiar. Routine. Empty of real intention.

She exhaled slowly and hugged her knees to her chest, the soft whoosh of the tide filling the space he'd left behind.

Laundry.

Wasn't she more important than laundry?

The thought stung more than she wanted to admit. But before she could follow it down too far, she felt it—a shift in the air. The subtle awareness of someone nearby.

She turned her head slightly.

And there he was.

The man from earlier.

Barefoot in the sand. Linen shirt rolled to his elbows, the fabric whispering in the breeze. There was a quiet in him, the kind that came from knowing he never had to chase attention to have it. He just... existed, and the world adjusted.

His gaze wasn't intrusive, but it was steady. Observant.

He looked at her like he noticed things.

Noticed her.

And Olivia, suddenly aware of the sunflower dress and the frizz in her hair and the ache in her chest, sat a little straighter.

He didn't speak right away.

But the silence between them wasn't heavy—it held something quiet and curious, like the pause before a page turns.

Then, finally, he said, "Hello."

Chapter Four

Jack hadn't meant to slow down.

His afternoon walks were a ritual—solitary, predictable, a stretch of sand where he didn't have to think, didn't have to talk. Just the tide, the salt wind, and the endless hush of the sea.

But today… he paused.

She was sitting on sand in front of a driftwood log.

The girl from the lobby.

Sunflower dress. Barefoot. Arms wrapped around her knees like she was trying to hold herself together, even if she looked calm from a distance.

And then there was Wyatt—striding out of the surf like a man who knew the world watched him and didn't mind one bit. Sun-slicked skin, board under his arm, hair dripping salt and arrogance.

Jack knew him. Knew the type.

Wyatt was one of his instructors—water skiing, surfing, whatever else the guests requested. A favourite among the thrill-seeking crowd. Charming, laid-back, golden as the sand he walked on.

Jack recognised the swagger, the casual confidence. He'd worn it once himself—before he understood the price.

Before he knew what it cost to live that lightly.

He watched the exchange from a distance.

A cheek and forehead kiss. Both brief. Thoughtless.

A line about laundry.

Laundry?

Jack's brow twitched faintly.

She smiled anyway. Tried to, at least. He saw it—the flicker of disappointment, the way her body leaned just slightly forward before pulling back. The ache she didn't hide quite fast enough.

And the way she looked at Wyatt as he jogged away.

That got him.

There was something in her eyes—tenderness, longing. Hope she didn't even seem aware she was wearing.

Jack's chest tightened, inexplicably.

He didn't know her. Didn't owe her anything. It wasn't his business who she waited for, or how easily her affection was wasted. But still, he didn't like it. That look. That quiet ache aimed at someone who clearly didn't notice—or didn't care.

He turned to walk past and nearly did.

But his feet slowed.

And then stilled.

He told himself it didn't mean anything. That he was being ridiculous. That it was none of his concern.

She was just another new hire. Young. Idealistic. The kind who hadn't yet learned the world didn't move just because you wanted it to.

And yet…

There was something about her—the way she stared out at the waves like she'd dropped something in them and couldn't swim out far enough to get it back.

Jack exhaled and stepped forward, brushing the silence clean.

He almost didn't say anything. Almost turned back toward the path and left her to her thoughts.

But something in the way she was looking after Wyatt—like she'd just handed over a small piece of herself and wasn't sure he'd even noticed—got under Jack's skin.

So, he stepped closer, letting the sand shift beneath his bare feet, and said quietly, "Hello."

She startled slightly, looked up. Her expression softened when she recognised him.

"I'm Jack," he offered. No title, no explanation.

Her eyebrows lifted a fraction, as if she already suspected he wasn't just another guest. But she nodded, polite. "Olivia."

He smiled. "Nice to meet you, Olivia."

A beat passed between them. The hush of the waves, the late sun stretching gold across the water.

"You're new here," he said—not a question, just an observation.

She nodded. "First day. I start at the kids' club tomorrow."

He let that settle. "Big day?"

She huffed a soft laugh. "Bigger than I expected. This place is…" Her gaze drifted toward the horizon. "It's a lot. Beautiful. Kind of overwhelming."

Jack tilted his head, studying her. She wasn't trying to impress him. She wasn't trying at all. And somehow that made her presence feel more solid, more real, than anyone he'd spoken to all week. Maybe longer. Maybe ever.

"Do you like it so far?" he asked.

"I do," she said honestly, looking back at him. "It feels like the kind of place where things change."

He found himself smiling again. "That's one way to put it."

Another silence stretched between them, but it wasn't uncomfortable.

"Your friend," he said carefully, nodding in the direction Wyatt had gone. "He seems… busy."

Olivia looked down at her knees, brushing a bit of sand off her shin. "Yeah. Laundry waits for no one."

Jack raised a brow. "That so?"

She glanced up, caught his expression, and let out a short, rueful laugh. "It's fine. We're not… anything. Not really."

Something in the way she said it—clear-eyed, unguarded—made Jack's chest ache in a way he didn't expect.

"You deserve better than 'not really,'" he said, surprising himself.

Olivia blinked, clearly not expecting that from a stranger in linen. "Well," she said softly, "sometimes 'not really' is all there is."

Jack didn't respond right away. He just looked at her. Not in a way that made her shrink, but in a way that told her he'd heard her.

Really heard her.

She sat up a little straighter under his gaze, like something inside her was remembering its worth. The way he looked at her—calm, curious, without any agenda—made her feel unexpectedly seen.

"Do you mind if I sit?" he asked, his voice low, unhurried.

She blinked, then shook her head. "No, not at all." She shifted up to sit on the driftwood log, brushing sand from her skirt as she made space.

He settled beside her, not too close, but close enough that she could sense the quiet steadiness of him.

"Do you mind if I ask how you know Wyatt?" he said after a moment, his tone casual but genuinely interested.

"We used to live next door to each other," she replied, glancing out at the water. "In Sydney."

"Australia?"

She nodded. "Yeah. Just a small suburb near the northern beaches. We grew up together, more, or less."

Her voice held no embellishment, no attempt to impress. Just simple honesty. Jack found it… disarming.

Refreshing.

He hesitated for a moment, then said, "Please don't take this the wrong way." He turned to look at her more directly. "But… you like him, don't you?"

She let out a small, mortified laugh and buried her face in her hands. "Oh God," she groaned. "Is it that obvious?"

Jack smiled, something soft tugging at the corner of his mouth. "Only a little."

She peeked at him through her fingers; her cheeks flushed with equal parts embarrassment and humour. "It's stupid, I know."

"I didn't say that."

"But you're thinking it."

He shrugged, still watching her. "No. I'm thinking you seem like someone who feels things deeply. And that's not stupid."

Her hands dropped to her lap, and her expression shifted—just slightly. Like a window opening.

"That's… not what most people say," she murmured, her voice soft but tinged with surprise.

"Most people aren't paying attention," he said simply.

And just like that, something passed between them—quiet but unmistakable. A kind of understanding. A thread of truth neither had expected but both instinctively recognised. He didn't press, and she didn't shy away.

Jack leaned forward slightly, resting his elbows on his knees, then glanced sideways at her. "So… does he not notice when you flirt with him?"

She let out a startled laugh. "Flirt?" She blinked at him. "Oh, I wouldn't even know how to do that."

He straightened a little, thrown. "Excuse me?"

She turned toward him with a grin that caught him off guard—radiant, unguarded, a burst of sunshine cutting through the last threads of late afternoon light.

"My friends at uni used to say I couldn't flirt my way out of a wet paper bag," she said with a self-deprecating chuckle. "They said I was too honest. Too earnest. No mystery."

Jack watched her closely, the edges of his composure softening. God, she was luminous when she wasn't trying to be. "Sounds like your friends were idiots."

She laughed again, but there was a flicker of uncertainty in her eyes. "I think they meant well. I was just… the girl you went to for tutoring. Or help with your essay. Not the girl you asked to the bar on Friday night."

He shook his head, a slow smile spreading as he studied her. "That's their loss."

She looked at him then—really looked—and something in her expression shifted. The breeze lifted a strand of her hair, carried the scent of salt and something softly floral— plumeria, maybe. Her smile didn't vanish, but it changed. Softened. Became contemplative.

Then it clicked. The recognition bloomed slowly across her features like sunlight cresting a wave.

"You're not... Jack Alden, are you?"

Jack tilted his head, a small smile tugging at the corner of his mouth. "Does it matter?"

She sat up straighter, a little awkward now, her body language shifting as her mind caught up to the name. "I'm sorry, Mr. Alden— I didn't realise. I shouldn't be taking up your time."

He leaned in slightly, his voice low and calm but threaded with amusement. "I approached you, remember?"

Her eyes met his, uncertain but searching. "Yes, but I didn't realise you were you."

"Still just Jack," he said. "Same guy who watched you watch the ocean like it might tell you a secret."

That startled a laugh from her—small but real. "You saw that?"

"I see a lot more than people think," he said simply. "Especially when they're not performing."

She looked down at her hands for a moment, then back up at him. "Most people would've led with the whole billionaire resort owner thing."

"I try not to introduce myself with a balance sheet," he said dryly. "It tends to ruin the conversation."

Her smile returned, genuine this time. "Well... thank you for not ruining it."

"You're welcome," he said, eyes steady on hers. "So. Are you going to keep treating me like a press release, or can we go back to being Olivia and Jack?"

She exhaled slowly, the tension easing from her shoulders. "Okay," she said softly. "Olivia and Jack."

He nodded once, satisfied, and rubbed his feet into the sand beside her. "Much better."

"So..." Jack's voice was gentle, but there was a note beneath it. Something cautious. "What are you going to do about Wyatt?"

She didn't answer right away. Her gaze drifted toward the tide, where a lone crab scuttled sideways across the wet sand, leaving delicate imprints behind. The sky was beginning to soften with the blush of approaching sunset, casting gold across the waves.

"I guess..." she said slowly, wistfully, "I just have to hope one day he'll open his eyes and see me."

Jack said nothing, but something in his chest twisted. He hated the way she said it—not desperate, not dramatic. Just honest. As if she'd accepted that maybe he never would.

He looked at her, really looked—at the quiet curve of her smile, the unguarded way she watched the ocean, the sincerity she carried like breath. She didn't know how rare she was. She didn't even try to be rare.

And yet here she was, waiting for some man who couldn't see past his own reflection.

"That could be a long time to wait," he said finally.

Her laugh was soft, self-deprecating. "Yeah. But I've waited for less."

Jack's jaw tightened, just a little. "You deserve more than that," he said. "To be seen without having to wait. Or hope. Or prove something."

Her eyes met his, surprised by the intensity in his voice. "Do you really think so?"

"I do," he said. No hesitation. No bravado. Just truth.

A quiet settled between them, heavy with something unnamed. And for a moment, Jack wanted to take her hand—just to see if it grounded her the way her presence grounded him. But he didn't.

Instead, he glanced toward the surf. "That crab's going to end up back where it started if it's not careful."

She smiled. "Aren't we all?"

"Maybe." He looked at her again, his voice low. "But not everyone's meant to stay stuck in the same loop."

And though she didn't fully understand what he meant, something in his gaze made her feel like—he saw her already.

Before Wyatt ever did.

Before she even saw herself.

A strange flutter stirred in her chest. Not nerves. Not attraction. Something quieter. Something that felt like being recognised.

Jack leaned back slightly, his eyes still on her. "You know... I could help you. With getting Wyatt to notice you."

He didn't even know why he was offering. The words slipped out before he could stop them, and the moment they did, he regretted it. Because deep down, he didn't want Wyatt to notice her. Not now. Not ever.

Olivia blinked, startled. "Oh—no, no, you're much too busy to worry about my silly hopes."

"They're not silly," he said, his voice low but certain. "And I wouldn't have offered if I didn't mean it."

She gave a small, embarrassed shake of her head. "Still... it's not your problem."

He tilted his head, thoughtful. "Coming from a man's point of view," he said, "guys like Wyatt usually don't start noticing things… until another man does."

She gave him a sceptical look. "That's ridiculous."

He grinned, one corner of his mouth curving up in that lazy, confident way that shouldn't have made her stomach flutter—but did. "Maybe. But it's also true."

She rolled her eyes, but she was smiling now—a little uncertain, a little shy. "So, what, you're going to flirt with me in front of him?"

Jack chuckled, low and amused. "Not if it makes you uncomfortable. But I could make him wonder… why I'm talking to you. Why I'm looking at you."

She turned to him then—really turned—and her gaze held his like she wasn't afraid of what she might find there. "Why are you looking at me?"

The question hit him harder than he expected. For a beat, he almost defaulted to charm, to something clever and detached. But the honesty in her eyes demanded something real in return.

"Because you're interesting," he said, his voice quieter now, more careful. "And you're not trying to be."

Olivia blinked at him, surprised, her cheeks warming. "I'm not sure I know how to be anything else."

"Good," he murmured, without hesitation. "Don't change."

The words hung in the air between them, soft and oddly weighted.

She hesitated, then looked down at her hands, fidgeting with the edge of her shirt. "But… wouldn't you pretending to like me—just to get Wyatt's attention—wouldn't that be dishonest?"

Her voice was quieter now, almost reluctant to voice the thing that didn't sit right inside her.

Jack's smile faded, his amusement sobering. He looked at her then—not the way most men looked at beautiful women, but like he was seeing her for the first time.

And he realised—she's probably never been dishonest a day in her life.

The thought stopped him. Slowed him down. In his world, pretence was currency. Games were just how things were played. But she… she was different. She wouldn't know how to manipulate someone even if she tried.

"No," he said after a moment, his voice thoughtful. "It would only be dishonest if I didn't actually like you."

Her eyes lifted to meet his. Wide. Cautious. Hopeful.

"And you do?" she asked, almost disbelieving.

Jack held her gaze. "Yeah. I do."

She didn't answer right away. But her smile—small, quiet, and more real than anything he'd seen all week—was answer enough.

And just like that, the game they were pretending to play—about Wyatt, about favours—slipped into something quieter, more intimate. The air between them shifted.

The kind of shift that made her suddenly aware of how close they were sitting.

And made him wonder why the hell he'd offered to help her win another man.

Chapter Five

The kids' club wasn't just a building—it was a world of its own. Tucked into the jungle canopy, it looked like something from a child's most enchanted dream, with treehouses on stilts, swaying rope bridges, tide pools, and breezy beachside art huts. Everywhere Olivia looked, there was colour, creativity, and the soft hum of magic.

And today, it was her turn to step inside.

Her first shift ran from nine to one. Margaret, a stout, no-nonsense woman with warm brown eyes, deep laugh lines, and a whistle that looked like it had survived a hundred summers, met her at the entrance with a clipboard and a brisk nod.

"Ready?" she asked, already scanning the attendance list.

Olivia smoothed the hem of her sunflower-yellow polo and smiled. "As I'll ever be."

Margaret gave her a once-over—curious, maybe even hopeful—but said nothing. She handed over a name tag that read Miss Olivia in bold blue letters and gestured toward the cubbies. "Eight kids today, ages four to ten. The shy ones hide in the beanbags. The loud ones'll be climbing the rafters by ten. Just keep 'em safe and happy."

"I can do that," Olivia said, slipping on the name tag with quiet confidence.

She did more than that.

Within thirty minutes, she'd built a pillow fort tall enough to impress even the oldest kids, turned a near-meltdown over spilled juice into a giggle fit, and somehow convinced a pair of rowdy twins to turn their wrestling match into an interpretive underwater dinosaur ballet.

The kids were smitten.

Little Ava clung to Olivia's waist like a baby koala during story time, her curls bouncing as she laughed at Olivia's animal voices. Charlie, a gap-toothed eight-year-old with boundless energy, claimed her as his scavenger hunt partner and declared loudly, "Miss Olivia has the BEST hiding spots in the entire universe!" Even Zoe—the aloof ten-year-old who usually read alone—started hovering nearby during snack time, asking shy questions about Australia and the Southern Cross.

By eleven, Margaret was leaning against the back wall, arms crossed, her expression slowly shifting from cautious to impressed.

She didn't say much. Just watched as Olivia calmly bandaged a scraped knee and convinced a stubborn four-year-old to eat a banana by pretending it was a magic phone delivering messages from mermaids.

When the last child settled into a sunbeam with a box of crayons, happily sketching mermaids and sharks, Margaret walked over and handed Olivia a paper cup of water.

"You've done this before," she said—not quite a question.

Olivia accepted the cup with a modest smile. "Yeah. I got a job straight out of uni, then did a nanny stint in New Zealand."

Margaret raised an eyebrow. "You're what—twenty-three?"

"Twenty-four next month."

"You've got the steadiness of someone twice your age."

Olivia hesitated, glancing down. Her voice dropped, soft and careful. "I had to go home. My mum got sick right after I started the nanny job. I looked after her full-time for six months."

Margaret's expression shifted—her tough exterior giving way to quiet understanding. "Cancer?"

Olivia nodded. "Yeah. It was awful. But I'm glad I could be there. She was everything to me."

For a moment, they stood in silence—not awkward, just honest. A pause filled with mutual understanding.

"Well," Margaret said, clearing her throat, "that explains a lot."

"Explains what?"

"You don't treat kids like problems to manage. You treat them like people. Like they matter."

Olivia blinked, touched. "They do."

Margaret nodded slowly, then gestured toward the lunch chart pinned to the wall. "We'll take them to the restaurant at noon. The next shift starts then, so all four of us'll be there. Karen and Helen will meet us at the doors."

"Perfect," Olivia said, already checking the list. "I'll take the littlies if you want the older ones."

Margaret looked at her for a long moment, then gave a short, satisfied nod. "You're going to be very good for this place, Miss Olivia."

Olivia's smile bloomed—unguarded and bright. "Thank you."

Just before noon, the kids lined up in their usual chaotic formation—shoelaces untied, chatter nonstop, a few still clutching glittery crafts. Olivia took one end of the line, Margaret the other. They set off toward the restaurant, small hands in theirs, a chorus of questions trailing after them:

"Do jellyfish sleep?"

"Can I have two desserts?"

"Are there pirate pancakes today?"

And for the first time in what felt like forever, Olivia didn't feel lost or invisible.

She felt needed. Seen. Like she belonged.

It was a good feeling.

One she hadn't realised she'd been missing—until now.

After the children had eaten and the last spoonfuls of ice cream had been scraped from their bowls, the lunchtime buzz began to fade. Olivia helped a little boy wipe ketchup from his cheeks, returned a fallen flip-flop to its rightful owner, and gently reminded Ava not to feed the seagulls again.

All four of them walked them back to the kids' club and when Margaret gave her a small nod from across the restaurant, Olivia knew her shift was done.

She crouched beside the table where the kids were still chattering, crouching to their level. "Alright, gang, that's me for today."

The reaction was instant.

"Nooo!"

"Don't go, Miss Olivia!"

A pair of arms wrapped around her leg—Ava again, her curls tickling Olivia's arm as she clung tightly. "Can't you stay all day?"

"I wish I could," Olivia said, smiling as she gently untangled herself. "But now it's my turn for lunch. Grown-ups need food too, you know."

Charlie folded his arms. "You could eat with us."

Olivia laughed. "Tempting, but I'd never get a bite with you lot stealing my chips."

That earned a chorus of giggles. She straightened, waved to the group, and called over her shoulder, "I'll see you all tomorrow. Be good for Karen and Helen, yeah?"

As she walked away, she could still hear their voices trailing after her.

"Bye, Miss Olivia!"

"Tomorrow!"

"Bring more pirate stickers!"

The path to the staff section of the restaurant curved gently through a row of palms, the sunlight dappling the sand underfoot. Olivia felt a strange ache beneath the hum of satisfaction in her chest—something like tired joy. She'd been nervous this morning, unsure if she'd fit in, unsure if the kids would take to her. But now, as she stepped into the quiet, shaded dining space reserved for staff, she knew she had done something right.

She grabbed a tray, skipped the heavier options, and opted for a fresh mango salad with a squeeze of lime. She wasn't starving—just in need of a few quiet moments and something light.

She had just taken a seat near the window, the ocean breeze drifting lazily through the slatted shutters, when a familiar voice cut through the hum of the fans.

"Hey, Liv."

Olivia looked up, her face brightening instinctively. "Hey, Wyatt."

He was still in his board shorts and resort-branded polo, his sun-streaked hair messy from salt and wind, his smile as casual as ever.

"Busy day?" she asked, setting down her fork.

Wyatt sank into the chair across from her with a dramatic sigh. "Back-to-back waterski sessions. One dad tried to race his ten-year-old daughter and nearly wiped out into a sandbar. Classic."

Olivia chuckled. "Sounds like a good show."

"Oh, it was." He leaned back, stretching one arm over the back of his chair, gaze flicking to her salad. "What about you? First day at the jungle circus. How was it?"

Olivia smiled, but it wasn't just a smile—it was something deeper, softer. "Honestly? Kinda magical. Exhausting, but… really lovely."

Wyatt raised an eyebrow. "Magical?"

"I know, it sounds cheesy." She shook her head, laughing at herself. "But I don't know. The kids were amazing. One of them made me pretend to be a banana on a mermaid's magic phone, and I just… went with it."

He grinned. "Let me guess, Margaret didn't yell at you. That means you passed the ultimate test."

"She actually said I'd be good for the place."

"High praise," he said, leaning forward on his elbows now. "She once made a yoga teacher cry just for asking if the kids liked aromatherapy."

Olivia giggled, stabbing a piece of mango with her fork. "Well, she did watch me clean a scraped knee and negotiate a truce between twin dinosaurs, so I guess I earned my stripes."

Wyatt studied her for a beat, then gave her a nod—genuine, warm. "Glad you're here, Liv. The kids' club needed someone like you."

Olivia looked out at the view for a second, the sea glittering in the distance. "Thanks. I think I needed it too."

Something about the way she said it made Wyatt go quiet for a moment. Then he leaned back, gave her a teasing smile, and said, "So… you doing anything later? There's a bonfire on the beach tonight. Staff only. You should come."

Her eyebrows lifted. "A bonfire?"

"Yeah. Music, drinks, half the team turns into barefoot philosophers after two cocktails. Could be fun."

Olivia smiled, tilting her head. "That would be great. Lucky it's not my turn to babysit tonight."

"Excellent," Wyatt said with a grin, already pushing to his feet. "Pick you up at seven. Bonfires are sacred, you know."

He threw her a playful wink as he backed toward the door. "Catch you later, Miss Banana-Phone."

She laughed, shaking her head. "See you, wave boy."

When the doors swung shut behind him, Olivia leaned back in her chair with a soft exhale. Her half-eaten salad sat forgotten in front of her, but she didn't care. Her cheeks were warm, her pulse still slightly elevated, and for the first time in a long time, she felt like maybe—just maybe—she was beginning to belong.

It had been a very good day.

And now, with a bonfire invitation from Wyatt hovering on the horizon, Olivia felt both happy and a little nervous. There was a flutter in her stomach she hadn't expected, and a restless energy in her limbs she couldn't quite shake.

She needed to move.

A swim, she decided. A solo plunge into the ocean to clear her head and cool her skin. She returned to her modest little bungalow, pulled on her one-piece swimsuit—it wasn't designer, a little faded from too many summers in the sun, but it still fit her snugly and made her feel like herself. No pretences. No performances.

She slipped a soft, crinkled cotton sundress over the top, grabbed her towel, and headed toward the beach.

The resort shoreline was dotted with guests in wide-brimmed hats and designer sunglasses, sipping cocktails from coconuts and reclining on chaise lounges. Olivia bypassed them all, walking barefoot along the water's edge until the crowds thinned, and the only footprints in the sand were her own.

She found a quiet curve of beach tucked behind a low rise of rocks and sea grape bushes. It was private enough—out of sight from the guests, secluded enough to exhale fully.

The breeze tugged gently at her dress as she spread her towel out on the sand. With a quick glance around to make sure no one was watching, she pulled the sundress over her head and folded it neatly, placing it atop her towel.

The swimsuit clung to her in all the right places—understated, but quietly stunning. The soft navy blue hugged her curves with a kind of effortless grace, the colour setting off the golden warmth of her sun-kissed skin. It wasn't flashy, not something designed to turn heads—but on Olivia, it did. Not because it demanded attention, but because she didn't.

She stood on the sand for a moment, toes curling into it, her arms loose at her sides as she took in the view. The waves shimmered with afternoon light, the sea stretching out like a sheet of silk, and the breeze lifted the damp tendrils of hair at her neck. She tilted her face to the sun, eyes closed, as though breathing in happiness.

There was no rush. No posing. Just a young woman alone with the ocean, and perfectly at home in her skin.

Then, with a sudden grin, Olivia took off running—barefoot and laughing, her laughter caught and scattered by the wind. The waves licked at her ankles, then climbed her legs, cool and welcoming. She splashed through the shallows, dove forward in one fluid motion, and disappeared beneath the surface.

Below, the world changed. The salt stung her nose, but she didn't mind. It was quiet down there—peaceful. Like being wrapped in a cool, blue cocoon where no one expected anything of her. She let herself float, suspended, untethered for a few heartbeats.

What she didn't know was that she wasn't entirely alone.

Chapter Six

Jack had been walking the shoreline with no real destination in mind, his mood frayed, his thoughts loud and restless, crashing through him like waves on stone. The island—his island—felt particularly hollow today. The guests were predictable, the business endless, and he was tired of the same smiles and shallow conversations.

He needed air. Space. Silence.

But when he rounded the curve past a tumble of sun-bleached rocks, he stopped dead in his tracks.

She was there.

Olivia.

At first, he didn't register it was her. Just the shape of a woman silhouetted against the surf—bare shoulders, long legs, the gentle curve of her waist. She stood with her back to him, loose and unguarded, looking out at the sea as if it were something sacred. Then she moved, and he saw her more clearly.

Recognition hit like a pulse.

So that's what had been hiding beneath the plain sundresses and oversized polos. That easy beauty she seemed to hide without even meaning to. But it wasn't just her body that made him stare—it was the way she carried it, the freedom in it. Like she wasn't performing for anyone.

How did he ever think this woman was plain?

She was breathtaking.

Jack stood frozen, his linen shirt fluttering slightly in the breeze. His gaze traced the curve of her back, the soft slope of her shoulders, the way her damp hair clung wetly to her neck. She ran forward and dove into the surf without hesitation, vanishing beneath the surface like some wild, free creature born of salt and sun.

He let out a breath he hadn't realised he'd been holding.

This wasn't supposed to happen.

She wasn't supposed to get under his skin like this.

She was just one of the new staff. Temporary. Background. A distraction at best.

But there was something about Olivia that defied categories—something raw and unpolished in a world where everything around him was filtered, curated, and choreographed to perfection. She didn't perform. She just… existed. And somehow, that made her impossible to ignore.

Now, watching her swim in his ocean, laughing as if it belonged to her, moving through the water like it was her natural element—it stirred something in him.

Desire, yes.

But more than that.

Curiosity.

Longing.

A spark of connection he hadn't felt in far too long.

He told himself to walk away. That he didn't care. That this meant nothing.

But instead, he found himself wandering closer. Drawn like a tide he couldn't fight.

He reached her towel, still warm from her body, and sat beside it, elbows on his knees, eyes on the waves. He told himself he was just resting. Just thinking. But the truth pressed quietly against his ribs:

He wanted to know more.

He wanted to know her laugh up close. He wanted to know what she thought about when she stared out to sea like that. He wanted to know what made her leave wherever she came from and land here, on his island, shaking things loose inside him with nothing more than a crooked smile and a navy-blue swimsuit.

She had a spectacular body, yes—curves that didn't need designer swimwear to make them unforgettable. But it wasn't just that. It was the way she moved, unselfconscious and free. The way she surfaced with water dripping from her lashes and pushed her hair back without a second thought. The way she smiled like the ocean was a secret only she understood.

She was radiant.

Not because she tried to be—but because she didn't.

And Jack, for the first time in a long time, felt like maybe he'd been sleepwalking through a world of silk and glass… and had just now stumbled into something real.

So, he stayed.

And waited for her to come back.

The ocean shimmered beneath the afternoon sun, the waves sighing against the shore in gentle, rhythmic pulses. Jack watched her swim with effortless grace, her movements fluid, untamed, and wholly unaware of the spell she was casting from a distance.

When Olivia finally began to wade out of the water, her hair slicked back and droplets gleaming on her skin like pearls, she spotted him near her towel. He was sitting casually, legs stretched out in the sand, one hand bracing behind him, the other running distractedly through his hair as he looked out at the sea. Relaxed. Sun-drenched. Barefoot.

She blinked in surprise, but the moment quickly melted into something warmer. Her face lit up with a smile so bright, so genuine, it hit him in the chest like a wave.

"Hello again," she said as she approached, her voice playful and light, the salt air clinging to every syllable.

Jack's breath caught—just for a moment—on the sheer happiness in her expression. Like she was actually glad to see him. No calculation. No agenda.

"Hello," he said, rising to his feet with an easy smile. "Did you enjoy your swim?"

"I did," she said, reaching for her towel. "It's wonderful out there—just what I needed."

She didn't fumble for modesty or try to hide herself, but neither did she flaunt anything. She was comfortable in her skin in a way that unnerved him a little. Grounded. Natural. She simply dried herself off with calm efficiency, standing in the sunlight like it belonged to her.

Jack watched her, not in a way that would make her uncomfortable, but with an intensity he couldn't seem to switch off. "How'd your first day go?" he asked.

Olivia beamed again, tugging the towel around her hips. "It was wonderful, thank you. The kids are amazing—chaotic, sticky, loud… but amazing."

He chuckled, the sound low and genuine. "I don't know many people who could use the word sticky and wonderful in the same sentence."

"That's childcare in a nutshell," she quipped. "One minute you're singing about turtles, the next you're wiping glitter off your eyelids."

"I can't say I've ever wiped glitter off anything," he said with a mock-serious nod. "But I admire your courage."

She laughed, and he felt it—that shift in the air, subtle but undeniable. A thread of connection pulling tight.

He looked at her a little longer than he should have. "You seem… good here."

Olivia glanced at the sea, then back at him. "Yeah. I think I am."

For a moment, neither of them said anything. The silence wasn't awkward. It felt suspended—like something might happen if one of them leaned just a little closer.

Jack cleared his throat and dropped his gaze to the sand, as if trying to anchor himself there. "Well. I didn't mean to intrude."

"You didn't," Olivia said quickly, her voice soft but certain. "It was a nice surprise."

He lifted his gaze to meet hers again, and for a moment, the space between them pulsed with something quietly electric—unspoken, tentative, but unmistakably real.

Then she tilted her head, the edges of her mouth curling with something like mischief. "Oh—I should tell you. Wyatt asked me on a date."

The words hit him harder than they should have. A flicker of something sharp twisted in his stomach. Jealousy, maybe. Possession. Something far too primal for a woman he barely knew.

"Really," he said, voice neutral, too neutral. "When?"

"Tonight," she replied, brushing a damp curl behind her ear. "He invited me to the staff bonfire."

Of course. The bonfire. Jack had heard about those—once a month, strictly staff-only. No management. No guests. Just barefoot dancing on the sand, music and laughter and a bit too much rum. A chance to unwind. To bond.

And now Olivia would be there. With Wyatt.

Jack looked out toward the horizon, jaw tight. He didn't want her bonding with Wyatt.

"So, we don't have to follow through with the plan we made last night," Olivia said lightly, her voice laced with amusement. She gave him a bright smile—the kind meant to say thank you, but your help is no longer needed.

Jack offered a casual shrug, one shoulder lifting with studied ease. But the way his eyes lingered on her, just a fraction too long, gave the moment a quiet, unspoken weight.

"Seems like you're halfway there already," he said, his tone teasing—but only on the surface.

Beneath it, something simmered. Not quite jealousy. Not quite amusement. Something murkier. More complicated.

"Well," she said after a pause, running her fingers through her damp hair, "I didn't expect it. But… it felt nice. Being asked. Being seen."

Something twisted inside him—sharp and unexpected.

"I see you," he said, the words slipping out—quiet, raw, unguarded. The words slipped out, honest and low.

Olivia looked up at him, a flicker of surprise in her eyes. Then she smiled—warm, appreciative, but not quite understanding. "I know," she said gently. "You've been really kind to me. I appreciate it. It's made things… easier. Starting here. Finding my feet."

She meant it. She was genuine. And yet… she hadn't really heard him. Not the way he'd meant her to.

Jack looked away, out toward the endless ocean, his jaw tightening just enough to betray the tension behind his calm façade.

He wasn't used to this—wanting to be understood. Wasn't used to not being understood.

He was Jack Alden. Billionaire. Resort owner. A man who moved through the world with practiced charm and flawless control. Women didn't misunderstand him—they worshipped him, studied him, tailored themselves to his moods. They wanted what he could give them. They knew what he meant.

But Olivia didn't. She was just herself. Bright and unfiltered. She didn't see him as a man to want. She saw him as… *nice.*

He let out a quiet breath, almost a laugh, and shook his head. "Well," he said, tone light again, "I'm glad I could make it a little easier."

Her smile widened, genuine and radiant. She didn't hear the undertow beneath his words. She didn't need to—at least not yet. That was what made it sting.

"Can you walk me back," she asked casually, slinging the towel over her shoulder with easy grace, "or do you need to be somewhere?"

He glanced at her, catching the way her damp hair clung to her neck, the flush of sun on her cheeks. "It would be my pleasure," he said, and with a sudden grin, gave a mock bow, one hand across his middle.

She giggled, eyes lighting up. "You're funny. I don't think anyone's ever bowed to me before."

"Then you clearly haven't been spending time with the right people."

They began walking side by side, the sand soft beneath their feet, the hush of waves and the distant cry of seabirds filling the space between their words. The late afternoon sun was warm on their backs, painting everything in golden hues.

They didn't speak for a while. But it wasn't an awkward silence—it was full of quiet thoughts neither of them had the courage, or the language, to name.

"I didn't expect to like it here so quickly," Olivia said at last, her voice contemplative. "It's different than I imagined. Warmer. Less... intimidating."

Jack glanced sideways at her, his expression softening. "That's good. You've settled in fast."

"Well, it helps when the locals are kind," she said, flashing him a smile and nudging his arm gently with her shoulder.

That small contact jolted through him more than it should have. And it lingered, long after they neared the edge of the resort, where the beachfront path branched toward the staff bungalows.

"Thanks for the company," she said, pausing at the turnoff. "And the bow. That might be the highlight of my day."

He slid his hands into his pockets, giving her a smirk that barely masked the truth behind it. "Then I clearly need to raise the bar."

"You're welcome to try," she replied, tossing him a cheeky grin before she turned and walked away, her towel swinging casually over her shoulder.

He watched her go until she disappeared around the bend, her laughter echoing faintly behind her.

And for the second time that day, Jack Alden stood perfectly still—chest tight, breath shallow—wondering why it mattered so damn much that she hadn't heard what he meant. And why it mattered even more that she might never.

Chapter Seven

As Olivia walked away from Jack, her damp towel slung over her shoulder and the sand cool beneath her feet, she couldn't stop thinking about Jack.

Jack Alden.

A billionaire.

And not just a billionaire—him. The one with the unreadable eyes and the tailored shirts and the quiet, amused way of listening when you spoke. The man whose resort she was working at, whose name was whispered with awe by the staff, whose reputation was tied up in boardrooms and glossy magazine profiles and wealth that felt like another language.

And yet… he'd walked her back like a friend. Bowed to her like a fool. Stood still on the beach like a man who hadn't wanted to say goodbye.

He's such a nice guy, she thought, baffled by it even now.

She never imagined she'd have a conversation with someone like him, let alone enjoy it. Let alone feel—whatever it was she'd felt when she nudged him with her shoulder, and he looked at her like that.

There'd been something in the contact. A flicker. A spark. Something that jumped from her shoulder straight to her stomach, warm, immediate, and hard to ignore.

But she did ignore it.

Because tonight was about Wyatt.

She picked up her pace and shoved Jack's smile, his voice, his impossible kindness to the back of her mind. She had just enough time to shower and get ready.

An hour later, Olivia stood in front of the small mirror above her sink, running a brush through her freshly dried hair. Her white shorts fit snugly, paired with a soft blue top that brought out the colour of her eyes. The look was casual, breezy—effortless, but cute.

She gave herself a little nod. Carefree. That was the vibe.

At exactly seven o'clock, a knock came at the door.

She opened it to find Wyatt standing there in a white linen shirt and sandals, his tanned skin glowing in the last of the daylight. He smiled, not quite sheepish, not quite charming—somewhere in between.

"Ready?" he asked.

"Ready," she said with a smile, tucking her key into her pocket.

They walked down the winding path together, the sky turning lavender above them, torches flickering along the beachfront. Music drifted from the direction of the bonfire—something rhythmic and light-hearted. Laughter echoed. Someone whistled.

When they reached the clearing, Olivia felt her stomach flip. It was beautiful—casual but magical. Tiki lights strung between palms, people dancing barefoot in the sand, a makeshift bar glowing at the far end. Staff milled about in loose clothes, drinks in hand, faces flushed with the freedom of a night off.

Wyatt slowed just before they reached the edge of the crowd.

"Well," he said, giving her a crooked smile. "Have a good night, Olivia."

Then he turned and walked away—straight toward a group of other men, already calling out greetings and clapping someone on the back.

Olivia stood there for a second, blinking.

That was it?

Her smile faltered before she could stop it. Did I misinterpret the invitation? she wondered, heart sinking. Maybe he'd just meant she should come tonight—on her own. Maybe she'd projected the whole "date" angle. Maybe…

"Olivia!" a familiar voice called, and she turned gratefully to see Karen waving.

Relief crashed into her like a wave.

Karen slipped her arm through Olivia's as she reached her, her eyes scanning Olivia's outfit with an approving grin. "Well, don't you look cute," she teased, giving her a playful nudge.

Olivia offered a small, tight-lipped smile. "Thanks."

Karen's smile softened, sensing something behind the flatness of the reply. But she didn't press. "I'm really glad you made it. And good news—Helen and Margaret are stuck with babysitting duty tonight, which means we are officially off the hook."

Olivia managed a more genuine smile. "So, we're the free birds tonight?"

"Exactly. Our turn to wrangle the little monsters is tomorrow night."

"Lucky us," Olivia said dryly, letting Karen guide her into the warm glow of the bonfire, the thrum of music and laughter wrapping around them like a blanket.

She smiled, nodded, chatted—did her best to enjoy herself. But the sting of Wyatt's nonchalance clung to her, quiet and sharp beneath her ribs.

Jack walked the shoreline alone, heading back toward his villa as the last of the daylight faded. The sky was turning ink-blue above the palms, and the path was lit by low, warm lanterns that cast soft glows over the sand.

He didn't know what he was doing exactly—walking, yes. But also thinking. Feeling.

Olivia had unsettled something in him earlier. He couldn't name it. Didn't want to.

As he reached the steps leading up from the beach, he slowed at the sound of a little girl's voice behind him.

"Miss Olivia is so nice, Mummy. Can I go to Kids' Club tomorrow?"

A woman laughed softly. "Of course you can, sweetheart. You like this, Miss Olivia?"

"Yes! She's great!"

Their voices faded as they passed behind him, walking further up the path toward the guest villas.

Jack stood still, one hand resting lightly on the railing, his chest tight with something he didn't understand.

She's great.

She was.

And the worst part—the most dangerous part—was that Olivia didn't even know it.

She didn't know the effect she had. Not on kids. Not on guests. Not on him.

And somehow, that made it harder to forget her.

Jack stood on a rise just beyond the curve of the main path, half-shrouded in the shadows of palm trees, the soft hum of the ocean behind him. From where he stood, he could see the flicker of firelight dancing across the sand, hear the rise and fall of laughter and music floating on the night breeze. Staff bonfire night.

He didn't know why he was here.

He shouldn't be.

This wasn't his world—not tonight. The unspoken rule was clear: management kept their distance, let the team unwind without the weight of eyes watching. And yet, here he was, hands in his pockets, jaw tight, eyes scanning the fire-lit crowd for one particular face.

Olivia.

It took him a moment to find her. She was standing just off to the side, near the drinks table, wearing white shorts and a blue top that caught the firelight like sea glass. Carefree. Bright. Like she belonged here.

His gaze flicked toward the group of men clustered near the fire—and there he was. Wyatt. Laughing with two others, drink in hand, body turned away from Olivia as if she didn't exist.

Jack frowned.

So that was it.

She'd said it was a date. Had believed it. But Wyatt hadn't even stayed with her. No smile. No conversation. No effort.

Jack's shoulders tensed.

He didn't know what he'd expected—he told himself it didn't matter—but still, something coiled low in his chest. Restlessness. Frustration. An edge of something darker he didn't care to name.

He shouldn't be here.

But he couldn't seem to walk away either.

Not yet.

Then Jack saw it.

A male staff member—one he vaguely recognised from the maintenance team—stumbled up to Olivia. The guy was clearly drunk, his gait loose, his smile too wide. Jack's eyes narrowed as he watched the exchange from the shadows.

Olivia smiled politely, but even from a distance, Jack could see the shift in her body. Tension. Her shoulders pulled tight, her stance edging back a fraction.

The man leaned in, too close, saying something Jack couldn't hear. Olivia shook her head with a small laugh, clearly trying to deflect, to keep things light. But the man didn't take the hint. He reached for her—hands on her arms—then lurched forward in an unmistakable attempt to kiss her.

Jack's chest went tight.

Olivia pushed him away firmly, her expression no longer friendly.

But the idiot tried again, stumbling toward her with persistence born of too much rum and too little sense.

Jack didn't think. He moved.

By the time he got close enough to the circle of firelight, the man had Olivia in a clumsy bear hug, his arms locked around her waist, mouth slurring something too low for Jack to hear. Olivia was twisting in his grip, her hands braced against his chest, trying to push him off, her face a mask of polite panic.

"Please let me go," she said, her voice tight but steady, clear even above the crackle of the flames and the hum of music in the background.

Jack's blood turned to ice.

He didn't shout. He didn't make a scene. He just reached them in three long strides, grabbed the man by the back of his shirt, and yanked him off Olivia with one sharp, practiced pull.

The drunk stumbled, barely catching his balance.

Jack stepped between them, calm but unmistakably cold, his voice like steel. "That's enough."

The man blinked up at him, uncomprehending at first—then paling as recognition dawned.

"Mr. Alden—I didn't mean—she didn't—"

"I don't care what you meant," Jack cut in, his tone quiet but lethal. "You don't put your hands on anyone who hasn't invited it. Especially not my staff."

The man opened his mouth, then closed it again, swaying slightly.

"Go sleep it off," Jack said, pointing toward the path that led back to the staff quarters. "Before I have security walk you there."

The guy hesitated, then muttered something unintelligible and shuffled off, head down.

Jack turned to Olivia, his gaze softening the instant it landed on her. "Are you okay?"

She nodded, but it wasn't convincing. Her arms were folded tightly across her stomach, her expression shuttered. She looked shaken. Angry at herself, maybe. Embarrassed. Jack hated that look on her.

"I'm fine," she said. "It's… fine."

"No, it's not," he replied, his voice still low. "But it's over."

Their eyes met, and something unspoken passed between them. Gratitude. Frustration. And something sharper—more intimate, more dangerous—something neither of them could name, but both felt like a current in the air between them.

The bonfire party crackled behind them—music rising and falling, bursts of laughter rolling across the sand, bottles clinking like wind chimes. But in that moment, it all felt distant. Dull. As if the firelight didn't quite reach where they stood.

Jack's body still thrummed with tension, his jaw tight, hands flexing at his sides. He wasn't used to feeling helpless—not here, not ever—but something about the way Olivia had looked in that man's arms, stiff with discomfort, trying to smile her way out of it… It unsettled him more than he wanted to admit.

But he didn't touch her.

He stood close enough that she could feel his presence, steady and quiet, but left the space between them untouched. He didn't want to crowd her—didn't want to make her feel boxed in by another man, even if every instinct in him was shouting to reach out, to do more.

After a beat, she spoke, her voice soft and tired. "I think it's time I left."

"I'll walk you back," Jack said without hesitation.

She turned to him, and in the firelight, he saw the faint shimmer of vulnerability in her eyes. She looked… relieved. "Thank you," she murmured.

He nodded once, falling into step beside her as they left the circle of light, the sound of the party fading with each step.

Neither of them spoke as they walked, the only sounds the crunch of sand beneath their feet and the distant hush of waves. The silence between them wasn't awkward—it felt necessary. Grounding. Olivia glanced sideways at him once, as if she wanted to say something more, but she didn't. And Jack didn't push.

What they didn't know—what neither of them saw—was the pair of eyes watching from across the fire.

Wyatt stood half in shadow, drink in hand, a slow frown carving across his face. He hadn't missed how Jack had appeared out of nowhere. Or how Olivia had looked at him afterward—trusting, like he'd saved her.

He took a long sip of his drink, his jaw tight.

So, Jack Alden wanted to play hero.

Interesting.

Chapter Eight

Jack walked beside her in silence, the path gently curving between tall hedges and flickering lanterns. The night air had cooled, brushing against them with the salty breath of the sea, but Olivia hadn't said much since they'd left the bonfire.

When they reached the modest staff housing wing tucked behind a cluster of palms, she slowed in front of her door, her fingers finding the key in her pocket.

She turned to him, her expression soft, shadows of the night playing at the corners of her eyes.

"Thank you, Jack. For pulling him off me. And for walking me back. I don't think I would've felt safe walking alone."

Jack's jaw clenched. He hated that any woman—especially Olivia—had to feel unsafe on a night that should've been carefree.

"I'm just glad I could help," he said quietly.

"You did." She smiled—small, but sincere. Then she laughed softly, brushing a strand of hair behind her ear. "I didn't want my first kiss to be with a drunk."

That pulled him up short.

He blinked. "Excuse me?" His voice was calm, but his brows lifted. "You've never been kissed?"

She laughed again, more self-consciously this time. Her gaze dropped to the ground.

"Not properly, no. I mean, there was a spin-the-bottle kiss at a primary school party, and one awkward peck after senior dance that barely counted. But no one's ever—"

She caught herself, cheeks warming. "I know that sounds ridiculous."

Jack didn't laugh. He didn't even smile.

His gaze was steady. Thoughtful. A touch of something sharper beneath it.

"It doesn't sound ridiculous."

She looked up at him.

"I think it sounds... honest. Rare. Kind of beautiful, actually."

Her lips parted, surprised by his response.

"Beautiful?"

He nodded; eyes locked with hers.

"You deserve your first kiss to mean something. Not be stolen by some drunk idiot who didn't even ask your name."

She exhaled, something in her shoulders loosening.

"I guess I was waiting for it to feel... right. Maybe that's stupid."

"It's not," Jack said. "And for what it's worth… I think you were right to wait."

A wry smile ghosted across her face. "I actually thought Wyatt might kiss me tonight," she admitted, eyes dropping. "But that was a bust."

She tried to sound nonchalant, like it didn't sting. Like it hadn't mattered.

But Jack heard it anyway—the edge beneath her words. And he hated it.

Not just the disappointment, but that she'd wanted the kiss at all. From Wyatt.

The thought of anyone kissing her made his chest tighten.

But the idea of it being him…

That stopped him cold.

He didn't like that thought.

He shouldn't like that thought.

But it was there—sudden, undeniable, and strong.

He didn't want anyone kissing Olivia.

Except him.

And the intensity of that realisation startled him.

"Well, thanks again, Jack," Olivia said softly.

Before he could respond, she rose onto her toes and pressed a quick kiss to his cheek—light, fleeting, warm.

Jack froze.

She was already turning, her fingers fumbling with the key. The door creaked open, and without looking back, she stepped inside and closed it behind her.

Leaving Jack standing there, one hand still in his pocket, the ghost of her kiss lingering on his skin.

And no words left in his mouth.

The next morning, Olivia arrived at Kids' Club right on the dot of nine, dressed in her sunny yellow polo and worn-in denim shorts, her hair neatly braided down her back. Despite the strange, tangled feelings left over from the night before, everything softened the moment the children tumbled through the door—sticky-fingered, wide-eyed, full of energy and wonder.

She smiled before she even realised it.

Little Connor proudly presented her with a seashell "with zebra stripes," as he put it, and the ever-curious twins, Ava and Mia, begged to braid her hair while their paintings dried. The hours flew by in a blur of finger paints, off-key singalongs, and wild games of hide-and-seek that left her breathless and laughing.

By the end of her shift, her voice was hoarse, and her legs ached—but something inside her had settled, like a jar of glitter finally sinking to stillness. She felt like herself again.

That evening, she and Karen were on babysitting duty, a routine part of the weekly roster. Every other night, they supervised the resort's youngest guests whose parents wanted a kid-free evening. From eight until midnight, the children would curl up on little mattresses in a quiet room, munching on popcorn and watching animated movies under the soft glow of fairy lights until they either nodded off or were picked up early.

It sounded peaceful. Sweet. And Olivia found herself genuinely looking forward to it.

At half past one, she wandered over to the staff restaurant, a breezy, no-frills space with long wooden tables and the scent of grilled vegetables in the air. She grabbed a salad sandwich and a cold bottle of water, then slid into a seat by the window, relishing the hush of mid-afternoon.

It was the first real pause she'd had all day.

She took a bite, savouring the quiet—until a familiar voice broke it.

"Hey, Liv."

She looked up. Wyatt had dropped into the seat across from her, sunglasses pushed onto his head, that same easy grin tugging at his mouth.

"Where'd you get to last night?" he asked, cracking open a soda. "I turned around and you were just gone."

Olivia blinked, her expression calm. "I left early," she said, managing a small smile. One that didn't quite reach her eyes.

Wyatt didn't seem to notice. "Yeah? Thought we were gonna hang out." He shrugged, like it didn't matter. "Karen said you'd already taken off by the time she came back with drinks."

"I didn't realise we were hanging out," Olivia said, keeping her voice even. "You kind of disappeared as soon as we got there."

Wyatt raised an eyebrow. "I figured you'd find me. You know… mingle a little."

She let out a quiet breath and looked down at her sandwich. "Right."

He leaned back in his seat, stretching an arm across the back of the bench. "You mad or something?"

Olivia met his gaze, her expression unreadable. "No. I just… thought it was going to be more of a date."

Wyatt blinked, like that possibility had never occurred to him. "Oh." Then, casually— too casually—he added, "Yeah, well… maybe next time."

She gave a polite smile, tight at the edges, her appetite gone.

Jack had just left the construction site of the still-in-progress wellness centre, the sound of drills and hammers still echoing in his ears. His mind was preoccupied with work, but as he walked past the staff restaurant, his gaze fell on a familiar sight: Olivia and Wyatt. They were sitting across from each other, Wyatt lounging in his seat with that cocky, too-confident smile that Jack had seen one too many times.

Olivia, on the other hand, was staring down at her sandwich, her fingers lightly tracing the edges of the bread as if trying to find a way to focus on it instead of the conversation happening across the table. There was something in the way she sat, her posture slightly hunched, her face devoid of the usual spark Jack had seen in her before. She didn't look happy.

Jack's gut tightened.

The sight stirred something in him—something sharp and unwelcome. His first instinct was that Wyatt was stringing her along again, and before he knew it, he'd taken a step toward her. Then stopped.

He didn't know the full story between them. From what he'd seen, their interactions barely scratched the surface—casual, fleeting, nothing substantial. But now, watching Olivia sit across from Wyatt, shoulders slightly hunched, her expression careful and closed off... something twisted in his chest.

It wasn't jealousy. Not exactly.

But it burned.

He found himself stopping just a little too long, his mind swirling with thoughts he wasn't ready to acknowledge. He had no reason to feel anything other than distant indifference toward their situation, but the reality was, seeing her like this, caught up in some game Wyatt was playing, didn't sit right with him.

Jack tore his eyes away from them and continued walking. But the image of Olivia looking so distant, so small, stayed with him.

Wyatt finally stood, slinging his bag over his shoulder with a casual flick of his wrist. He shot Olivia one last smile—half-hearted, as always. "I'll see you around, Liv."

"Yeah," Olivia replied, her voice flat. She didn't look up from her sandwich, her gaze lingering on the half-eaten food. She didn't need to watch him leave; she could feel the way his presence faded, as if it had never really mattered in the first place.

As Wyatt strolled away, Olivia pushed the remains of her sandwich aside and stood. The usual buzz of the staff restaurant—the chatter, the clinking of silverware—felt muffled now, as if the world was still spinning, but she was standing outside of it. Her thoughts were tangled, a mixture of frustration, confusion, and something she couldn't quite name. The words he'd said, the way he'd left without much of a second thought, still stung. She had hoped for something more. Maybe not a fairy tale, but at least more than what he had given her.

With a soft exhale and made her way out of the restaurant. The cool, salty air of the island felt like it was waiting for her. She needed space. Needed to clear her head. Her feet carried her instinctively toward the beach, the soft sand beneath her toes a comforting contrast to the restlessness stirring inside her.

The waves lapped gently at the shore as she walked, the rhythmic sound soothing, yet her mind was anything but calm. Olivia let the breeze tug at her hair, her thoughts drifting like the foam rolling in from the ocean. She had spent the last few weeks trying to convince herself that Wyatt was just another passing distraction, but somewhere deep inside, she'd let herself believe that maybe, just maybe, he could be more. And now… now it felt like everything she had hoped for was unravelling.

She found a quiet spot near a rock formation, where the beach curved gently around the bay, giving her some privacy. She sank down onto a smooth rock, hugging her knees to her chest as she stared out at the horizon. The sun was beginning its slow descent, casting a golden glow over the water, but even its beauty couldn't lift the weight from her chest.

What was she doing? Waiting for someone who didn't even seem to notice her? She could feel the frustration bubbling up again, and it was easier to focus on the ache than to admit the deeper wound. It wasn't just about Wyatt—it was about something she hadn't quite realised until now. She had spent so much time waiting for someone else to show her her worth. Maybe it was time to stop waiting altogether.

But even as she thought it, something pulled at her. A quiet whisper inside that told her she wasn't entirely ready to give up yet. She wasn't sure who she was hoping for anymore—Wyatt or someone else—but the tug at her heart was undeniable.

Her phone buzzed in her pocket, snapping her out of her thoughts. She pulled it out to see a message from Karen.

Babysitting tonight. You good?

Olivia glanced up at the fading light, the water sparkling in the distance, before typing a quick reply.

Yeah, all good. See you soon.

With a soft sigh, she stood and dusted the sand off her shorts. The beach had offered her a brief moment of peace, but now she was ready to return. Tonight was another shift with the kids. Maybe that was exactly what she needed. Something simple, uncomplicated. Just the way she used to like it.

As Olivia walked back to the resort, the sound of soft footsteps on the sand mingled with the distant rush of the waves. She was lost in her thoughts when she spotted Jack approaching from the other direction. His tall frame was unmistakable, the sun glinting off his sunglasses as he walked with that confident, easy stride of his.

Her heart gave a little flutter, but she pushed it down. Smiling, she lifted her hand in greeting. "Hello."

Jack's lips curved into a warm smile when he saw her. "Hey there. Where are you off to?" His voice was casual, but there was something in his eyes that softened when he looked at her, as if he was genuinely interested in what she had to say.

"First babysitting shift tonight," she replied, her face lighting up as she spoke. The excitement was clear in her voice, a sparkle that came to life whenever she talked about the kids.

He raised an eyebrow, clearly noticing her enthusiasm. "You really like your job, don't you?"

Olivia grinned. "Yes, I do," she said, nodding earnestly. But then her expression faltered, and she grimaced. "Don't get me wrong, you can occasionally get some naughty kids." She paused, then let out a small laugh, her shoulders relaxing. "But mostly they're great. It's one of those things where the good outweighs the bad."

Jack chuckled, clearly amused by her honesty. "Sounds like you've got a real passion for it."

She shrugged lightly, then leaned in, lowering her voice to a whisper, as if to share a little secret. "Ava and Mia are my favourites at the moment," she said, her face lighting up with mischief, the corners of her lips curling up. "They're just so full of energy and imagination. I swear, they could talk your ear off for hours about their adventures."

Jack's smile deepened as he leaned in slightly, his voice softening in response. "I promise I won't tell anyone," he whispered back, a teasing glint in his eyes. His gaze lingered on her for a moment longer than usual, the playfulness between them building in a way that felt different, warmer.

Olivia chuckled, feeling the tension between them shift into something lighter. "Good," she replied, her eyes sparkling. "Because they'd probably come after you if they found out you knew their secret."

Jack laughed in return, a deep, rich sound that made her heart skip. "I think I can handle a couple of pint-sized troublemakers," he said, the teasing tone still in his voice. "But I'll take your word for it."

They both fell into an easy silence, the kind that didn't beg to be filled. The rhythmic sound of the ocean washed between them, soft and steady, like nature's own lullaby. Olivia felt a strange warmth settle in her chest, a quiet comfort she hadn't expected. This thing between her and Jack—their gentle teasing, the way he listened without interrupting, how he actually seemed to see her—it was… easy. Too easy, maybe. And that made her heart flutter in a way she didn't quite trust.

"Well," she said, with a little laugh, "I should let you go. You probably have a hundred more important things to do than stand here talking to me."

Jack shook his head slightly, that thoughtful look still lingering in his eyes. "Not as many as you'd think," he said, his voice soft. Then he added, "Have a good night, Olivia. Have fun with the little ones. I'm sure they'll be thrilled to see you."

"Thanks, Jack," she said, her smile warm and real. "I'm sure I will. It's always a good time with the kids." She gave him a small wave as she turned to go, already feeling the tug of the evening ahead.

He didn't move right away. Just stood there, watching her, his hands casually in his pockets, gaze thoughtful. "Take care, Olivia," he called after her, his voice quieter now, but rich with something she couldn't name.

She glanced back over her shoulder and waved again. "You too," she said, her tone light and breezy—though her chest felt anything but.

As she walked the winding path back toward the resort, the fading light casting long shadows across the sand, Olivia couldn't shake the feeling buzzing under her skin. Her mind should've been on the evening ahead—on popcorn and sleepy children and finding the remote—but instead, it kept circling back to Jack. To the way his eyes softened when he looked at her. The way he made her feel seen.

She hadn't realised just how much she'd enjoyed talking to him… until now.

Chapter Nine

Wyatt watched as Jack walked away, his jaw tightening.

There was something about the way Jack had lingered—hovering like he was just waiting for the right moment to step in—that left a bitter taste in his mouth. He glanced toward Olivia, catching sight of her retreating figure as she headed back toward her bungalow. A flicker of something unfamiliar stirred in his chest—uncertainty.

What the hell is going on between them?

He'd seen it before. The quiet glances. The subtle shifts in her posture—how her body seemed to tilt instinctively toward Jack, like she didn't even know she was doing it. It was understated, maybe even nothing. But it had started to gnaw at him, threading its way into his thoughts when he least expected it.

Why is it every time I turn around, they're together?

He didn't like it. Not one bit.

Jack had never looked twice at the staff—especially not sweet, open-hearted girls like Olivia with messy ponytails, wide eyes, and an awkward little laugh that didn't belong in Jack's curated, high-gloss world. Jack only ever went for the polished types—icy, untouchable women in stilettos and silk, who spoke in low, calculated tones and always knew how to play the game.

Olivia wasn't that. She wasn't trying to be anything but herself.

That used to be what Wyatt liked most about her.

But now? Now it just made her stand out more. Especially to someone like Jack.

Wyatt shifted on his feet, heat crawling beneath his skin. Maybe it was nothing. Maybe Olivia was just being friendly.

Still, he couldn't shake the growing unease coiling in his gut.

Because Jack was watching her differently now.

And worse—Olivia was starting to watch him right back.

Olivia walked down the winding path toward her bungalow, the moon casting a silvery glow across the trees. Her steps were light, a soft smile still lingering on her lips. Her first babysitting shift had gone better than she'd hoped—the twin girls had been sweet, endlessly curious, and full of giggles that still echoed in her mind.

She was replaying one of their sillier jokes when a voice cut through the quiet.

"Liv."

She turned, startled, as Wyatt stepped out from between two tall palms, his hands buried deep in his pockets. His usual easy grin was nowhere in sight. Instead, he looked… uncertain.

"I've been thinking about what you said at lunch," he began, his voice low and careful. "About the bonfire. About how I left you."

Olivia's smile faded, softening into something quieter. Her heart gave a flutter—equal parts nerves and old ache.

Wyatt took a slow step closer. "I shouldn't have left you like that."

She nodded, unsure what to say. She had spent years waiting for him to realise she was worth staying for. Now that he was standing in front of her, regret in his voice, it felt like a memory playing out differently than she'd imagined.

"Can I take you out?" he asked, his tone gentler now. "Tomorrow night. A real date."

The words hung in the still air between them, brushing against old dreams she hadn't quite let go of.

Olivia's breath caught. She'd imagined this moment so many times—when she was younger, when she first arrived at the resort. Wyatt had always been the charming golden boy, sun-drenched and impossible not to look at. The idea of him had been safe, familiar. Easy to want.

But now, something about this felt fragile. Not wrong, exactly—just… not what it used to be.

She searched his face. "A real date?"

He smiled, hesitant but sincere. "Dinner. Just you and me. No distractions. No games."

Her heart fluttered—but it wasn't the swooping kind she expected. It was a smaller, quieter beat. And behind it, uninvited, came another face. Jack. The way he had looked at her that morning—not with charm or ease, but with something raw. Something real. That look had unsettled her in a way Wyatt never had.

Still, she pushed the thought aside.

"Okay," she said, nodding. "Dinner sounds nice."

Wyatt's grin bloomed, relief loosening the tension in his shoulders. "Great. I'll come by around seven?"

"Seven's good," she said, offering a smile that felt like muscle memory more than emotion.

As he disappeared down the path, Olivia stood still, the warmth of the night pressing in around her. She had just agreed to go on a date with the man she'd once dreamed about.

So why did it feel like something in her had just taken a step in the opposite direction?

The sun was high and unrelenting by the time Olivia finished her morning shift at the kids' club. Her ponytail sagged to one side, the elastic barely holding through the chaos of finger painting, papier-mâché, and a glitter explosion she hadn't seen coming. Smudges of colour streaked her forearms like battle scars, and a faint dab of purple marker sat stubbornly on her jaw.

She was bone-tired—but content. Being with the kids always grounded her. In a world that so often felt tangled and uncertain, this part made sense. It was simple. Honest.

She stepped off the path toward the staff bungalows, humming under her breath, shoes kicking up soft clouds of dust—when a familiar voice cut through the heat.

"Olivia."

She turned, blinking into the bright light as Jack approached from the direction of the main resort. He looked maddeningly composed in a crisp white button-down, sleeves rolled to his elbows, and pale linen trousers that whispered quiet luxury. But his face was harder to read—serious, watchful. And his eyes…

His eyes betrayed something else entirely.

"Hey," she said, brushing glitter from her elbow, suddenly conscious of the mess she was. "How are you today?"

Jack's gaze swept over her—taking in the stained shirt, the glitter, the streak of marker. His lips curved slightly, like he wasn't sure if he should smile or frown.

"You look…" he tilted his head, voice low and dry, "like you survived something."

She laughed, tucking a strand of hair behind her ear. "The glitter apocalypse. One of the twins had a vision and about six bottles of glue."

Jack's mouth twitched. "Brave girl."

She was about to make a joke—something easy, something light—when the words came out before she could stop them.

"Wyatt asked me out."

Jack stilled.

"On a real date," she added, her voice flatter than she intended.

Jack's expression didn't change, not really. But something in the set of his jaw sharpened.

"Oh," he said, too casually. "A real date?"

She nodded, fingers fidgeting at the hem of her shirt. "Dinner. Just the two of us."

A silence stretched between them, filled only by the hum of cicadas and the rustling of palm leaves in the breeze. The warmth of the day suddenly felt heavier, clinging to her skin like tension.

Jack looked past her for a moment, then back. "That's… good," he said slowly. "You must be happy."

But the words came out clipped, like they didn't sit right in his mouth.

Olivia swallowed. "I guess so. I mean, I was. I think I still am."

Jack's eyes flicked to hers, unreadable again. "Sounds like something you've wanted for a long time."

"It was," she said, quieter now. "It is."

But even as she said it, the certainty in her voice wavered. Jack noticed—of course he noticed. He always did.

A gust of wind swept through, catching the loose strands of her hair and lifting them across her face. Jack reached out before he could stop himself, brushing them back gently, fingers grazing her temple.

The touch was brief, almost accidental—but it sent a jolt through her chest.

He pulled his hand away, looking as if he regretted it instantly. "Sorry. You had… paint or something."

She nodded, though there was nothing there.

Jack stepped back, hands sliding into his pockets. "Well… enjoy your date."

She opened her mouth to say something—she wasn't even sure what—but he was already turning.

And just like that, he was gone.

She stood there a moment longer, still, and quiet in the humid air, surrounded by sunshine and glitter… and the ache of something she couldn't name.

Jack walked briskly down the path that curved behind the staff bungalows, his strides long, controlled—too controlled. His hands were jammed into his pockets, knuckles tight, his pulse a slow, steady thud in his ears.

He didn't know what he'd expected. Maybe nothing. Maybe just the sight of Olivia covered in paint and glitter, laughing about glue and chaos, would've been enough to brighten the day. Maybe he'd just wanted to see her.

But then she'd said it— *Wyatt asked me out.*

The words had landed with more force than they should have, knocking the wind out of something he hadn't realised was still forming. And worse? She'd said it like it mattered. Like it meant something.

A real date.

Jack let out a quiet breath through his nose, forcing himself not to react, even now. Because it wasn't his place, was it? He wasn't her boyfriend. He wasn't even her friend, really. He was the boss. The billionaire. The guy who didn't do messy emotions or accidental attachments.

But none of that stopped the tight, sour twist in his stomach.

Wyatt.

Of all the people on this island. The golden boy with the easy charm and ocean-blue eyes. The kind of guy girls like Olivia fell for without a second thought. And Jack had seen the way she looked at him—wide-eyed, hopeful, like he'd hung the stars just by showing up on a paddleboard with his shirt half-buttoned.

Jack scowled at the memory, stepping off the path and into the shadow of an overgrown banyan tree. He leaned against the trunk, folding his arms, but it didn't soothe the restlessness under his skin.

He couldn't shake the image of Olivia's face when she told him. She'd tried to sound casual. But her smile hadn't quite reached her eyes. There'd been hesitation there. Doubt.

And that doubt—it had lodged itself in Jack's chest like a splinter.

What was he doing?

He had no business interfering. She wasn't his. He wasn't even sure what this was—the thing between them. A flicker of curiosity? Chemistry? Something he'd talked himself out of a dozen times since she arrived.

But she made him feel something.

Something unfamiliar. Something real.

Something he hadn't felt in a long time—maybe ever.

And now she was going to dinner with someone who wouldn't think twice about breaking her heart. Jack knew Wyatt. Knew the way he moved through the world like nothing could touch him, how girls blurred into one another like background noise. Olivia wasn't background noise.

But who was he kidding?

He'd probably break her heart too.

Because Olivia wasn't the kind of girl you had a fling with.

Not with that soft honesty in her eyes.

Not after the way she'd looked at him, vulnerable and wide open, when she told him she'd never been kissed.

A true innocent.

Not in the naïve sense—Olivia was smarter than people gave her credit for. But untouched by the world in a way that made Jack's chest ache. She deserved something gentle. Something sure. Something safe.

He ran a hand through his hair, fingers catching at the back of his neck. The sun pressed down through the canopy above, heat prickling against his skin, but the real discomfort was under it—in his chest, twisting.

Maybe this was a good thing.

Maybe it would settle things.

Give her the closure she needed. Give him the clarity to walk away.

To stop thinking about her.

To stop wondering how her laugh would sound pressed against his shoulder, or how it would feel to hold her just a moment too long.

Except…

He didn't want her to go.

He didn't want to watch her sit across from Wyatt in some candlelit corner of the island, nervous and hopeful, smiling at all the wrong things. He didn't want her mistaking surface-level charm for something deeper. For connection. For care.

And he sure as hell didn't want to wonder whether Wyatt's hands would graze that delicate spot behind her ear—or if she'd laugh that soft, breathy laugh, the one she saved for moments when she felt safe.

With him.

Jack's exhale came out rough and low, his jaw clenched hard enough to ache.

This wasn't jealousy. He refused to call it that. Jealousy implied ownership. Possession.

This was something else. Something quieter, more dangerous.

It was fear.

Fear that she'd give her heart to someone who wouldn't know how to hold it.

Fear that he'd convinced himself for too long that he didn't want a heart to hold at all.

Fear that he'd already started falling for the one girl he had no business wanting.

Because Olivia Clifton —messy ponytail, glitter-streaked arms, and all—mattered.

And he might already be too late.

How the hell had this happened?

He'd only known her for three days. *Three.* And yet, here he was—tied up in knots, unravelling over a girl who hadn't even been on his radar a week ago. A girl who didn't fit into his world, didn't play by its rules.

But maybe that was exactly why she was getting under his skin.

Because she didn't try to impress him.

Because she saw him, not the fortune or the name.

And because, against all odds, she'd made him feel again.

Damn it.

Three days. That's all it had taken.

And he was already wrecked.

Chapter Ten

The restaurant sat tucked beneath a canopy of string lights and swaying palms, the flicker of candlelight dancing across linen-draped tables and the soft strains of acoustic guitar weaving through the warm night air.

Olivia smoothed the fabric of her sundress as Wyatt pulled out her chair. He'd shown up at her door right on time, all easy charm and sun-kissed confidence, dressed in a crisp button-down and linen pants rolled at the ankle like some catalog dream. He smelled like ocean wind and salt. Familiar. Safe.

So why did her stomach feel like it was balancing on the edge of something she couldn't name?

"Table by the water," Wyatt said with a grin, motioning toward the view. "Best seat in the house."

She smiled and nodded, lowering herself into the chair. "It's beautiful."

He settled across from her, gesturing to the server with a practiced ease. "Two mojitos," he said without asking. "Trust me—you'll love them."

She didn't correct him. It was a small thing—barely worth noticing. But Jack would've asked.

She pushed the thought away, like brushing lint from a sleeve.

The conversation began light, easy. Wyatt launched into a story about a chaotic water-skiing lesson with a hungover hedge fund manager who face-planted four times in ten minutes. She laughed—genuinely, at first. But as he kept talking, a subtle unease crept in, curling around the edges of her mood.

He was trying. Trying to amuse her. Trying to recapture a spark that had never really ignited. He asked her questions, but they skimmed the surface—nothing that lingered, nothing that dug deeper. Not like Jack's questions. Jack asked as if the answers mattered.

She shook off the thought.

Wyatt leaned in, propping his elbows on the table with that familiar boyish grin. "So," he said, "what brought you here, really? You said it was for a job, but I always figured there was more to it."

Olivia stirred her drink slowly, watching the mint leaves spiral in the glass. "I needed a change. Something quieter. I thought… maybe I'd find something that made sense."

Wyatt chuckled. "And instead, you found kids with glitter and glue."

She smiled, but it didn't quite reach her eyes.

He tilted his head, studying her. "You always had a soft heart. That's what I liked about you back then."

Liked. Past tense.

And maybe that's when the realisation settled in.

Wyatt didn't know her anymore. Maybe he never had.

The girl he'd once "liked" had been quiet, uncertain—grateful for crumbs of attention. She'd moulded herself to fit the moment, never daring to ask for more.

But the woman sitting here now? The one who had learned to laugh again, who had started to believe she was worth being seen—she hadn't been shaped by Wyatt.

That had been Jack.

The thought startled her. She blinked, her gaze drifting toward the path outside the restaurant. She imagined Jack walking there, hands in his pockets, eyes searching for her even if he pretended, they weren't.

She liked him. More than she should.

"Olivia?" Wyatt's voice cut through the haze.

She turned back to him. "Sorry. I was just… thinking."

He smiled, but a flicker of something passed through his expression—doubt, maybe. Or disappointment. "You've been a little quiet tonight."

She parted her lips, ready to explain, to ease the tension, but the words tangled in her throat.

Because how could she tell him the truth?

That she was sitting here with a man she could maybe build a life with, while her heart kept wandering back to someone who would never be hers?

Jack was a billionaire. Kind, complicated, and completely out of reach. Olivia knew he liked her—but not enough. Not in a way that would ever make sense in the real world.

She was just an employee. He was… him.

And Wyatt—Wyatt was safe. Familiar. Possible.

So, she forced a smile and pushed Jack aside. "Just a little tired," she said lightly. "Kids can do that to you."

She laughed, a little too brightly, and leaned into Wyatt's story.

And for the rest of the meal, she tried—really tried—to be present.

But a part of her heart had already gone walking down that path, chasing someone who would never be hers to keep.

By the end of dinner, the effort of pretending had worn Olivia down. Her laughter had grown thin, her temples throbbed with the dull thump of an oncoming headache, and even the candlelight, once warm and romantic, now felt too bright—too revealing.

She was drained. Emotionally and physically.

Wyatt didn't seem to notice. Or maybe he didn't want to.

He walked her back through the winding paths of the resort, making casual conversation that barely registered in her mind. Crickets chirped in the trees above, the night air thick with salt and heat. She kept nodding along, offering polite smiles, but her heart wasn't in it.

By the time they reached her door, she just wanted to go inside, crawl under the covers, and disappear into the silence.

But Wyatt didn't stop walking when she did.

He stepped in close—too close—blocking her in as her back met the door. His hand braced beside her head, his eyes searching hers.

And before she could react, he leaned in and kissed her.

His lips were warm, firm. But the moment they touched hers, something in her recoiled. It felt wrong—like wearing someone else's clothes, like trying to step into a memory that no longer fit.

She pulled away, gently but decisively, placing a hand on his chest to create space.

"Goodnight, Wyatt," she said softly. "Thank you for dinner."

There was a flicker of surprise in his eyes, maybe even anger, but he didn't press.

He stepped back, hands falling to his sides. "Yeah… sure. Sleep well."

She slipped inside, quietly shutting the door behind her. And as she leaned against it, the silence hit her like a wave—cool and bracing.

She exhaled slowly, eyes closed, one hand still resting on the wood.

It shouldn't have been so hard.

But it was.

Because her heart wasn't confused anymore. It already knew where it wanted to be.

Jack spent the night trying not to think about Olivia.

He failed spectacularly.

He told himself it didn't matter. That what she did with Wyatt was none of his business. That she was free to make her own choices, and he had no right—none at all—to care.

But he did care.

And it made him furious.

He paced the length of the villa more times than he could count, a low thrum of irritation simmering beneath his skin. Not at her—never at her—but at himself. For letting it get this far. For thinking about her when he should have been reviewing expansion plans. For wondering if she laughed with Wyatt the way she laughed with him. If she let Wyatt touch her hand across the table. If she'd wear that same soft expression she wore when she talked about the kids, or the ocean, or that stupid lavender tea she liked so much.

It was madness.

He didn't do this. He didn't linger over women who didn't fall at his feet. That wasn't arrogance—it was experience. They always did. Always had. And when they didn't, he moved on.

Even Charlotte hadn't occupied this much space in his mind, and he'd been seconds away from marrying her at one point. With Charlotte, everything had been planned— practical. Calculated. A partnership that made sense on paper.

But Olivia…

She was chaos wrapped in quiet. Kindness, he didn't know how to hold. She looked at the world like it still had magic in it—and damn it, she made him want to believe in it too.

That terrified him.

By the time the clock struck midnight, Jack had poured himself two fingers of scotch and stood at the edge of his terrace, staring out at the dark stretch of ocean. Somewhere on the island, Olivia was with Wyatt. Laughing. Talking. Maybe more.

The thought tightened something sharp and bitter in his chest.

He set the glass down with a thud and walked away from the balcony, jaw clenched.

Enough.

He had come here for the wellness centre. For the launch. For the future of his company.

Not for a woman who didn't want him.

His decision was final.

He would focus. He would keep his distance. He would bury whatever this was before it became something he couldn't undo.

No more Olivia.

He told himself that again when he lay in bed, staring at the ceiling.

No more Olivia.

And again, just before he closed his eyes.

No more—

But even in sleep, she didn't leave him.

Jack was up before dawn.

He hit the gym like a man trying to outrun himself. Pushed through a brutal circuit until his muscles burned and his breath came in ragged pulls. Showered quickly, mechanically, like scrubbing off whatever part of him still gave a damn about a girl in a sundress with stars in her eyes.

He buttoned his crispest linen shirt with military precision. It felt too stiff, too structured for island life—wrong against his skin—but he wore it anyway. A statement, maybe. To himself, more than anyone else.

He had work to do. The wellness centre fit-out was in its final stages, and he planned to be across every detail. No distractions. No deviations.

No Olivia.

Focused. Sharp. Unshakable.

That's what he told himself.

He was walking past the staff dining area on his way to the site when he heard it—low male voices, laughter, chairs scraping. He didn't mean to slow his step, but something in the tone pulled at him. Then he heard the name.

"Hey, Wyatt, I saw you out with the new childcare worker."

Jack stopped. Just for a second. Just long enough to hear Wyatt's unmistakable voice, arrogant and laid-back.

"Yep."

"How'd it go? Seal the deal?"

A pause. Then, cockier still: "Of course. What, you think I've lost my touch?"

There was a ripple of laughter.

Jack's jaw tightened. He didn't move.

"So, you gonna see her again?" another guy asked. "'Cause I wouldn't mind taking her out."

Silence. Then Wyatt's reply, casual and cutting in equal measure:

"Nah. She's mine for a while. I'll let you know when I'm done."

Jack's teeth nearly cracked with how hard he clenched them.

A red haze crept in behind his eyes, hot and unfamiliar. He wasn't the possessive type. He didn't do jealousy, didn't care who anyone else slept with. He especially didn't lose sleep over women who weren't his.

But there was something about the way Wyatt said it.

'She mine for a while. I'll let you know when I'm done.'

Like she was a toy. A temporary thrill. A warm body he could pass around.

And maybe the worst part was—Olivia wouldn't even know. Wouldn't see it. She'd believe Wyatt when he turned on that beach-blond charm and said all the right things. She'd trust him. Because Olivia was good like that.

Too good.

Jack turned on his heel, walked away before he did something stupid. Like storm in there and rearrange Wyatt's face.

He shoved his hands into his pockets as he stalked toward the construction site, trying to ignore the way his heart pounded against his ribs like a warning.

She's not yours either, something in his head snapped.

You made that choice. You said no more.

But that line was already blurred.

Because Jack couldn't stop thinking about her laugh. Or the way she tilted her head when she was curious.

And now, the thought of Wyatt—Wyatt—putting his hands on her made Jack's blood boil.

He wasn't focused. He wasn't sharp.

And he sure as hell wasn't unshakable.

Not anymore.

The cracks were showing, and worse, he didn't know how to seal them. He was a man who controlled outcomes, who managed expectations, who walked away clean. But this—this thing with Olivia—it was beginning to feel like a landslide.

He raked a hand through his hair and stopped by the construction site, staring at blueprints he couldn't focus on. His eyes didn't register the details. All he saw was Wyatt's smug face and Olivia's soft smile—and how wrong they looked in the same frame.

He should tell her.

He should walk right up to her, look her in the eye, and say exactly what he'd heard. Give her the truth before she got pulled any deeper into something she didn't deserve.

But then the doubt crept in.

Would she believe him?

He barely knew her, not really—not the way Wyatt did. She might think Jack was jealous. Or worse, interfering out of some misplaced sense of control. It could backfire. Push her closer to the very man he was trying to protect her from.

And what gave him the right, anyway? He'd already decided to keep his distance. Already chosen logic over longing.

It's her business.

It wasn't his job to play the hero. Olivia was smart. She was kind, yes—but not naïve. If there was something off about Wyatt, she'd see it.

Eventually.

Hopefully.

It's something she needs to sort out for herself.

But the thought made his stomach twist.

Because while she was figuring it out, Wyatt was laying on the charm, making promises he wouldn't keep, touching her like she belonged to him.

And Jack—Jack was standing on the sidelines, pretending it didn't matter. Pretending he could focus on wellness centres and business plans and linen shirts that didn't fit right anymore.

He told himself to let it go. To stay out of it.

But every time he closed his eyes, he saw her.

And every time he opened them, he wanted her more.

Chapter Eleven

It had been two weeks since the date with Wyatt.

Not that Olivia was counting.

She hadn't seen him since that awkward goodnight at her door, and honestly? She hadn't missed him. The date had confirmed what her gut had been quietly whispering all along: Wyatt wasn't the man for her.

He was charming—sure—in that glossy, easy sort of way. The kind of man who looked like a postcard and sounded like a promise. But beneath the sun-kissed skin and surfer drawl, there was nothing real. Nothing to hold on to.

Shallow. Self-absorbed. Empty.

There was no heartbreak. No sting. Just clarity.

And yet, clarity came with a cost.

Because while she hadn't spent the last two weeks thinking about Wyatt, she had spent them thinking about someone else.

Jack.

She hadn't seen him either. Not once.

He was busy, she told herself. He was Jack Alden—billionaire resort owner, head of an empire, master of a million moving pieces. He was overseeing the launch of a world-class wellness centre. He had meetings to attend, investors to impress, helicopters to board, luxury problems to solve.

He had no reason to cross paths with her anymore.

Still, that didn't stop her from hoping.

Every morning when she walked through the staff entrance, her eyes flicked automatically toward the main building. Every evening, she found excuses to linger— by the pool, near the beach bar, beside the path lined with white lanterns. Just in case.

Just in case he might be there.

Each time she caught a glimpse of dark hair, a tall figure in crisp linen, her breath caught. And each time it wasn't him, the breath left her chest a little heavier than before.

She missed him.

More than she wanted to.

It wasn't about the flirtation or the thrill, or even how wildly, unfairly attractive he was. It was the way he'd seen her. Really seen her. Like she wasn't just some girl in a borrowed uniform trying to keep up—but someone worth looking at. Someone worth knowing.

That feeling… that quiet, impossible magic… had vanished with him.

The nights were the hardest. When the island slipped into hush and the ocean whispered just outside her window. When her thoughts turned traitor in the dark, circling back to the sound of his voice, the sharp curve of his smile, the way his eyes lingered like he was memorising her.

She'd lie awake in her little bungalow, staring at the ceiling fan turning slow overhead, and wonder if he thought about her at all.

He probably doesn't, she'd whisper into the dark. Of course he doesn't.

Jack Alden could have anyone. He belonged to a world she couldn't even imagine—wealth, power, influence. She was a childcare worker from a nowhere town with freckles on her nose and a habit of talking too much when she got nervous.

Why would he give her a second thought?

But no matter how many times she reminded herself of that truth, it never made her miss him less.

It had only been two weeks.

And it already felt like forever.

The sun was beginning its slow descent as Olivia wandered down the beach, the sky painted in strokes of orange and rose. She'd meant to head to dinner, but her feet carried her here instead—down the stretch of shoreline that felt more like memory than sand.

Then she saw it.

That spot. The place where, on her second day here, he'd appeared beside her towel like some perfectly timed apparition. The image was burned into her mind—the lazy smile, relaxed posture, the unshakable sense that he saw her.

She stared at it now, and the ache in her chest throbbed like a bruise pressed too hard.

She missed him.

More than she should. More than she wanted to.

And then—

She turned.

And there he was.

Just a few feet away.

Walking toward her along the shoreline, barefoot, sleeves rolled to his elbows, hands tucked into his pockets like he hadn't planned to find her here… but couldn't help hoping he might.

The air shifted.

Time slowed.

The breeze stilled around them.

Jack stopped when their eyes met. And in that long, quiet moment, he looked at her like he hadn't seen her in years—not days.

Like he'd missed her, too.

Jack told himself he was fine.

He had work to do. The wellness centre was finally taking shape—glass walls installed, lighting fixtures arriving, and his project manager waiting for sign-off on the next budget approval. The staff was performing well. Guest feedback was glowing. Everything on the island was running like clockwork.

And yet… he felt unmoored.

Restless.

It had been two weeks since he'd seen Olivia.

He knew exactly how long it had been because every morning when he shaved, he caught himself looking in the mirror and wondering if today might be the day he ran into her.

And then it wasn't.

He hadn't intended to avoid her, not at first. He'd told himself he was just giving her space. After all, she had gone out with Wyatt—twice, he thought bitterly, though he didn't know if that was even true. And she hadn't come looking for him, hadn't reached out, hadn't done anything to suggest she even noticed he was gone.

So, Jack had stayed away.

But it was getting harder by the day.

He didn't like this version of himself—moody, distracted, short-tempered with his team. He didn't like waking up thinking about a woman who didn't belong in his world. A woman he had no business wanting.

But he did want her.

God, he wanted her.

And so, on a humid Wednesday afternoon before dinner, Jack decided to go for a walk along the beach.

And then he saw her.

Standing right where she had been that second day—next to the towel, near the edge of the surf—like time had folded in on itself.

Jack stopped breathing.

It was like being punched in the chest and kissed at the same time.

She turned. Their eyes met. Just for a beat.

Then she smiled.

That brilliant, heart-stopping smile—like she was actually glad to see him.

It knocked the breath clean out of him.

"Jack," she said, her voice soft and warm, as if it had been waiting for him. "It's so good to see you."

He swallowed. Hard. "Hi, Olivia."

"I haven't seen you around," she said, still smiling, but there was a thread of something beneath it—something just shy of disappointment.

He gave a dry, practiced smile. "I've been… busy."

Her smile faltered, just slightly. "Of course."

She nodded, like she understood all the things he wasn't saying.

Things he didn't even fully understand himself.

Silence stretched between them, the kind that felt too heavy for two people standing on a beach under a golden sky.

"I missed talking to you," she said quietly, like it had slipped out without permission.

Jack froze.

His chest tightened, breath caught somewhere between relief and longing.

Then, slowly, he said, "Yeah. Me too."

The pause that followed was thick with everything they weren't saying. The waves kept rolling in, careless and constant.

Jack cleared his throat. "How are things going with you and Wyatt—"

"There's nothing going on," she cut in quickly. "There was that one dinner. That's it. I figured out pretty fast he's not for me."

Jack blinked. He hadn't expected that. So, Wyatt had lied that day to save face.

And just like that, something hot and reckless surged in his chest—hope.

God help him, it flared so fast it nearly took him down.

"I see," he said, voice low.

She looked up at him, uncertain now. Her confidence had shifted into something raw, unguarded.

"By the end of that dinner, I had a splitting headache," she said with a small, self-deprecating laugh. "He kissed me, and—" she shook her head— "I think there's something wrong with me."

He frowned. "Why would you say that?"

Her eyes met his, steady now. "Because I hated it."

Jack's breath caught.

There was no flirtation in her voice, no drama—just the truth, dropped between them like a stone.

He stared at her. The sea. The fading sun. The sudden, fierce desire to touch her—really touch her—nearly undid him.

"I don't think there's anything wrong with you," he said, quiet but certain.

She smiled again. Smaller this time. But real. It hit him like sunlight after too long in the dark.

And in that moment, Jack knew—with terrifying, bone-deep certainty—he wasn't going to be able to stay away.

Not now.

Not from her.

"Have you eaten yet?" he asked, his voice low, careful.

She shook her head. "Not yet."

A pause.

Then, quietly, "Would you have dinner with me?"

Her eyes searched his for a moment, like she needed to make sure he meant it—not as a boss, not as a friend, but as a man who'd missed her.

And then she smiled.

That radiant, breathtaking smile that knocked the air right out of him.

"I'd love that," she said.

They started walking, side by side along the shoreline, their bare feet sinking into the warm sand. The silence between them wasn't awkward—it was easy, filled with the kind of quiet that only existed between people who didn't need to rush the moment

Chapter Twelve

When they reached the private path to Jack's villa, she glanced at him. "You live here?"

He gave a modest shrug. "For now."

The villa sat on a rise overlooking the water, partially hidden by lush greenery and lit by warm, ambient lighting that glowed softly as the sun dipped below the horizon. He opened the door and held it for her, letting her step inside first.

Olivia stopped in her tracks.

"Wow," she whispered. "This is beautiful."

The inside was modern, but not cold. Sleek lines met warm wood, floor-to-ceiling windows framed the sea, and soft linen drapes billowed slightly in the ocean breeze. A long, low sofa faced a sculpted fireplace. The open-concept space flowed from a cozy sitting area to a chef's kitchen with matte black fixtures and stone countertops that gleamed under the pendant lights. Art—real art—hung on the walls: abstract brushstrokes in earth tones that somehow made the room feel both elevated and grounded. One entire wall was glass, with a sliding door that opened onto a private terrace with an infinity-edge plunge pool that seemed to spill directly into the ocean beyond.

She turned in a slow circle, taking it all in.

"I'm glad you like it," Jack said quietly.

She laughed, a soft, surprised sound, like his words had caught her off guard. "How could anyone not? I've never seen anything so lovely."

He watched her as she spoke, but it wasn't the villa he was admiring.

"It's just a place," he said, his voice low. "What would you like to eat?"

She glanced over at him with that easy, open smile that always seemed to catch him off guard. "You can decide. I trust you. When I eat by myself, I usually just have a salad."

Jack raised an eyebrow. "Salad? That's criminal."

She laughed, the sound bright and unguarded. "I know."

"Well, let's see if I can do better than a salad."

"I'm sure you will." She grinned, then turned slightly and pointed toward the glass doors. "Can I go look at the view before it's too dark?"

"Of course," he said, already reaching for his phone to place their order. "I'll be out in a minute."

Olivia stepped out onto the terrace, barefoot, drawn by the soft hush of the waves and the fading blush of the sunset. The view was unreal—like something from a dream. The ocean stretched endlessly toward the horizon, the water glimmering with the last kiss of sunlight. Palm trees swayed in the evening breeze, and the air smelled like salt and something sweet—hibiscus maybe. She braced her hands on the railing and closed her eyes for a moment, letting the quiet settle into her bones.

It had been so long since she felt peace like this.

She heard the soft slide of the door behind her and turned as Jack stepped onto the terrace, holding two delicate stemmed glasses. He handed one to her without a word.

"Thank you," she said, taking the glass and lifting it to her lips.

The wine was crisp and cold, with a subtle hint of peach. Olivia let it linger on her tongue before swallowing, then sighed softly, eyes drifting back to the view.

"This place is spectacular," she murmured.

He leaned against the railing beside her, close but not quite touching. There was space between them—but only just. The kind of space that hummed with awareness.

"I like it," Jack said, his gaze fixed somewhere out over the water. "It's quiet. Private. The kind of place where things make sense."

She glanced at him, curiosity flickering in her eyes. "So… do you have any brothers or sisters?"

His brow lifted, surprised by the question. "You don't know?"

She blinked. "Know what?"

"Most people look me up before they even meet me. Tell me things I've forgotten about my own life," he said with a wry, slightly tired smile. "I figured you might've googled me by now."

Olivia laughed—a genuine, delighted sound that made something tighten in Jack's chest. "Sorry," she said, playful. "I'll remember that for the next time I meet a rich guy. Do the full online stalk beforehand."

He chuckled, the corner of his mouth lifting. "You're not even a little curious?"

She shrugged, swirling her wine. "Of course I'm curious. But I would prefer to get to know you, not your Wikipedia page. All I know is that you're a billionaire… and you own this incredible resort. That's it, I'm afraid."

His expression softened, surprised again—but this time in a way that looked like it actually mattered to him.

"Well," he said, after a beat, "in that case… yes. I have one sister. Younger. She's married with two little boys who've completely stolen my heart."

"That's sweet," Olivia said, smiling. "So, you're the cool uncle?"

"I try. I fly them in every few months, spoil them with candy, take them to feed the stingrays, and then send them home when they're completely wired."

She laughed again, this time more softly. "Bet they adore you."

He didn't answer right away. His eyes were on her again, quietly studying the way her hair moved in the breeze, the way she looked around like she was actually seeing everything.

"Maybe," he said at last. "But not as much as I think I'm starting to adore this."

She glanced at him, caught off guard.

"This?" she asked, breath catching a little.

Jack tilted his head, watching her. "You. This. Talking like this. Not knowing what's coming next."

Her heart skipped. Just once. But it echoed all the way down.

She took another sip of wine, hoping it would calm the way her pulse had just leapt.

"So," she said, her voice a little lighter, "what else don't I know about you?"

He grinned. "That's a long list."

"Good," she said, smiling over the rim of her glass. "I'm not in a rush."

There was a beat of quiet between them, the kind that didn't feel awkward, only full of possibilities.

"What about you?" he asked, turning toward her a little more. "Do you have family?"

A shadow passed through her smile, softening her expression. "No siblings. And... no parents."

Jack's brow furrowed gently. "I'm sorry."

She gave a small nod, eyes drifting to the horizon. "My dad died in a car accident four years ago. It was... sudden. I was at uni at the time. One phone call and everything changed." She paused, then exhaled softly. "And then my mum got sick. Cancer. It took her quickly. Two years later, I was standing in another hospital room holding her hand, knowing I was about to say goodbye all over again."

Jack didn't speak right away. He didn't offer platitudes or apologies. He just listened— really listened.

"She told me," Olivia went on, her voice quieter now, "just before she passed, that she was going to find my dad. That he'd be waiting for her. I like to think she was right. That maybe wherever they are, they're together."

Jack's chest tightened. Not just at the words, but at the way she said them—with that quiet strength, the kind that only came from walking through fire and still being able to speak of love.

"I believe she found him," he said, voice low.

She turned to look at him, and something passed between them—something unspoken but powerful. Gratitude. Understanding. A kind of closeness that had nothing to do with time and everything to do with truth.

"I don't talk about them much," she admitted. "Most people get uncomfortable. Or they try to fix it."

"I'm not trying to fix anything," Jack said, his voice steady. "I just want to know you."

Her lips curved slowly, and that smile—smaller than before, but no less breathtaking—made his heart skip a beat.

"Then you're already doing it right," she whispered.

The ocean rolled in gently beneath them, and for a moment, the world held its breath.

Jack lifted his glass and touched it lightly to hers. "To your parents."

She blinked, surprised, then smiled again. "To my parents."

They drank, and the silence that followed wasn't empty.

It pulsed with something quiet and intimate—something warm, delicate, and very, very real. The kind of silence that didn't need filling. That said more than words ever could.

From the terrace, the golden light filtered through sheer linen curtains, casting soft shadows across the polished floors as the sun slipped lower behind the horizon. The air was laced with salt and citrus, the clink of ice in her glass, the occasional murmur of the waves below.

Dinner arrived shortly after—a discreet knock, a pair of servers in crisp uniforms wheeling in a tray, all efficient and wordless. Jack led her back inside, and Olivia followed him barefoot across the cool stone tiles.

The dining table had been set with casual elegance—no fuss, just quality. A bottle of white wine in a silver bucket. Two linen napkins folded into soft triangles. Plates already arranged with grilled sea bass resting on a bed of herbed farro, blistered cherry tomatoes, and a delicate salad of arugula, citrus, and goat cheese.

Olivia's eyes widened. "Wow. This is… a little more impressive than a salad."

Jack grinned as he poured her another splash of wine. "Good. You deserve more than iceberg lettuce and croutons."

She laughed, but her cheeks flushed slightly, the compliment landing somewhere deep.

They sat across from each other, the soft clink of cutlery filling the quiet. Olivia took a bite, then paused, eyes wide again.

"This is incredible," she said around a smile. "I can't cook, what about you?"

"I can toast bread without burning it," Jack said dryly. "Beyond that, I outsource."

"Well, whoever made this, tell them I'm sending fan mail."

Jack watched her, amused. She wasn't shy about enjoying her food—she took real bites, closed her eyes to savour. And for some reason, that struck him deeper than it should have.

Most of the women he dined with in his world—models, socialites, influencers—picked at their meals with apologetic smiles and sipped at wine they barely touched. Watching Olivia eat like this, fully present, unselfconscious… it was refreshing. Grounding.

"You actually eat," he murmured, almost to himself.

She looked up, surprised. "Of course I eat. Why wouldn't I?"

Jack hesitated, then gave a small smile. "You'd be amazed how rare it is."

Olivia tilted her head, eyes narrowing in curiosity. "Is that what they're like? The women you usually…?"

He gave a short, low laugh. "Let's just say you're a pleasant surprise."

There was no edge to the compliment. No flirtation. Just quiet truth.

Their conversation moved easily after that, threading through stories of their childhoods—Olivia's summers at her grandmother's house in Gosford, Jack's boarding school days in Switzerland. She asked about the first business he ever started, and he surprised her by saying it was a lawn-mowing service at twelve years old. She told him about the kids she looked after in the kids' club, how one of them had tried to sell her a shell for twenty dollars because it was "enchanted."

He laughed, deeply, and she felt the warmth of it all the way to her toes.

After they'd eaten, Jack leaned back in his chair, watching her with a softness in his eyes that hadn't been there at the beginning of the evening.

"Would you like dessert?" he asked, his voice low and warm.

Olivia tilted her head, a mischievous glint in her eyes. "Depends," she said, swirling the last sip of wine in her glass. "What's on offer?"

He smiled slowly, like he knew exactly what she was doing—and didn't mind in the slightest. "Anything you want."

She bit her lip in mock contemplation, then said, "I love cheesecake."

Jack nodded, his gaze never leaving hers. "Cheesecake it is."

"Do you always give women whatever they ask for?" she teased, resting her chin on her hand.

"Only when they ask so sweetly," he said, standing and pulling out his phone. "And especially when they smile like that."

She laughed softly, the sound like a bell in the quiet villa, as Jack walked toward the kitchen to make a call.

Jack returned a moment later, sliding his phone into his pocket. "It's on its way."

"You just happen to have cheesecake on standby?" she asked, arching a brow.

"I own the place," he said with a shrug. "I can make cheesecake appear."

She leaned back in her chair, impressed. "That's a very dangerous power, Jack."

He met her gaze. "You have no idea."

The dessert arrived not long after, delivered on a silver tray with two small forks and a dollop of fresh cream on the side. The cheesecake was pale gold, its texture impossibly light, with a buttery crust and a hint of citrus that made Olivia's eyes widen with the first bite.

She let out a soft moan of delight. "Oh my God. This is the best cheesecake I've ever eaten."

Jack grinned, watching her with open amusement. "I'll let my pastry chef know you approve."

She laughed—really laughed—and it was the kind that lit up her whole face. "You're fun, you know that?"

Jack tilted his head, pretending to consider. "I'm also devastatingly handsome, fabulously wealthy, and an excellent listener."

She laughed again, shaking her head. "Don't forget modest."

Jack raised his fork in a mock toast, his eyes gleaming with mischief. "Modesty. It's my best quality."

Olivia chuckled, shaking her head as they polished off the last bites of cheesecake. The plates were nearly spotless by the time they leaned back in their chairs, sated and smiling.

The conversation flowed easily between them after that—unforced and open. Jack found himself learning things he hadn't expected. That Olivia wasn't just kind and genuine, but sharp-witted and deeply thoughtful. That she read classic novels to the kids in her care because she believed they deserved magic. That she once volunteered at a community shelter for a year after her mother died, needing to be near other people's hearts when her own was breaking.

He couldn't remember the last time he'd been this genuinely curious about someone. Or this effortlessly drawn in.

"I've really enjoyed myself tonight," she said softly, tucking a strand of hair behind her ear. Her eyes met his, steady and sincere.

"So have I," he said, his voice low, honest. "More than you know."

She smiled. "Thank you… for all of it."

Jack hesitated, then asked, "Just curious—what went wrong with your date with Wyatt?"

Olivia let out a slow breath, her smile fading a little. "He spent most of the evening talking about himself. His career, his body, his social media following… Honestly, it was like sitting across from a mirror he couldn't stop admiring."

Jack smirked. "That sounds about right."

"And he didn't ask me a single question about myself," she added, shaking her head. "I wasn't joking when I said I had a splitting headache by the end of the night. I did. One of those dull, persistent ones that starts behind your eyes when you're trying too hard to be polite."

Jack's expression softened. "I'm sorry you went through that."

She shrugged lightly, but her eyes darkened with memory.

"And the kiss?" he asked gently.

She paused, her body giving a small, involuntary shiver—the kind that had nothing to do with temperature.

"I felt… wrong," she admitted, her voice barely above a whisper. "Like I was acting out someone else's scene. I was standing there, letting it happen, and every cell in my body was screaming this isn't it."

She looked down at her hands. "Then afterward, I thought maybe there was something wrong with me. Because Wyatt is handsome, right? Charming. He's kissed more women than I can probably count. So, if I didn't feel anything… maybe it meant I was broken."

Jack sat still for a moment; his eyes fixed on her face. His jaw tightened, something unspoken flickering in his gaze—a quiet storm held just beneath the surface. Then he leaned forward slightly, his voice soft but steady.

"There's nothing wrong with you, Olivia. You just haven't been kissed right."

Her breath caught.

The air between them shifted, thick with meaning. The warmth of the room, the intimacy of the evening—it all seemed to press in around them like a secret waiting to be spoken aloud.

"Thanks, Jack," she said quietly, a flicker of something unreadable in her eyes. Then she stood, smoothing her hands down the front of her dress. "I better go, or I won't get up for work. My boss will sack me."

He laughed, rising to his feet. "Wouldn't want that. I'll walk you to your bungalow."

She gave a small smile. "There's no need—"

"I insist," he said, already moving toward the door.

A beat passed. She nodded. "Okay."

They reached the door, the cool evening air spilling in as Jack pulled it open. But before they crossed the threshold, he paused, his hand still resting on the doorknob. His voice was lower now, almost reverent.

"Olivia… can I kiss you good night?"

She turned to face him, her eyes wide—startled, caught off guard like a deer in headlights. For a heartbeat, she just looked at him, her lips parting with something close to wonder. Then, silently, she nodded.

Chapter Thirteen

Jack didn't rush.

He released the doorknob, letting the door close.

He stepped toward her slowly, like she was something precious—fragile and fierce all at once. His hand rose to her cheek, brushing a loose strand of hair behind her ear with a touch so gentle it made her shiver. She came to him willingly, breath hitching, her heart pounding so loudly she was sure he could hear it.

He pulled her into his arms, one arm circling her waist with a quiet certainty, the other settling lightly at the curve of her back. She fit against him like a breath held too long finally exhaled. Her hands found the front of his shirt, clutching the fabric as if grounding herself—and still, she trembled.

Then he kissed her.

And everything else disappeared.

The world slipped away—the ocean, the wind, the soft glow of the terrace lights—all of it faded into nothing.

His lips moved against hers with exquisite patience, not demanding but discovering, coaxing rather than taking. It wasn't urgent or showy. It was deep and devastatingly tender. A kiss that said, I see you. I feel you. I've been waiting for this.

And Olivia melted.

The moment their mouths met, something inside her unlocked. The doubt, the ache, the quiet loneliness she hadn't even realised she carried—it all cracked open in that single, searing kiss.

It was electric.

Not in the way she thought kisses were supposed to feel—fast and dizzying—but in the way it reached inside her and rearranged something. A current that lit her up from the inside out.

When they finally pulled apart, her eyes fluttered open, dazed and searching.

Jack's forehead rested lightly against hers, their breaths mingling.

"I've wanted to do that since the day I met you," he whispered.

She smiled, breathless, her voice barely a whisper. "I think I've been waiting for it."

Jack's forehead still rested against hers, his eyes closed, breathing her in. The scent of her—warm skin, sea air, a hint of vanilla—wrapped around him like a drug. He was drowning in her.

He wanted to kiss her again.

God, he wanted *to.*

His hand skimmed up her spine, fingers pressing lightly between her shoulder blades, and her body responded—melting a little closer, fitting even more perfectly into his arms. His lips hovered just a breath from hers, and her eyes flicked to his, wide, open, and waiting.

One more kiss. Just one.

But Jack knew himself too well.

If he kissed her again here—he wouldn't want to stop. And this wasn't the time.

Not now.

Not yet.

He pulled in a breath, slow and steady, and forced himself to take a half-step back. Her body swayed toward him for the briefest moment before she caught herself.

Her cheeks were flushed, lips parted, eyes soft with something that unravelled him.

"We should get you home," he said, his voice low, a little hoarse.

She nodded slowly, as if coming back to earth. "Yeah… yeah, okay."

They walked in silence for a while, the soft thud of their footsteps against the sand the only sound. The moon cast silver ribbons across the waves, and the night air was warm against their skin. Olivia walked beside him, arms loose at her sides, her fingers occasionally brushing his. She didn't pull away when they did.

Jack didn't speak. He couldn't. Not yet. His body still hummed with the taste of her, the feel of her trembling against him, the echo of that kiss in every nerve ending.

By the time they reached her bungalow, nestled at the edge of the staff cottages beneath a canopy of palm trees, Jack was aching with restraint.

She stopped at her door, turning to face him. The porch light spilled gold across her face, catching the curve of her smile, the shine in her eyes.

"Well," she said, quiet and soft.

"Well," he echoed.

Neither moved.

For a second, Jack's hand lifted again—reaching for her cheek, her waist, her hand, anything—but he caught himself. He didn't trust himself not to press her against the door and kiss her until morning bled through the trees.

So instead, he smiled. "Goodnight, Olivia."

She tilted her head, watching him with a look that made it very hard to walk away.

"Goodnight, Jack."

He started to turn, then paused, one last look.

"I meant it, you know," he said. "There's nothing wrong with you. In fact, I think there's a lot that's incredibly right."

Her breath hitched.

And then—before she could answer—he stepped off her porch and into the dark, leaving her standing there, heart racing, pulse thrumming, the echo of his kiss still burning on her lips.

Olivia hardly slept. Every time she closed her eyes, she was back in Jack's villa—back in his arms—his mouth claiming hers like he had every right to it. Every stolen breath, every brush of his lips, had wrecked her in the most unexpected way.

That kiss had undone her.

It wasn't just the heat of it, though that alone had scorched through her like wildfire—it was the feeling behind it. The way it anchored her, like for one fleeting moment, she wasn't invisible or temporary or second choice. She felt real. Seen. Desired in a way that had nothing to do with performance or pleasing or chasing someone who barely noticed her at all.

Jack had kissed her like she mattered. Like he meant it. Like she was the only thing in the world he wanted.

She lay tangled in the resort's linen sheets long after dawn began to stir at the edges of the sky, her body still humming with the memory of his touch. His hands had curled around her waist like he was afraid she might disappear. His mouth—God, his mouth—had known just where to go, just how to make her unravel.

She'd never been kissed like that. Not by Wyatt. Not by anyone.

And that terrified her.

Because if that kiss had been nothing to Jack, then it had meant far too much to her.

Finally, with sleep impossible and her thoughts an endless loop, she threw off the covers and dressed in jean shorts and a loose, worn t-shirt. The air was already warm, the sky brushing soft gold against the sea as the sun crept above the horizon. She slipped on her sandals and wandered toward the beach, needing the solitude, the quiet rhythm of the waves, the feel of sand beneath her feet to clear her head.

She walked slowly, toes nudging at broken shells and pieces of sea glass, head down, trying—failing—to stop thinking about him. About that kiss.

She'd told him she thought she was broken—that something inside her didn't work right—because when Wyatt kissed her, she'd felt nothing. But now... now she knew the truth.

It wasn't her.

It was Wyatt.

Wyatt's kiss had felt wrong because he was wrong. He didn't see her. He didn't really want her. Not the way Jack had looked at her like she was some kind of miracle he didn't expect to find.

She paused in her steps, staring down at the foamy edge of the surf. Her heart clenched. She had let Jack in—really in—and that was dangerous. He was a billionaire playboy. She was a girl with sand between her toes and a heart held together with tape and hope.

She didn't belong in his world.

But he had kissed her like maybe—just maybe—she belonged in his arms.

A shadow stretched across her path, and suddenly, a pair of feet appeared in front of hers.

Her head snapped up, heart jolting.

"Jack."

His eyes were warm, unreadable in the early light. "Morning."

Olivia's breath caught in her throat. He was barefoot, his khaki joggers rolled at the ankle, a white t-shirt clinging to his chest in the soft morning breeze. His hair was tousled like he'd just rolled out of bed—or hadn't slept either.

Maybe she wasn't the only one haunted by that kiss.

"Didn't expect to see anyone out here this early," she said, voice thin and a little too high. She looked away, shielding her eyes from the rising sun—and from him.

Jack studied her for a moment. "I couldn't sleep." His tone was quieter than usual. Less smug, more human.

She nodded, arms crossing over her chest like a shield. "Yeah. Me neither."

A few seconds passed in silence. The ocean whispered beside them, soft waves curling toward their feet.

Jack took a cautious step closer. "About last night..."

Olivia's heart skittered. She shook her head quickly, backing up a step. "You don't have to say anything. Really. I get it—it happened, it was a moment. You were being nice. I was... confused."

"No." His voice was firmer now, his brow knitting. "That's not what it was."

She blinked, surprised. "It wasn't?"

He exhaled like he'd been holding his breath all night. "I didn't kiss you because I was being nice, Olivia." He stepped toward her again, slowly, like he was afraid she might run. "I kissed you because I couldn't not kiss you. I've been trying to fight it since the day you got here."

Her mouth parted. "Jack..."

He gave a soft, humourless laugh. "This wasn't my plan. I don't ever get involved with staff." His eyes softened as they dropped to her lips. "But you walked into my world like you didn't give a damn who I was. You weren't impressed or intimidated. You made me feel like just... a guy. And last night—"

He broke off, stepping even closer now, his voice lowering.

"Last night scared the hell out of me. Because that kiss—you—felt like more."

Olivia's throat tightened. She stared up at him, all the oxygen sucked from her lungs. Her fingers curled at her sides as emotions tumbled in her chest—fear, longing, disbelief.

"I don't know what this is," she whispered. "Or what you want from me."

"I want you to stop looking at me like I'm some mistake you're going to regret." His hand lifted, fingers brushing a strand of hair from her face. "And I want to kiss you again. Right here. With the sun rising and the world still asleep."

She swallowed, her heart slamming against her ribs. "And then what?"

Jack's hand lingered at her jaw, his thumb brushing the corner of her mouth. "Then we figure it out. One step at a time."

For a beat, neither of them moved. The waves rolled in, warm and slow. And then Olivia leaned forward—just enough.

That was all it took.

Jack closed the space between them and kissed her like he had all the time in the world. His hands found her waist—steady, warm, grounding her like she was something precious, something he couldn't bear to lose. There was no urgency in the first brush of his lips, no firestorm of impulse—just a slow, reverent tenderness that stole her breath more completely than any heat ever could. It was as if he were memorising her—her taste, the curve of her lips, the rhythm of her breath, the way she tasted like salt and sunrise.

The kiss began soft, almost hesitant, as though he wasn't sure she would let him in. But then something shifted, something deep and undeniable. The moment deepened—richer, hungrier. Jack's arms tightened around her, drawing her flush against him, and his mouth pressed more firmly to hers. The tenderness gave way to intensity, a wave of raw desire rising between them like a tide breaking free.

Olivia's response was instant—primal. Heat bloomed in her chest and swept through her, dizzying and fierce. Her heart pounded as his kiss turned bold, persuasive, a demand and a promise wrapped in velvet fire. Her knees went weak beneath her, but she didn't care. She clung to him, letting the kiss consume her, letting herself fall into the space where everything else faded but him.

A soft, involuntary moan slipped from her lips as her hands found their way up his chest, fingers trembling slightly as they slid to his shoulders, then up around his neck. She wrapped herself around him, holding on like he was the only solid thing in her world. Her fingers threaded into his hair—thick and silken—and he shivered beneath her touch, the sound of his breath deepening as her body pressed closer.

His tongue teased at her lips, coaxing them open, and when she let him in, the world tilted. He kissed her deeper, tasting her like a man starved. She was sweetness and fire, soft and unrelenting, and he couldn't get enough. Her scent wrapped around him—

warm skin, wild air, something that felt like home and danger all at once. Every inch of her drove him mad.

His hands slid down the curve of her back, anchoring at her hips, strong fingers guiding her against him with aching precision. As if even a millimetre of space was too much to bear. Olivia moved without thinking, her body attuned to his, surrendering to the pull she no longer wanted to resist.

When their lips finally parted, they stood locked in each other's arms, breathing hard, their foreheads resting together. Silence stretched between them, charged and intimate. Neither of them spoke—but they didn't have to.

That kiss had said it all.

Neither of them moved or spoke. The world felt suspended—just the hush of waves and the echo of their shared breath hanging between them.

Then reality hit Olivia. *Hard.*

What was she doing?

Kissing a billionaire on the beach of his exclusive island resort like she belonged there— like this was her world. Like she was someone who could survive falling for Jack Alden.

But she wasn't. She was just a girl from Sydney. A childcare worker with sand in her shoes and a heart that bruised too easily. This—him—was never supposed to happen.

She pulled away, her breath still shaky. Jack didn't stop her.

"I have to go to work," she said, her voice clipped, barely holding together.

He opened his mouth, maybe to say something, maybe to stop her—but she didn't wait.

She turned and walked away, fast, like if she didn't move now, she never would.

Jack watched her go, every step she took away from him carving a hollow ache deep in his chest. He wanted to follow her. Wanted to stop her, pull her back into his arms, kiss her until that worried look vanished from her eyes.

He'd scared her.

She was innocent—not in the way people usually meant it, but in the truest sense. Untouched by the games, the expectations, the guardedness that came with his world. She hadn't come looking for him, hadn't tried to impress or manipulate or charm. She'd just... been herself.

And that terrified him.

Because what he felt holding her wasn't just desire—it was something deeper. Something that settled in his bones like truth.

Jack dragged a hand through his hair and exhaled shakily.

He had to admit it—to himself, at least.

He was scared too.

Because he had never felt so right with a woman in his arms. Never felt his body respond the way it did to Olivia—like every nerve ending came alive the moment she touched him. Like his heart had been asleep until she kissed him back.

She felt like she belonged.

And that was the most dangerous feeling of all.

A little further down the beach, half-hidden behind a cluster of palms, someone was watching.

Wyatt.

He stood frozen, the early morning sun casting long shadows across his face, but the flicker of disbelief in his eyes was unmistakable.

He'd seen everything.

Olivia. His Olivia. Kissing Jack Alden like she meant it—like she'd been waiting her whole life to be kissed like that. Out in the open, on the damn beach, where anyone could see them.

Wyatt's jaw clenched.

His stomach twisted, fists balling tight at his sides.

Two weeks ago, she'd dodged his kiss like it meant nothing. He'd leaned in, certain she wanted it—confident, even—and she'd pulled away with some mumbled excuse that hadn't made a damn bit of sense.

But now it did.

That kiss wasn't hesitation. It was rejection.

And watching her now, melting into Jack Alden like her body was made for his—like she couldn't get close enough—Wyatt felt something bitter twist inside him.

It didn't sit right.

Not because Olivia had kissed someone else, but because she'd kissed him like that. So openly. So… freely.

That wasn't the Olivia he thought he knew—the one who blushed when he looked at her too long, who fumbled for words when he got close.

Chapter Fourteen

The chatter of children filled the kids' club like a tide Olivia didn't mind being swept up in. It was mid-morning now, the island sun filtering through the wide windows and casting golden light over the bright playroom. Blocks lay scattered across the mat, glitter-glue projects half-dried on the craft table, and the sweet, shrieking giggles of sugar-hyped six-year-olds echoed off the walls.

Olivia knelt beside a tower of foam bricks, helping four-year-old Rosie rebuild after her older brother had bulldozed it moments ago.

"Let's make it even taller this time," she said, her voice cheerful despite the gnawing ache in her chest. "Maybe even taller than me."

Rosie's eyes widened. "That's so tall!"

Olivia smiled and reached for another block. Her hands moved automatically—building, guiding, soothing. It helped. Being here, surrounded by little lives full of big emotions and tiny triumphs, grounded her in a way nothing else did.

Even as her thoughts tried to pull her back to that beach—to Jack's lips, his hands, the sound of his voice whispering that he wanted her—Olivia forced herself to stay present. She wasn't going to get lost in that mess again. Not now.

But the memories clung to her like humidity in the air. The taste of him. The way her body had come alive in his arms. That terrifying, exhilarating moment when she'd felt like she actually mattered.

She caught herself staring at nothing, heart racing.

Get it together.

After the kids had eaten lunch and were safely handed off to the afternoon team, Olivia clocked out and made a beeline for her bungalow. She felt hollowed out—bone-weary and emotionally raw.

She hadn't slept. Not really. Just lay there all night, staring at the ceiling, replaying every word, every look, that kiss.

As soon as she stepped inside, she dropped her bag and sank onto the edge of the bed, letting the silence settle over her like a heavy blanket. The ceiling fan spun lazily above her, its soft hum the only sound in the room. Through the open window, a breeze slipped in—warm, salted, and scented with frangipani.

She leaned back; hands braced behind her and stared up at the ceiling as the morning played on repeat in her mind.

Jack Alden.

Billionaire. Playboy. Owner of the damn island.

And somehow… the man who'd made her feel more seen with one kiss than Wyatt ever had with all his charm and empty promises.

It should've been simple.

But it wasn't.

Because despite everything—his money, his reputation, his world so far removed from hers—she'd let herself feel something. Real. Raw. Terrifying.

And now she couldn't stop asking the questions she didn't want answers to.

What if it hadn't meant anything to him?

What if she was just a distraction—something shiny and unexpected in a life that rarely surprised him?

What if she were just another story he'd forget the moment he flew back to wherever billionaires went when they got bored of paradise?

She exhaled shakily and flopped backward onto the bed with a groan, one arm slung over her eyes. Her mind was a battlefield. Every hopeful thought was met with doubt. Every memory, a warning.

And yet…

Beneath the static of her worry, the echo of his words kept tugging at her.

'Then we figure it out. One step at a time.'

God help her, she'd wanted to believe him.

She still did.

And maybe that was the scariest part of all.

Wyatt had just finished up his last surfing lesson of the morning, his board tucked under one arm, saltwater dripping from his hair, when he spotted Jack Alden walking along the path that cut between the beach and the resort grounds.

Perfect.

Wyatt slowed his pace, angling toward his rental hut. Just as he passed Jack, he couldn't help himself.

"Slumming it with the staff now?" he drawled, eyes narrowed, his tone deliberately casual but laced with venom.

Jack paused mid-stride and turned, his expression unreadable behind his aviators.

"Excuse me?" His voice was calm—too calm. That kind of dangerous stillness that hinted at a fuse burning low.

Wyatt shrugged, letting his board drop with a soft thud into the sand beside the hut. "You know what I mean. Olivia. Sweet, naïve, working-class—your type now?"

Jack took a step closer. "Be careful," he said quietly. "You're talking about someone who deserves a hell of a lot more respect than you're capable of giving."

Wyatt scoffed. "Sure. Until you get bored and toss her aside. Or maybe that's your idea of charity—dabbling with the hired help."

Jack's jaw flexed. "You don't know a damn thing about me."

Wyatt folded his arms, cocky and careless. "I know you go through models like cocktails—one every other week. I know you'll get bored with a girl like my Olivia."

Jack stepped in closer, voice low and lethal. "She's not your Olivia. And I heard you in the staff restaurant the other night—bragging about how you 'sealed the deal' with her. Telling your buddies she's yours for now, and you'll let them know when you're done."

Wyatt faltered, the cockiness slipping. "I was just joking."

"Didn't sound like a joke to me." Jack's eyes narrowed. "Let me be clear—if I hear you speak about any female staff member like that again, it's grounds for immediate dismissal."

Wyatt's smirk wavered, just for a second.

Jack turned without waiting for a reply, smooth and deliberate. "Enjoy your waves," he said over his shoulder. "They're the only thing around here still willing to let you ride them."

And then he was gone, leaving Wyatt standing there, jaw tight, pride stinging under the morning sun.

The last of the children had finally drifted off, their soft breathing filling the room like the tide easing in. Olivia tucked a light blanket over one of the little boys who had kicked his off, then settled beside Karen on the oversized floor cushions.

Karen sipped from her water bottle and nudged Olivia with her elbow. "So, what are you planning to do with your week off?"

Their schedule worked on a rotation—three weeks on, one week off—and Olivia's break was just around the corner.

She sighed, keeping her voice low. "I'm not sure, honestly. Got any ideas?"

Karen leaned her head back against the wall. "There's a boat that runs from the marina. Takes you to some of the other islands—quiet beaches, caves, waterfalls… all the pretty postcard stuff."

Olivia gave a soft smile. "That sounds perfect, actually. I'll check it out."

"When do you start your break?"

"Day after tomorrow."

Karen grinned. "Same. I'm meeting my boyfriend on one of the other islands."

Olivia nodded, her thoughts already drifting—salt air, open sea, and maybe, just maybe, a few days to untangle the knot her heart had become.

Olivia had just finished her final shift of the month, the weight of exhaustion settling in her bones. A whole week stretched ahead of her—her first real break since arriving on the island. She planned to explore, maybe visit one of the outer islands Karen had mentioned. Anything to distract her from the emotional mess she'd found herself tangled in.

But first… she just needed a moment to breathe.

Skipping the staff restaurant, she made her way straight to her bungalow, craving silence more than food. The midday sun beat down and sweat clung to her skin. She reached her door and had just pulled her key from her pocket when she heard it.

"Liv."

She froze.

Wyatt.

Turning, she forced a polite smile. "Hi, Wyatt." Her voice was cool, guarded. "What's up?"

He shoved his hands in his pockets, eyes darting behind her, then back to her face. "Can we talk?"

She didn't want to. Every cell in her body screamed for solitude, but something in his tone made her hesitate. She exhaled. "Okay, fine."

She opened the door, stepping inside. He followed, uninvited.

Olivia stood just past the threshold, arms crossed. "What's on your mind, Wyatt?"

He didn't waste time. "I came to warn you."

She stiffened. "About what?"

"Jack Alden," he said, voice low and serious.

She rolled her eyes, instantly regretting letting him in. "I don't want to do this with you, Wyatt."

"I'm serious, Olivia," he said, stepping closer. "He's playing you. That's what he does. Guys like him, they don't stick around. You're just the flavour of the month."

"Enough," she snapped, moving away from him. "What I do isn't your business."

Wyatt's expression darkened. "You think he's going to date you? Bring you into his world? He'll toss you aside the second he gets bored. Just like he does with everyone else."

"I said that's enough." Her voice sharpened.

His jaw clenched. "You don't see it. You never did. You brushed me off to chase him—after everything I—"

"I think you should go," Olivia said, her voice firm as she moved toward the door.

But before she could reach it, Wyatt's hand shot out and clamped around her arm, hard.

She froze. "Let go of me, Wyatt."

He didn't. His fingers dug deeper into her skin. "I'm just trying to make you see—"

"Let me go!" she snapped, fear rising like bile in her throat.

Instead, he yanked her closer, his eyes wild and desperate. "He doesn't want you like I do. He never could. I'm the one who's real. I'm the one who—"

"Stop it!" she shouted, struggling against his grip.

Then he leaned in and tried to kiss her.

Revulsion surged through her. She twisted hard, managing to shove him back a step, her voice cracking as she screamed, "Get out!"

Outside, footsteps crunched rapidly on the path. Then the door burst open.

"Get your hands off her."

Jack.

He stood in the doorway like a storm, eyes locked on Wyatt, voice low and lethal.

Wyatt froze, guilt and fear flickering across his face.

Jack didn't raise his voice. He didn't have to.

"If I ever see you touch her again," he said, stepping inside, "you'll be on the first boat off this island. And you won't like how fast I make that happen."

Wyatt looked between them, then backed away, his face pale. "Fine," he muttered, brushing past Jack and out the door.

Silence fell.

Olivia stood trembling, heart pounding, eyes brimming with unshed tears.

Jack stepped closer, gentle now. "Are you okay?"

She nodded shakily, but her body betrayed her—her shoulders sagging, her lip trembling.

And Jack, without asking, pulled her into his arms.

She hadn't meant to cry. Not really. But the moment Jack's arms wrapped around her, the weight of everything came crashing down.

The fear. The shock. The violation.

Tears slipped silently down her cheeks as she pressed her face to his chest, trying to breathe past the panic tightening in her lungs. Her whole body trembled. Jack held her tighter, one hand moving slowly, gently along her back—steady, grounding, the way someone might soothe a frightened child… or someone they couldn't bear to see hurt.

"I didn't think he'd—" she started, but her voice cracked, the words dissolving into a broken breath.

"You don't have to explain," Jack murmured, pulling back just enough to look at her face. His thumb brushed beneath her eye, catching a stray tear. "It's over now. He won't come near you again."

She nodded, but her breath was still shaky. "I shouldn't have let him in. I didn't want to deal with him, but I thought… I don't know, maybe he just needed to say whatever it was and leave."

"You don't need to justify anything. You gave him a chance to speak—he abused it."

He was so close now. His gaze searched hers, and she could see the flicker of restrained anger still simmering in him—not at her, but for her.

"Are you hurt?" Jack asked, his voice low now, gentler.

"No," she whispered. "I… don't think so."

He let out a long breath, like he'd been holding it for too long. "I was looking for you," he said after a beat. "Didn't want to crowd you yesterday. But today… I don't know. Something told me to come."

Despite everything, her lips curved faintly. "Lucky for me you did."

His mouth twitched, but the smile didn't quite reach his eyes. They darkened again, serious. "If you want me to leave, I will. But if you'd rather not be alone…"

Olivia hesitated. She probably should ask for space. Take time to breathe, cry, untangle the knot of emotions inside her.

But she didn't want to be alone.

"Stay," she said quietly.

He nodded. No questions. No expectations. Just stayed.

They sat together on the edge of the bed, her head finding its place on his shoulder, his arm around her—a quiet shield. Outside, the island moved on. Waves rolled against the shore; palm trees rustled in the breeze. But in the hush of her bungalow, everything stilled.

He felt her body grow heavier against him, her breathing deepened. She'd fallen asleep.

Jack didn't move. He just held her, his jaw still tight with everything he hadn't said. When he'd heard her scream, it had ripped through him like a gunshot. He'd wanted to hurt Wyatt—wanted to break something, someone—but he knew Olivia wouldn't have wanted that.

Instead, he shifted gently, easing them both down so she could rest more comfortably. She didn't stir.

Lying beside her, he watched her for a long moment. Then finally, his eyes closed too, and the tension in his body slowly melted into sleep.

Chapter Fifteen

Olivia opened her eyes slowly, the familiar weight of exhaustion still tugging at her limbs. But something was different. The panic had faded into quiet. The storm inside her had stilled.

Jack was asleep beside her, facing her, his features softened in rest. The afternoon light filtered through the thin curtains, casting a soft glow across his jawline, the curve of his cheek, the dark lashes resting against his skin. Without the sharp edge of his usual guarded expression, he looked almost boyish. Vulnerable. Human in a way that few ever got to see.

She watched him for a long time, her heart a tangle of awe and confusion.

How had they gotten here?

How had the man who owned everything—this island, his reputation, a string of fast cars and faster relationships—ended up holding her through the worst moment she'd had in years?

Her fingers itched to reach out, to trace the edge of his brow, to map the planes of his face. She didn't move. Just watched. Just… felt.

She'd be twenty-four in four days. Twenty-four and still trying to figure out what it meant to be brave—not just in the face of danger, but in the quiet choices too. Like letting someone in. Like trusting the way your heart thudded when a man looked at you like you were something rare, something fragile and strong all at once.

She had never been with anyone. Not like that. Not intimately. The thought had always made her feel awkward, exposed, unsure of herself.

But with Jack, the fear wasn't that she wouldn't be enough. The fear was how badly she wanted to be. How deeply she felt everything when he was near. Her body, her heart, her mind—they were all tangled up in this impossible man with his quiet fury, his unexpected gentleness, his relentless drive.

She bit her lip and blinked against the sudden rush of emotion.

What if she let herself believe—just for a second—that he meant what he said? That this wasn't some game, some temporary thrill? What if… this could be real?

Wasn't a chance at happiness worth the risk?

Olivia exhaled softly, her gaze drifting to the space between them. There wasn't much of it left. One shift of her hand, one breath too deep, and they'd be touching. Skin to skin. Heart to heart.

She was terrified.

But maybe… maybe she was more terrified of never trying. Of walking away before she ever found out what it meant to be loved the way she'd only dreamed about. To be seen, completely, and not have the other person flinch or pull away.

Jack stirred then, his brow furrowing slightly before his eyes fluttered open. Sleepy, soft, still hazy.

His gaze met hers. And held.

"Hey," he said, voice thick with sleep.

Her lips lifted faintly. "Hey."

He blinked a few times, registering their proximity, the way she was watching him. His hand moved instinctively, brushing her hair behind her ear, fingers lingering at her jaw.

"You okay?" he asked.

She nodded, though her heart was thundering in her chest. "Yeah," she whispered. "I think I am."

His thumb moved gently, tracing the line of her cheekbone. He didn't speak. Just looked at her like he was waiting—for her to speak, to move, to decide what this moment would become.

Olivia's breath caught.

She didn't know what would happen next. Didn't know if this would last, or if it would break her. But right now, she knew this much:

She didn't want to run.

Not from him.

Not from this.

So, she leaned in, slowly, giving him every chance to pull away.

He didn't.

When her lips met his, it was soft. Tentative. Like a question whispered against skin.

His answer came in the way he kissed her back—reverent, aching, sure.

And in that kiss, she found her answer, too.

Yes.

It was worth the risk.

The kiss was fragile. Like they both understood the weight of what it meant. When Jack finally pulled away, it wasn't because he wanted to—it was because he needed to look at her. See her. Make sure she knew this wasn't a game.

His hand lingered at the side of her face, thumb brushing lightly across her cheek.

"Spend your week off with me?" he asked, his voice low, rough with emotion.

Olivia blinked, caught off guard. "Where? Here at the resort?"

Jack shook his head, the corners of his mouth lifting into a soft smile. "No. On my yacht."

Her eyebrows lifted. "I've never been on a yacht."

"You'll have your own room," he added quickly, gently. "No pressure. No expectations. Just us… getting to know what this is."

There was something unguarded in his face as he said it—something that made her heart turn over. For all his confidence and charm, this was Jack laying down his armour. Inviting her into his world without conditions, without demands.

She smiled, slow and genuine. "Okay."

His grin broke wide across his face. Then, without warning, he kissed her—hard, quick, full of relief and adrenaline and something like joy. And then he jumped up from the bed, running a hand through his tousled hair, looking like a man who knew staying another minute with her on her bed would lead to decisions she might not be ready for.

"Can you be ready in an hour?" he asked, voice already lighter, urgent with anticipation.

Olivia sat up, blinking at him. "An hour?"

"Yes." He was already halfway to the door, barefoot and grinning. "Meet me at the marina. I'll have everything arranged."

She shook her head in amused disbelief. "You move fast."

His eyes flicked back to her, warm and playful. "Only when it matters."

Then he was gone, the door clicking shut behind him.

Olivia stared at the empty space he'd just left, her heart pounding in her chest. Her fingers pressed to her lips, still tingling from his kiss.

'Just us, getting to know what this is.'

She whispered the words aloud, then stood and crossed to the window. Outside, the sea sparkled beneath the early afternoon sun, endless and open.

Something inside her shifted—like possibility had just stepped through the door with Jack Alden and asked her to come find out what might happen next.

And for once, she was ready to say yes.

Jack was excited—for the first time in years.

It wasn't the kind of fleeting thrill he got from closing a major deal or taking delivery of a new toy. This was different. Sharper. Deeper. A low, steady thrum in his chest that had started the second Olivia said "okay."

He paced the deck of his yacht like a man who didn't know what to do with himself, glancing toward the dock every few seconds, scanning for a flash of sun-kissed hair or the swing of a familiar stride.

God, he thought, raking a hand through his hair. What if she changes her mind?

He wouldn't blame her if she did. He wasn't exactly a safe bet. His reputation preceded him—billionaire, playboy, emotionally unavailable. And Olivia... she was something else entirely. Honest. Warm. The kind of woman who saw things clearly and still believed in the best parts of people.

She deserved better than a man still figuring out what it meant to be real with someone.

But he couldn't stop hoping.

The moment she'd said yes, something had cracked open inside him. A space he hadn't realised was empty until she looked at him like he might be worth trusting.

He stopped pacing, stood at the rail, and looked out at the sun-drenched marina. Boats bobbed in their slips. Voices carried on the wind. Somewhere behind him, the engines hummed low, ready.

And then—there she was.

Walking down the dock like some impossible vision, wind in her hair, dress fluttering around her knees. A small bag slung over one shoulder, her expression open and maybe a little unsure, but beautiful. So damn beautiful it nearly dropped him to his knees.

She came.

She hadn't changed her mind.

Jack exhaled for what felt like the first time in an hour and smiled—a real, unguarded smile that stretched across his face and settled somewhere deep in his chest.

Whatever happened next... whatever this week brought...

He knew one thing for sure:

He was all in.

Olivia walked toward the marina with the wind tugging at her sundress and her nerves fluttering like a thousand tiny wings. Her bag was light, but everything inside her felt weightless.

The dock curved like a ribbon into the turquoise sea, and at the end of it, gleaming in the golden light, was Jack's yacht.

It wasn't just impressive—it was breathtaking. Sleek lines, crisp white decks, and polished chrome that winked in the sun. It looked like something out of a dream, like a place people went when they were no longer afraid to chase joy.

Jack stood at the edge of the gangway, one hand in his pocket, the other lifted in a casual wave. He was barefoot, wearing navy linen pants and a white shirt with the sleeves rolled up, and he looked… *happy*.

The moment her feet hit the dock; he moved toward her.

"I wasn't sure you'd come," he said, voice low and a little husky, like he hadn't quite dared to hope.

"I said I would." She smiled, shy and sure all at once. "I don't say yes unless I mean it."

His eyes searched hers, and something softened in his expression.

"Welcome aboard," he said, and offered his hand.

She took it. His fingers closed gently around hers as he helped her onto the yacht. As soon as her sandals touched the deck, she turned in a slow circle, taking it all in—the wide lounge area with its shaded canopy, the glass doors leading into a gorgeous salon, the stretch of open sea all around them.

"Wow," she breathed. "This is… not the world I'm used to."

Jack grinned, but there was no smugness in it—just quiet pleasure at sharing it with her. "It's just a boat, Olivia."

"It's a floating palace, the size of a football field," she said, laughing. "And you're barefoot on it."

"Well," he said, brushing a strand of hair from her face, "I figured if I was trying to convince you this wasn't about seduction and champagne… socks would ruin the mood."

She giggled, the tension inside her melting away. "You're impossible."

He leaned in, brushing his lips against her temple. "You'll get used to me."

Then he stepped back and gestured toward the front of the yacht. "We'll be cruising for a few hours. Captain says we'll anchor just off a quiet cove by dusk. You hungry?"

"A little."

"Dinner will be ready soon. Come inside. Let me give you the tour."

Olivia followed Jack through the sleek glass doors, the sea breeze tugging at her sundress as the teak deck gave way to polished marble underfoot. The interior of the yacht opened up in a sweep of understated elegance—modern, luxurious, but surprisingly warm. Sunlight poured through oversized windows that lined the main salon, bouncing off soft ivory walls and cream-coloured furnishings. Tasteful art—abstract ocean scenes, vintage nautical maps—adorned the walls, while a pair of deep leather armchairs flanked a low coffee table with a vase of fresh orchids.

"This is the main lounge," Jack said, glancing over his shoulder to make sure she was still with him. "It's where most people hang out when they're not sunning themselves or in the water."

"It's beautiful," Olivia murmured, her fingers grazing the back of a curved linen sofa.

Jack smiled, his hand brushing his jaw. "Thanks. I didn't want anything too flashy—just clean, comfortable. Peaceful."

He led her forward, past a dining area set for eight, with pale wood chairs and soft pendant lighting. A few crew members moved quietly in the background, preparing for the evening meal, their steps efficient but discreet.

They descended a wide, floating staircase to the lower deck, where the ambient light softened and cool air hummed quietly from hidden vents. Jack paused beside a glass door that slid open with a whisper to reveal a sleek media room. "Movie nights, if you're into that," he said, gesturing at the oversized screen and plush recliners.

Olivia blinked. "This is like a private theatre."

Jack chuckled. "Yeah, but I mostly use it to fall asleep watching documentaries I'll never finish."

She laughed, and he seemed to relax even more, the earlier tension in his shoulders dissolving with every shared smile.

They moved through a corridor lined with guest cabins—each one more elegant than the last, outfitted with neutral tones, natural textures, and ocean views. "There's a spa room, a gym, a wine cellar… and even a little library, though I'm the only one who ever seems to use it."

Olivia raised a brow. "A man of culture."

Jack grinned, not cocky, just boyish, and genuine. "I try."

At the far end of the corridor, he opened a final door and stepped back to let her in. "This one's yours."

The room was sunlit and serene, with a queen-sized bed framed by sheer white drapes and windows that offered a sweeping view of the endless blue. A small writing desk sat in the corner; a cozy armchair nestled beside it. The en suite bathroom gleamed—glass, stone, brushed gold fixtures, and a rainfall shower that looked like it belonged in a luxury spa.

Olivia turned in a slow circle, her breath catching. "Jack, this is…"

"It's yours for as long as you want it." His voice had softened, his expression earnest. "I meant what I said—no pressure, no expectations. Just time. Together. However, that looks."

She looked at him, and for a moment, said nothing. Then she nodded, her voice warm. "Thank you."

Jack's smile deepened. "Freshen up if you like. Dinner will be served on deck in about thirty minutes. I'll be up top."

And with that, he turned and left her alone in the quiet elegance of her private cabin—his footsteps fading down the corridor as the soft hum of the ocean surrounded her.

Chapter Sixteen

Olivia smoothed the fabric of her sundress as she stepped out of her cabin, taking one last glance down the hallway. She had freshened up—washed her face, added a touch of gloss to her lips, and brushed her hair—but now she was second-guessing every choice. The yacht was quiet, serene, but also completely unfamiliar. Had Jack said to go left? Or—

She turned right, trying to follow the soft hum of ambient music in the distance. But every hallway looked the same—sleek wood panels, modern lighting, polished finishes. She passed the media room, then what looked like a massage suite. Definitely not the way to dinner.

She turned another corner and stopped, unsure.

"Everything all right, miss?"

She looked up to see a man approaching—tall and composed in a navy polo with the yacht's insignia on the chest. He had a calm presence, sharp eyes that noticed everything, but his tone was kind.

"Oh, hi," Olivia said, cheeks blooming with embarrassment. She extended a hand, hoping to recover some dignity. "I'm Olivia. I'm supposed to meet Jack for dinner on deck… but I think I got a little turned around."

The man offered a small, patient smile and took her hand in a firm, no-nonsense shake. "Nice to meet you, Olivia. It happens more often than you'd think. This boat's a bit of a labyrinth the first time around."

He released her hand and gestured down the corridor. "Lachlan. Chief Officer. I'll walk you up."

"Thank you," she said, falling into step beside him, grateful for his calm presence.

They moved through the softly lit corridor, the quiet hum of the yacht and the muffled hush of the sea their only companions. Olivia stole glances around her—sleek lines, warm wood panelling, polished steel, and glass. It was like walking through a luxury hotel on the water.

As they approached a narrow turn, Lachlan subtly stepped ahead, positioning himself on the side closest to a swinging door just before it opened with a quiet hiss. He didn't break stride or comment on it, but Olivia noticed the quiet attentiveness in the gesture—it felt instinctive, almost protective.

"This yacht is incredible," she said, awe still lacing her voice.

Lachlan gave a quiet nod. "She's something, all right. We're proud of her. It's not every day you get to serve on a vessel like this."

"I believe it. It's my first time on a yacht," Olivia admitted with a soft laugh. "I think it shows."

"You'll be fine," Lachlan said, with a reassuring edge to his voice. "The crew's here to help. Just don't be afraid to ask—we're used to showing people around."

She smiled at that, the tension in her shoulders easing. "Good to know."

As they reached the staircase that led to the upper deck, the scent of grilled seafood floated down, mingling with a breeze that carried music and the salty tang of the sea.

Lachlan stepped aside, gesturing upward. "You're just in time. Sunset's putting on a show tonight."

Olivia paused at the first step, glancing back at him. "Thanks for saving me from wandering into the engine room or something."

He chuckled softly, dipping his head. "Anytime. Enjoy your evening, Olivia."

She offered him a warm smile, then ascended the steps, heart fluttering not from nerves now—but from anticipation.

The evening air had softened, the sun just beginning to set, casting a warm golden hue over everything.

She found Jack standing near the edge of the deck, his gaze scanning the horizon. He straightened as soon as he saw her, a smile tugging at the corners of his mouth. He got up, his voice low and warm. "There you are. Everything okay?"

Olivia smiled, her eyes lighting up. "I met Lachlan, while wandering around..." She paused, trying to find the right words, but she couldn't help it—she laughed, her voice light and genuine. "I think I got a bit lost, but he was kind enough to show me how to get here."

Jack raised an eyebrow, his smile spreading as he reached out to gently take her hand. "Lachlan, huh? I hope he wasn't too much of a gruff tour guide. He's... a bit protective of the yacht and the crew."

Olivia chuckled, shaking her head. "No, he wasn't gruff. He's just... a bit serious, but in a good way. It was nice of him to take the time."

Jack's eyes softened at her words, a touch of pride flickering in them. "Yeah, he's been with me for years. I trust him with everything, especially when it comes to running this ship." His gaze lingered on her for a moment longer before he gave her a teasing smile. "Though, next time, I'll make sure you don't get lost, so I don't have to worry about who's showing you around."

Olivia couldn't help but laugh again, a warmth spreading through her chest. "I'm sure I'll get my bearings,"

Then Jack's gaze dropped to her arm, and his expression shifted in an instant.

"Olivia," he said quietly, taking her arm gently in his hands.

She followed his gaze and saw what he was looking at—faint bruises, blooming like shadows just beneath the edge of her sleeve. The memory of Wyatt's grip flashed through her mind, and her stomach sank.

Jack's jaw tightened, a muscle twitching along his cheek. "He had no right to put his hands on you," he said, his voice low and tense.

She placed her hand lightly on his arm, trying to soothe the storm rising behind his eyes. "It's okay, Jack. I don't think he meant to hurt me… he was just upset."

"That doesn't make it acceptable," Jack said, his gaze locked on the bruises as if willing them to vanish. "You shouldn't have to explain it away."

Her touch tightened slightly on his arm. "I'm not," she said softly. "I'm just trying not to carry the weight of his anger. I left that behind when I walked away from him."

Jack looked at her then, really looked—his anger tempered now by something deeper. Respect. Admiration. And a fierce protectiveness that seemed to wrap around her like a quiet promise.

Olivia felt the weight of his gaze, the unspoken things between them lingering in the air like the softness before a storm. Her heart thudded in her chest, but instead of meeting his eyes again, she turned her head toward the horizon.

"Oh," she whispered, her voice a breath. "Isn't that beautiful?"

The sky was ablaze with colour—burnished gold melting into rose, lavender streaked across the ocean like watercolour. It was the kind of sunset that made the world feel paused, like it was holding its breath.

Jack followed her gaze, and the tightness in his shoulders eased. "It is," he said quietly.

But he wasn't just talking about the sunset.

He was still watching her.

She turned to him, catching the way his eyes lingered on her face, warm and intent. A flush crept up her cheeks, and she laughed softly, nudging his arm with her elbow.

"You need to stop that," she said, smiling. "I'll get a big head."

Jack chuckled, the sound low and unhurried, like the tide kissing the hull. "I don't believe that for a second."

His eyes still held hers, a spark of amusement and something else—something quieter, more serious—beneath the surface. He wasn't just teasing her. He meant it.

Jack's smile deepened, the playful tension between them still lingering. He led her toward the table set for dinner on the deck, the setting sun casting a breathtaking glow over everything. As they reached the table, he pulled out her chair, gesturing for her to sit. "Dinner should be just about ready."

Olivia nodded, settling into her seat, the anticipation of the evening wrapping around her like a soft blanket. Jack took the seat across from her, his gaze steady—warm with affection, but laced with something deeper, something that made her pulse stutter in a way she wasn't prepared for.

The soft clink of silverware and the gentle hush of the waves filled the space between them as the first course arrived—seared scallops nestled on a bed of citrus risotto. Olivia took a bite, closed her eyes, and let out a quiet hum of delight.

"Oh wow," she murmured, her eyes widening. "This is incredible."

Jack's grin was slow and satisfied, as if her reaction was the real reward. "I'll tell Chef you approve. He's picky about who gets to try that dish."

The courses drifted by like chapters in a perfect story—grilled sea bass, roasted vegetables, warm, crusty bread. Conversation flowed just as easily, carried along by shared laughter and sips of wine. They swapped childhood memories, favourite movies, and stories about the oddest jobs they'd ever had.

Jack recounted sneaking into his father's boardroom as a boy, pretending to fire imaginary executives with dramatic flair. Olivia confessed to accidentally locking herself in a church basement during a wedding reception, only to be rescued by a five-year-old with a juice box and a lisp.

By the time dessert arrived—dark chocolate mousse with a swirl of raspberry coulis—the sky had deepened into a velvet blue, stars pricking the horizon like scattered diamonds. The music softened into a romantic hush, the deck glowing beneath string lights that swayed with the breeze.

Jack leaned back in his chair, wine glass in hand, his eyes fixed on Olivia with quiet intensity.

"I love this," he said, his voice low. "Just talking. Laughing. Being with you."

Olivia blinked, her heart stuttering at the sincerity in his tone. "You'll get bored," she said softly, a smile tugging at her lips. "That's all I know how to be... me."

His smile deepened, and without a word, he stood and offered his hand. She slipped hers into it without hesitation, letting him guide her to the curved daybed tucked along the edge of the deck.

He sank onto the cushions first, pulling her gently down with him until she was nestled against his side, her back to his chest. His arm curled around her, and he ran his fingers slowly through her hair, his touch unhurried, intimate.

"Mmm, this is nice," she murmured, her voice soft, drowsy from wine and comfort and the heady closeness of him.

Jack didn't answer right away. He just held her there, steady, and quiet, as the stars turned slowly overhead. His fingers combed gently through her hair, tracing the silk of it as if memorising the feel.

The sea whispered around them, the yacht swaying gently beneath their bodies like a lullaby. Olivia let her eyes drift closed, her body melting into his—into the stillness, the warmth, the quiet sense of safety that wrapped around her like a tide she didn't want to resist.

Jack's arm tightened slightly around her, his breath brushing her temple. "You feel good in my arms," he murmured after a long pause, his voice low and honest, like the thought had just settled into him. "Like you belong here."

Olivia opened her eyes, her heart fluttering—not just at the words, but at the way he said them, not rehearsed, not polished, just raw and real.

She shifted, turning in his arms until her chin rested on her folded hands atop his chest, her gaze lifting to his like it always did—trusting, searching, quietly hopeful.

"You make me feel special, Jack."

He didn't smile right away. Instead, he looked at her for a long, quiet beat, his thumb brushing a lazy line across her temple. The wind tugged gently at her hair, but his fingers kept it in place like it belonged there—like she belonged here.

"You are special," he whispered, the words sliding from his lips like they'd been waiting a lifetime to be said. Not a compliment. Not a line. A fact. A revelation.

Olivia's breath caught, her throat suddenly thick with something tender and unspoken. She could feel his heartbeat beneath her cheek, steady and strong, echoing the rhythm rising in her own chest.

She tilted her head just slightly, her voice barely more than a breath. "When are you going to kiss me, then?"

Jack's lips curved into the faintest smile—but his eyes, oh, his eyes stayed locked on hers, fierce and full of something deeper. "I wasn't sure if you wanted me to."

"I wouldn't be this close if I didn't," she said, her smile soft, teasing—but her voice trembled slightly, full of anticipation.

He let out a quiet breath, like she'd just given him permission to exhale. Then he leaned in, slow and unhurried, brushing his nose against hers, his mouth hovering just a heartbeat away.

"You have no idea how long I've been wanting to," he murmured.

Then finally—finally—his lips met hers. Not rushed. Not demanding. Just warm and reverent, like he was discovering her for the first time and wanted to memorise everything. Olivia melted into the kiss, her hands sliding up to his chest, fingers curling into his shirt like she never wanted to let go.

The sea whispered around them, stars overhead blinking like silent witnesses, and the world narrowed to the space between their hearts.

The kiss deepened, growing more urgent, more consuming, like a tide pulling them under. Jack shifted with deliberate care, gently guiding her onto her back without ever breaking the connection. Her arms wrapped around his neck, holding him close, as if she could anchor herself to the moment.

His body settled half across hers, warm and solid, shielding her from everything but the rhythm of their shared breath. One hand slid to her hip, grounding them in place, while the other cradled her cheek with a tenderness that contradicted the growing heat between them.

Olivia's fingers threaded through Jack's hair, her heart racing as his lips moved over hers with a slow, aching intensity. The stars above seemed to blur behind her closed eyes, the world reduced to the warmth of his mouth, the strength of his body, the way he touched her like she mattered.

A soft moan escaped her lips, unbidden.

"Olivia…" Jack breathed against her mouth, the sound of her name breaking on his lips like a wave.

"Yes," she whispered, already aching for the next kiss.

He kissed her again, slower this time, almost reverent—and then pulled back, his forehead resting gently against hers. "We need to stop."

Her eyes fluttered open. "Why?"

His hand slid from her hip to her waist, lingering. "Because if I don't… I won't be able to."

She held his gaze, her voice barely above a breath. "I don't want you to stop."

His jaw flexed, eyes darkening with the war between restraint and raw desire. "You're making this very difficult."

Olivia cupped his cheek, her thumb brushing just beneath his eye. "I want to be with you, Jack," she said softly, her voice steady despite the thunder in her chest.

She kissed him again—gentle, lingering, a whisper of promise. "Don't you want to be with me?"

He let out a breath—ragged, low—as if her words had cracked something open inside him that he hadn't realised he was holding back. "I do," he said, the confession raw and heavy with meaning. "God, I do… but—"

"No buts," Olivia interrupted gently, her voice a mix of tenderness and quiet certainty. Her hands framed his face, grounding him. "When I said I'd spend the week with you, it wasn't just for sunsets and dinners and pretending." She paused, her eyes searching his. "It was because I knew I wanted to be with you. Really be with you."

Chapter Seventeen

Her honesty struck him like a wave—steady, undeniable, and achingly beautiful. He stared at her, breath caught in his chest, as if the world had slowed just for this moment. And maybe, in some way, it had.

Jack rose without saying another word. He extended his hand to her, silent but certain, offering her the choice.

Olivia didn't hesitate. She slipped her hand into his, and he closed his fingers gently around hers.

Without a word, he led her through the quiet corridors of the yacht. The soft glow of sconces lit their path, the muted hum of the sea a steady rhythm beneath their feet.

They stopped at a door Olivia hadn't noticed before—sleek, understated, with a subtle curve of steel at the handle.

Jack turned the handle and gently pushed it open.

She stepped inside—and her breath caught.

It had to be Jack's cabin, but it felt like something out of a dream. Floor-to-ceiling windows framed the moonlit ocean, casting silver light across a space both elegant and quietly personal. Dark wood and cream fabrics softened the modern edges, and everything carried the faint scent of cedar and salt. It was beautiful. Masculine. Intimate.

Olivia turned to him, heart thudding, eyes wide with something between wonder and anticipation.

He closed the door behind them, his gaze never leaving hers.

"Are you sure, Olivia?" His voice was low, almost rough, as if the weight of his desire warred with his restraint.

She stepped closer, placing her hands gently on his chest. The steady thrum of his heartbeat pulsed beneath her palms.

"Yes, Jack," she said softly. "I'm not here to play games. I want to be with you. No one else. Only you."

Jack didn't speak. He didn't need to.

His hands rose slowly, brushing her hair back from her face with a tenderness that felt almost reverent, as if he were memorising her features. His fingers lingered along her jaw, tracing its delicate curve. Then, without rushing, he lowered his head, his lips just brushing hers—once, twice—before he finally kissed her.

It was soft at first. A question. A promise.

Olivia answered with a breathless sigh, her hands gliding up his chest to clutch at his shirt. He deepened the kiss, still slow, still steady, but weighted with longing—like he'd been holding back for far too long.

When they finally parted for breath, Jack rested his forehead against hers. "I've wanted this," he murmured. "You. From the moment you looked at me like I wasn't who the world thinks I am."

Her hands slipped beneath his shirt, finding warmth and muscle, the real man beneath the polished billionaire exterior. "I see you, Jack," she whispered. "Only you."

Something shifted in his eyes—vulnerability, desire, wonder. He kissed her again, more urgently this time, pulling her closer until their bodies were flush.

He guided her back until the edge of the bed met her knees. They paused—gazing at each other, breathing the same breath, suspended in that sacred in-between.

Jack reached for the hem of her dress, giving her every chance to stop him. She didn't. The fabric slipped over her head and fell to the floor, leaving her bathed in moonlight and lace.

"You're beautiful," he said, his voice low and full of awe. "I want this to be perfect for you."

"It already is," she whispered. "Because it's with you."

She pulled his shirt over his head, revealing the strong lines of his body beneath. Her hands roamed his chest, and he inhaled sharply, his muscles tensing under her touch. He kissed her again—deeper, hungrier—his need no longer something he could temper.

Without breaking their kiss, he lifted her effortlessly and laid her on the bed. He stripped quickly and joined her, hovering above her as his eyes drank her in.

"Do you have any idea what you do to me?" he asked, voice thick with want.

"Show me," she whispered.

He did.

His hand cupped her breast, and her breath caught in a gasp. He groaned, dragging his thumb over the peaked nipple, again and again, as she arched into him. Their mouths tangled—hungry, searching—her arms around him, her body yielding with reckless abandon.

He trailed hot, open-mouthed kisses down her neck, to her chest, and then lower, worshipping her with his mouth. When he finally reached her breast, he took it into his mouth, teasing and licking until she cried out, her fingers threading into his hair.

His kisses moved lower—over her ribs, her belly, until he peeled away the last scrap of lace and slid his tongue over the slick heat of her. She gasped, bucking beneath him as pleasure overtook her.

"Jack... please," she panted.

"You taste like honey," he murmured against her, and then he gave her exactly what she asked for.

His tongue moved with devastating precision—licking, circling, sucking—until she was sobbing his name. And when he slipped a long finger inside her, slow and sure, Olivia shattered. Her body tensed, hips lifting from the bed as waves of ecstasy overtook her. He stayed with her, tender and patient, riding out every tremor.

When her cries softened into sighs, Jack kissed his way back up her trembling body, lavishing every inch with devotion. He hovered above her, kissed her deeply, then reached for a condom and rolled it on.

She could feel the heavy weight of him pressing at her entrance. Her body was ready— aching, welcoming, wholly his.

He thrust slowly, carefully—and she cried out when he breached her innocence.

Jack froze instantly, his eyes locking with hers. "I'm sorry," he whispered, breath ragged, concern etched across his face.

Olivia cradled his face in her hands, pulling him down for a kiss, her voice barely a breath. "It's okay. I want this. I want you."

He began to move, slow and gentle, his breath coming in uneven gasps as the heat of her body welcomed him fully. Olivia clung to him, her fingers digging into his shoulders as a wildfire of sensation tore through her. Their rhythm built—fluid, hungry, desperate, and sweet all at once.

The tension coiled tight between them. Her moans turned into broken cries, his name falling from her lips like a prayer. Jack moved harder, deeper, every thrust taking her higher. Her body convulsed again, a storm of sensation tearing through her. Jack followed, his body stiffening, a low growl torn from his throat as he spilled into her, lost in the depths of her pleasure.

Afterward, he held her close, pressing soft kisses to her cheeks, her eyelids, her temple. When she felt the sting of unexpected tears, he kissed them away.

A while later, Jack rolled onto his side and drew her close, cradling her in the crook of his arm. He pressed a tender kiss to the top of her head, whispering something soft against her hair—words she couldn't quite hear, but felt deep in her chest.

Wrapped in his warmth, Olivia surrendered to sleep—deep, dreamless, and safe in his arms.

Jack slipped out quietly a short time later to clean up. When he returned, he found her still curled among the rumpled sheets, her face serene in sleep. He climbed back into bed and gently pulled her against him once more, her back fitting perfectly against his chest.

Holding her like this, her skin still warm from their lovemaking, something settled deep in him—something he hadn't known he was missing.

Making love to Olivia had been a revelation. She'd given herself to him so openly, so honestly, meeting every touch with trust, every kiss with unguarded feeling. No pretences. No games. Just her.

It had never felt like this before. Not with anyone.

And he wasn't sure it ever could again—with anyone but her.

Sunlight streamed in through the floor-to-ceiling windows, casting golden lines across the bed. Olivia stirred, the scent of cedar and salt still clinging to the sheets, to him.

Jack was already awake, propped on one elbow beside her, watching her with an expression so quiet and tender it made her heart flutter.

"Are you staring at me?" she murmured sleepily, eyes still half-closed.

He gave a small, crooked smile. "Maybe."

She stretched like a cat, the sheets slipping down to reveal bare shoulders. "Creepy."

"Beautiful," he corrected gently. "You looked peaceful. Like you belonged here."

Her lashes fluttered open, and she met his gaze. "And do I?"

Jack brushed a loose strand of hair from her cheek, his fingers lingering. "You did last night. And you do now."

That softened her completely. She tucked herself closer to him, her head fitting beneath his chin like it had always belonged there.

"I don't usually wake up in men's beds," she murmured.

Jack smiled, his fingers tracing idle patterns along her bare back. "I don't usually wake up with a woman still in mine."

Olivia let out a soft laugh, then tilted her face up to him. "Last night was…"

"Incredible," he said, finishing for her, his voice low and sincere. "You were."

A pause settled between them—quiet, warm, and intimate.

"You hungry?" he asked, brushing his lips against her hair.

"Mmm… only for you." Her lips found the curve of his neck, and she pressed a slow, lingering kiss there.

He chuckled, the sound rumbling in his chest. "Have I created a monster?"

She smiled against his skin. "Are you complaining?"

Jack rolled her gently beneath him, the heat between them reigniting as her body welcomed his touch.

"Not even a little," he murmured.

And then there were no more words—only breathless laughter, whispered names, and the quiet rhythm of two bodies rediscovering each other in the soft hush of morning.

Later, Olivia slipped quietly back to her cabin to shower and dress, her skin still tingling from his touch, her heart light. When she emerged, the sun was high, casting golden ribbons across the deck where Jack waited for her.

"Good morning," she said, greeting him with a quick, sweet kiss on the lips.

His smile was easy, content. "Good morning."

She sat down across from him, tucking her legs beneath her, and reached for a buttery croissant. She began tearing it apart absently, her eyes scanning the endless stretch of ocean around them.

"So," she said casually, "what's the plan for today?"

Jack took a sip of his coffee, watching her over the rim. "Jet skiing."

Her head snapped up, eyes lighting with delight. "Really?"

He grinned. "Thought you might like that."

The sun glittered across the waves, the air rich with salt and freedom. Olivia stood at the edge of the platform, eyeing the jet skis bobbing gently on the water.

"I've never actually done this before," she admitted, adjusting the straps of her life vest.

Jack raised a brow, already looking unfairly good in his navy swim trunks and sunglasses. "Never?"

She shook her head. "Not unless you count the time I was dragged behind one on an inflatable banana boat."

He laughed. "That's criminal. All right—come here."

She stepped closer, and Jack moved behind her, his hands brushing over her shoulders as he adjusted her straps. His fingers lingered a moment too long on her arms, and her breath hitched.

"This should be snug," he said, voice low near her ear. "We can't have you falling off."

"I'm starting to think you'd enjoy rescuing me," she teased, glancing back at him.

"Oh, I definitely would." His smirk was wicked.

They mounted separate jet skis, Jack leading at first, cutting across the waves like he was born for it. Olivia followed, shrieking as she hit a swell, then laughing when she caught air. The wind tore through her hair, and adrenaline surged through her veins. Every time she glanced over at Jack, he looked back—grinning like a kid.

They raced in loops, circling each other, splashing like teenagers. At one point, Jack came dangerously close, and Olivia deliberately turned into his wake, sending a cascade of water over him.

"You're gonna pay for that," he called, laughing.

"I hope so," she shouted back.

Eventually, they drifted together near a quiet cove, floating side by side in the sunlight.

"Okay," she said, breathless. "That was amazing."

Jack took off his sunglasses and looked at her, something softer in his expression now. "You looked free out there."

"I felt free."

He reached over, threading his fingers briefly through hers. "That's how you make me feel."

"Good."

And for the first time in a long while, Olivia wasn't looking ahead or behind—only at the man beside her, and the way the sunlight caught in his eyes.

Chapter Eighteen

Time on the yacht slowed. Softened. Stopped needing definition.

For three days, Jack and Olivia existed in a kind of blissful in-between—floating somewhere between sunrise and moonlight, between laughter and shared silences, between two hearts learning how to trust.

They swam in hidden lagoons, their bodies cutting through water so clear it felt like air. Olivia clung to Jack's back during their first snorkelling adventure, shrieking through her snorkel when a curious fish got a little too close. He laughed until he choked on saltwater, then kissed her under the surface.

They watched old movies in the yacht's private theatre—sometimes curled up together with a bowl of popcorn, sometimes tangled in blankets, too distracted by each other to follow the plot. Jack confessed he'd never seen The Princess Bride. Olivia demanded a double feature. He never complained.

There were moments with music—his playlists, her favourites, songs they discovered together. Slow jazz during breakfast. Classic rock while sunbathing. One evening, as the sun melted into the ocean, they danced barefoot on the deck, her head resting on his chest, his fingers gently tracing the curve of her spine.

Other times, they didn't speak at all.

They read. Together. Just the quiet flip of pages and the occasional glance over the edge of a book when Olivia caught Jack watching her with that soft, unreadable smile.

She didn't ask what it meant. She didn't want to break the spell.

Each night, they made love without rush, without pretence. Jack worshipped her, like every part of her mattered—her thoughts, her fears, her skin, her laughter. And every morning, she woke up tucked under his arm, her name a sleepy murmur on his lips.

By the third afternoon, Olivia stood at the railing, watching the horizon as the yacht gently glided toward open water. The sky was smeared in gold, sea spray brushing her cheeks.

Jack came up behind her, wrapping his arms around her waist, resting his chin on her shoulder.

"We're going out tonight," he said casually.

She blinked, surprised. "Out? Like… off the yacht?"

"To Tahiti," he said. "There's an exclusive restaurant I think you'll love."

Her heart skipped. "Jack, I don't have anything to wear to some glamorous Tahitian restaurant."

He grinned, stepping in front of her and brushing a windblown curl behind her ear. "There's a dress waiting for you in your cabin. And a stylist coming on board in about an hour to help you get ready."

Her eyes widened. "What's the occasion?"

He didn't answer at first. Just stared at her like she was his favourite secret. Then, slowly, his smile deepened, the corners of his eyes crinkling.

"Did you really think you could hide that it's your twenty-fourth birthday tomorrow?"

She gaped, her eyes wide with surprise. "How did you even—"

Jack's lips curled into a playful grin. "I have my ways."

He couldn't help but marvel at how she didn't make a big deal of it. Any other woman would have dropped hints, given him clues, or at the very least, pointed out what she wanted. But not Olivia. She was different—content just being with him, savouring the moments without any expectation.

Olivia laughed, her cheeks colouring with warmth as she shook her head. "You are impossible."

"Only for you." He pressed a soft kiss to her lips. "Now go get ready. I want to take your breath away."

"You already did," she whispered.

And as she turned toward the cabin, heart racing and eyes stinging with emotion, Olivia couldn't help but feel that this—whatever it was between them—was real. And growing.

Maybe even too fast to stop.

Olivia's cabin was filled with golden afternoon light, after she had showered, when the light knock came at the door.

"Miss Clifton?" a warm, accented voice called.

She opened the door to find two women standing there—both polished, smiling, and effortlessly chic.

"I'm Elodie," said the woman holding a sleek black case. "I'm here to do your hair and makeup." She gestured to the woman beside her. "And this is Cami. She'll help with your dress and accessories."

Olivia blinked. "Oh… wow. Okay. Come in."

Before she knew it, the room had been transformed. Elodie set up her brushes, compacts, and curling wands like an artist prepping her canvas. Cami laid the dress carefully across the bed: a deep teal silk gown with a thigh-high slit, delicate draping, and tiny beads that shimmered when the light hit them. It was elegant but daring. Sophisticated but still youthful. Olivia's stomach fluttered.

She sat at the vanity while Elodie worked her magic. Her hair was styled into soft, romantic waves swept to one side, a few tendrils left loose to frame her face. Her makeup was natural, glowing—her skin luminous, her eyes subtly defined in smoky taupe and gold, her lips painted a soft berry rose.

Cami returned with a box that held silver drop earrings and a matching bracelet. "Minimalist," she said in a French lilt. "Just enough to make him stare."

Olivia laughed nervously. "I think he already does that."

When Elodie stepped back and said, "Voilà," Olivia turned toward the mirror.

And froze.

She barely recognised herself.

The woman staring back was radiant. Effortlessly elegant. The gown hugged her curves and flowed like water. Her eyes sparkled, her skin glowed, and for the first time in her life, she felt like the leading lady in one of those classic films Jack liked to watch with her.

Her voice came out in a whisper. "I've never felt... this beautiful."

Cami smiled knowingly. "You've always been. You just needed to see it."

The sun had just begun to dip below the horizon when Olivia stepped onto the deck.

Jack stood at the railing, staring out at the sea. He wore a crisp white shirt, open at the collar, and navy trousers tailored so perfectly they looked like they'd been made just for him. His jacket was draped casually over one arm. The breeze lifted his hair, tousling it just enough to make him look even more devastatingly handsome.

He turned at the sound of her heels against the deck.

And then he just... stopped.

His expression shifted slowly—first confusion, then awe. His lips parted slightly, as if the breath had been knocked out of him.

"Olivia..." he said, his voice husky, as though the air had thickened between them. He couldn't tear his eyes away from her.

She stood there, bathed in the fading golden light of the setting sun. She wore the deep teal silk gown that shimmered with each subtle movement, the fabric hugging her curves in all the right places, then flowing softly at her feet.

The thigh-high slit teased just a hint of her leg, making her look both elegant and seductive. The gown's delicate beadwork caught the light, casting a warm glow that only seemed to enhance her beauty.

Her skin—radiant and smooth—was the perfect contrast to the rich colour of the dress, and her wavy hair, swept gently to one side, framed her face like a work of art. A few stray curls softly kissed her shoulders, and her eyes—framed by the softest smoky makeup—seemed to glow with something between surprise and delight.

She smiled shyly, tucking a curl behind her ear, her lips curling up in that warm, sweet way that always made his heart race. "Too much?" she asked, her voice soft but teasing, the quiet breeze lifting the hem of her gown slightly as if to add its own touch to the magic of the moment.

"Too much?" he stepped toward her, eyes devouring every inch of her. "You look like every wish I never knew I was making… all at once."

She let out a nervous laugh. "You're just saying that."

"I'm not," he said quietly, reaching for her hand. "I mean it. You are… breathtaking."

She felt it then—warmth rising through her chest, something tender and almost unbearable in the way he looked at her, like she was rare. Precious.

He lifted her hand and pressed a kiss to her knuckles. "Happy almost-birthday, Olivia."

And with his fingers laced in hers, they walked together toward the waiting launch boat, the night unfolding like a dream yet to be written.

The evening in Tahiti was more than Olivia had imagined—it was a dream painted in golden twilight and kissed by the sea. The exclusive restaurant Jack had chosen perched on a cliff, offering a panoramic view of the endless Pacific. As the sun dipped beneath the horizon, twilight draped the world in soft indigo, and hundreds of flickering candles bathed the terrace in warm, golden light.

The air was fragrant with plumeria and jasmine, blending with the gentle salt-kissed breeze. Olivia stood at the edge of the railing, taking in the breathtaking view, and Jack watched her—utterly captivated. She looked radiant, the sea wind catching her hair, her dress fluttering softly at her calves. But it wasn't just her beauty that struck him. It was the lightness she brought to the world around her. The way she smiled, truly listened, the way she never demanded anything. She simply was, and that was more than enough.

They sat down to dinner at a table lit by candlelight, the soft notes of a live jazz band drifting through the evening air, tinged with an island rhythm. Course after course arrived—delicate, flavourful, and artfully plated—but Jack hardly tasted a thing. Olivia's laughter, her joy, the glow in her eyes as she sipped her wine and leaned toward him across the table—that was what he savoured.

Dessert had just been cleared when a slow song began to play—romantic, languid, full of promise. Jack stood and extended his hand to her.

"Dance with me?" he asked, his voice low, intimate.

Olivia's smile grew soft and shy as she slipped her hand into his. He led her to the centre of the open-air dance floor, stars glittering above them like scattered diamonds. The night wrapped around them as they moved together, her body warm against his, their rhythm easy and instinctive.

And yet Jack couldn't ignore the way other men were looking at her—appreciative, lingering stares that followed her every graceful step.

"The men can't take their eyes off you," he murmured into her ear.

She looked up at him, her gaze unwavering. "I don't care," she said simply. "You're the only one I have eyes for."

His heart clenched at the sincerity in her voice. She meant it. She wasn't trying to impress anyone. She didn't even realise the effect she had. There was no artifice. Just grace. Just her.

The music wrapped around them like silk, and Jack guided her gently off the floor, his arm tucked around hers as they returned to the table. But he was already leaning in, brushing his lips close to her ear.

"Let's get out of here," he said softly, his tone shifting to something quieter, deeper.

Olivia glanced at him, curious. "Where are we going?"

Jack smiled, his expression tender. "To a hotel. I want tonight to be just us."

They left the restaurant hand in hand, candlelight and music fading behind them as they stepped into a sleek black car waiting nearby. The drive was short, and when they arrived, Jack helped her out of the car with quiet care.

The hotel was a secluded gem—perched high above the water, with windows that opened to the sound of waves crashing far below. The suite was luxurious yet intimate, bathed in golden lamplight and decorated in creamy whites and golds, the ocean shimmering through the wide glass doors.

Olivia turned to him, her arms looping around his waist as she gazed up at him, eyes luminous.

"Jack…" she whispered, rising on her toes to kiss him gently. "Make love to me."

And he did—with reverence, with tenderness, with the depth of emotion he could no longer hide. He touched her like she was something sacred, held her like he couldn't bear to let go.

Later, as the night deepened and they lay tangled in the soft sheets, Jack pulled her into his arms, brushing a kiss to her temple.

"Happy birthday, Olivia," he whispered against her skin.

She smiled, curling closer to him, her heart full. "Thank you, Jack. This has been the most perfect birthday I've ever had."

But as his arms tightened around her, Jack didn't see the flicker of worry that passed across her face.

She loved him—completely, without question. And she knew, with an ache that bloomed quietly in her chest, that if he didn't love her back… it would break something in her she might never mend.

A single tear slipped down her cheek, silent and unseen, as she buried her face against his shoulder, willing the moment to last just a little longer.

Chapter Nineteen

The morning sun poured in through gauzy curtains, casting golden streaks across the cream-coloured sheets. Outside, the ocean whispered against the rocks far below, the world soft and slow, as if reluctant to intrude on the stillness inside.

Olivia stirred, her body warm and sore in the best way. Jack lay beside her, one arm curled under his head, watching her with that lazy, contented smile she was quickly becoming addicted to.

"Happy birthday," he murmured, brushing a kiss to her shoulder.

She turned toward him, grinning sleepily. "That's not fair. You already said that last night. You don't get credit twice."

"I could say it every hour today and it still wouldn't be enough."

She laughed, stretching like a cat beneath the sheets before slipping out of bed. He followed soon after, both of them wrapping themselves in robes and stepping out onto the private terrace. Breakfast waited for them—fresh papaya, buttery croissants, steaming coffee, and delicate pastries dusted with powdered sugar.

They ate barefoot in the golden light, Olivia's hair still tousled, her cheeks flushed with the kind of happiness that made her glow. Jack poured her more coffee, watching the way she tucked her legs beneath her and smiled into her cup.

Then he reached beneath the table and slid a small velvet box across the linen.

She blinked. "Jack..."

"Don't argue yet. Just open it."

Her brow furrowed with a soft laugh. "You really didn't have to get me anything. Last night was..." She looked at him, eyes warm. "More than enough."

"I know," he said, his voice low and sincere. "But I wanted to. Just—open it."

She hesitated, then slowly lifted the lid.

Inside was a delicate diamond bracelet—thin, elegant, shimmering with quiet extravagance. The diamonds caught the morning light and scattered it in a thousand directions. It was the kind of gift that whispered both wealth and devotion.

Olivia didn't say anything.

She just stared at it, her smile fading slightly, her fingers hovering but not touching.

Jack leaned forward, heart beginning to beat faster. "You don't like it?"

She looked up at him, eyes wide and conflicted. "It's not that. It's beautiful. It's..." She shook her head softly. "Jack, I can't accept something this expensive."

His brows pulled together. "Why not?"

"Because it's too much," she said gently. "This bracelet probably costs more than I make in a year. I'd be afraid to wear it. And…" Her voice faltered. "I don't want this to be about… money."

He was quiet for a beat, then said softly, "Olivia, it's not about money. It's your birthday. I wanted to give you something that reflects how I see you."

She offered a fragile smile, her fingers brushing the edge of the box. "You already do that… in the way you look at me. The way you treat me. Last night, this whole trip— that's what I'll remember. Not diamonds."

His chest tightened. He reached for her hand. "So let me give you both."

She didn't answer right away. Just sat there in the soft morning light, the bracelet between them, and him watching her like she might slip away if he blinked too long.

Finally, she closed the box gently and rested her hand on his.

"I love that you thought of me. I really do. But… maybe just hold onto it for now. Let's see where this goes first."

There was no accusation in her voice. No bitterness. Just honesty wrapped in grace.

And Jack—so used to women chasing his wealth and status—realised with a quiet, aching certainty: Olivia Clifton might be the most valuable thing in his life.

And she didn't even want anything… except him.

The sun had climbed high by the time they returned to the yacht. The sea sparkled around them like it held secrets, and the breeze carried the clean scent of salt and something floral drifting from the island.

Olivia stood at the stern railing, arms folded loosely, her hair twisted into a messy bun that danced in the wind. Her sundress fluttered around her knees, soft and simple, and she stared out at the waves as if they might answer the questions swirling in her mind.

Lachlan approached quietly, his heavy boots making almost no sound against the deck.

"You alright, Liv?"

She turned, startled for a moment, but her expression softened when she saw him. "Yeah. Just… thinking."

He nodded and leaned beside her on the railing. "Heard it's your birthday."

She smiled faintly. "Word travels fast on a boat."

"Especially when the boss orders champagne with lunch." Lachlan grinned, then let the quiet stretch for a beat before his tone shifted. "Something bothering you?"

She hesitated, then sighed. "He gave me a gift this morning. A diamond bracelet."

Lachlan gave a low whistle. "Sounds like Jack."

"That's just it," she murmured. "It does sound like Jack. And I'm not sure I fit in a world where someone gives diamond bracelets like it's nothing."

"You tell him that?"

"I tried." Her arms tightened around herself. "He looked… hurt. Like I was rejecting him, not the gift. But I just… I don't want to be some story he tells later. 'This girl from nowhere who didn't know what to do with diamonds.'"

Lachlan was quiet, eyes on the horizon. Then he said, "You know, the first time I saw Jack fall off a jet ski, it was because he was trying to impress a girl by doing a handstand."

Olivia blinked. "Seriously?"

"Face-first into the bay. Looked like a seal falling off a dock. We laughed so hard we couldn't breathe. Point is—he's not used to someone who doesn't want his money. Maybe you scare him a little."

She gave a short, surprised laugh. "Me? Scare Jack Alden?"

"You didn't take the bracelet," Lachlan said simply. "That's a first."

She looked at him then, her gaze searching. "Do you think I'm being ungrateful?"

"I think," Lachlan said with that steady, brotherly calm she was learning to trust, "you're being honest. And that's what's going to make all the difference—if he's ready for someone real."

Jack sat alone in his study, the velvet box resting on his desk. The bracelet was back in the safe, untouched. He stared at the box like it might explain where he'd gone wrong.

She hadn't accepted it.

She didn't like it.

No—that wasn't quite true. She thought it was beautiful. He'd seen it in her eyes; in the way her fingers hovered over the diamonds. But she didn't accept it anyway. And that hit harder than it should have.

He wasn't used to this.

He'd spent years giving women whatever they wanted—jewels, designer clothes, trips around the world. But none of that had ever made him nervous. None of that had ever felt this personal.

But Olivia—with her messy hair and warm laugh and honest eyes—she looked at him like he was the gift.

And for the first time, he didn't want to impress someone. He wanted to deserve them.

Her voice echoed in his mind:

'You already do that… in the way you look at me. The way you treat me.'

He leaned back in his chair, fingers steepled under his chin, and watched the sun shimmer across the sea.

Then slowly, a smile tugged at the corner of his mouth.

He had an idea.

That night, the yacht rocked gently beneath a canopy of stars. The water whispered against the hull, and a soft jazz melody floated from hidden speakers—low and intimate, like a secret only the two of them shared.

Jack found Olivia near the bow, wrapped in a shawl, her hair loose and glowing silver in the moonlight. She hadn't said much since breakfast. He'd given her space.

She turned, calm but a little cautious. "Hey."

"I owe you an apology," he began. "Not for the bracelet. But for putting you in a position where you felt like you had to apologise for who you are."

Her lips parted slightly, surprise flickering across her face.

"I don't want to impress you," he continued. "I want to know you."

He stepped forward and held out a small object wrapped in brown paper and tied with twine.

She blinked. "What is this?"

"Open it."

She unfolded the paper carefully. Inside was a dog-eared paperback novel.

Little Women.

Her breath caught. "How did you—?"

"You mentioned it at our first dinner on the island," he said. "Said you used to read it when you couldn't sleep. I asked Lachlan to find a copy. That one's been read a dozen times—underlined, notes in the margins. Someone loved it before you. I figured you'd like that."

She opened the book, turning the pages with reverent hands. Inside the cover, in Jack's slanted handwriting:

Happy birthday, Liv.

No diamonds. Just words—like the ones that shaped you.

Maybe someday, we'll write a few of our own.

Tears welled in her eyes. She didn't even try to blink them away.

When she looked up, her voice was thick with emotion. "Jack…"

He stepped closer, gently brushing a strand of hair behind her ear. "This isn't me trying to buy your heart. This is me trying to deserve it."

She didn't respond with words.

She just reached for him, wrapped her arms around his neck, and tucked herself against his chest.

He held her there, steady, and warm beneath the stars, as the music swelled softly around them.

This time, she didn't feel like she was falling.

This time, she felt like she was home.

Later, after the stars had climbed even higher in the sky, Olivia followed Jack down the staircase that led to the lower deck. She thought they were just heading inside for a drink, maybe a nightcap in the lounge. But when the final step gave way to the main salon, she stopped in her tracks.

The space had been transformed.

Soft lights twinkled from strings draped across the ceiling, casting a warm glow over everything. A small table for two had been set near the wide glass windows that looked out over the sea, dressed in white linen and a scattering of fresh jasmine and gardenia. Candles flickered in glass votives, their scent mingling with the salty breeze that filtered in from the open doors.

A gentle instrumental version of "La Vie en Rose" played from a nearby speaker, as if the moment needed a soundtrack.

Olivia turned to him, wide-eyed. "What is this?"

Jack smiled, slipping his hands into his pockets. "Your real birthday dinner."

"But we already had—"

"Breakfast on the hotel terrace. Champagne with lunch. Your favourite book," he ticked them off with a wry smile. "Lovely. But this… this is the part I wanted you to remember."

She looked around again, stunned by how intimate it felt. Not flashy. Not grand. Just thoughtful. It was the kind of celebration built not from money, but from knowing someone deeply.

He pulled out a chair for her, and she sat slowly, like she wasn't sure she could trust the ground under her feet.

A steward appeared quietly with two covered plates, then vanished just as silently. When they lifted the domes, Olivia gave a startled laugh.

"Grilled cheese?" she asked, eyes bright.

"With tomato soup," Jack confirmed, lifting his wineglass. "You once said it was your favourite comfort food. I figure birthdays should be about comfort. And joy."

She blinked down at the plate, then back at him. "You remember everything I say."

"I'm trying to," he said softly.

They ate slowly, savouring the simple meal in the candlelight, pausing between bites to laugh, to talk, to linger in the kind of silence that felt full instead of empty.

After dinner, he guided her outside again—only this time, to the far edge of the deck where a mattress of cushions and soft blankets had been arranged beneath a wide canopy. Dozens of little lanterns glowed like captured fireflies and nestled beside the pillows sat a small projector and screen.

"A movie?" she asked, her voice barely above a whisper.

Jack nodded. "You said you missed drive-in theatres. I can't offer you a truck bed or popcorn in a paper bag... but I can give you this."

She looked up at him, overwhelmed.

"What movie?" she asked, sitting down amid the pillows.

He handed her the remote. "Your pick."

She scrolled through a small, curated list: Roman Holiday, Pride and Prejudice, The Secret Life of Walter Mitty, even Tangled. She laughed when she reached the last one.

"You added this on purpose."

"You said once it was your guilty pleasure."

She clicked play without hesitation.

They lay side by side, her head resting on his chest, the movie flickering above them. Jack said nothing when her fingers found his and laced them together. He just held her tighter.

Halfway through, she turned her face toward his.

"I didn't think today could get any better," she whispered.

"And yet," he murmured, brushing his lips to her temple, "here we are."

The yacht swayed gently beneath them, the ocean a soft hush all around, and above them, the stars watched silently.

She hadn't needed diamonds.

She'd needed this.

And he had given it to her.

Chapter Twenty

Breakfast was quiet in the best way—just the clinking of silverware, the occasional murmur of conversation, and the easy silences that came when two people had nothing to prove. Jack had ordered banana pancakes for her, claiming they were the only acceptable birthday breakfast even a day late, and Olivia hadn't argued.

They ate on the upper deck, the sun bright above them, the breeze cool and laced with salt. Everything felt softened by the afterglow of the night before.

Jack kept stealing glances at her—messy bun, oversized white linen shirt she'd borrowed from his closet, bare feet tucked up beneath her. She was radiant, and she didn't even know it.

He reached across the table to touch her hand. "I was thinking… we could take the tender over to that private cove this afternoon. Swim, snorkel. Hide from the world a little longer."

Olivia smiled. "Hide with you? Sounds suspicious."

He grinned. "Only if we bring champagne."

She was about to tease him again when his phone buzzed on the table.

He glanced at the screen and stiffened, the smile fading just slightly. "I need to take this."

"No problem." She offered a shrug, casual, but something in his expression made her stomach twist.

Jack stood, phone in hand, and walked toward the interior of the yacht. Not the main lounge. Not the deck. His study.

A space he rarely used. A space he locked.

She told herself not to care. He was a billionaire. He had business. Private things. The world didn't stop just because they were living in this bubble of sun and sea and lazy mornings.

Still… when she returned to her cabin a few minutes later to grab her sunglasses, she heard him.

His voice, low and urgent, drifted down the corridor from the study, the door slightly ajar.

"Charlotte, it's not like that…" A pause. "You know you—"

Olivia slowed for just a moment, her fingers brushing the sunglasses on her nightstand. The name floated in her mind, unfamiliar and lingering.

Charlotte.

She didn't linger. Didn't eavesdrop. Just noted the shift in Jack's voice—quiet, personal—and filed the name away with a tilt of curiosity. If it mattered, he'd tell her. *She trusted him.*

Just after lunch the tender cut smoothly across the water, its sleek hull gliding over turquoise waves as the afternoon sun shimmered on the horizon. Jack sat at the helm, one hand steady on the wheel, the other reaching occasionally for Olivia's knee like he couldn't help but touch her.

She sat beside him, wind in her hair, a loose white shirt tied at her waist over her swimsuit. Her bare feet were tucked beneath her, and she leaned back with her face tilted to the sun, eyes closed, looking utterly content.

They rounded a rocky outcrop and slipped into the hidden cove—secluded, untouched, the kind of place that felt like it had been carved out of the world just for them. The water here was calmer, deeper blue, cradled between cliffs cloaked in wild green vines.

Jack dropped anchor in the shallows, then turned to her with a boyish grin. "Race you in?"

Olivia laughed, already pulling her shirt over her head. "You'll lose."

She dove in first, her body slicing clean through the water. Jack followed a heartbeat later with a splash that echoed against the rocks. They surfaced together, breathless, grinning, sunlight bouncing off their shoulders.

They swam and snorkelled, chasing schools of silver fish that scattered like confetti in their wake. Olivia pointed excitedly at a sea turtle gliding past, its movements lazy and graceful, and Jack caught himself watching her more than the reef—how she looked so alive out here, untethered.

Later, they climbed onto a smooth, sun-warmed rock, stretched out to dry beneath the sky. Olivia lay on her stomach, water dripping from her hair, her cheek resting on her folded arms.

"We should hide here forever," she murmured.

Jack shifted closer, brushing his hand down her spine. "Tempting."

She turned her head, meeting his gaze. "What would happen if we did?"

"I'd finally learn how to cook," he said seriously. "You'd get tired of fish. And we'd both be absurdly tan."

She smiled, her eyes soft. "I think we'd be happy."

He leaned in and kissed her shoulder. "I already am."

The world beyond the cove didn't exist for a while—not the yacht. Just the two of them, sun-drenched and salt-kissed, hidden in a place that felt like a secret only they knew.

And for a few golden hours, they let themselves believe they could stay there forever.

The next day was just as perfect—sunlit and slow, filled with stolen kisses, shared laughter, and the quiet comfort of two people who'd found something rare. They made the most of every moment, knowing that tomorrow they would return to the real world.

Not that Olivia minded. If she and Jack were going to have a future, it had to include real life—the chaos, the questions, the unknowns. The past six days had been a dream, beautiful and intoxicating, but dreams fade. What mattered was what came after.

She knew she loved him. The truth of it settled in her chest like something fragile but certain. But she hadn't told him. Not yet.

Maybe he wasn't ready to hear it.

Maybe he didn't want her to love him.

So, she held her secret close, not out of fear, but out of respect—for him, for herself, for the delicate thing blooming between them. And instead of worrying about tomorrow, she chose to stay in the moment, treasuring every glance, every touch, every soft, golden hour they shared.

Because love didn't always need to be spoken to be real. Sometimes, it just needed to be lived.

Their last night together was just as magical—because Jack made it so. At Olivia's suggestion, they shared an early dinner, something simple and quiet, as if they were already beginning to say goodbye to the dream. Then they spent the rest of the night wrapped in each other's arms, tangled in sheets and whispers, holding on to every moment like it might slip away with the dawn.

When they woke, the yacht was already docked back at Motukava. The island shimmered in the morning light, beautiful as ever, but something in the air felt different—like reality had quietly crept in while they slept.

After breakfast, Jack had to leave for an early meeting with the crew finishing construction on his wellness centre. He kissed Olivia softly, lingering just a little, and promised he'd see her later.

Olivia packed the few clothes she'd brought, said warm goodbyes to the crew—Lachlan included, who hugged her like a sister—and stepped off the yacht for what felt like the end of a chapter.

The walk back to her bungalow was slow. Quiet. The sea breeze tugged at her hair as she crossed the beach, her sandals sinking into the warm sand.

Tomorrow, she'd be back at work. Back to routine. Back to the version of her life that had existed before Jack Alden had turned it upside down.

Olivia got back to her bungalow, unpacked her clothes slowly, folding each item with care more out of distraction than neatness. The silence felt heavier now, the stillness unfamiliar after six days of laughter and whispered conversations in bed.

Restless, she decided to go for a walk. The sun was high, the breeze warm, and the path toward the staff restaurant took her through the reception foyer. She figured a coffee might help ease the strange ache tugging at her chest.

As she stepped into the cool, airy lobby, she noticed a woman at the front desk—a tall, strikingly beautiful blonde dressed in crisp designer linen. Her sunglasses were pushed up on her head, and her expression could cut glass.

"I need to speak to Jack Alden," the woman said, her tone clipped with entitlement.

"I'm sorry," the receptionist replied politely. "Mr. Alden is currently in a meeting."

The woman scoffed, her voice rising sharply. "Then interrupt him. He won't mind. I'm his fiancée."

Olivia stopped dead.

The word hit her like a slap, echoing in her ears, stealing the breath from her lungs.

Fiancée?

The woman didn't even glance in her direction. She stood there—elegant, furious, sure of her place in Jack's world.

Olivia's heart thundered in her chest. She couldn't move. Couldn't think. Just stood there, hidden in plain sight, trying to make sense of what she'd just heard. The sound of the lobby suddenly becoming muffled, her pulse in her ears.

Fiancée.

No. There had to be a mistake.

Jack wouldn't do that to her.

He cared about her. Maybe he didn't love her—not yet—but he *cared.* She knew that much. She felt it, in every touch, every look, every word whispered into her skin during the nights they'd spent tangled in each other.

He wouldn't lie to her. Would he?

At the front desk, the receptionist, ever composed, asked gently, "Can I have your name, please?"

The woman lifted her chin, her red lipstick flawless, eyes cool with confidence. "Just tell him Charlotte is here."

Olivia's stomach dropped.

Charlotte.

The name echoed like a warning bell in her mind— *'Charlotte, it's not like that… you know you—'*

She felt the colour drain from her face. Her fingers, still curled loosely at her sides, turned cold.

She turned away quickly before anyone could see her expression. Each step toward the back exit felt like walking through water. Her chest ached with the weight of something she wasn't ready to name yet.

But deep down, Olivia already knew.

This wasn't just a mistake.

This was something else entirely.

Olivia couldn't breathe. Couldn't think.

Her chest ached, tight and heavy, like someone was standing on it.

Fiancée.

Charlotte.

The words slammed into her, sharp and unforgiving.

No.

She shook her head, as if that could make it all go away.

I refuse to believe this. Jack wouldn't hurt me like this. He just… he wouldn't.

She held onto that thought like a lifeline, trying to steady the storm that had erupted inside her. He cared about her. She wasn't some fling. She wasn't just passing time in his bed.

He kissed me this morning like he meant it. He looked at me like I mattered.

Yes. She would wait. She'd talk to him. There had to be an explanation. Something that made sense.

But her body didn't believe what her mind was saying.

Her hands were trembling. Her throat was thick with unshed tears. She needed air.

Olivia turned and walked blindly, out of the lobby and down the winding path toward the beach. Sand clung to her feet as she reached the shore, but she barely noticed. The breeze rushed over her skin, salty and warm, but it didn't soothe her.

She stood there, facing the ocean, wrapping her arms around herself as if she could hold her heart together that way.

The waves rolled in and out, calm, and indifferent.

But Olivia couldn't find calm.

Not when the name Charlotte still echoed like a ghost in her ears.

Jack's meeting had gone better than expected. The wellness centre was just days from opening—sleek, serene, and destined to bring a new kind of guest to Motukava.

Everything was running on time, the staff were prepped, and the vision he'd dreamed up months ago was finally becoming real.

It was perfect. Every detail.

But even standing in the centre of something he'd worked so hard to build, Jack's thoughts drifted.

He missed her.

He hadn't even been away from Olivia for more than a few hours, but he felt her absence like an ache under his skin. He couldn't wait to tell her the news, to see her eyes light up the way they always did when he shared something with her.

He should've told her this morning.

He was going to. He'd kissed her goodbye, and the words had hovered on the tip of his tongue. I love you. Three syllables that terrified him and grounded him all at once.

She had taken his heart so completely, so effortlessly, he couldn't imagine ever giving it to anyone else. No one else would be worthy now. Not after Olivia.

His phone rang. He glanced at the screen and answered distractedly. "Hello?"

"Mr. Alden, your fiancée has arrived. She asked me to let you know."

He froze. "My fiancée?" he repeated, confused. "I don't have a fiancée."

Not yet, he thought, but if Olivia will have me...

"She said her name was Charlotte, sir."

Jack let out a groan and ran a hand down his face. "Where is she?"

"We put her in your villa, sir. She said she'd wait there for you."

"Thank you," he said, though the words were clipped.

He ended the call and swore under his breath.

What the hell does she want now?

Charlotte had called him the other day, bitter and furious, accusing him of cheating back when they were together. Somehow, news of another woman being on his yacht had reached her—and that, combined with Charlotte's talent for dramatics, had clearly turned into some fantasy where she could show up and reclaim something that never really existed.

But this wasn't about her anymore.

And there was no way in hell he was letting Charlotte anywhere near Olivia. He wouldn't expose her to Charlotte's cold, manipulative presence. Not after the way Olivia made him feel—open, vulnerable, alive.

He was going to handle this. Fast.

And then he was going to find Olivia.

Because the only woman who mattered—the only one who had ever truly mattered—was probably somewhere wondering where he was.

Jack found her exactly where he expected—on the terrace, lounging against the balustrade like she owned the view. The late morning sun painted the beach gold, but all he could see was red.

"What the hell are you doing here?" he demanded, striding onto the terrace with clipped, angry steps.

Charlotte turned slowly, a calculated smile spreading across her flawless face. "Jack don't be like that," she purred, her voice soft and syrupy.

The sound of it sent a chill down his spine.

God, what the hell was I thinking when I asked her to marry me?

That had been a lifetime ago. A version of him that didn't know better. That hadn't met Olivia.

"Whatever this is, it's over. You need to leave."

"Jack, we need to talk."

"No," he said, his voice cutting through the air like a blade. "We really don't."

He stepped forward, close enough for her perfume to reach him, but stopped just short of touching her. She held her ground, chin lifted, lips curled in that infuriating smile that once had him under its spell. Like she still believed this was all a game—and she was still winning.

"When you ended things," she said, her tone velvet-smooth, "I figured you just needed time. A little space. You've had your fun, Jack. Your... fling." She leaned in slightly, voice dropping to a purr. "Now it's time to come home. To me."

Then she did something that didn't register at first.

Her hands glided up his chest in a slow, familiar motion, slipping around the back of his neck—and before he could react, she pressed her lips to his.

The shock hit first. Then the fury.

Jack grabbed her wrists, firm but controlled, and yanked her arms away from him, taking a step back like she'd burned him.

"What the hell, Charlotte?" he barked. "No. I'm not interested. I've moved on. You need to."

The warmth drained from her face, but her eyes glittered with something—anger, maybe. Or denial.

He didn't care.

Whatever game she thought she was playing, he wasn't part of it anymore.

Charlotte's heels clicked sharply against the villa's polished tiles as she stormed inside behind Jack, the air between them crackling with unresolved fury.

"You can't just dismiss me like this," she snapped, arms folded across her chest, her eyes narrowing as she followed him into the open living area. "We were engaged, Jack. You don't just throw that away."

Jack turned slowly, his expression unreadable. But his eyes—those cool, focused eyes—left no room for misunderstanding.

"I didn't throw anything away, Charlotte. You did, the moment you started treating our relationship like a competition you had to win." His voice was even, but underneath, the steel was unmistakable. "It was never love; it was greed."

She scoffed. "Oh please, don't act like you were some poor victim. You're the one who asked me to marry you."

"Yes but…," he said calmly. "I woke up. There's a difference."

She stared at him, shaking her head. "And now what? You've moved on with some—some girl you met here? A fling on your yacht and suddenly you're in love?"

"Her name is Olivia," Jack said firmly. "And what we have is real. Something you and I never had. I didn't know what it was supposed to be like until her."

The words landed like a slap, and for a moment, Charlotte's composure faltered. Her jaw tightened, and her voice dipped. "So that's it? You just toss me aside for some island girl and pretend the last year never happened?"

"It did happen," Jack said. "But it's over. And I won't let you use it to hold me hostage. You're in my past, Charlotte. And you won't be in my future."

She stared at him, searching his face for some hint of hesitation. Some weakness she could use.

There was none.

After a long, seething silence, she snatched her designer handbag off the sofa. "You'll regret this."

"I won't," Jack replied without missing a beat. "But you'll regret staying any longer than this."

With one last glance—half fury, half wounded pride—Charlotte swept toward the door.

She didn't look back.

And Jack didn't watch her go.

He was already thinking about Olivia.

Chapter Twenty-One

Olivia ran to her bungalow, tears blurring the path beneath her feet.

She couldn't breathe. Couldn't think. Only one image replayed in her mind, over and over—the one now seared into her heart.

Jack.

Charlotte.

On the terrace.

The way Charlotte's hands had slid up his chest, curled around his neck—then that kiss.

She couldn't watch another second.

It was all a lie. He had lied. She couldn't stay here.

She flung the door open and stumbled inside, pressing a hand to her chest as if that might somehow calm the storm raging inside her.

"Liv?"

She froze.

Wyatt.

"Go away, Wyatt," she said hoarsely. Her voice cracked as the tears continued to fall, hot and fast.

But he didn't leave. He stepped inside slowly, concern softening his features. "Liv—"

She turned away.

He came closer anyway, his hand gently reaching for her chin, tilting her face toward him.

"Don't say it," she whispered. "You warned me. I know I'm an idiot. You don't have to rub it in."

Wyatt's brow furrowed. "Oh, Liv… I'm not here to rub anything in. I'm sorry."

She blinked, thrown off. "You're… what?"

"I'm sorry for what I said the last time we talked. I was angry, jealous, stupid. I didn't mean it."

Olivia swallowed hard, her throat burning. "It doesn't matter now. You were right. He has a fiancée."

Wyatt's jaw tightened. "That bastard," he muttered. "You don't deserve that. No one does."

Her gaze drifted downward and landed on the small duffel bag near his feet. "Where are you going?"

"Home," he said with a sigh. "My contract's up. I have a month off. I've got a boat off the island in half an hour. I just… I wanted to say goodbye."

Her heart twisted, already broken, and now pulled in a new, unexpected direction. "Oh, Wyatt… I'm sorry."

He gave a soft, lopsided smile. "Don't be. I just didn't want to leave without seeing you. No matter what happened between us… you still matter."

"I can't stay here," Olivia said, her voice barely above a whisper. "I just can't—not after what happened."

"Then come with me, Liv. Come home. Forget this place. Forget him."

She hesitated. "I… I can't. I'm still on contract."

Wyatt looked her straight in the eyes. "After what he did to you, do you really think he'd hold you to that contract?"

A long beat passed.

"No," she said quietly.

"The boat leaves in thirty minutes. If you want to come, you need to come now."

Her heart felt like it had been cracked open and tossed into the sea. She thought of the kids. The work she loved. But she couldn't breathe here anymore. Not with Charlotte roaming the island. Not with the image of that kiss burned into her mind.

"Okay," she whispered. "I'll come. I need to pack."

Wyatt nodded, and they moved through the bungalow together. She hadn't brought much. Everything went into her suitcase except one thing.

The book.

The one Jack had given her for her birthday.

She held it for a moment, her fingers trembling. Then she set it gently on the bed.

Wyatt glanced at her but said nothing.

She couldn't take it with her. Not now. Not after the way he'd broken her heart.

It didn't belong to her anymore.

They reached the marina with ten minutes to spare. Olivia was still crying—quiet, steady tears slipping down her cheeks as they neared the boat.

Then—

"Olivia!"

She turned.

Lachlan.

He was striding toward her; concern etched deep into his face.

"What's wrong?" he asked, his eyes darting to the suitcase Wyatt held. "Where are you going?"

"Home," she said shakily. "I can't stay here."

"Why? What's happened?"

A loud whistle blew—the final boarding call.

"Jack lied to me," she choked out. "I can't stay here."

Lachlan blinked. "What did he lie about?"

She started toward the boat, her steps quickening.

"He didn't tell me he was getting married. Charlotte showed up this morning."

Lachlan's expression twisted—confusion turning to disbelief. "Olivia—Jack's not with Charlotte. He's not marrying her."

"I saw her, Lachlan. Kissing him." Her voice cracked again. She turned away, eyes stinging, and hurried aboard just as the boat began to pull from the dock.

And then she was gone.

Jack took the winding path toward Olivia's bungalow, his steps quicker than usual. The island breeze tousled his hair, but he barely noticed—he felt happy. Charlotte was gone. Her departure was final, the sound of a helicopter fading into the sky.

Good riddance.

He had barely waited ten minutes after she left before deciding to find Olivia. He wanted—needed—to tell her. About the new wellness centre that was almost finished. About how damn much he had already missed her this morning.

Jack reached the bungalow and frowned. The door was slightly ajar.

He knocked gently.

"Olivia?" he called, peering in.

No answer.

He pushed the door open.

The room was empty. Neat, quiet, but undeniably empty. The scent of coconut lotion still hung in the air, and the curtains danced lazily in the breeze, but Olivia was gone.

Jack's eyes swept the room and caught on something resting in the centre of the bed.

The book.

Little Women.

He crossed the room and picked it up. It was the one he'd given her for her birthday. He frowned. What's going on? Where is Olivia?

But something about the sight of that book sitting there, alone, filled him with a strange sort of dread. She wouldn't have left it behind. Not unless…

He turned slowly, scanning the room again, as if he'd missed her somehow. Everything was gone.

Jack's throat tightened.

Jack stood in the centre of the room, the book hanging limply in his hand, and for the first time in a long while, he felt unsure.

He walked out, dazed, the sunshine too bright, the air too loud. Confusion spun in his chest like a storm.

Maybe they moved her, he told himself. Maybe the bungalow had an issue—plumbing or power—and they moved her somewhere else.

That had to be it. He'd go find Kate. She'd know.

But before he could make it two steps down the path, he heard someone call his name.

"Jack!"

He turned.

It was Lachlan. And he did not look pleased.

"What's wrong?" Jack asked, alert now. "Has something happened?"

Lachlan walked toward him, jaw tight. "Please," he said grimly, "tell me you didn't kiss that ice queen."

Jack blinked. "What?"

Lachlan's voice lowered. "Charlotte."

Jack's stomach dropped. "I didn't—" He stopped, remembering. That brief moment. Charlotte leaning in. The kiss. A second too late, and he'd pulled away.

But someone could've seen it.

"Olivia…" Lachlan started.

Jack's breath hitched. "You saw her? Where is she?"

"Gone."

Jack stared at him. "Gone? What do you mean gone?"

"I saw her at the marina about half an hour ago. She was crying, Jack."

Jack stepped forward, the book still clenched in his hand. "Why?" he asked, already fearing the answer.

"She said you lied to her. That you were getting married." Lachlan's gaze sharpened. "That she saw you kiss Charlotte."

The words hit Jack like a punch.

"No," he muttered. "No, that's not what happened—Charlotte ambushed me, I didn't—" He looked down at the book, his chest tightening. "She saw that?"

"She did," Lachlan said quietly. "And whatever it meant to you, Jack… to her, it meant everything. She looked like her heart had been ripped out."

He didn't say anything, he couldn't.

Finally, Jack broke the silence, his voice low. "She's really gone."

Lachlan nodded grimly. "Yeah."

"She saw Charlotte… it wasn't what it looked like."

"It never is," Lachlan said, not unkindly. "But Jack… she believed what she saw. Did you even tell her about Charlotte?"

Jack's jaw clenched. "No. I wanted to forget about that stupid decision. I was going to tell her I loved her—she just left."

"She left because she thought you didn't care," Lachlan said. "You know how that feels?"

Jack looked away, jaw working. "I didn't mean for this to happen. I didn't—"

"You let it happen," Lachlan said quietly. "You didn't lie. But you didn't tell her everything, she deserved to know all of it."

Jack didn't answer. He just stared at the empty horizon where the boat had disappeared, the book still gripped in his hand like a lifeline.

Minutes passed.

The sun climbed higher. The island buzzed around them. But Jack remained rooted to the spot.

"She loved it here," he said eventually, his voice hollow. "She loved the kids. The water. The way she looked at me when she was happy… God."

His voice broke.

Lachlan watched him for a long moment before speaking. "What are you going to do?"

Jack swallowed. "I don't know."

"You should figure it out," Lachlan said, softer now. "She's the best thing that's ever happened to you."

"I know."

Olivia stepped off the bus that had carried her and Wyatt from the marina in Papeete to the airport, her heart still splintered.

The air was heavier here—warmer, clinging to her skin. The scent of hibiscus drifted in on the breeze, mingling with the tang of jet fuel. A soft murmur of French floated over the hum of travellers moving through the open-air terminal at Faa'a International Airport.

She pulled her suitcase behind her, her eyes hidden behind dark sunglasses, but her posture betrayed her. She was wrecked.

Wyatt walked beside her, unusually quiet. He hadn't pushed or pried. But his glances toward her were frequent—worried, steady, like someone who wanted to offer more than silence but didn't know how.

They moved through the airport with practiced ease, but then Olivia stopped. She stood still as Lachlan's voice echoed in her mind.

'Jack's not with Charlotte. He's not marrying her.'

What if he was right?

What if she'd gotten it wrong?

This morning—this morning—she had woken up in Jack Alden's bed, his breath warm against her neck, her heart wrapped around his. She'd smiled into his shoulder, anchored in the certainty that they were becoming something real.

And now?

Now she felt unmoored. Like a boat that had slipped its tether in the night and drifted out to sea.

Wyatt turned to her gently. "Are you okay?"

She didn't answer at first. Then, soft as breath, she said, "No."

The tears had stopped somewhere between Motukava and Tahiti, but the ache hadn't. It had only settled deeper, a dull, constant throb—like a bruise pressed against bone.

"I thought I was sure," she whispered. "This morning, if you'd asked me, I would've sworn Jack loved me. That I—me, Olivia Clifton—was enough."

Wyatt didn't speak. He didn't need to. She wasn't done.

"But now?" Her voice cracked. "Now I don't know. I saw her—Charlotte—put her hands on him. Then she kissed him. And I didn't stay. I didn't wait to see what he did. I just... left."

She turned to him, anguish raw on her face. "Lachlan said Jack's not with her. That he's not marrying her. He wouldn't lie to me. So... did I get it all wrong?"

Wyatt hesitated. He'd never liked Jack. The man had everything—money, charm, the power to make someone like Olivia fall fast and hard. But in this moment, none of that mattered.

"You said you saw them kiss," he said carefully.

"I thought I did," she murmured, voice trembling. "But maybe... maybe he pulled away. Maybe I didn't see the whole thing. I don't know anymore. It all happened so fast and—and I panicked."

Wyatt exhaled, dragging a hand through his sun-bleached hair. "Look, I'm not Jack's biggest fan. That's obvious. But Olivia…" He held her gaze. "If there's even a chance what you had with him was real—*truly real*—then maybe you owe it to yourself to find out."

She blinked at him, startled.

"I saw the way you looked at him," Wyatt continued, his voice low. "He was it for you. And the way you spoke about him… even when you didn't mean to, even when you tried not to. You love him, Liv. And this pain you're carrying?" He gestured gently. "It's not from betrayal. It's from doubt. Because deep down, you still think he loves you too."

Olivia pressed her fingers to her lips as tears threatened again.

"You could be wrong," Wyatt said softly. "But you could also be right. And if you are… isn't that worth fighting for?"

Her chest rose and fell, slow and uncertain, her emotions warring beneath the surface.

"I don't even know where to start," she whispered.

Wyatt's lips curved, the barest hint of a smile. "You'll figure it out. You're not exactly the giving-up type."

She turned her face toward the terminal's edge, where the ocean shimmered in the distance like an unreachable dream.

But maybe it wasn't unreachable.

Maybe she didn't have to run away.

Maybe—just maybe—it was time to run toward something.

Toward the truth.

Toward him.

Because what if she'd been wrong?

What if she'd walked away from the only man who ever truly saw her—because of fear, heartbreak, and a single, misunderstood moment?

The ache in her chest pulsed again.

But this time, it wasn't despair.

It was hope.

The yacht sliced through the waves like a blade, relentless and single-minded—just like the man standing on the deck.

Jack gripped the railing, the wind whipping against his face, salty and sharp, but he barely felt it. His jaw was locked; eyes fixed on the fading horizon as if he could force Tahiti to rise from the sea by sheer will.

He had to find her.

He had to.

His fingers raked through his hair in a restless sweep, then clenched into fists at his sides. His heart hadn't stopped pounding since he'd walked into her bungalow and found it empty. No scent of her shampoo. No humming from the bathroom. No suitcase by the door.

Just silence.

Just gone.

Lachlan's words echoed through his mind.

'I saw her at the marina about half an hour ago.'

'She was crying, Jack.'

Those words had landed like a gut punch.

'She looked like her heart had been ripped out.'

Jack had swallowed the ache in his throat. "That means she cares," he whispered hoarsely. "That means… maybe I still have a chance."

Now, as the peaks of Tahiti began to cut through the misty blue ahead, desperation clawed at him like fire under his skin. He braced his hands on the railing, knuckles bone-white, his mind caught in an endless loop—her laughter, her warmth, the way she'd looked at him like he was someone worth loving.

She didn't know.

She didn't know that he loved her more than he'd ever thought himself capable of loving anyone.

And now she was gone, believing he'd betrayed her.

"God, Olivia," he murmured, his voice breaking. "Please still be there."

She hadn't planned to leave. That much was clear. She'd run—panicked, heartbroken. Which meant if she hadn't managed to get a last-minute flight out of Faa'a International, she was still somewhere in Papeete.

There was still time.

"She's the best thing that's ever happened to me," Jack muttered, as if saying it aloud could anchor the truth in his chest.

Lachlan appeared beside him on the deck; his usual composure edged with something softer. He studied Jack a long moment before speaking. "You told me once that money can buy anything."

Jack didn't flinch. "I was wrong."

"She's not for sale," Lachlan agreed quietly.

Jack nodded. "No. She's the best kind of woman. The kind you don't deserve—but pray to hell you get to keep anyway."

If she was still on the island, he would find her.

And when he did?

He'd tell her everything.

That she wasn't a fling. She wasn't a mistake. She wasn't someone to get over.

She was everything.

And if fate was on his side—if love still lived in her heart—then maybe, just maybe, she'd let him prove it.

Chapter Twenty-Two

The yacht pulled into the dock, sleek and fast, drawing curious glances from tourists and locals alike. Jack didn't wait for the yacht to dock properly. He was already airborne, leaping down onto the weathered planks, landing hard with a jolt that shot up his spine. He didn't care. Adrenaline was the only thing keeping him upright.

He spotted the nearest driver and strode toward him with laser focus. "Airport," he barked. "Now."

But as he reached for the car door, something made him pause.

A glint of familiar sun kissed hair caught his eye.

A small, hunched figure on a bench by the dock.

Jack blinked, heart stalling in his chest.

No. It couldn't be.

But it was.

Olivia.

There.

Still here.

His breath left him in a rush. He stepped back from the car like a man in a dream, walking toward her slowly, afraid any sudden movement might shatter the moment and make her disappear.

"Olivia."

Her head jerked up. Eyes wide, wet with tears.

"Jack?" Her voice was barely a whisper.

He took another step, heart pounding. "You didn't leave."

She rose to her feet, legs unsteady. "I tried to go back. But there were no boats. Nothing until tomorrow."

His chest ached. "I thought you were gone. I was on my way to the airport. I was going to stop you."

"I didn't want to go," she said, her voice cracking. "But I thought I had to. I heard Charlotte… she said she's your fiancée."

"She's not. Hasn't been for a long time." His voice was firm. "It was—months ago. That ended long before I ever met you."

"But I saw her. Kissing you."

"I pushed her away," he said, jaw tightening. "Not fast enough, apparently. But I swear to you, Olivia, it wasn't what it looked like."

Her voice trembled. "Do you still love her?"

Jack closed the distance between them in two strides, gently cupping her face in his hands. "No, I never did. I love you, Olivia. I love you more than I ever thought I could love anyone. What you saw—it wasn't what you think. She kissed me. I didn't kiss her back. I didn't want it. I want you."

Tears welled in her eyes again, spilling down her cheeks.

"I thought I ruined everything," she whispered.

Jack wrapped his arms around her, holding her to him like he'd been drowning, and she was air. "You didn't. But if you had left, I would've chased you across every ocean to bring you back."

She pressed her face to his chest, breathing him in. The scent of him wrapped around her—salt, sunlight, and something undeniably Jack. It felt like home.

He rested his cheek against her hair, his voice low. "What stopped you from going?"

She hesitated, then murmured, "Wyatt."

Jack pulled back slightly, just enough to look down at her. His brow furrowed. "Wyatt?"

She nodded. "He told me if I thought what we had was real, I should fight for it."

Jack blinked, surprised. "He said that?"

Her eyes glistened as she gave a small, tearful laugh. "Turns out he's not as much of an idiot as I thought."

A slow, incredulous smile touched Jack's lips. "Remind me to thank him."

"I can't believe you found me," she breathed.

He lowered his lips to her temple, his voice ragged and full of feeling. "I'd find you in every lifetime."

Jack picked up her suitcase. Olivia didn't resist when he reached for her free hand next, intertwining their fingers as he gently guided her down the dock toward the waiting yacht.

The sun dipped low on the horizon, painting the water in shades of rose and gold. The breeze tugged at Olivia's hair, but she barely noticed. Jack was beside her. Solid. Real. And somehow, miraculously, still hers.

Once they were aboard, the crew melted away with silent efficiency, as if sensing the moment's intimacy. Jack led her up to the top deck where a wide daybed waited beneath a canopy of gauzy linen. He sat first, pulling her down with him until she was tucked into his side, her head resting on his shoulder, his arm wrapped protectively around her.

The quiet swelled between them, warm and thick with unspoken feelings. The yacht swayed gently, and the ocean hummed its lullaby, but neither of them were ready for sleep.

"Why were you even engaged to Charlotte," Olivia asked softly, her voice muffled against his shirt, "if you never loved her?"

Jack exhaled slowly, his thumb tracing small circles on her arm. "I met Charlotte at a charity gala in Monaco—she was beautiful, poised, and impeccably connected. On paper, she checked all the boxes."

Olivia tilted her head up to look at him. "But you didn't love her?"

"No," he said without hesitation. "And I didn't realise how little I knew about her until I saw what she really wanted."

"What was that?"

"My name. My money. The life she imagined came with it." He gave a bitter chuckle. "I think she loved the idea of being Mrs. Jack Alden more than she ever liked me."

Olivia's brows knit together. "Oh, Jack. I'm sorry."

He looked down at her, and a gentle smile curved his lips. "I'm not."

She blinked. "You're not?"

"If I hadn't woken up—if I hadn't called off the engagement—I never would've met you. I'd still be sleepwalking through my life. Building empires and attending parties, never knowing what I was missing."

She tucked her hand against his chest, over his heart. "But I still don't understand why you were willing to marry her in the first place. You had to know it wasn't love."

He sighed, his gaze drifting toward the darkening sky. "I thought love was a fairytale. A luxury for poets and dreamers. Not something that happened in the real world. Not for people like me."

He looked at her then, eyes deep and unguarded. "But then I met you, Olivia. And you ruined every lie I ever told myself."

She swallowed hard, her heart thudding loud in the quiet night. "Good."

He laughed softly. "Good?"

She smiled, tears shining in her eyes. "Because I love you and I only want you, not what comes with you."

Jack kissed her forehead, his voice low against her skin. "I never thought I could meet anyone like you, but I'm so glad I did."

The soft hum of the electric cart hummed through the night air as Jack steered it up the winding path to his private villa. Olivia sat beside him, her hand in his, her suitcase tucked in the back. She hadn't protested when he insisted, she come with him—hadn't even tried. After everything, there was a quiet comfort in letting him take the lead, in letting herself belong to this moment with him.

Jack parked the cart and turned to her.

"You're not going back to your bungalow," he said firmly, his voice low. "I need you with me. I need to know you're here."

She nodded wordlessly, heart thudding. "Okay."

He carried her suitcase in one hand, his other never leaving hers. Inside, everything smelled like cedar and sea air. He led her through the spacious living area, past the floor-to-ceiling windows that looked out over the moonlit ocean, and into the master suite.

"I'll get you something to sleep in," he said, already moving toward the dresser.

"I don't need anything," she said quietly. "Just you."

He stopped. Turned.

His eyes darkened, not with lust, but emotion. "Olivia…"

She stepped toward him slowly, barefoot on the cool floor. "I'm tired of running. Of doubting what I feel. What we feel."

Jack reached for her as if he couldn't help himself, his hands sliding to her waist as he pulled her gently to him. She looked up, eyes wide, vulnerable, and sure all at once.

"I want to be here," she whispered. "With you. If you still want me."

He let out a soft, strangled breath. "More than anything."

Their mouths met, slow and deep. It wasn't the heat of their stolen kisses from before—this was something else. Something rooted. Anchored. His hands slid up her back as she clung to his shoulders, her body moulding to his as if they'd been made to fit.

He kissed her like a man who had almost lost everything—and knew now how to cherish it.

Clothes slipped away between touches and quiet gasps. They tumbled into bed beneath the open shutters, the breeze cool against overheated skin. Jack moved with reverence, his touch both tender and desperate. Olivia's fingers threaded through his hair, her lips finding his jaw, his throat, his mouth again.

"I love you," he breathed against her skin. "I love you, Olivia."

She cupped his face, eyes wet with tears that had nothing to do with pain. "I love you, Jack."

He held her like she was the most precious thing he'd ever touched, and made love to her like it was the last night of the world.

Later, they lay tangled in the sheets, the ocean murmuring just beyond the open doors. Olivia rested her head on Jack's chest, listening to the steady beat of his heart beneath her ear.

"I'm not going anywhere," she murmured.

Jack tightened his arm around her, pressing a kiss to her hair.

"Good," he whispered. "Because now that I have you, I'm never letting you go."

The next morning came with the soft wash of golden light and the gentle sound of waves brushing the shore. Olivia woke nestled in Jack's arms, the linens tangled around their bodies, his breath warm at her temple. She wanted to stay like that—forever if the world would let her.

But real life called.

She had the early shift at the kid's club, and despite Jack's playful attempts to convince her to stay in bed a little longer, she kissed him softly and began to get dressed.

At the door, he walked her out, his bare feet padding across the wooden floor. When she turned to say goodbye, he pulled her close and brushed a lingering kiss over her lips.

"No more running, okay?" he said, his voice low and teasing, but with a hint of seriousness in his eyes. "Make sure I see you later."

She smiled up at him, her heart full. "You will."

The day passed in a blur of laughter, finger paints, and story time. Olivia felt lighter than she had in weeks. The ache of heartbreak had been replaced with a quiet joy, something fragile and real. The kids noticed too—more than one of them asked why she was smiling so much.

When her shift ended, she stepped out into the sunshine, brushing sand from her shorts. Jack was already waiting outside the kids' club, leaning against a golf cart like something from a vacation brochure—white linen shirt, sunglasses, and that smile that made her insides flutter.

"Hey," she said, walking toward him.

"Hey, yourself." He held out his hand. "Come with me. I want to show you something."

She raised a brow but took his hand without hesitation. "What?"

Jack grinned. "You'll see."

He drove them across the resort, past familiar paths, and winding gardens until they reached a secluded section tucked between palms and flowering vines. A sleek new building stood there, its architecture both modern and organic—floor-to-ceiling glass walls framed by wood and stone, open terraces spilling into lush greenery. A gentle water feature trickled beside the entryway, the sound calming and rhythmic.

"The new wellness centre," Jack said as he helped her down from the cart.

Olivia looked around in awe as he guided her inside. The scent of eucalyptus and lavender hung in the air, instantly soothing. The reception area was bathed in natural light; soft neutral tones offset by lush plants and art from local artists.

He led her through the space, pointing out different rooms. "That's the yoga pavilion, open-air with retractable walls for rainy days. Over there's the meditation deck—it looks out over the ocean. The treatment rooms have private plunge pools and outdoor showers. And there's a rooftop tea bar with herbal infusions."

"It's absolutely beautiful, Jack," she said, wonder in her voice, threaded with awe as she turned in a slow circle, taking in the tranquil, sun-drenched space. "You should be so proud."

Jack didn't look at the walls, the gardens, or the glass that shimmered in the light—he only looked at her. "I am," he said. "But mostly because you're here to see it."

They stood in the quiet for a moment, the kind of silence that didn't need to be filled. It felt easy. Natural. Like breathing.

Then Jack's mouth moved before he could think better of it.

"Marry me."

Olivia froze, eyes wide as they snapped to his. He wasn't smiling now. Just watching her—carefully, hopefully.

"What?" she whispered.

"Marry me," he said again, firmer this time. "Olivia Clifton, marry me and make me the luckiest man alive."

Her heart thudded in her chest. "Jack…" she breathed, tears already gathering in her lashes. "Are you sure?"

His smile faded slightly, a flicker of vulnerability crossing his face. "Don't you want to marry me?"

"I do," she said, stepping closer. "I want to. But I'm not from your world. I'm just… a simple childcare worker who followed a guy to an island and fell in love with a man she never expected."

He reached for her hands, gripping them tightly. "Thank God you're not from my world. If you were, I don't think I could love you as much as I do."

That broke something in her.

Tears spilled over, her voice catching. "I love you, Jack. I love you so much it scares me."

He smiled then, eyes glinting with emotion. "So, is that a yes?"

She nodded, tears rolling freely now. "Yes. Yes, I'll marry you."

Jack pulled her into his arms, holding her against his chest as the rest of the world fell away.

Epilogue

Five Years Later...

Charity Gala — Monaco

Jack Alden stood beneath a crystal chandelier, sipping champagne and pretending not to watch his wife.

But of course, he was watching.

In a sea of glittering gowns and black-tie elegance, Olivia blazed like a flame—effortlessly radiant in a ruby-red dress that skimmed her curves and moved like liquid silk. The diamond and ruby necklace at her throat shimmered under the ballroom lights, a piece he'd spent nearly an hour convincing her to wear.

"You know I don't need you to spoil me," she'd said, rolling her eyes as she turned her back for him to clasp it.

"I like spoiling you," he'd murmured, pressing a kiss to her bare shoulder.

Now she was dancing with a European prince or a shipping heir—he hadn't caught the name and didn't, particularly care. Whoever the man was, he was grinning like he'd just discovered treasure. Jack didn't blame him. Olivia Alden had a way of lighting up a room. Over the years, the elite had come to see what Jack had known from the start—she was a breath of fresh air. Authentic. Witty. Kind to her core.

His eyes drifted to the modest engagement ring still sitting proudly on her finger. Not a massive diamond. Not a statement piece. Just something timeless and quietly stunning. He'd tried—God knows he'd tried—to give her the biggest rock money could buy, but she'd just shaken her head and said softly, "Find something that feels like me, not like a price tag."

He had. And she wore it like it was priceless.

At least she let him buy her clothes... *sometimes.*

Her dance partner was finally escorting her back, still looking slightly dazed. Jack bit back a smirk as the man bowed low.

"Your wife is an absolute delight, Jack," the man said, reverently.

Jack took Olivia's hand and pressed a kiss to her knuckles, his gaze never straying from hers. "I know."

The man offered a final, dazzled smile and drifted back into the crowd.

She giggled softly as Jack drew her close.

"What are you laughing at, Mrs. Alden?"

"I still can't get used to men bowing to me," she said, eyes alight with mischief. "You did it, remember? That second day on Motukava. You bowed and said, 'It would be my pleasure.' It was the highlight of my day."

He wrapped his arms around her, his hand settling at the small of her back. "I remember." He kissed her temple. "I'll never forget."

She leaned into him, fingers brushing the lapel of his tuxedo. "You always look at me like that."

"Like what?"

"Like I hung the stars."

Jack smiled. "You did."

They swayed to the music, the world falling away, wrapped in the kind of quiet joy that only comes after weathering storms. They'd had their trials. Their heartbreaks. But in the end, love had been louder. Fiercer. Unbreakable.

She looked up at him and whispered, "It still feels like a dream sometimes."

He touched his forehead to hers. "It's real. Every second of it."

"And you're still not sick of me?"

Jack chuckled. "Ask me again in fifty years."

She grinned. "Deal."

Across the room, the gala host took the stage, calling guests to gather for the auction. But Jack didn't move. Neither did Olivia.

He leaned down, his lips brushing her ear. "Let's sneak out. Jessica's waiting."

Olivia's eyes lit with warmth. "Think she stayed up?"

Jack nodded. "Lachlan said she was too excited to sleep. Probably still out on the deck in her pyjamas, giving orders."

They both laughed, picturing their three-year-old daughter aboard the yacht moored in the Monaco marina—curly-haired, barefoot, and full of opinions. Very possibly the next CEO, if her bedtime negotiations were any indication.

She was already the princess of Jack's world—her mother, his queen.

As they stepped out into the warm Mediterranean night, Olivia's hand drifted gently to her stomach. Jack's fingers slid over hers.

"Soon," he said, wonder threading through the single word.

She nodded, her smile soft and secret.

And as they walked toward the harbour, toward the quiet gleam of their yacht and the sound of the sea, Jack Alden knew one thing for certain:

The best chapters of their love story were still unwritten.

The End

Before You Go…

If you fell for these characters and want more love stories filled with emotion, passion, and second chances, my newsletter is where I share them first.

You'll receive:

💕 Early access to new releases

💕 Exclusive reader-only content and extras

👉 **Join my reader list here:** https://alisonreidauthor.com

I'd love to welcome you.

Alison Reid

Thank you for reading Guarded Hearts!

If you enjoyed this collection of irresistible heroes, keep an eye out for more upcoming romance collections by Alison Reid, including:

Alpha Kings - *A Billionaire Alpha Male Romance Collection*

Cautious Hearts - *A Trust-After-Heartbreak Romance Collection*

Dark & Dangerous - *Brooding Heroes Romance Collection*

Final Surrender - *Alpha Heroes Yielding to Love Collection*

Forbidden Hearts - *A Forbidden Love Romance Collection*

Forever Mine - *A Longing-for-Love Romance Collection*

Hearts & Secrets - *Small Town Romance Collection*

Hearts in Peril - *A Suspenseful Romance Collection*

Hidden Truths - *A Secret Identity Romance Collection*

Lies & Hearts - *A Lies, Secrets & Betrayal Romance Collection*

Love After Regret - *A Second-Chance Redemption Romance Collection*

Misjudged Hearts - *A Love After Judgement Romance Collection*

Torn Between Hearts - *A Love Triangle Romance Collection*

All of Alison Reid's books feature standalone stories, swoon-worthy heroes, and guaranteed happily-ever-afters.

Books by Alison Reid

A Billionaire for Christmas

A Heart in Florence

After The Storm

Always You

Before I Fell

Before the Thaw

Beneath the Lies

Billionaire Bodyguard

Billionaire Rancher

Blueprints of the Heart

Branlow

Collide

Echoes of Deception

Falling for the Billionaire

Forever Yours

Heart of the Outback

Hearts on the Line

Hidden Gem

Kept Promises

Mended Hearts

Mistaken Hearts

New Year's Eve Kiss

Quiet Danger

Reckless Hearts

Reflections of Deception

Second Glance

Shadows of the Past

Shattered Dreams

Shattered Hope, Stolen Kisses

Still Yours

The Billionaire's Accidental Legacy

The Billionaire's Bargain

The Billionaire's Mistake

The Billionaire's Regret

The Billionaire's Secret Baby

The Billionaire's Unexpected Heir

The Blood Debt

The Playboy's Surrender

The Wrong Sister

Trust in Time

Undercover Billionaire

Until you Loved Me

Vows of Vengeance

Wife in Name Only

Find all my books on Amazon:

https://www.amazon.com/author/alisonreid1970

About the Author

Alison Reid writes contemporary and small-town romance filled with heart, passion, and second-chance love stories. Her novels often feature strong heroines, irresistible heroes, and the happily-ever-afters readers adore. When she's not writing, Alison enjoys reading, spending time with her family, and imagining new love stories. She hopes her books give readers a few hours of escape, joy, and swoon-worthy romance they won't forget.